Escape to Nowhere

The two men in front got out. A moment later the officer called to my guards. They got out too. I could see we were in a quarry, and for some reason gooseflesh began creeping over me. All around us were high stone walls glistening with damp. Pools of water at the foot of the quarry gleamed sinisterly in the moonlight. I tried to stop thinking why we had come here. A few yards away were five armed men, and it didn't do to get over-imaginative.

The officer lifted the flap and beckoned to me. 'Get out', he said. 'We want you.' I obeyed slowly. I wasn't scared now. There wouldn't be a dog's chance, and when all hope has gone a man isn't frightened of death. There was only dull resentment that it had come like this, and in such a place.

Also by Francis S. Jones

HIT OR MISS
NO RICE FOR REBELS

Escape to Nowhere

Francis S. Jones

Triad
Mayflower

Published in 1977 by Triad/Mayflower Books
Frogmore, St Albans, Herts AL2 2NF

Triad Paperbacks Ltd is an imprint of
Chatto, Bodley Head and Jonathan Cape Ltd
and its associated companies

First published in Great Britain by
the Bodley Head Ltd 1952

Made and printed in Great Britain by
Richard Clay (The Chaucer Press) Ltd
Bungay, Suffolk
Set in Monotype Plantin

To

HUGH

that he may never have to
do better than his Dad

AUTHOR'S NOTE

I regret to record that since this book was written, Lt. Col. Francis Gilbert Macaskie, M.C. has died as a result of his wartime privations. So passes a very brave and honourable man.

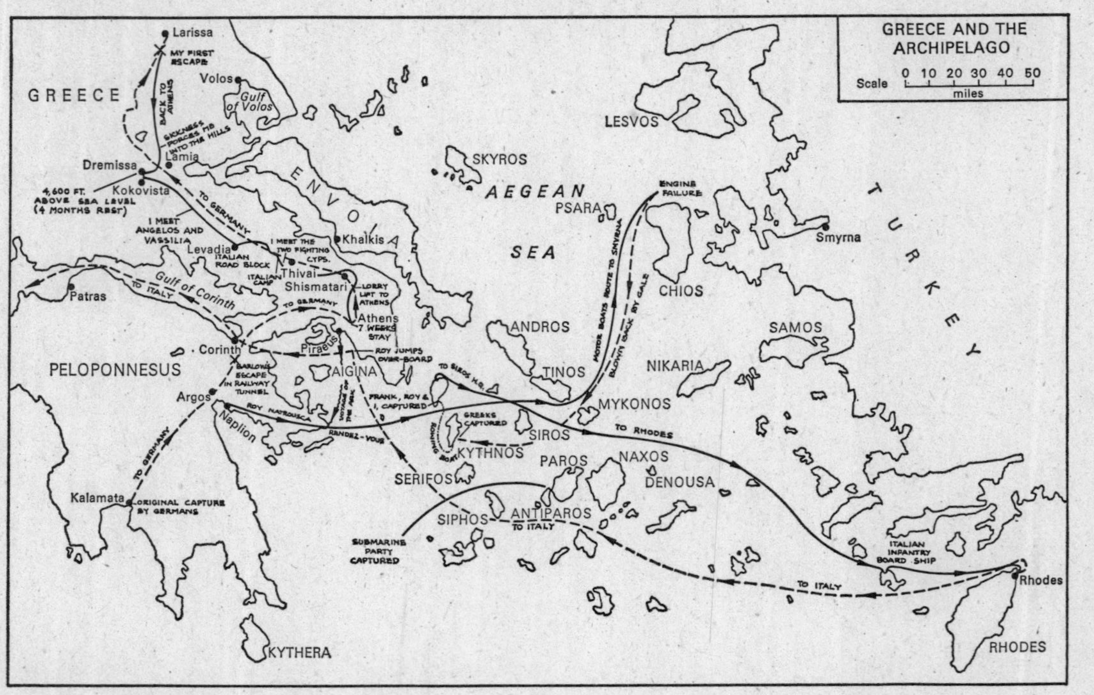
GREECE AND THE ARCHIPELAGO
Scale 0 10 20 30 40 50 miles
GREECE
Larissa
MY FIRST ESCAPE
BACK TO ATHENS
Volos
Gulf of Volos
SICKNESS FORCES ME INTO THE HILLS
Lamia
Dremissa
Kokovista
4,600 FT. ABOVE SEA LEVEL (4 MONTHS REST)
TO GERMANY
I MEET ANGELOS AND VASSILIA
EVVOIA
Khalkis
Levadia
ITALIAN ROAD BLOCK
I MEET THE TWO FIGHTING CYPS.
ITALIAN CAMP
Thivai
Shismatari
LORRY LIFT TO ATHENS
Athens
7 WEEKS STAY
Patras
TO ITALY
Gulf of Corinth
TO GERMANY
Corinth
Piraeus
ROY JUMPS OVER-BOARD
PELOPONNESUS
AIGINA
BARLOW'S ESCAPE IN RAILWAY TUNNEL
Argos
ROY NATROUSCA
VOYAGE OF THE ARK
FRANK, ROY & I, CAPTURED
RENDEZ-VOUS
Naplion
TO GERMANY
Kalamata
ORIGINAL CAPTURE BY GERMANS
KYTHERA
SKYROS
AEGEAN
SEA
LESVOS
PSARA
ENGINE FAILURE
MOTOR BOATS ROUTE TO SMYRNA
BLOWN BACK BY GALE
CHIOS
Smyrna
TURKEY
ANDROS
SAMOS
TINOS
NIKARIA
TO SIROS H.Q.
MYKONOS
GREEKS CAPTURED
ROWING BOAT
SIROS
TO RHODES
KYTHNOS
PAROS
NAXOS
DENOUSA
SERIFOS
ANTIPAROS
SIPHOS
TO ITALY
SUBMARINE PARTY CAPTURED
ITALIAN INFANTRY BOARD SHIP
TO ITALY
Rhodes
RHODES

ONE

Two o'clock in the morning is a God-forsaken hour. It's a time when all honest men should be asleep, with consciences clear and sins temporarily forgotten. There's only one place for it. That's bed.

I wished I was there. It was like a bad dream trudging up and down the Grecian hillsides with guards holding a trigger-brief on every move. What made it worse was knowing there wasn't anything I could do about it. I wasn't sure I wanted to do anything just then. The three Australians lower down the road, with their backs shattered, had put a damper on everyone's enthusiasm for escaping.

I did have one consolation. Barlow was safe. He'd got away as he said he would, which made us one up and one to go. Right now Barlow was somewhere in the Central Peloponnesus. Probably he was snoring his head off. Six weeks had passed since, but the nervous tension still mounted in me every time I thought of that break. When the train chugged into one of the last tunnels before Corinth, Barlow had gathered his kit and edged to the side of the truck. Just before we plunged into the smoky blackness he nudged me. 'This one'll do,' he said. 'You coming?' I heard one bump as his kit hit the ground, and then another as he leapt out of the truck himself. The Germans never missed him. If I'd had more guts I'd have gone myself.

But that was all of six weeks ago. Now we were on the move again, still one up and still one to go: and this time it wasn't going to be so easy. I had more courage screwed up, but I was going to need it. Six weeks at Corinth had educated the Germans. My pal's voice came back to reassure me: 'You'll do it, son,' it said, confidently. 'Just watch your chance. It'll come. And remember, it's not as risky as it looks. There's only one thing. When you *do* move off, for Christ's sake move fast.'

For a moment or two I felt more cheerful. After all, this was Greece, not Germany. All I had to do was dodge the column, and once clear I was safe. And if it comes to that, I thought, what better time than now? It's dark and we're dog-tired, but there's more than a grain of comfort in that. The guards will be dog-tired too. I took a quick glance up and down the column.

The big German walking just ahead seemed to sense the decision. He snapped out of his lethargy, surveyed the column of prisoners in sudden alertness, and hitched up the strap of his Schmeisser. Fat bullets in the magazine winked at me and my resolve weakened. I felt my knees going queer. A sudden vision came of three khaki figures sprawled grotesquely at the side of the road. I shuddered. Those Aussies had also gambled on the guards being too sleepy to shoot.

It was nine hours and twenty-odd miles later before the chance came. By then it was midday, and a Greek sun was sending heat-hazes rippling off the road. Everyone was grey with fatigue. Even the guards were parched with thirst, but the column stumbled on. We were nearing the last village before the repaired railway line. There were only two miles left, with every yard in dead flat country.

The commotion began farther up the line. I saw the front men surging around a roadside pump, filling bottles, pushing their heads underneath, taking huge gulps and sluicing layers of grey dust off their faces. I walked quicker in sudden, fierce exaltation.

The first part couldn't have worked out better. Men drifted away from the pump and straggled up the road in ones and twos. The foremost guards were halting them just around the bend. The other Germans were either filling water bottles or watching the crowd still fighting to get at the pump. Momentarily, the vigilance slackened. Ahead of me, a clear fifty yards of road lay unpatrolled. I took one look behind and turned sharp right. Nobody took any notice. My knees wobbled a bit as I got down by a pile of wood, but that was allowable. It was those three Aussies again. One of them had stopped and put up his hands, but it hadn't influenced the Germans.

Guttural voices were reassembling the column when the real ordeal began. Footsteps sounded at the side of the house and I waited in a tense agony of expectation: but it wasn't a guard. An old crone appeared, saw me, and began screeching at the top of her voice. From her gestures I gathered she was warning me there were Germans about. In greater anguish than before, I implored her to be quiet. 'Shut up, you old fool!' I hissed. 'Pipe down for Christ's sake. You'll have me shot. Go on, beat it! Don't stand there gawping. Beat it! Shove off!' Fragments of Arabic gushed under the strain. 'Imshi!' I urged. 'Yellah!'

The old woman stood her ground, not understanding. I dug feverishly in my kitbag and found a coloured scarf. 'Look,' I pleaded. 'Here's a present for you. Now for the love of God, beat it! Get the hell outa here!'

A moron couldn't have failed to grasp the idea. The old lady took the scarf, looked at it and walked away. I breathed again. A moment later she was back, this time with a swarthy middle-aged man who knew his own mind. He made his point crystal clear. Either I went or he called the guards. One look at that beetling brow ruled out scarves, and very slowly I got up. It looked like this was it. I set off across the flat field. There was no point in waiting for a bullet.

Both ends of the long file came into sight. I was only thirty yards from the column of prisoners, and harsh German voices tortured my ears; but I didn't run. A running man is a mark miles away. It could be any time now. . . .

The file stretched interminably. Seconds passed, each of them an age. I was too tense even to pray, but the expected shouts and rifle cracks didn't happen. Suddenly the ground began to dip. In another few seconds I was out of sight, and out of range. I walked into the wide stream ahead and on the far bank, dived into a clump of bushes and hugged the roots. A moment of two later the tension snapped. I'd done it. I was free, and on the first step of a retreat to our own lines.

From the top of the bank, the railway station didn't seem much more than a mile distant. The column was now clear of the village, and once again close-packed. I could see guards strung out on either side of the marching men. For those chaps, Germany lay ahead, with perhaps years of captivity. For me – well, that depended.

But it was a warm day, and for the moment the future could look after itself. The present was good enough. It was Friday, the 13th June, 1941, the only combination of Friday and the 13th in the whole year. It seemed that omens would be nothing to go by on this venture.

As the last of the column breasted a small hill and disappeared from sight, I began thinking about getting back to Egypt. It shouldn't be too hard, I decided. I'd been over the route a hundred times during those six weeks at Corinth, and if I had no other advantage, at least the geography was familiar. Turkey was the best way out. I opened a pencilled map and took another look at the cluster of Aegean islands that marked the route. They were all there – Andros, Tinos, Mykonos, Nikaria, Samos – all neatly bridging the gap between Greece and Smyrna. There was one wide stretch in the middle, but with any kind of a boat it should still be fairly easy. With real luck, I might find a caique travelling straight to Smyrna.

A voice interrupted the chain of thought. It spoke English that had a strong American flavour. 'Where've you come from?' it demanded. I looked up and saw an elderly Greek not more than a yard away. He must have come through the bushes like a cat. I pointed towards the railway station. 'I've just got away from that lot,' I said. 'And who are you, and where d'you learn English?' The Greek smiled, 'Been in the States twenty years, son,' he said grinning, 'but that's a while back. You'll be hungry, I guess.'

I was, but just now there was something more important than food. A man doesn't jeopardize his freedom for a full belly. 'I'd like to get out of uniform,' I said. The Greek smiled again. 'Sure,' he agreed. 'You stay right here. I'll be back in ten minutes. And my name's Giorgos.'

I moved to another spot when he left, to be on the safe side. But it wasn't necessary, Giorgos came back alone, and dumped a parcel at my feet. 'There's a suit here might fit you,' he said, 'although you're bigger than I am. And you needn't be scared. I won't turn you in. Didn't the Greeks fight against the Germans?'

I felt a bit ashamed at that reminder, but Giorgos laughed at my confusion. 'Try the suit on,' he suggested. I did. It was tight under the arms, and the top trouser buttons were inches out, but they were minor points. It was civilian wear, not khaki, which was all that mattered. I clapped the old man on the shoulder. 'It'll do fine,' I said. 'I wouldn't ask for better. And I'm very grateful to you.' That part was true enough.

After dark Giorgos came back again, and led me through a quietened village to his house. By this time the rest of 'B' Company were probably nearing Yugoslavia. The sharp night air seemed to emphasize my freedom, and I felt sympathy for them. Sixty men in one cattle truck, with no sanitation, no food, and precious little water, isn't the best way of travelling. So far as I knew, Barlow and I were the only ones who were missing.

The stone house was full of people. Giorgos had gathered the clan together, and as soon as we went in a dozen Greeks began pumping my hand and slapping me on the back. The English were welcome in Greece. The old man restored order, and sat me at the low table. The others crowded round, pressing all manner of strange foods on me, and toasting the Anglo-Greek alliance in lashings of red wine. Giorgos interpreted: 'They're glad you escaped,' he said. 'They don't like Germans any more than you do. But they want to know what your plans are. Where will you make for?'

I took another pull at the wine. It was good stuff. 'Egypt,' I said, 'as quick as I can.'

'How will you get there?'

I shrugged my shoulders. I'd like to know the answer to that one, too. 'By boat, probably,' I told him. 'Via the islands. But I might go to Athens and get on a caique. There'll be plenty going to Turkey from there even now. It'll be some time before the Germans start checking up. I'm not sure yet. I'll think about it to-morrow.'

A criss-cross of voluble Greek followed, and then the old man spoke up again. 'They say Athens is best,' he summarized, 'but it's a big place. D'you know anyone there?'

This put me on firmer ground. 'Yes,' I said. 'There's a man in Kephissia I know well. Very well. He's like a blood brother. If I can get to Athens, I'll be all right.' That seemed to convince the Greeks. We had another round of handshaking and good wishes, and then they left. Women stretched blankets on the wooden floor. I took my boots off and was asleep in an instant.

Next morning I gave Giorgos my uniform, all my kit, and what money I had as a token of thanks. In turn he presented me with a cartwheel loaf and a flask of wine: and as the sun topped the nearby hills, I set off for Athens and Liberty. I felt fine. The morning sunshine seemed to bring Cairo and Shepheard's Hotel all the nearer. Corinth, tightly-jammed cattle trucks, even the unhappy men of 'B' Company, were fast becoming memories. I was as free as a bird. Somewhere down South, my pal was free too. Maybe I'd find him again before long.

Athens had been an obvious choice. It was about 200 miles away, and at least eight days' walk. That was along the main roads, where it would be policy to keep a weather eye open: but it was still the best bet. I didn't know just one Greek there, as I'd said. I knew six. Of those six, Rosebud and Pedro alone should be able to 'fix' a caique.

The tracks were easy enough to follow. I kept to those which ran parallel with the road, and at first made surprising progress. On the first day I covered about 30 miles. On the second I walked 25: but on the third, my good luck deserted me. I doubt if I walked five miles that day. An increasing stiffness was seizing my legs, and as the day wore on, it got worse. Soon after I started, the former brisk pace began to slow down. By mid-day, it wasn't a pace any longer. It was a crawl. I began to get alarmed. Two days' march shouldn't knock me up like this; but it was doing. At dusk I gave up the Athens trip altogether. I couldn't go on. It was painful now even to walk.

The sudden lameness was probably an after-effect of the Corinth camp. The Germans had packed us in like sardines – five thousand men into a barracks built for eight hundred. The Luftwaffe had already blasted whatever sanitary system the place originally had, but that didn't count. There was no water, except from a few deep wells, but apparently that didn't matter either. In we went, and before long the inevitable happened. Dysentery ran riot through the camp. Diphtheria followed on its heels, but the medical staff pleaded in vain. Red Cross officials came and promptly condemned the place. The German authorities weren't so quick off the mark, but when they did come, even they agreed it was unhealthy. That was considerable understatement. By this time prisoners were dying rapidly.

The plague hit me without warning. In the space of ten minutes I was unconscious. The hospital was full, so I stayed unconscious on the stone floor for three days. Someone pushed a kit bag under my head, and another Samaritan covered me with a great-coat. Apart from that, nobody did anything. They couldn't. Live or die, I was fighting this battle on my own. Probably the only person interested was the chap who used my rations to ensure his own health.

I came to about noon on the fourth day. In an hour or two I was up and about: by the evening I was weak, but quite better. Why and how remain mysteries; but I do remember getting mad at the cook-sergeant's refusal to refund the missing rations.

Very likely the present paralysis dated from that illness. It was getting worse, too, which frightened me; and realizing I'd have to rest a few weeks I headed away from the main road towards the hills. The Greeks were souls of kindness and generosity. They fed me with all kinds of delicacies, massaged the numbed legs, asked hundreds of questions I wished I could have understood, and in short, did their best. Some wanted me to stay with them, but I said 'No' to those offers. It was too near the road yet for safety.

I pushed on. On the flat I went slowly. When the tracks began to climb, I went slower still, and the pace kept slackening until a village carpenter made me a pair of crutches. They were a big help. My arms were strong, even if my legs were three-quarters dead. On the fifth day I was numb from the waist down, and had to use the crutches to hoist myself up: but I was getting used to the idea. That night I slept between sheets in a schoolmaster's house, and dreamt I was home. In the morning I found I couldn't see. My eyes were stuck together with some kind of discharge, and had to be bathed before they would open. It seemed I'd got conjunctivitis as well.

This more or less put the top hat on things. It was bad enough being a cripple, but up to now I could at least see where

I was going. I pressed on despite the double difficulty. Before I could accept any lodging offers, I had to be out of reach of German patrols; as much for the villagers' sakes as for my own.

I was beginning to understand some of the weird language these people spoke. 'Penas?' meant 'Are you hungry?' and was fired at me a dozen times a day. It was easy. All I had to say was 'Penow,' and out came a feast. I liked 'Penas.' 'Ap po poo eiste?' which meant 'Where've you come from?' was harder. I could get as far as 'Ichmalotus – Anglia' – 'Prisoner – England,' but after that I stuck and had to rely on arm waving. The positive and negative bothered me too. If I wanted to indicate 'Yes' I had to shake my head and say 'Nay'. For 'No,' the drill was to wag the head up and down, and say 'Oiche'. It was confusing, but I got into it.

I stayed with the schoolmaster for two days, mostly because there was no choice. I could neither see nor walk during that time. I would have stayed longer still, but on the third day word came that the Germans were searching villages lower down. They knew some prisoners had escaped. They also knew that a good many more had never been captured, and from what we heard, the searching seemed to be thorough. I had been expecting something like this. The schoolmaster, who spoke French, told me the news, and agreed the best course was to get moving again. His wife gave me half a loaf and a packet of olives, and wept as I hobbled away. I could have wept, too, in annoyance. I didn't want to go. I wasn't nearly fit enough to travel, and what was more, those blasted Huns were chasing me from the best house I'd yet been in.

I plodded on for another three days. Each morning I had to prise my eyes open with finger and thumb, and then wait for a sympathetic Greek to bring the bathing water. I was well up in the hills now. The tracks were poor, and growing fainter, and the district seemed safe enough from patrols. I felt more cheerful. My eyes were all right as soon as I got them opened and bathed, and vision wasn't affected. As regards the paralysis, well, I'd stopped worrying about it. It would be hard put to get any worse than it was. I swung along between the crutches and reached Dremissa in fairly good shape. It was a village about 4,500 feet up in the Parnassus Mountains.

Dimitrion Theodoron stopped me. He had been watching me struggling along the track for over an hour, but he'd let it rest at that. I was coming his way, and these days it didn't pay to be inquisitive with strangers.

The crutches reassured him, but he was still cautious. He pushed his hat back and looked at me for a while. Then the usual preliminaries began. 'Ap po poo eiste?' he asked: but I wasn't feeling strong enough for Greek. 'I'm an English soldier,' I said. 'Escaped a week ago. I'd like a drink of water.' I put a thumb to my mouth and tilted my head back. 'Nero, chum,' I explained, 'water. Nero.'

The Greek's interest quickened. This time he spoke in English. 'What's wrong with you?' he asked. 'You look bad.'

'I am bad,' I assured him. 'You'd be bad too if you were me. And now how about that water?'

Dimitrion ignored the request. 'You've done well to get this far,' he pointed out. 'We're a long way from the road here. Where did you escape?'

I waved backwards. 'Larissa, I think. There's a river there.'

Dimitrion thought again. 'Have you seen any Germans since?' he asked. 'I hear they're hunting you fellows.'

It struck me that this conversation wasn't getting us anywhere. What I wanted was a bed for the night, not a discussion on Huns or my health. I might as well carry on. 'No, I've seen no Germans,' I said. 'I don't think they'll get this far. You're safe enough. Cheerio.' I turned away, but the Greek jumped after me.

'Hey!' he shouted, suddenly becoming human. 'You can't go like that! God damn it, man, you'll be out all night. You come home with me and we'll eat.'

This was more like it. Once I got sitting down, I would hardly be asked to leave before morning: and sleeping out wasn't my idea of comfort. I'd been trying it the last two nights. But I needn't have worried. I wasn't to know then, but this was Journey's End for a while. At least until I was fit again.

Dimitrion helped me along the cobbled lane towards the village, and stopped at one of the nearer houses. A boy of about seven saw us coming and promptly vanished inside. He reappeared with a pleasant-looking woman who glanced at me, first in alarm, and then more in pity as she saw the crutches. She took a few steps towards us.

'This is Maria,' said Dimitrion. 'My wife.' He patted the lad's head. 'And here's Cristos. He's a chip off the old block. Now let's go in.'

Maria was a sensible woman. She got out a bowl of water, and began bathing my eyes as soon as her husband had manœuvred me on to a stool. The lad vanished again, but after a minute or so he was back, this time with a glass of goat's milk. I smiled at him and took a long drink.

Over the meal Dimitrion told Maria who I was and what had happened to me. Then he told me about himself. I gathered he had been born in Dremissa – in this very house, to be exact – but had left for America when he was sixteen. He stayed there twenty-four years, changed his name to Jim Thompson and, like most Greeks, did well. Very well. At one time two restaurants bore the name 'James Thompson', and a dozen men were pedalling his ice cream carts all over Chicago. I took another glance at the sparsely furnished room and felt a bit doubtful about that one.

'Then what in the world brought you back?' I asked.

Jim grinned. 'I didn't expect you'd believe me,' he said, 'but it's true. A good many of us came back. I suppose you've met some of them?'

He was right there. I had. One or two of the older Greeks did speak English, but so far I'd not bothered to be inquisitive. 'Well why did you come back?' I persisted.

Jim smiled again. He didn't exhaust conversation too quickly. 'The '29 crash,' he said ruefully. 'Ruined every Goddam one of us. Fellows were shooting 'emselves left and right. I took a boat home instead.'

'But what made you stay here?' I was going to get to the bottom of this.

This time Jim laughed outright, and explained the question to his wife. She laughed too. 'I met Maria,' he said chuckling. 'And just when I've got her persuaded to go back to the States, along comes Cristos. I guess we've never made it since.' Maria showed her white teeth in a wide grin. Little Cristos, not understanding anything, but wide-eyed with the novelty of a stranger, and not wanting to be left out of the joke, thumped the table in delight. I decided I liked this family.

Later on, Jim suggested I stayed with him until I was fit again. I didn't argue. 'You can stay till the war's over, if you like,' he added. 'It's quite safe. As you said, we're too far from the road for patrols, and there'll be three feet of snow when winter comes. That should stop them. It stops us going anywhere. What d'you say?'

I didn't have to ponder for long. 'I'll stay,' I said. 'My legs are not too good. I don't suppose I'd get much farther if I did leave you. I'll stay till I'm better, anyway. Then we'll see. And it's damn decent of you. Thank you.' That little speech made me embarrassed. It sounded an almost casual answer to the princely offer Jim was making: but he wasn't looking for thanks.

I spent my first week in Dremissa wrapped in blankets and recuperating on the wooden floor. The Theodorons' daily life went on as usual. It was a Spartan life, but there was no lack of variety in it. The house had only two rooms, one above, level with the path, and one below. Jim and his family lived, ate and slept in the top room. Underneath was a mule (ex-army), an aged donkey named Jericho, a hen, three chicks, and a mountainous heap of odds and ends. Originally there had been nine chicks, but stray cats had so far got six of them. Maria guarded the survivors as if they were her own children. The mere sight of her was enough to send any cat in the village racing for its life. Through cracks in the floorboards I could see the old hen cluck-clucking around, with the chicks hard on her heels. Periodically Maria did a sentry turn on the wooden verandah, and now and again Cristos let out a yell and hurled stones at possible marauders. Life didn't get much chance to grow stagnant.

The bugs worried me at first. Every house in the hills is full of them. The climate, the design of the houses, and their owners' tolerance, make them inevitable. And Greek bugs are big and bite hard. The first night I was nearly eaten alive. After that I slept on the verandah, where it was colder. The few that still troubled me walked a long way to do it.

TWO

Time passed quickly. The conjunctivitis cleared up in a week, and soon after, a little strength began trickling back into the numbed legs; but it was a slow job. A month had passed before I could use a stick in place of crutches. Another went by before I could throw the stick away. I was slow and clumsy even then, but I kept improving. 'Maybe another month,' I thought, 'and I'll be fit. Then we'll see about the trip to Athens.'

In the meantime I studied Greek. The proposed trip to Athens made it more or less essential, but the knowledge didn't come easily. Greek has more complications to the square inch than any language bar Chinese. Like Chinese, it is written in code, presumably to keep students at a distance. It was hard going.

Cristos gave me the first lessons. We opened his school primer and did *alpha beta gamma delta* all the way to *omega.* The lad was hazy himself about some of the harder letters like *psi* and *epsilon,* but we persevered. He had the right pronunciation, which was what I wanted. When we finally closed his book, there was a double sigh of relief: but we were both a good deal wiser.

As soon as Cristos reached his limit I transferred to a couple of adult tutors. One was Tyki, an Athenian undergraduate and son of the village Papas. The other was Costas, the schoolmaster. They were both eager to help. Both understood French, too, which made things easier, and all told, I put in about five or six hours' study a day. About half the time was spent in teaching them English, which was fair exchange, but I made the best progress. That was mainly because a dozen or so amateur teachers pounced on me at all hours of the day and insisted on putting me through my paces. It was a wearing business, but good for the vocabulary.

There had been no sign of Axis troops during these two months. It didn't surprise me. Dremissa was almost inaccessible, and in the July and August of '41, both Germans and Italians had other things to think about. Russia was being overrun by the Wehrmacht, Crete had fallen, and the Libyan see-saw was in full swing. Almost every day saw some tremendous event, but only the vaguest whispers reached us. We were too secluded, too cut-off, for important news to filter through. And because none came, I let the war look after itself, concentrated on Greek and getting well, and thought only about people I knew. By now, the rest of 'B' Company were probably getting accustomed to barbed wire: those who had missed the draft would either be sunning themselves in Alexandria or moving up into the 'blue', and my friends in Athens would be getting familiar with German method the hard way. As for Barlow, God alone knew where he was. I could only hope he had found as sweet a billet.

During these days I felt as secluded as a Trappist Monk. Only the mail plane droning high overhead each day on its way to Berlin even hinted there was still a war on. We knew nothing, we learnt nothing, and I was glad when the village fête came to interrupt the even tenor of our life.

It took up a whole day. The Greeks have a number of patron Saints, and each one gets his due recognition. The ceremony is called 'Kronia polla.' Literally it means 'Many Years,' colloquially 'All the Best' – and the wine flows. Every family with the Saint's namesake in its ranks holds open house.

It was St. Cristos' day, which meant there would be a good many 'open' houses; and as custom decreed we should visit all of them we didn't waste time. At the third house I was giving the salutation 'Aseyean' as correctly as Tyki. At the eighth, being a more seasoned toper than the young undergraduate, I was doing it better. We took three glasses at each stop, and enjoyed the sweet-tasting wine more with every glass. Before we were halfway through the village I was doing the greetings for both of us. It was new wine, not very strong, and they were small glasses, but forty odd packed a punch. For all his college upbringing Tyki couldn't take it: but he was no quitter. It was polite to go the round, and Tyki didn't intend to miss anyone. He grew aggressive about this. He, son of the Papas, would visit the whole damn flock, if he did it on his hands and knees.

Towards ten o'clock he was on his hands and knees, and by this time I was swaying myself. We pulled in at Epthemios' house to give our legs a chance to recover.

Epthemios was stone sober. He hadn't been visiting, but he was full of a great rambling yarn that flowed pleasantly over our heads. We sat down and let him talk. He could talk his head off for all we cared. You could relax with a man like this.

But eventually the flow ceased and reluctantly Tyki and I got up to go. Epthemios saw us to the door. 'You do understand, Vassiliou, don't you?' he asked earnestly. It dawned on me that his harangue must have been addressed to me. 'It's your big chance,' Epthemios went on. 'Go tomorrow. Don't forget. To-morrow certain, or it'll be too late.' I leaned on Tyki, and turned round to face Epthemios. Tyki felt the hand on his shoulder and promptly collapsed. He vanished over the low verandah rail, and robbed of support, I went backwards down the wooden steps.

A tremendous hullabaloo arose. Epthemios shouted in alarm, his women screamed, and two dogs below began barking like mad. A dozen others joined in, and doors and windows flung open. One would have thought the war was over: but it was unnecessary fuss. Providence looks after drunks with a special and benign care, and neither Tyki nor I were scratched. We missed the hard cobbles by a few feet and landed on a patch of grass. Our anxious host helped us up, and began feeling for broken bones. The warning about to-morrow was forgotten, Tyki got back on his hands and knees, grunted ' 'Nicta, V'siou,' and set off home without any more ado. An hour later I found Jim's house.

The heady influence of the wine wore off soon afterwards. New *cressi* is a grand drink. It tastes good, it can make a man as drunk as a lord, but it never leaves any trace of a hangover. I felt fine. Jim was waiting. I knew why as soon as I got through the door. 'Did you get that message from Epthemios?' he asked. 'His wife's just been here.'

I shook my head. 'No,' I admitted, 'I didn't. He gave me some message, but I wasn't listening. I was with Tyki and we'd just been round the houses. You should see Tyki now.' I grinned at the thought. 'What was the message, anyway?'

Jim's answer cleared away the last mists. 'There's a chap in Kokovista,' he said. 'He's from the Underground. He wants to see you to-morrow night.'

I timed the journey well. In the hills distances are measured in hours, not kilometres, because walking is the only way to get anywhere. I knew Kokovista was two hours distant, and by allowing three for the journey, I got there just after dark. That was according to instructions. I found the house and gave two long and two short knocks, also as per instructions. Somehow I didn't feel too optimistic about this business, but it had the right atmosphere.

A girl opened the door, and showed me in. I stood for a minute or two in the living room, probably whilst unseen eyes checked up on me. A tall Greek then came into the room. 'You're Vassiliou?' he asked, offering his hand. I nodded. Vassiliou Zoneras was the nearest anyone had got to my name. 'I'm George Mathias,' said the Greek. 'Call me George. And don't bank too much on it yet, but I may be able to help you. Fill this in, will you?' He gave me a sheet of paper, with the words 'Name, Rank, Number' printed in English. I wrote down the details and handed the paper back. There might be something in this yet. George glanced at it, and folded it away in his wallet. 'Well, that's all right,' he said cheerfully. 'Now let's see about some clothes.'

With that, he opened a trunk and brought out four or five suits. I chose one and tried it on. It fitted. 'This'll do nicely,' I said. 'Now suppose you tell me what it's all about. Or if you can't answer that, when do we start?'

George smiled. 'No, I can't tell you much,' he admitted, 'except that this is a big business. I'm only a pawn in it. I can't tell you when we start either, but you're guessing right. When we do start the idea is to finish in Egypt. Let's leave it at that, shall we? Don't leave Dremissa for a while. Maybe I'll send you a message in a week or two. Now let's have some supper.'

I gave him back the suit, and saw it put away separately from the others. After that neither of us mentioned Egypt or the Underground, until I was leaving. 'I'll be waiting, George,' I reminded him. The Greek made the Victory sign with his fingers. 'Don't worry. I'll not forget,' he promised.

One result of that Kokovista episode was a 'get-fit' campaign. My legs were almost better now, but they pained if I walked too far. A mile or so was as much as I could do in comfort. It wasn't enough. I wanted to be able to run. If George Mathias' trip did come off, it would involve some brisk walking. If a few bullets started flying about, which might easily happen, I would need a pair of legs in sound working order. Even if the whole scheme fell flat, it still left that trek to Athens; and 150 miles is no joke.

I called next morning on Panagioti, the village *Proitherus*. He had a flock of fifty sheep, and for some time past had been short of a shepherd. He jumped at my offer. At first he wanted to pay me, but I explained that I wasn't interested in money. What I wanted was to develop leg muscles like a kangaroo. I'd been shot at before many a time, but on those occasions I'd always had something to shoot back with. Next time I wouldn't have any answer but speed and the grace of God.

Panagioti's job certainly promised an abundance of exercise. The sheep roamed high up in the hills, sometimes as far as ten miles away. Two shepherds, working in shifts, looked after them; but the men had to walk to and from Dremissa as well. They could put thirty miles into a day and think nothing of it: and most of it was over rough ground. It struck me that a month on the job should be sufficient.

Panagioti would have agreed, but he was worried about the pay packet. He was headman of Dremissa, and had a position to uphold. He didn't like the idea of cheap labour. For my part, I still didn't want any money. As I told him, I didn't want for anything and had no use for it. In the end we compromised. As well as being *Proitherus*, and possessing a big flock of sheep, Panagioti was ahead in other directions. He owned the village pub, too. For my services I got the freedom of the place and a retainer for Jim. I clinched on that offer.

It was a grand job. Each morning, just after dawn, I called at the side door of the Kafineou, and greeted the new day with a glass of wine and a slice of hot bread. The ouzo and absinthe could wait till I got back. A loud snore coming from the room above indicated that the publican was at peace with the world, but his wife was always up. Mrs. P. was a curious woman. She did her baking at odd hours too, but she had no rival in the village. Her wits weren't too keen, but she cooked like an angel: and after greeting her, and sometimes getting a special pastry for the trouble, I picked up my freshly-baked loaf, the parcel of figs and olives, the bottle of wine, and the dogs' can of porridge and set off to find the flock.

I worked from dawn till dusk. Thakis, Panagioti's son, took the night shift, and was often hard to find in the early morning. Usually his cheery bellow 'Kali mera, filimou!' greeted me when I was least expecting it, and the two dogs would come bounding up for their breakfast. They were huge animals, more like bull-mastiffs than sheep-dogs. They weren't brainy, but then they weren't expected to be. That was the shepherd's prerogative. Greek sheep-dogs are bred more for size and ferocity than intelligence. 'They guard the flock from wolves,' Thakis told me, 'and my God, you should see them fight! But there's two-legged wolves in these parts,' he warned. 'You'd best keep your eyes open.'

At first they would have eaten me, but for Thakis, and it took a full day before the idea penetrated that I was a friend. Now we were great pals. The morning porridge was cementing the friendship, and although the brutes weren't over-bright, they could smell breakfast a hundred yards away. They would race towards me, tongues out and tails wagging, rear up and thump affectionate paws on my shoulders.

Whilst they ate, Thakis and I got our own breakfast ready. The reluctant ewes contributed a bowlful of milk. Into it we dropped pieces of still-warm bread, and took turns with the single spoon. There never was such a breakfast. There never will be again. Mrs. P.'s angelic bread, made from whole wheat, and rich ewes' milk, and an Arcadian glade in which to eat. Who could ask more? We squatted on our heels in the grass, and ate from the communal bowl until we were both full. The dogs lapped up the rest, and then, with a belch of contentment, Thakis got up and set off for home. For the next twelve hours I was a shepherd in my own right.

The work made me move about more than I had expected. The sheep were active at this time, and I was continually bounding up and down the hillside searching for strays. The dogs would obey whistles and round up stragglers, but they were dense over locating them. They reckoned that was my job. By the time the sun peeped over the high mountain ridge, I was tired out; but fortunately the sheep then began taking things easier. They worked up the steep hillside and towards midday grouped together and lay down. It was the slack part of the day. The two dogs also settled down for one of the short naps they took in lieu of regular sleep; but each kept an ear cocked, and like the half-wild brutes they were, they dozed lightly.

This was the time I always looked forward to. Up here in the mountains there were no wars and no worries. I was my own boss. I did what I liked in a kind of animal happiness that knew no conventions. I had no money, possessed nothing, and neither state worried me. The sun shone and it warmed me. I had food and drink, and when I needed it, shelter. I had the dogs for company, and felt more contented probably, than many a millionaire.

It wasn't the first time the war had put me in Easy Street. There was that month in Palestine for instance, when I drove the Brigadier's car: and again, in Cairo, when I got a fortnight's duty as a medical orderly in the Berka Street brothel area. I was furious over the insult at first; but the anger cooled quickly. Life at the Early Treatment Centre was soon making me wish I could finish the war there. It was the soldier's idea of bliss – no parades, no inspections, nobody rooting about interfering – nothing whatsoever except six hours a day 'condy-walloping'. Even that wasn't unpleasant. There was an air of dignity to it. We wore long white gowns, operating theatre hats, and a professional air. On evening shifts, which were busy, we sterilized little nozzles, handed out ointment, gave advice and mothered odd drunks. Customers came from The Garden of Paradise next door, from Tiger Lil's above us, and from half a dozen houses in the vicinity. We got to know people. We got to know the prostitutes quite well. Fat old harridans like Tiger Lil weren't easy to stomach, but some of the girls were good company: and during the slack day shifts, with a shooting war only a hundred miles away, we gallant soldiers of the King lounged outside a bawdy house drinking coffee with a pack of prostitutes.

Here in the mountains I found the other extreme. There was peace and purity in these hills, and the war seemed far away. The German advance had by-passed all the remote mountain villages. The odds were against them ever being visited. An army needs roads, and not even a bicycle had got to Dremissa yet.

My thoughts wandered on. How about staying here? Permanently? Why not settle down in this village, and live at the easy tempo that hadn't changed in centuries? Other places were full of the frenzy of war. Here was peace and leisure and safety. Again, why not stay?

But it was only a pipe-dream. At the end of the month Epthemios brought a message that sent me once again hot-foot to Kokovista. George Mathias greeted me warmly, but he didn't seem very happy. 'It's bad news, Vassiliou,' he said, tersely. 'The organization's being watched by the Gestapo. I'm afraid the trip's off.' My face dropped. This really was bad news; but if the Gestapo were on the track, the people in Athens couldn't do other than drop the whole project, and drop it fast. Which left me precisely where I had started a month ago. It looked as though I'd have to go back to my original plan after all. That meant going to Athens for a passport, and then either finding a boat or walking the 600 miles to Turkey.

But George hadn't finished. He seemed a bit more cheerful than before. 'There's still a way out,' he said. 'It's just as safe, but it means we have to wait another fortnight. My brother has a caique at Piraeus, and he's sailing to Turkey in two weeks' time. Now listen to this. Suppose I go to Athens and get a passport for you? If I start to-morrow, I'll be back in a week. Then we'll go there together by train. That'll save you a pretty long walk. We'll go on the caique as part of the crew, and in Turkey you can take over and help me get to Egypt. What d'you say?'

It sounded good. I thought hard about the idea, trying to foresee snags, and then said 'Yes.' George was now full of enthusiasm. He picked up a camera, took my photograph outside the house, and slapped me on the shoulder. 'I'll see you again in a week's time,' he promised. 'I'll bring the passport with me.'

Back in Dremissa Jim agreed it was the best thing to do. 'If it works out as Mathias says, you'll be in Turkey inside three weeks,' he commented. 'That's quicker than walking. But don't forget the winter's not far off. If anything goes wrong this time, you might have to stay here till next April.'

He was right, there. It was now September, and in the North the first snows were only a month away. If Mathias was wrong about the caique, and I had to go the hard way, it was still 600 miles: and I didn't want any snowstorms on that journey.

I went back to the sheep with my fingers crossed, but trouble came after the first day. As usual the ubiquitous Epthemios brought it. I was walking back to Jim's when a sibilant 'Psst!' greeted me from Epthemios' door. The Greek stood inside, beckoning urgently. This man thrived on mysteries. I went over and the door shut behind me. 'Well, what do you know now?' I asked. 'Got a submarine?'

Eph. shook his head. 'No, Vassiliou,' he said, quite seriously, 'there's no submarines around here. But there's something almost as good. An English major is in Ligorias.'

I looked up. 'What? Are you sure?'

The Greek nodded eagerly. 'Yes. He got there this morning. Maybe he's from a submarine. He could be. And there's something else. The Italians are sending out patrols. You'd better watch you don't walk into any of them.'

Poor Thakis had to do a double shift next day. I told Panagioti about the Ligorias major, and sunrise saw me heading towards the high mountain that separated the two villages. Ligorias, on the other side, was much nearer the main road than Dremissa. According to Eph. it was six hours away, but he was thinking of the recognized route. Because of his alleged patrols I was following a little known path that meandered all over the hills.

It soon got me into trouble. The path was difficult to see even in broad daylight, and several times I had doubts whether I was still on it or not. When it petered out altogether at the bank of a river, I knew for certain. Still, it wasn't important. I knew the direction of Ligorias and losing the track only meant the going would be harder. The river was also deceptive. I walked in, expecting it to be waist deep and it came up to my shoulders. On the far bank I squeezed out a gallon of water and began wishing I'd risked those patrols. More so, five minutes later. I came out of a small wood and found the river had made a neat horse-shoe turn and was in front of me again. The mountain loomed up encouragingly just ahead. I slithered down the bank and made towards it. This time I stepped into an unseen hole and had to swim a few yards.

I was still using strong words when I reached the top of the mountain; but at the summit all the murderous feelings were stilled. To a doubly-soaked mountaineer in a bad temper, any view would need be good to be noticed at all. It would have to inspire. The one that awaited me was all-compelling.

It was the Balkan scene I had always imagined. The wooded mountainside dipped sharply at first and then shelved into a wide valley. Taller trees towered above their fellows like church spires. Their lofty plumes nodded gently over a solid green mass which descended each side of the valley and encroached right to the edges of the tiny cultivated areas far below. Clusters of Lilliputian houses glinted in the sunlight. Along the bed of the valley a narrow ribbon of water twisted in tortuous fashion, winding towards, and finally losing itself in the open plain beyond. Opposite, another mountain rocketed upwards, its summit reaching clear and gaunt into the sky. Wisps of cloud caressed the snowcap. It was the tallest peak in the Parnassus.

The majesty and grandeur compelled a halt. For a while I forgot my quest, but recollection came sharply. Somewhere below was Ligorias, and in Ligorias an English major, perhaps with the key to freedom for both George Mathias and myself. I began the long descent. It was a dangerous business. A narrow path ran along the mountainside, sometimes through the stifling heat and pungency of the pine trees, but more often along ledges where the way was perilous and open precipices, hundreds of feet deep, yawned and waited for a careless step.

But somehow word went ahead of me. I reached Ligorias and found the major had gone to earth: and from the reception it seemed he had briefed the villagers first. 'What?' they asked, incredulously. 'An English major? Here? In Ligorias? No, you're mistaken. We've seen no English major. And it won't do you any good staying here.'

They spoke in hard unfriendly tones. I sought out the *Proitherus* and worked on him for a while. In the end I got him convinced I was neither a German nor an Italian agent, but I had to name half the people in Dremissa to do it. Even that got me no further: and after two days in the village the major was as remote as ever. Most of the villagers came over to my side, but none would discuss him. They had been briefed too well. In the end I gave up. Someone was there, I knew that, but I was having doubts about his rank. Probably the 'major' was just another escapee trading on a spurious crown, and too ashamed to come out and admit it.

On the other side of the mountain I got lost again. A Red Indian would have had his work cut out keeping to that track; but it was no more serious than before. The Parnassus is a maze of paths. If you lose one, you're bound to strike another before long, and so get the general direction. Normally it wouldn't have worried me: but after the Ligorias hoax I wasn't in too good a mood. What I wanted was home and the sound of familiar voices. This was no time to get lost.

The prospect of a night in the open made things worse. The sky had become overcast, and presently, the rain came down. I walked on and ignored it. I was still well off the track when the river came in sight. I said a few things and walked through. The rain began pelting down, but by now I was past caring. There is a degree of wetness beyond which you don't get wetter. I had reached it.

But the bad luck was ending. I came out of a clump of trees and saw a well-defined path a few yards ahead. A minute later a Greek came striding along. He was an elderly man, dressed in a huge shepherd's capa which enveloped him from head to foot. He looked like an outsize gnome, but he was a friendly type. A bushy red beard, glistening with rain drops, jutted out from the hood of the cape. Above it, a pair of twinkling eyes surveyed me interestedly.

'You're wet,' he declared. 'Where are you going?'

'Dremissa,' I answered. 'Is this the right road?'

Redbeard looked puzzled. 'No, Dremissa's six hours away. Over there.' He pointed to a range of hills behind me, and looked closer. 'You're English,' he asserted. I nodded. If he had said I was Chinese, I wouldn't have argued. Redbeard smiled. 'Well, you'd better come home with me,' he invited. 'You'll not make Dremissa to-night. Not in those wet clothes. And a meal wouldn't hurt you either. Did you fall in the river?'

I let that pass, and fell in step with him. I was feeling happy for the first time in three days, and willing to overlook a lot.

THREE

The inside of Redbeard's home was a real haven. Outside, the weather was steadily growing worse, and dark skies offered no promise of relief. I took off jacket and jersey, and sat down by the huge wood fire. A group of children, perched nearby, watched curiously as little clouds of steam began to rise from me. The old man, dry as a bone beneath his hair armour, busied himself helping his wife. Soon a pot of thick porridge appeared on the low table and appetizing odours began to fill the room. Everything looked fine.

It was good porridge. The warmth of it crept through me in little glows, as if to emphasize that all's well that ends well; but the day wasn't done yet. As we were finishing, a neighbour burst into the room. 'The Italians are here!' he hissed. 'They're searching the houses.'

We got up abruptly. I put my half-dry clothes on and made for the door, but the old man stopped me. 'Where d'you think you're going?' he demanded.

I looked at him, astonished. 'Where d'you think?' I asked. 'I don't know any more than you, but I'm not stopping here. Why, you'll get shot if they find me.'

But Redbeard blocked the doorway. It seemed he didn't scare easily. 'You can't go,' he objected. 'You'll be out all night. Listen to that rain.' He argued for a minute or two, but it was time wasted. I knew the Italians would be checking identity cards, and I hadn't got one. And I wasn't going to get this Greek into trouble just because he was obstinate. Nor myself, either, come to that.

In the end we compromised. The old man pulled on his capa, and we cleared the village by a side track. Ten minutes later both of us were in a stone hut half a mile from the village. It was nearly full of sweet hay, and seemed about as safe as any hide-out could be. In day-time two windows commanded a wide view of the approaches. At night the place was invisible. Only a villager would ever have found it, but that was all right. I could trust the villagers.

Redbeard had now come round to my way of thinking. 'You were right,' he acknowledged. 'I was over-hasty.' He scowled and spat viciously on the floor. 'Damn all Italians!' he muttered.

It was a natural feeling. There wasn't a man of the Hellenes who didn't resent the coming of the new Cæsar; and bitterly, at that. Unlike his great predecessor, Mussolini had never earned his conquest. Italy's crack divisions had been hurled out of Greece, in one of the most signal defeats in military history, only to be rescued in the nick of time by the Nazi hordes. And now these would-be legionaries were lording it as masters of the Hellenes. The Roman press was using all its superlatives about their alleged battle prowess, and worse, was boasting of victories which had been degrading routs. It got the Greeks on the raw. They fumed savagely at their humiliation; and gave escaped British prisoners devoted and fanatical support.

I enjoyed that night in the hayshed. It was like sleeping on a warm cloud, and none of the little creatures that went exploring had anything but the friendliest intentions. I woke up bone-dry and refreshed. From one of the windows I saw a woman, with a creel on her back, approaching the hut. It was Mrs. Redbeard, as the old patriarch had promised: and at the bottom of her creel was a half a loaf, some apples, a big piece of *tiropeta* – a kind of mountain cheese pie – and a flask of wine. She had done me proud, but there was something else – a battered copy of the New Testament. Where it came from was a mystery.

'Giorgos says to stay in the hut,' warned Mrs. R. 'The Italians are still in the village. He'll come and see you to-night.' That forced me to wait until the old man came. I had been hoping to see him about dinnertime, and then be on my way, but I couldn't go without saying 'Thank you.'

It was a bad day. It was too slow. From one window I watched the sun rise, and from the other saw it sink, and the hours crawled by. I read the Bible as far as St. John, made a collection of twelve different kinds of insects, and wove a rope from hay. After dusk old Giorgos came with a can of soup, and another warning. 'They're still there,' he said, 'and there's two more patrols in the neighbourhood. It looks like you'll be here awhile yet.' I began to object, but the old man cut in. 'I know what you're going to say,' he smiled. 'You'd rather take a chance. And you can pass as a Greek. Well, perhaps you can, but you've no passport. You know that. And they're checking up on passports. No, Vassiliou, it's too dangerous. You stay here another day or two. Better that than get captured. Eh?'

He won the argument, and I agreed to stay one more day. Giorgos beamed. He said something derogatory about Italians, gave me a cheerful 'Kali-nicta' and left in great humour. The private vendetta was going well.

I had another comfortable night, but the second day was punishing. I finished the New Testament, read most of it again, found six more insect specimens, and wove a rope forty feet long. But the minutes still crept past on tip-toe. Before the day was gone I had one point settled. This wasn't the life for me.

Giorgos made less fuss than I had expected. He shook his head philosophically, said the Greek for 'Ah! Well!' and when I pressed him, admitted that he too might prefer to risk patrols rather than skulk in a barn. 'But be careful,' he urged. 'Keep off the tracks and keep a look-out. And God be with you.' I said my thanksgiving speech, and we shook hands. He was a good man, old Redbeard.

I left before dawn, and headed over the hills for Dremissa. By midday I stood on the last remaining crest. Stromei lay behind, and through the trees below, Dremissa's church tower was gleaming whitely. An hour later I tapped on Jim's door and went inside.

I sat down gratefully. Jim's look of alarm got me up again. I reached for my stick resignedly and prepared to go. 'They're in Kokovista,' Jim said. 'About twenty of them. We're expecting them here any time. You'd better not stay.' I turned at the door. They were all over the place, these Italians. 'What about George Mathias?' I asked. 'Any word?' Jim shook his head. 'No, he's not been here,' he said. 'There's no news at all.' That was a blow. I'd been banking on George Mathias and that caique, but perhaps it was only a temporary delay. 'I'd better go,' I agreed. 'Look, Jim, Mathias should have been here yesterday. If he comes, tell him to wait. I'll be back in three or four days. That'll give us plenty of time to get to Piraeus, and maybe the Italians will be gone then. Cheerio!'

I couldn't have chosen a better time for leaving. There didn't seem to be any hurry, and a little way up the hillside, I sat down by some bushes and took out a packet of bread. It was long past dinnertime. Below me the village houses spread out in their disorderly array. I could see children playing in little groups, and Maria's washing fluttering in the breeze. Panagioti came out and began walking towards the Kafineou. It was opening time. He was almost within hailing distance. Immediately below me was the path from Kokovista, but except for a few foraging goats, it was deserted. I was thinking of going back and having a few glasses of wine with the boss when another glance at the path banished the idea. The goats were no longer alone. Striding along towards the village were six blue-clad figures, each with a rifle on his shoulder.

Luckily the bushes hid me. I was about twenty feet above the Italians, but none looked up, and so none of them saw the interest in my face. Except in prison camps in Egypt, this was the first time I had ever seen Italian soldiers.

They passed the outlying houses, and the news spread like wildfire. Children were snatched up from doorsteps, villagers appeared from nowhere, and the Kafineou emptied. The customers stood and watched the invaders sullenly. One of the soldiers stepped forward and began delivering a harangue. I got up. It was time to go.

Towards dusk I was standing outside a small cemetery eight miles away, feeling very tired. I had been walking up and down steep hills since before dawn, without ever once getting a decent rest or a proper meal: but it was still too early to go into the village. For all I knew it might be the patrol H.Q. I crawled into a little stone hut in the cemetery and lay down. The floor was damp, but there was a long wooden box on one side offering itself as a couch. It was a pity it wasn't long enough. I got a recurring crick in the legs, and after about an hour, opened my eyes and gave up trying to sleep. It was now almost dark. I looked up, and in the dim light saw what looked like a row of white faces peering down at me. I shuddered, suddenly realized that this was a charnel house, and shuddered again. I had been trying to doze in a room full of ghosts and long-dead people. I took a skull down, and the jawbone waggled on its hinges. I put it back quickly, and turned to the box. The far end was open. Inside lay a motley assortment of human bones – ribs, pelvises, vertebrae by the dozen, thigh bones, big bones, little bones, all in a glorious mix-up.

But I knew what it was all about. The Greeks don't believe in wasting cemetery space. They dig up corpses after five years or so, and lodge the remains in these huts. It takes about thirty years to fill a hut, and by that time everyone in it is anonymous. The enterprising Greeks then cart the bones away, rebury them at some distant spot, and forget about them: and much can be said for the practice.

I left the hut and went into the village. An old lady, sitting outside her door, stopped me, and the usual pleasantries began. These mountain Greeks have none of the aloofness of city folk. They take an interest in strangers. They like to know who you are, where you are going, and something about you; and they are not frightened of asking questions. If you care to give a few family details, so much the better.

My old lady opened up in the approved style. 'Poo tha pass?' she enquired. 'Nowhere special,' I replied. 'Maybe I'll stay here to-night. (If I'm asked, I thought.) I've come a long way to-day.' 'Where from?' 'Dremissa. And before that Ligorias. Over all the hills. They were very steep hills.' There was no harm in laying it on a bit. The old lady took a closer look. 'Are you English?' she ventured. She seemed keen that I should be English. I agreed with her. 'Yes, I was a prisoner, but I've been free a few months now.'

In time, I thought, we'll get on to the question of digs. But you mustn't hurry these folk. My prospective landlady's eyes were now filled with tears. 'Your poor mother,' she grieved. 'She'll be wondering about you. She won't know where you are.' That was another nail struck bang on the head. My mother had no idea where I was. She couldn't have had any news at all for over six months, but there was little I could do about it. I'd send word at the first opportunity, but what was immediately important wasn't sympathy, but dinner. In due course, it came. Still weeping, the old lady took my arm and escorted me into the house.

I stayed there two days. No patrols came near the village but one visitor appeared who interested me very much. He was Gerald Mills, the first New Zealander I had yet seen since the German victory.

I liked that Kiwi. Like me, he had been captured at Kalamata, at the foot of the Peloponnesus, and like Barlow, he hadn't stayed to see what Corinth had to offer. He reacted in much the same fashion by jumping off the train en route from Kalamata. He crossed to the mainland, and since then had been wandering about the Parnassus, keeping an eye open for the mysterious agents we heard so much about. So far, his vigilance had brought no reward. 'I'm fed up,' he confessed. 'There's supposed to be Secret Service chaps in these parts, but I never meet them. They're too damned secretive. That's the trouble. I keep hearing of submarines too, but nobody ever tells me where they are. Not until it's too late, anyway.' He thought for a moment and then smiled. 'I think I'll join up with the hill troops,' he added. 'Coming?'

It was my turn to grin. Mills knew as well as I did that there weren't any hill troops. Not at this time. The Greeks hadn't yet split into their rival factions, and the Partisan movement was in the embryo stage. Everywhere we heard whispers of hidden 'opla' – weapons – but never of warriors wanting to use them. The men who were later to become Andartes and Elas troops, and to be yet another thorn in the German flesh, were still villagers. Their heyday was two years distant.

I found Mills an unusual type. For a start, he was making no effort to learn Greek, although it would have helped him considerably. He had the brains, and would have been fluent if he had tried, but his moral convictions wouldn't allow it. They forbade any attempt to learn foreign lingos.

I had never met such a rabid Nationalist. His world was composed of two classes, with the dividing line as sharp as a needle. You were either a white Britisher, said Gerald, or you were a Wog, and no half measures about it. The Greeks were good folk, he allowed, but they were still Wogs, and ever would be, along with all the rest.

For most of his conversation – the Wog dictum and so on – I didn't argue, but the Kiwi had a surprise up his sleeve. I was telling him about George Mathias and the caique when it struck me he might like to come too. I sounded him. 'Maybe George can fix up another passport,' I suggested. 'He's got something to do with the Underground. He should be able to.'

Gerald shook his head. 'No, Bill,' he said. 'Thanks all the same, but I've got a better idea of my own. I'll let you in on it, if you like. Ever heard of Zante?' I was puzzled. 'No, who's Zante?' I asked. The Kiwi smiled. 'It's not a he, fathead. It's a place. Over on the West coast. There's a port near there the Wops are using as an M.T.B. base. Well, I'm going to take one.'

My eyes opened wider. This man took some getting used to. 'You're going to what?' I said.

Mills was quite calm. 'I'm going to take one. A motor torpedo boat. To Malta.'

'You're going to pinch an M.T.B. and go to Malta?' I stuttered. 'And who the hell's going to let you?'

The Kiwi remained unruffled. 'I shan't ask,' he said. 'I'll just take it. If I can. It's only 400 miles, so I'll be there by daylight. Like to come?'

It left me blank. It was some time before I realized he was serious, but he was. This harebrained idea had been turning over in his mind for weeks now, and he had the pros and cons all weighed up. He knew something about marine engines, and enough astronomy to use the stars as a compass. The only uncertainty lay in getting the boat: but that should be possible. Zante was a quiet place. The M.T.B.s were probably not guarded all night long, but they would almost certainly be fuelled and ready for action. Gerald intended to swim out, reconnoitre, board an unattended one, and make a beeline for Malta. So far, so good. He paused a moment and then went on. 'By the time the Wops wake up I'll be ten miles away,' he calculated. 'Malta's 400 miles due West, so about ten hours should do the trip, and you can rule out interception once I get started. Planes won't be any use. I'll be three quarters of the way there before it's light. In any case an M.T.B. at full speed makes a bad target. D'you think it sounds any better now?'

Frankly I didn't. There were far too many 'ifs' about the whole business. If the boats were there, to start with: if the Italians were as sleepy as Gerald made out: if the engine would start: and if by any chance he did get near Malta, whether the British garrison would be kind enough not to blow him and his boat out of the water. No, this idea wasn't for me.

Temperamentally the Kiwi and I were poles apart. He was a gambler, prepared to stake his all on the one chance. My long suit was caution. Probably I was just as ready to face a risk, but I did like to know what it entailed. There would be risks, of course, if either of us intended to get back. We knew that, and we were prepared for them, but here the resemblance stopped. Mills was willing to stick his neck out like a giraffe. I wasn't.

He left early the next morning. I never saw him again, but it is unlikely that the scheme went off according to plan, or the world would have acclaimed it. What other ideas followed I shall never know: but I would wager the intrepid Kiwi tempted the gods with every one. He had queer notions in some ways, but he had a bellyful of guts to go with them.

FOUR

I went back to Dremissa the same day. The excitement had died down, and what I heard exasperated me beyond all measure. Jim was wearing a peculiar expression on his face. 'It seems you needn't have gone after all,' he said gently. 'They weren't looking for prisoners or passports. They were doing mountain exercises. Now they've gone back to Lamia.'

Words failed me. So the whole thing had been a mare's nest. The man-hunt had been a myth. There never had been a man-hunt except in the fertile brains of some of the Greeks: and I had been hiding in barns and cemeteries, and skipping up and down mountains for no purpose at all. I felt mad: but worse news was coming. 'Mathias has been here,' Jim continued. 'He wants another fortnight. There's some hitch over your passport. He says to wait for him.'

At this I rebelled. 'I'm not waiting any longer for anyone,' I said emphatically. 'Mathias will want another fortnight when this one's up. Well, he'll go on wanting. I'm going to Athens to-morrow. I can't afford to wait any more. Time's too short.'

Jim shrugged, but he didn't argue. He would be sorry to lose me, I knew, just as much as I would be sorry to go, but both of us were aware it had to come. 'I think it's the best idea,' he agreed. 'If you don't go very soon, you'll be here all winter, like I told you. But we'll miss you, Bill. I don't know how Cristos will take it.'

I hadn't realized before just how close the Theodoron family had grown to me. There was a lump in my throat when the parting came, and Jim was uncommonly quiet. Maria wept, but little Cristos made loud demonstrations. He refused to be comforted. Recollections of all the new games we had played flooded his small mind, and he howled for Vassiliou to stay. Jim tried his hand at diplomacy, but the little chap ignored him, and sent up fresh roars of protest. Who would play horses, he sobbed, when Vassiliou had gone? Maria baked a special *tiropeta* as a parting gift, and bade a tearful goodbye. I kissed her and the little lad and walked out and up the lane with Jim.

I wore my ordinary clothes for the trip. One Pedro, a rich and influential friend in Athens, had sent two suits, an overcoat and 10,000 drachmae via the Underground. The rank-name-number delegate's suit was still brand new, and various other people had also made donations, but the shepherd's kit was best. It made me look a genuine hillman. I wore my own army boots, now resoled with pieces of old motor tyre. The *changaris* at Kokovista had made a new pair to measure for 500 Dm, but he used wooden rivets in lieu of nails. I knew that one day on rough tracks would be enough for them. For the rest I wore Greek army breeches, putties, a heavy jersey and jacket, a woolly capa like Redbeard's, and a battered cap. A black beard added realism. All I needed to be a genuine hillman was the precious *taftotita* that only Athens could supply.

I shook hands with Jim and waved to him from the bend of the track. Below me lay the road, eight hours distant, with Athens 160 miles to the South. I called in at Kokovista, told George I was leaving, and at dusk saw a white ribbon gleaming faintly below. The track from Dremissa had descended 4,500 feet, every yard rough and boulder-strewn, and the smooth highway beckoned enticingly.

But the main road had none of the security of the mountain tracks. There were patrols on this road, and far too much military traffic. And knowing that one request for a passport would be more than enough, I decided to go canny, and walk only by night.

It was easy going. Long treks in the mountains had built reserves of stamina into my legs, and the now sturdy members made child's-play of the level road. I walked all through the night. Several cars and lorries passed, but none stopped. An hour after dawn I left the road, followed a track, and came eventually to a fair-sized village. Dremissa was thirty-five miles behind. The night trek had covered twenty miles, and I was still fresh. It was encouraging. At this rate I could be in

Athens in a week.

The villagers were up and doing, despite the early hour. I weighed up the chances of a good breakfast, and decided they were bright. An old man standing by a tub of steaming water gave me a cheerful 'Kali mera,' and followed it with the routine 'Where are you going?' He looked a friendly old boy. 'Athens,' I told him, 'but not just yet. After breakfast, perhaps. I've been walking all night.' The Greek looked closely at me, and then offered his hand. These old folk could tell every time. 'My name is Angelos,' he said. 'I like Englishmen. You'll have breakfast with me. I've to kill a pig first, but it won't take long. Then we'll eat. Come!'

I followed him to the back of the house, where a fat porker was snuffling about in the grass. The old man took a knife from his belt and put it between his teeth. He walked up to the pig, and began tickling its flanks until the pleasant sensation made the animal sit on its hindquarters. Angelos moved like a flash. He grabbed the pig's snout with one hand, and with the other, plunged the knife hilt deep into the exposed neck. Blood spurted, but the pig was held fast. In a moment or two it rolled over, and gave its first and final squeal as it died. It was remarkably neat slaughtering. It was humane, too, and quick, with none of the cacophony of squeals and blood-choked gurgles that stuck pigs usually make.

'Let's go inside,' Angelos invited, jerking his head towards the house. 'The women will fix this.'

Over breakfast I heard all about the family. Angelos had lost his son in the Albanian fighting and now had to work the farm with the help of his wife and three daughters. He felt the bereavement keenly. Occasionally his eyes would stray towards the photograph of a young man in uniform, and I could see the tears welling up. But the old man kept a grip on himself. He made the sign of the Cross and turned to me. 'Tell me about yourself,' he said abruptly. 'How did you get here?'

I was only too anxious to talk. His grief was very real and for the next ten minutes or so I did my best to take his mind off the tragedy. Before long the tension eased and we were joking again. Two comely girls came in to clear the table, and Angelos introduced them as his daughters. As we sat down I prophesied he'd have two men about the house before long.

The Greek laughed. 'I won't,' he said. 'When they get married they'll leave here. I suppose a good many of my sheep will go with them. There's Vassilia, too. You haven't seen her yet, but she's the best of the lot. I'll be sorry when she goes.' He fell silent for a while, ruminating over some idea of his own. Suddenly he looked up. 'Maybe she'll choose someone like you,' he said quizzically. His eyes held mine. 'If she did take a fancy to you, perhaps you'd stay here. If that happened you'd take the place of my son. And half of what I have belongs to my son.'

I said nothing. Angelos didn't believe in beating about the bush, and this chat needed digesting. It wasn't a light project. The old boy was saying he liked me, but I didn't put that down to good looks. What he wanted was a resident son-in-law, and a husky one for preference. I fitted that part, but it seemed a cold-blooded business. Still, he was making the offer, not me. And after all, I was a free-lance and liked this life. If Vassilia had half the virtues Angelos credited her with, she was better than I deserved, but I could overlook that. Supposing I did marry the wench? Well, on that basis I could stay here for good. The self-imposed journey offered a big reward, but there was the chance of being captured, too. And possibly being shot into the bargain. Here was safety and a blushing bride. And more than a spot of the ready to go with her. Yes, this business needed thinking about.

Angelos sensed what was going on. He was a shrewd old man, and an opportunist. He believed in striking whilst the iron was hot. 'You'd have plenty to do,' he said casually. 'There's about three hundred sheep to look after.'

If material things had been paramount that would have settled everything. In Dremissa, a man with twenty sheep was considered rich, and he rightly put on airs about it. Panagioti, the publican, who owned fifty, was lord of all he surveyed. An English bank manager and Panagioti were about equal in status. And now here was this Croesus, with his flock of 300, wanting me to be his heir apparent, with a lovely bride, a house to live in, and all found. It was temptation indeed.

I came out of the reverie. 'I don't know what to say,' I confessed. 'You're offering everything and I've got nothing. Let me sleep on it, will you? I'm dog tired now, and my head's fuddled. We'll talk again later.' It seemed to satisfy the old man. 'Come on then,' he said. 'I'll fix you a bed.'

I slept the clock round. Those 50 kilometres had taken their toll, and it was dusk before I woke again. A wash in ice-cold water made me as good as new, but by this time my mind was made up. I liked Angelos' idea. It seemed even more attractive than before, and visions of the unseen goddess almost swayed the issue. After all I was young and fit, and wanted a woman. More than that I wanted a girl upon whom I could lavish the affection that had been bottled up so long. Men don't think about girls all the time. When they do day-dream it doesn't always concern sleeping partners. The average chap likes his wench to shine out of bed as well as in it.

For all this philosophy I said 'No' to Angelos. It seemed to me he was getting a raw deal. 'I'm sorry,' I told him. 'It's generous of you to treat me as you have done. I'd like to stay too, and do my best, but I can't. I just can't. I don't know why. Maybe it's because if you start something, I suppose you have to finish it.'

I don't know what made me deliver that oration. It wasn't virtue or excess of patriotism, I was certain of that. I'd never yet managed to get worked up on patriotic issues. I had gone into 'this man's' army because the adventure of it appealed to me, and because I was glad of the chance to quit a humdrum job. There was another reason. It was vaguer, but roughly it meant I'd fight for those nearest to me. There was even a streak of vanity about that. I guessed there'd be the usual crew of dodgers, and thought the authorities would put out the flags for those who came running. As it happened, they didn't. They were aloof and inclined to be fussy; but it was too late then.

Angelos was more than disappointed. He had been banking on my accepting his offer, and I could see he was full of ideas about the new regime: but he took it well. His shoulders shrugged in the typical Greek manner. 'It's a pity,' he said briefly, 'but there it is. Let's have supper, shall we?'

We went into the kitchen. The low table was set for a meal,

with yesterday's pig occupying a place of honour; but I had no eyes for it. The pious resolution began to wilt. Vassilia, the third daughter was there, waiting to welcome us. A smile parted her perfect lips, white teeth flashed in the lamp-light, long silky hair gleamed over a face of consummate beauty, and the shadows played tricks with a figure that was at once alluring. Old Angelos was playing his ace of trumps.

I managed a polite greeting and sat down. I was feeling weak. Here was I doing my damnedest to obey the dictates of Conscience, and the old villain had to spring this on me. He had no right. It was enough to weaken a saint.

The young goddess sat down by me and Angelos began carving the pig. There was a twinkle in his eye. I ate my share and tasted nothing. Vassilia's charm and poise forbade that. I was joyfully heaving overboard the whole stupid idea of leaving when a little voice spoke in my ear. 'Selling yourself?' it asked. It was Conscience butting in again. I came back to earth with a bump.

The alert Angelos was watching closely, trying to read the answer to this complex riddle. I looked up, gave an almost imperceptible 'No', and the Greek gestured in despair. He did so need a man to take his son's place. But he was a brave old warrior. He filled the glasses and passed one to me. 'Well, Vassiliou,' he said, 'let's drink to your journey.'

We were both heavy drinkers. We also had brand-new sorrows that needed drowning and four bottles went in the next hour or two. It was strong stuff, and we rocked slightly on getting up. I paid my respects to the good lady and the three girls, and guided by Angelos walked out into the night. He was coming with me as far as the road. At least that was the intention, but after a few minutes it seemed doubtful if either of us would get there intact.

The sharp night air redoubled the effects of the wine. I fell into a ditch, and sat there feeling sad. It was bad enough leaving Vassilia without my legs giving trouble too. Angelos, who had gone on alone, came back and helped me out. Soon after, the rôles changed. I helped him up, and each of us put an arm around the other's shoulder for support. We continued this Rakes' Progress as far as the road. My opinion of the old

Greek had gone up tremendously. Never once during that journey did he mention a word about his disappointment, or even hint that I was a fool to go. If he had done either, we would have gone back together.

I started off again on the long trek to the capital. My feet were good, and the long sleep had restored all the spent energy. For four hours I kept a steady pace that ate up the miles relentlessly. One should never hurry on a long march. Haste preoccupies the mind, and the body demands rest before it should do. A consistent pace makes movement automatic and sets the mind free.

I hardly knew I was walking. My head was too full of Vassilia. I was conjuring up all sorts of visions of long slim hands, delicious smiles, captivating curves, and the marital bliss that might have been. The way I was feeling I could have walked to Kalamata and not noticed it.

The sound of an approaching vehicle brought me back again. The innate caution that warned by sight and sound of possible danger had temporarily relaxed. Now there was no time to do anything. Questing headlights had stabbed out, illuminating the road for a quarter of a mile ahead. I walked on without looking back. There was no option. Bare fields stretched on either side, and to run would invite shots. The lorry drew nearer and with a squealing of brakes stopped alongside me. I glanced up, half-expecting a guttural German challenge: but a woman's voice put my mind at rest. I breathed again. The Germans had a habit of throwing suspects into jail and forgetting about them: and what the Greeks knew of Averoff prison wasn't good to hear.

The woman spoke in the broad dialect of the mountains. 'Is this the way to Levadia?' she asked. A group of people in the back of the lorry stared down curiously.

'Yes,' I said. 'It's about 30 Km. straight on. You can't miss it. There's an Italian road barrier there.' The driver bent to engage his gears when an idea struck me. Here was a lift offering itself. 'Wait!' I shouted. 'I'll come with you.'

Willing hands helped me up, and the lorry restarted. It was packed tight. Something moved on the crossbar I was holding, and looking down I saw a fowl hanging by its legs. There were half a dozen all in the same sad plight. The wheels bounced in a pothole and one of the birds uttered a forlorn squawk of protest. Nobody took any notice.

The people were travelling at this hour to avoid the frequent halts of the day patrols. I knew none of them, but had no hesitation in saying I was English. The Greeks were completely loyal. The news travelled around and everyone jostled in the confined space trying to shake my hand. We all pledged the union of the two countries, and one enthusiast began singing the Greek anthem.

The driver had promised to stop half a mile outside Levadia. I had no papers and had to skirt the town to by-pass patrols: but our man was a bad guesser. He should have admitted he didn't know the route. He jammed the brakes on suddenly and the lorry pulled up almost in its own length. The sound of Italian voices floated up. . . .

It was as well that no one panicked. I edged to the back of the lorry as quickly as I could, and found a soldier standing below. A long bayonet gleamed dully on the end of his rifle. He stood there for a minute or more, leaving me to wonder what next, when a voice sounded. 'Ricco! Viene qua!' it ordered.

I knew no Italian, but this lesson was easy. Somebody, thank God, wanted this Ricco chap. He answered the summons, and like greased lightning I was over the tailboard and away. The rubber soles made no sound, and about a hundred yards down the road I stopped. Ricco was now back at his post. A dozen flashlights were flickering around the lorry.

I decided to pack in for the night. It was about 5 a.m. and dawn wasn't far off. Also, I was ahead of schedule, thanks to the lorry lift. A nip in the air warned me that this trip should have started a month ago: a fierce nip, that chased me out of the ditch almost before I had my head down. I abandoned the vagrant's standby, and searched for better shelter.

Farther along the road I found it. It was only a broken down old hut, but a welcome flicker of light was coming from within. Two very shabby old men were inside, sitting by a wood fire. I gave them a cheerful 'Kali spera sas!' got no answer, which surprised me, and sat down to warm my hands. The old men looked on suspiciously. Probably they were resenting the intrusion, but that couldn't be helped. I was easy about it. If they didn't like me, well, they could go find another place. I brought out bread and olives, and as a friendly gesture, invited them to join in. That changed everything. They were a pair of disreputable rogues but they were certainly hungry. Everything I had came out of the bag, and vanished down the old men's gullets. They were still looking hungry when the feed was over.

An Italian bugler awakened us with his 'Reveille'. It was light now, and the three of us prepared to leave the hut. I pulled on the capa and had another look at my sleeping partners. The daylight didn't flatter them. Nine magistrates in ten would have given them a couple of months on sight. They puzzled me, too. Neither spoke Greek, and both were far too surly to have anything in common with the hill folk. I felt glad I was leaving.

The old men had been talking in low tones, and eyeing me covertly. Suddenly the taller of the two spoke. 'We want some money,' he said. He had a harsh voice, and a pair of beady eyes that toned well with the rest of his features. 'We want some money,' he repeated, more truculently.

I began to feel annoyed. I had intended to give them a grubstake, despite their looks, but this tone was too peremptory. 'Go to the devil,' I said.

A passing patrol car slowed down for the barrier, and the beady-eyed tramp moved nearer. 'Give us money,' he threatened, 'or we call the guards. You're English.'

For a moment I thought of knocking their heads together. Then I thought again. They were old men, but both were wiry characters; and the Italians lounging at the gate were within earshot and rifle range. It wasn't a pleasant predicament. I dug in my pocket, and by pure bad luck, brought out the only 1,000 Dm. note I had. It was more than the rogues had expected. It was more than I had intended to give, too, but it wasn't a time for haggling. The second tramp caught hold of the capa, and got the heel of my hand in his face. Italians or no, that capa was staying where it belonged. The blackmailer picked himself up, and set off with his pal towards the barricade.

For the next five minutes I ran hard through a wood opposite.

I was furious, but still free; which was all that mattered. Except one other thing. No Greek had yet let me down. 'Those old bastards aren't Greeks,' I thought. 'Maybe they're Turks. Why, I spoke better Greek than they. They'll tell the Italians as sure as fate.'

A loud 'Kali-mera!' interrupted me. I turned, and saw a Greek, sitting on a fallen tree, beckoning. He had a huge loaf in his hand, and with true peasant hospitality called over, 'Come and eat!' Over breakfast I told him about the two Turks. At first he frowned, but soon his face grew red with anger. This was a proud and patriotic Greek.

'Let's go and knife them,' he offered. 'They won't have got far yet.'

I had some trouble dissuading him. It was a sporting gesture, that, if ever there was one, but I could hardly allow a stranger to champion me. 'Don't mind them,' I said, mollifying him, 'I'm still free, so what odds? Anyway, I may come across them again. Somewhere where there's no Italians. If I do, I'll fix them.'

That cooled the fiery Greek a little. He dived into his bag and pressed another loaf on me. His wallet was out next, but I made him put it back. I hadn't much use for money, and no intention at all of taking his. A bottle of cressi eased the tension further. We passed it from hand to hand, and it struck me once again what a good thing cressi is. The Greeks have a mercurial temperament. They fly into fierce rages over matters we might dismiss with a shrug. They are hot-blooded, and need the soothing balm of good wine all the year round.

My new friend controlled his wrath with the first bottle, and subdued it altogether with a second. We toasted Elatha and Anglia and dismissed the two tramps. They had it coming to them. It couldn't be long now before some self-respecting patriot would stiffen them, and do the world a good turn. And feeling my old self again, I shook hands with the now amiable Greek, got my bearings, and left.

I kept off the road after that incident and followed the railway instead; but the day had made a bad start. Nearing a bridge, I spotted the familiar blue uniform, and promptly got off the line to detour. It was wooded country, but a break in the trees revealed the stream that out of sheer cussedness had to be there. I walked through it. Something told me the day wouldn't be too good, so it was no use getting steamed up at this stage. Two minutes later the path emerged from the trees and continued through a neat line of tents.

Shirt-sleeved Italians watched interestedly as I passed. One of them shouted some remark that amused the others and brought out more Italians to see what was going on. Further sallies followed and then one or two catcalls, but nobody tried to stop me. After all it *was* a public path. I cleared the camp and carried on.

The track wandered over the hills and through odd villages in a roundabout haphazard manner. As usual, it was rough and stony, and hard to walk on, but I had good boots. George, the Kokovista cobbler, had put his best into them. During the day I met three ex-prisoners, all Cypriots. There were at least twenty Cypriots for every other escapee in Greece. Greek was their own language, and they had been quicker to seize their chances; which emphasizes what has been said before. If you are going to escape – go early and go fast. It's ten to one they'll never miss you.

One of the Cypriots had settled down permanently. He had papers to prove he was born in the village where I met him, he had a regular job, and was even engaged to a local girl. There was nothing wrong with his staff work.

The other two were birds of passage. They were friendly but formidable men who had chosen the harder course, and were doing all they could to get back to Egypt. They were trying all they knew, and they really were tough. Two nights before, they had gone down to a roadside house to contact an 'agent'. Unwisely, they decided to sleep there: and somehow the Italians got to know about it.

Near midnight a dozen armed carabinieri surrounded the house and called confidently for a surrender. They were a bit too confident. As they banged their rifles on the front door, the Cyps charged out of the loosely guarded rear, both blazing away with revolvers at the startled Italians. They saw two men go down before their own headlong rush carried them through the cordon. The darkness, ally of all hunted creatures, swallowed them up, but not before a machine gun burst caught one in the leg. He fell, but the uninjured Cypriot stopped, picked up his friend, and both escaped. The next day they lay low. A Greek doctor came to tend the injured man, and fortunately it was only a flesh wound. During the following night the two men put a dozen miles between them and the scene of battle; and the heavily-reinforced carabinieri searched high and low in vain.

FIVE

These were gallant deperadoes, but not all the Cyps were built that way. Nor, for that matter, were all the English. I met plenty of Cypriots in the hills, about half a dozen Colonials, and no Englishmen at all. Yet in Athens, hundreds of English, Anzac and Cyprian soldiers were being concealed from the Axis troops. Amongst them was a small band of renegades, who were working for the Germans.

I had been warned about these decoys. Usually they entered bars and cafés, had a few drinks, and then began bawling 'Roll out the Barrel' at the top of their voices. It was guaranteed to stop all conversation, but anyone unwise enough to warn the vocalist soon found his mistake. Several plain clothes Gestapo would conduct him to the door, where a car was waiting. The notorious Averoff prison was the first and only stop.

The traitors got a commission for each victim, but fortunately they weren't a brainy crew. Very few showed any initiative, and soon Greeks and British alike had every Judas marked after his first job. Not all the decoys went unrewarded. There were 'accidents', even whilst the Germans were about. I knew one Englishman, engaged in this vicious business, who betrayed half a dozen men. He died suddenly, just before the Liberation.

The intrepid pistol-packing Cyps were representative of the better type of escapee, but there were all too few of this calibre. The majority of us stayed hidden in Athens or wandered over the Grecian peninsula with less fiery ambitions. A good many abandoned altogether the idea of getting back to Egypt: and in this the Greeks aided and abetted them. They wanted very much to produce a live English soldier to our boys on Liberation day.

On the whole they did their guests well. The famine touched very few escapees. Their hosts were invariably rich, and when riches and shortages get together the offspring is a black market. Most of our lads had plenty to eat and drink, and had a roof over their heads, and all had a bed to sleep on. A minority who possessed a cat-like ability to land on their feet, went one better. They found lady friends who shared their beds and soothed away the anguish of being parted from Company Orders.

I met one of these happy warriors. 'You should stay in Athens,' he advised me. 'Y'know, you're a fathead trying to get back. It can't be done now. The Jerries are wise to everything. I'm not risking it. I get three meals a day here,' he produced a photograph and winked at me, 'and the nights aren't too long.' Judging from the looks on that very seductive wench, I didn't imagine they would be. And from this point of view, it did seem a little harebrained risking life and liberty in mad escapades.

The ramblers held a higher status. They were about midway between the Athenian bedroom battalion and fighting escapees like the two Cyps. Some of them took up roving in the hills because they reckoned it was safer; but most were genuinely trying to get away.

It was never impossible. Even at the height of Axis vigilance, boats still left for Turkey: but these trips weren't advertised. Would-be travellers had to find the details themselves. German agents were also on the scent, so it was not surprising that many a red-hot tip, given in good faith and conscientiously followed up proved to be a red herring. British submarines were also said to be evacuating ex-prisoners, but here the curtain really came down. Only men personally contacted and vetted by British agents ever stood a chance. Certainly no widespread search was made for passengers, nor could one have been expected. There were very few agents in Greece, and the bulk of them probably had more important work to do.

I hadn't a dog's chance of a submarine. The prospects of a boat weren't much brighter, but I intended to worry about that when I got to Athens. My Greek friends there would fix the passport, at all events. Maybe, I hoped, they'll fix a boat too.

By the sixth day the reunion was getting nearer. It was straightforward travelling now. I had walked about 25 miles each day, and all the food and shelter I wanted had come gratis. There were no more scares. Now it was merely putting one foot in front of the other for about ten hours a day. I skirted the big town of Thivai, dodged the last barrier at Shismatari, and rejoined the road, only forty miles from Athens.

I got there the same night. A lorry stopped for me, and the mob of civilians in the back did a further miracle of congestion. The end two hauled me up until I got astride the tailboard, with one leg in and one out. I clung like a limpet to this chancy hold all the way. It put years on me. The lift was saving two days' travel, but I would have walked for a week to have got off.

We had a lunatic at the wheel. He ignored all dangers. Road safety wasn't Greek to him, but it was something he'd never heard of. We charged down hills at 50 m.p.h. mostly in neutral and I shut my eyes against appalling drops at the side of the unfenced road. Near the bottom the horn blared continuously. Brakes screamed as the lorry slowed, and I shut my eyes again. If anything gave, we were done for, but strangely enough, none of the Greeks looked worried. We took open corners at full speed, blind corners a little slower and none of the steel-nerved passengers turned a hair. Miraculously nothing got in the way. Providentially the brakes and horn held out and in Omonoia Square the nightmare trip ended.

It was some time before the outside leg came to life again. At first I limped towards Pedro's house, and then changed the limp for a half-trot through five minutes of agonizing pins and needles. I was heading towards the rich suburb of Elevsis. Pedro, who owned several cafés, and who had sent me the clothes and money, lived there.

I liked this little Greek. I liked his wife more, but she was his wife, so it had to stop at that. Pedro was a small spare man of nearly fifty, with a generous disposition. Nina was tall and blonde, a graceful large-bosomed girl who contrasted oddly with her husband excepting on one count. She also had a generous disposition. She was still in her twenties, and at first Barlow and I thought she was Pedro's daughter. The way she looked at us made us both wish she were.

At first Nina failed to recognize me. I wasn't surprised. The rough, bearded man in shepherd's clothes was very different from the spruce soldier she had known six months before. 'It's Bill, Nina,' I said. 'I've come to see you. You asked me once. Remember?' The way her arched brows lifted incredulously made me smile, but the smile went quickly. The sound of cheerful chatter was echoing into the hall. It was the sound of men's voices, belonging to men who clearly weren't sorry to be in the house: and it was in German.

Urgently, Nina put a finger to her lips. She disappeared. The door closed behind her and I was left on the step waiting: but no longer wondering. I should have guessed something like this would happen. Pedro and his wife were playing a double game, entertaining the Huns and financing their guests' enemies at the same time. They were doing the entertaining for business reasons and because it was expedient. They were financing me because they were still loyal to Greece and Greece's allies. It was a risky business. Averoff yawned for the slightest mistake; but Pedro and Nina knew that and were on their guard. They were in good company. Most of the Underground leaders wined and dined with the Boche, and their secret work was all the more effective for the 'collaboration'.

After a minute or two, Maria, the maid, came out, and we walked away. I learnt more. German officers came to the house quite often. They seemed to like Pedro, and certainly drank enough of his wine, but Nina was the real attraction. She drew them like a magnet. Her Nordic full-bosomed attractiveness appealed to these blond young Aryans, and they wanted to be more than friendly.

So far, I gathered, Nina had kept them at a smiling arm's length, but it was getting difficult. Poor old Pedro was in a cleft stick, if ever a man was. He knew what the Germans were after, and if, maybe, he had felt he could trust me with his wife, he had no illusions about the new visitors. He had none about himself, either. He was a pathetic man, and he feared the husky virility of these unwanted guests. I felt for him there.

Still, Pedro had to keep those cafés open. If they closed, he was ruined, and the men who fawned so obviously and attentively on Nina held the business trumps. They decided who got supplies, and who didn't. Their good graces were essential and therefore Pedro welcomed them. He laughed at their cumbrous sallies and beamed when they ogled his wife. He had to pretend he liked it, too. That was the worst part of all.

Maria stopped at a house on the far side of Omonoia Square. A telephone message had preceded us, and the door opened and closed immediately. I found an old friend waiting inside. He was a Greek named Rosebud. His real name was Triandaferos Triandafilithes, which means Thirty Leaves, but on the day the first British contingent landed in Greece, Triandaferos changed to Rosebud. It stayed Rosebud. With British soldiers that was inevitable. There were other Greeks with queer names. One of Rosebud's cronies was Crio Vassilio – Cold Bean. He also had contact with our Army, but he stayed Cold Bean. There was no need to re-christen a man with a handle like that.

Rosebud saw through my hairy disguise quicker than Nina, and a smile crossed his face. It broadened when he found we could throw our hit-and-miss French overboard, and converse in Greek. We had a lot to say. I told him all that had happened since that night our trucks rolled through a deserted Athens and headed South, two days ahead of the Germans. He was sorry to hear the boys had been captured. He knew most of them quite well: but Barlow's escape brightened him up. Randle, who feared little this side of the Styx, was his favourite.

In turn, I had my eyes opened about our German successors. Athens wasn't enjoying this new occupation. Not by a long chalk. The business section, especially, was looking grim. The shops were empty. Almost on the first day, Wehrmacht soldiers moved in with fists full of newly printed banknotes. In no time the Athenian stocks were moving too, en route to Hansels and Gretels in the Reich. There was no question of further supplies. The Germans brought with them armour, printing presses and very little else. The currency crash-dived.

But the business people weren't the worst hit. They were mostly the well-to-do, with reserves tucked away. It was the ordinary folk who felt the squeeze most. To them the occupation was fast becoming a matter of life and death. Bread was now rationed to 30 drams a day – one thick slice – and other staple foods were at the same level. The people were getting weaker. Every day an increasing number were dropping in the streets from sheer starvation.

The rich still got by, of course. They patronized the black market, and managed to get enough to support even their British investments: but the poor were in desperate straits.

'The infant mortality rate's up 400 per cent,' Rosebud commented. 'It's still rising. The undertakers are busy, but they're complaining the money you pay them's no good. They're right, too. It's getting worse, Vassiliou. D'you know, there are Greek girls taking up with soldiers for a loaf of bread now. They'd starve if they didn't.' He spat. 'One day soon,' he muttered savagely, 'they'll pay all right.'

I lived better than most Athenians. Two sponsors were looking after me – Pedro, and one of the Underground organizations. Food and lodging came from both, although I rarely saw Pedro, and only heard vague whispers of the Underground. Athens was stiff with spies, and when men spoke together it was generally in whispers.

I trod softly until the passport came through. I changed lodgings about three times a week, and did the moving after dark; but the *taftotita* put a stop to that business. It was an easy job. I filled in a blank card, signed it Vassiliou Zoneras, stuck a street photograph on it, and gave it to Rosebud. Next day it was back. The official seals were impressed, and the card franked by an illegible signature. Vassiliou Zoneras had become a full-blooded Greek. He asked no questions. In Athens inquisitiveness was reckoned a bad social error.

I was ready to start the long trip to Turkey as soon as I got the passport. There had been no news of boats during the last few weeks, and I was chafing at all this delay. Now the passport had come through it was a much easier journey. I had a birth certificate as well, which corroborated everything on the passport, and meant I could travel by train without any risk; as far as Salonica, anyway. From there to the Maritsa River on the Turkish border, it was more advisable to walk, but most of the journey would be behind me. All I wanted was to get moving, but Rosebud put an effective stop to that idea. There was an air of repressed excitement about him that I guessed had nothing to do with phoney documents.

'Your Turkey trip's off, Vassiliou,' he announced exuberantly. 'You're going to Egypt instead. And I'm coming with you.'

It took some time to get the whole story. Rosebud was babbling on happily about boats and secret agents, and talking too fast for me to understand. I put a hand over his mouth and stopped the flow. 'Now listen,' I said. 'Don't talk so fast. What is it you've heard?'

The Greek wriggled away. He tried to speak slowly, and the news came out in little jerks. 'I've found a secret agent,' he said. 'A British officer. Here. In Athens. He knows about you.' I did my best not to smile. 'And what's he doing?' I asked. 'Building a boat?' Rosebud looked hurt. 'No. He's got one And it's not a boat. It's a submarine. All we have to do is wait.

But I had heard that one before. Frequently. 'I'm not waiting,' I said. 'You're a beginner in this game, Rosebud. I've had submarines promised me about once a week for the past six months, but I haven't seen one yet. No. You quit talking nonsense and come on the train with me. I'm going to-morrow. I bet you we'll be in Egypt a long time before your sub gets there.'

This really got Rosebud. He could see I was laughing at his idea, and it sobered him. He began talking in earnest: and in the next ten minutes I heard enough detail of this new venture to begin having doubts. The officer really was in Athens. Rosebud had seen him. The Underground, who could be relied upon, were hiding him until he found enough men for a motorboat run to Turkey. It wasn't a submarine – I did manage to get that corrected – but a motorboat was precisely what I had been searching for. My name was on the list, too. The officer had to stay until he got a full complement, so therefore he would be relying on me. That was another consideration. To cut the story short, I stayed. Often I wished I hadn't.

That night I moved to new quarters in a flat above a German garage. It was quite safe. I lived there alone, and was a legitimate Greek. Short of deliberate treachery there could be no suspicion I was English. Three more weeks went by. About every other day Rosebud came to give details of the round-up, and to urge patience. The officer was still six men short. He seemed to be having trouble getting those last six; and often I didn't wonder. There was every incentive to stay in Athens.

I was doing fine: but for the nagging feeling of inactivity, I would have been nicely set for the duration. Pedro wanted me for an investment, and Nina wasn't at all averse to my staying. The second time I saw her, she said as much and inferred more. Both did all they could to make life easy. I had a library of English books, a gramophone, and now and again access to the B.B.C. news. I played English records on the gramophone quite openly. It didn't matter. Lots of Athenians had them, and the Germans were used to hearing them. The mechanics working in the yard below often whistled the chorus of Walt Disney's 'Heigh-ho! Heigh-ho!' Sometimes they shouted up for me to play that particular record.

But there was more in the daily round than books and music. I went to the cinema about twice a week and enjoyed the American films that were still showing. Once I found myself between two Axis soldiers, explaining part of the plot to one of them in French. On Mondays I went to a lady's house for formal dinner, but there was another weekly visit to counterbalance that. It was to the barber's girl, who was informal.

The barber, who was one of 'us', had numerous lady friends. He introduced me to Zoie, and before long I was visiting her flat. She was a sympathetic girl, Zoie, the right type to make a man's worries seem smaller. I liked her very much. She had plenty of conversation, she could wear negligé without looking half-dressed, and she cooked a superb breakfast. No, it wasn't hard to stay in Athens if you knew the right people.

The three weeks spread to four. Christmas was now only a fortnight away, and I began worrying again. On December 11th, 1941, Athens and the free world got a body blow that started them worrying too. The morning papers headlined the sinking of *Repulse* and *Prince of Wales*. For fuller measure the Germans sent out a special edition that gave details of the Jap navy, wept crocodile tears about the Nipponic threat to the Far East, and summed up jubilantly on the very slim chance of Singapore holding out. In reply, Mr. Churchill delivered one of his best broadcasts. It uplifted all the secret listeners, but even his stirring words couldn't hide one fact. *Repulse* and *Prince of Wales* were at the bottom of the sea. He knew it, we knew it, and we all felt grim.

The ebullient Italians went to town. They splashed 'V' signs all over Athens, and crowed as loudly as if their own land-locked *Regia Marina* had done the deed. They crowed less next day. Some of the more resolute Athenians had moved around with them to watch the celebration. During the night they added huge question marks to every Italian 'V'. Even the Germans laughed at that.

I continued to kill time. I did it in my own flat with the books, more successfully in Zoie's flat with Zoie, and in occasional outings with Rosebud. We were careful on these trips. In one café someone behind me slammed down a glass, grunted, and said quite loudly in English, 'Now that's what I call good beer! Who'll have a drink?' The café quietened like magic. I didn't move. Only a drunk or a decoy would use English here, and in any case, it wasn't good beer. It was a foul brew. Rosebud looked up casually and asked a question with his eyebrow. I nodded. After a while we paid for our drinks and walked out. Two hard-looking characters were loitering near the door, but they made no move to stop us. Twenty yards down the road a private car was waiting, with another tough at the wheel. I noted the number.

My own wait was nearly over. Next morning Rosebud came to the flat, bringing Zoie with him. He was in one of his most expansive moods. 'Well, Vassiliou,' he chirruped, 'It's come at last. We got word about half an hour ago. To-morrow night you'll be in Turkey.'

A weight seemed to lift itself off my mind, but I was still puzzled. 'But aren't you coming, too?' I asked. 'And what's Zoie doing here? It's not safe for her, you know.'

Rosebud laughed. 'For the next hour or two Zoie's your wife,' he said innocently. Zoie blushed, and the little Greek went on. 'She's taking you to a rendezvous. I'm going too, but I've another call to make first. I'll see you later.'

Just before noon a dentist on the other side of the town admitted us through his private door, and being a thoughtful man, withdrew so we could make our farewells alone. And faced with a bravely smiling Zoie, I began regretting this haste to get out of Athens. What was the hurry, after all? I could come back, granted, perhaps during the war, perhaps afterwards, but in the meantime it meant leaving this very lovely and very gallant Greek maiden. Zoie had virtues other than her physical charms. She was intelligent and brave. She was resourceful with it, and like so many more of her type, willing to risk torture and death for the Cause. I seemed to be having more than my share of sad partings.

I stayed that night in the dentist's house. It appeared that the British agent was not travelling with us. The dentist was purposely vague, but he talked too much, and I gathered the agent was staying behind to organize another evacuation party. Nobody, remarked the garrulous tooth puller, knew any details. And as for me, all I had to do was wait. I would be called in due course. And aware of the etiquette of these matters, I let it go at that.

SIX

Now is as good a time as any to introduce the Jinx. His family crest bore the words 'Ill-omen', and he was to figure largely in my affairs during the next two or three years. A good many men who were in the Balkans about this time know all about the Jinx. They need no further explanation. Probably they are still wondering why they were singled out, too. I can't answer that one: but I do know this. On the 16th December '41, the day after Zoie took me to the dentist's house, my own name went on his list.

That morning found me waiting impatiently in a private room. I was told to expect a call at 10 a.m. At half past nine, I began fidgeting in the chair. Ten o'clock came, and then eleven. At six in the evening I was still waiting, but by now I hadn't sat down for three hours. I was in Redbeard's barn all over again.

At seven o'clock a messenger arrived to end the suspense. The scheme had come unstuck. Thirty men were waiting in houses all over Athens, the dentist said, and like me, had been waiting since the crack of dawn; but the all-clear had never come through. The first party had been stopped by the Gestapo. Somehow, two men escaped, and after hiding all day they crept back into the city with the bad news. Instantly, telephones hummed with innocent-sounding messages that brought dismay to the listeners.

The whole affair was abandoned immediately. How the Gestapo got wind of it remained ever a mystery. Somebody had talked – that was certain; but despite all their efforts the Organization never found who it was. And for good reason. The Jinx was clever at covering his tracks.

But the Athenian underground leaders were hard men to beat. Whilst the Gestapo were still crowing over their victory, another attempt was planned, this time in such secrecy that even the dentist knew nothing. Perhaps that was just as well.

He was told to keep me in his house, and when Rosebud called, a week later, we were equally surprised. At least one of us was over-joyed as well. Rosebud was like a clam, although I made no move to question him, and in all honesty, wanted no information. It was enough, to get clear of those four walls.

We set off towards Rouf Station. Here I was too engrossed, this time in recollection, to be curious. Eight months before, I had been at this very spot. Hundreds of newly-captured Britishers had stood here too, all gathered inside a menacing ring of field-grey. Nobody wandered far. The Fallschirm Jäger boys, flushed with victory, and inclined to be a little trigger-happy, were not men to take liberties with.

We crossed the now desolate square and boarded the electric train. Rosebud seemed carefree enough during the journey, but in Piraeus he was once again caution personified. We followed a devious and roundabout route that eventually brought us to a dark street near the waterfront. It was real cloak-and-dagger stuff, this. Rosebud looked up and down, and then tapped quietly on a door. It opened immediately. I would have been disappointed if it hadn't. It was a dark and dismal evening, and the very air seemed pregnant with mystery. It was also Christmas Eve 1941.

In a room upstairs a dozen men sat at a long table, all talking in English. We entered, blinking a little in the strong light, and I felt a dozen pairs of eyes upon me. These men knew Rosebud of old, but I was a stranger and therefore suspect. Very much so. A week ago someone had split to the Gestapo, and that someone was still undiscovered. If anything went wrong this time a dozen lives were forfeit: for with one exception, these men were all Greeks, four of them active partisan leaders.

Their familiarity with English puzzled me at first, but it was easily explained. George, who was the leader, was a Cambridge graduate. Alexis had got his M.Sc. degree at London University, and Panagioti had been educated in England since childhood. The fourth man, who was also George, was an Athenian professor in English.

The quartette politely grilled me. I stood facing them in the centre of the room, and did my best against a solid barrage of questions. I had already been checked once. Somehow they had contacted Jim Theodoron, and got all the details of my past life. There were nods of approval as the present answers tallied with those in the dossier, but I found the exchange difficult. I had almost forgotten my own language. And for fear they took me for an impostor, and I missed the boat or sub whatever it was, I told them why. For seven months now I had been speaking nothing but Greek. It had got to the stage when I was beginning to think in Greek, and the mother tongue was slipping away from sheer disuse. Abruptly the interrogators switched over to Greek, and I found the going easier. This final check must have satisfied them. The elder George closed the dossier, gave me a last long look, and then winked and offered a hand. His friends followed suit, and everyone relaxed.

I sat down by a burly young man in sports clothes who had so far been silent. 'I'm Jones,' I said in English, introducing myself. 'Railhead Company R.A.S.C. I don't like Germans and I'm genuinely Jones. You can say what the hell you like. It's O.K. with me.'

The burly man grinned. 'It's all right now,' he smiled. 'We believe you. I'm Macaskie, of the Leicesters. Captain. I'm more or less in charge here. I've been watching you, too. A chap pulling a fast one keeps his face straight, but you can tell a lot from his hands. Worth knowing, that.'

This was the first time I met Macaskie. If I had known him better then, I would have relished that long speech. Macaskie wasn't the talking type. At first it puzzled me why such men as the George-Alexis-Panagioti quartette accepted him as leader. They looked far brainer and more ruthless than he did. But for the alert eyes in his rather sleepy face Macaskie looked a stodgy individual. It was the impression he liked to give. It was also one of his greatest assets. For underneath this cloak of amiable nonentity was shrewdness and an astonishing courage. Frank Macaskie already had a reputation that any officer in the Middle East would have envied: ahead of him lay exploits that were to win him the title of 'Scarlet Pimpernel of Greece'.

He had been right through the ill-fated campaign of '40/'41.

In Crete he led his company in a bayonet charge against the German parachute troops. He stopped three bullets and was captured. The Germans flew him to a prison camp on the mainland, and Frank spent some weeks in hospital. One of the bullets had gone through his middle and missed the spine by half an inch. As soon as he was fit, he got away and got back to Egypt. There was nothing spectacular in that. Many officers had done as much. Some had made even more daring escapes, but the bulk of them were content to rest on deserved laurels. Frank returned to Greece. He knew that hundreds of men were on the run there, and his idea was to evacuate them. Cairo H.Q. gave him a boat and he did the trip to Piraeus without incident. There, he set up the organization that ultimately took over 250 men back to the British lines.

The system was nearly fool-proof in later days, but at the time we met it was very much in its infancy: and teething troubles were coming fast. The Gestapo noticed the unfamiliar boat in Piraeus harbour, and promptly confiscated it. Frank was as quick off the mark. He purchased another for 250,000 drachmae, which was a relatively low price. So far the dreaded Gesta Polizei knew nothing about it. I found myself nourishing hopes that they would remain in the dark. We needed that boat first thing in the morning.

Only a few of these details came that night. Frank was not like the dentist, and after the opening gambit he fell silent. Supper came and was finished: after that we all lay down in the hot room and tried to snatch some sleep.

Everyone was awake well before dawn. We had to be clear of the coast by daylight to dodge the harbour patrol boats and we needed an early start. George briefed everyone, and soon the first couple left for the quayside. We went in pairs to avoid attracting attention, but the mist that was rolling in from the sea and reducing visibility to five yards made the precaution seem unnecessary. Rosebud found it no hindrance. He threaded his way unerringly through the mean streets and we got to the waterside without trouble. The rest of the company turned up safely and towards four o'clock a low whistle floated in from the sea. A torch answered briefly, and soon we heard the gentle swish of water lapping the sides of a boat. It nosed in towards us and made fast to the quayside. Frank and George stepped aboard and exchanged a few words with the boatman.

I didn't speak. I couldn't. I was too dumbfounded at this monstrosity wallowing by the quayside. It must have been the hoariest old relic in the Aegean. Even in the half-light its age and infirmities were blatant. There was no engine, huge dun-coloured patches disfigured the two sails and about six inches of bilge slopped about in the bottom. And we were going to Turkey in this! I tackled Rosebud.

'This isn't our boat, is it?' I pleaded anxiously. 'Why, God damn it, we'll sink if it blows enough to fly a kite.'

The Greek smiled at the note of panic. 'Yes, Vassiliou, this is it,' he said, 'but only as far as the rendezvous. The motor-boat's coming to-morrow to pick us up. And don't you worry. The old tub's stouter than it looks. We're using it to fool the Germans.'

I began to see light, but I didn't feel much happier. It would be too dangerous of course, to leave Piraeus in the motorboat. I should have thought of that. The Germans would be watching it, but not our present craft. Nobody in his right mind would put to sea in a floating coffin like this. It could come and go as it pleased.

Rosebud enlightened me a bit further. 'Crio Vassilio is skipper on the other boat,' he explained. 'He's got authority from the Germans to go to Samos. He's sailing to-morrow morning. He is going to Samos, too, and there'll be a check there, but he'll drop us near Smyrna first. Then he'll go on and do his normal trip. We'll be arrested in Turkey, but I understand Kerie Macaskie has got that fixed. All we've got to do is dodge two Italian patrol boats near the Turkish coast. I believe Kerie Macaskie has arranged that, too. Everything's planned for this journey.'

I nodded approval. If I had known all this before, I wouldn't have been so worried. So Cold Bean was bringing the boat, was he? Well, Frank might have picked a better captain. I knew Cold Bean of old: but apart from that, everything did seem well thought out. So unless Cold Bean let us down, or the Ark foundered (which seemed likely), we would be in Turkey in two days' time. The thought warmed me.

The ancient craft left as stealthily as it had come. It glided through the still waters, and we were about four miles out before it was properly light. That seemed safe enough. The boatman hoisted another sail and our speed increased; but the flat calm was beginning to ruffle. A morning breeze had sprung up. It grew rapidly fresher. Before long it was a strong wind, and the boat wallowed in the troughs of the waves. Green seas, that kept increasing in size, smacked heavily against the blunt prow. The old Ark shivered and began to pitch alarmingly. Black bilge careered up the sides, and occasionally wave-tops cascaded into the boat so that someone was constantly bailing. The motion upset Frank. He leaned over the side dismally, but the mad antics and gyrations continued. By now it was blowing a half gale. One after another we all turned green and joined the unhappy Frank. My stomach was doing hand-springs inside me. To add to Frank's misery, a gust seized his hat and sent it helter-skeltering over the billows. It landed on the crest of a wave a hundred yards away, bobbed up and down a couple of times and then sank. The way I was feeling, just then, I envied it. And this was Christmas Day!

Suddenly we forgot the seasickness. The boatman had been straining his eyes into the distance. All at once he jerked up and his arms galvanized into action. 'Down!' he shouted. 'Get down! For the love of God get down!'

Like one man we slipped off the high seats and crouched in the bottom of the boat. A flood of bilge swirled up and lapped caressingly around my middle, but I sat motionless. Half a mile away a destroyer was coming in from the open sea. It neared us, and then sped past, flat out, at about a furlong's distance, with a great wall of water peeling from either side of its razor bow. We hugged the high wooden sides and remained hidden, but in the wash of the racing warship the Ark did everything but stand on its head. I found breath and opportunity to mutter to Rosebud, 'You were right. It's better than it looks.'

It was. The old boat belied its appearance. By rights we should have gone down with all hands long ago, but beneath the battered exterior, a tough heart was beating strongly. This old tub had guts. Age had withered it, perhaps, but it was defying the years.

With all this wind we were pushing and buffeting along at a good speed. I knew now the rendezvous was an island forty miles away, and there seemed every chance of getting there by midday: but these Elysian waters are temperamental. An hour later, the wind dropped completely and a hot sun emerged. The half gale quickly gave way to a flat calm and sails that had groaned at the mast hung lifelessly. The Ark stopped. It lay motionless in a glassy sea, too far from land to be in any danger, but much too far from the isle for comfort. We were becalmed until dusk. There was nothing anyone could do except hope that no coastguard on those distant shores would get curious. Once or twice motorboats did cruise past, forcing us back into the bilge, but they were all Greek boats. The danger passed.

The evening breeze took an age to come, but all things end sometime. In due course, and in its own good time, the breeze arrived. At first it was a mere breath, but it grew stronger and more robust, until at last the sails were filled, the ropes creaked and strained again, and the old tub careered merrily towards the isle.

We got there an hour after dark. The boatman left immediately and we climbed up to a stone house on top of the island. The launch was due first thing in the morning, and nobody worried much about the uncomfortable night ahead. Most of us would have gone willingly to Turkey on an iceberg. It did grow very cold. We were in a draughty hut on top of a hill, and it was winter-time, but even so the chill was fearsome. I lay and froze on the stone floor, mourning my heavy capa. Towards dawn an Arctic bitterness descended, and in desperation I went out to watch for the boat. It was due early, but with Cold Bean in charge, I hadn't much hope of seeing it for a few hours. With Cold Bean anything could happen.

After a while Frank and Alexis came up, both numb and blue, and eventually the dawn broke. We had intermittent spasms of excitement to warm us as boats approached, but none stopped. The morning dragged on. Towards mid-day there was still no boat. Towards three in the afternoon the sea was barren of all vessels. By now we all feared the worst.

Cold Bean had been arrested. He had forgotten his directions, and was searching for us twenty miles away. The boat had broken down. And so it went on. Certainly something terrible had happened. But how could it? The boat's papers were in order. George fixed that himself. A breakdown could be ruled out, too. Frank had given the skipper enough money to buy a new engine in spares. Two mechanics were travelling with Cold Bean, and all three knew where we were, so even with the skipper's slap-happy methods they could hardly miss us. But no boat came . . .

We slept in the hut again, and were again frozen. During the night a strong wind sprang up. By morning it was blowing a gale, and all hopes of the boat vanished. No small craft would have lived in this storm. For two days the screaming of wind and the roar of crashing waves never left us. We huddled in the bare shelter of the hut. Provisions ran out and we lived on boiled cabbage and potatoes, and blessed the narrow causeway that joined us to the mainland. We got the vegetables easily enough, but none of the peasants had any cigarettes. That caused real hardship, though not to me personally. I didn't smoke then, but three-quarters of the company went around with faces as long as to-morrow. On the first day of the storm all the ends and stubs went. On the second, the smokers were like bears with sore heads. They tried grass and herbs but got no satisfaction. One of them experimented with a cigarette made from dried sheep's dung. It puffed well, and had an encouraging aroma, but it was too rank. The failure saddened everyone. On the third day it rained hard, and the most doleful group of pessimists in the Aegean sat brooding in the leaky hut, without food, without tobacco, and almost without hope.

But relief was on the way. The rain increased to cloudburst proportions, and the sky grew murkier; and just as the smokers' spirits touched bottom dead centre, a packet of Papistratos No. 7 bounced on to the floor. For a moment none of them would believe it. Some turned their heads away sharply, not wanting to be tantalized with such a vision. Then the spell broke. The packet was snatched up and passed around like lightning. In no time the room was a fog of smoke, and nearly a dozen pairs of eyes turned gratefully towards the miracle man. He was standing in the doorway, peeling off a dripping jacket.

Roy Natrousch was a New Zealand sapper. It turned out later that he had a lot of Frank's qualities about him, but that will come. He also had a familiar but still exciting tale to tell. He was near Olympus when the Intelligence people used their heads and went back to Egypt: he was mining roads near Argos when the German spearhead raced unhindered down the opposite coast: he got to Kalamata in time for the street battle, and was finally captured there. After two days he left his captors and began searching for a way back. Since then he had walked twice around the entire Peloponnesus. It was the old familiar pattern – waiting for boats that never came, trying to contact agents who weren't there, and spending too much time and energy in chasing shadows.

During the last week Roy had travelled farther than usual. That was because of some bother at Argos. There were M.T.B.s there, all ready to sail, and sometimes not guarded too closely. Roy watched one crew for a few days until he knew their routine. There was no need to swim out to that boat. It was moored at the quayside, and he knew the guard would be anything up to twenty minutes late. It was getting dark too, which was all to the good. The idea, of course, was a quick one-way trip to Turkey. It was a good idea, despite what I had said to that other Kiwi, Gerald Mills, but Roy soon found his Jinx was on duty. He got into the boat, and was casting off, when a chance party of sailors appeared at the far end of the quay.

Roy got out again. In the gloom he made a poor target. The shots all missed, and the would-be mariner lit out as fast as he could for the back country. There he heard odd whispers about us (which wasn't comforting news), and came hotfoot to join our party.

He brought good luck as well as cigarettes. That night the gale blew itself out completely. It was even warm in the small hours, and for the first time in three days we managed to sleep. In the morning our luck went the whole hog. The long-delayed boat slid quietly into the cove, and barring Frank, who never got excited, we all ran whooping down to the water's edge.

Cold Bean had used his head in one respect. He brought ample stocks of food and cigarettes, and whilst the tobacco-hungry horde had a field-day, he explained what had kept him so long. It appeared that the Germans put a ban on sailing just as he was about to leave. They didn't lift it for two days. After that, the gale kept him in harbour until early this morning. All told, we had lost three days but it didn't really matter. The boat was here now, ready for the trip, and with any luck tomorrow would see us all in Turkey.

It was dark before we left. There was also an alteration in the sailing orders that took away half the pleasure. Rosebud couldn't come. Frank and George decided that the Organization would have to know what had happened, and they asked Rosebud to report. He was the obvious man for the job, but it didn't make our parting any easier. For once the cheery little Greek looked beaten. All the smiles were ironed off his face, and he looked heartbroken, despite an assurance of the No. 1 seat in the next boat. I didn't offer to go back with him. He would have refused, in any case. We both knew he was the only Greek who wasn't already suspect and that my company could easily put the two of us in jail.

The boat chugged away and Rosebud summoned back the familiar grin as he waved farewell. Within seconds he had melted into the anonymity of rugged cliffs. Only the fluttering of a white handkerchief showed he was still there. Then it vanished. I never saw him again.

We slipped past the coastline at a steady 10 knots, and soon the boat was rolling slightly in the swell of the open sea. At long last, after all the snags and disappointments, even after this latest most bitter blow, we were well and truly on the way. Cold Bean stood at the wheel, guiding his vessel on the route through the isles. He had been this way before, and knew exactly where the patrol boats would be. We would pass between them when they were at the farthest point of their beats. Smyrna lay just over 160 miles away. I listened to the comforting thud of Diesel engines and watched the miles slip astern in a creaming wake. The skipper moved his telegraph to 'Full Speed Ahead'. The healthy pom-pom-pom of the exhaust grew stronger. A squat outline, that was Kea, loomed up, and receded into the distance: and above the gloom of losing Rosebud came the thrill of approaching liberty.

I was sleeping below when the engines stopped. The sudden quiet roused me like a shot. It roused everyone else too, and even before the boat slowed down the small engine room was full of anxious enquiry. We were still living on our nerves.

Cold Bean seemed quite unperturbed. 'It's nothing,' he said, waving a hand deprecatingly. 'We're changing fuel tanks. Don't get worried. Two minutes, and we'll be off again.' But his nonchalance was wasted on the grim faces watching him. Some of us knew Cold Bean. Those who didn't were quite certain this was no place to be changing tanks.

The two minutes grew into ten. The boat rocked idly in the phosphorescent waters. Cold Bean was having trouble. It was a failing of his. He was always having trouble. I found myself wishing that Frank had known him as long as I had. Twenty minutes slipped past, and with each one the patrol boats cut down the safety margin. If the boat didn't start soon, we'd have to go back. Suddenly the hiss of compressed air died away, and the skipper gaped blankly at the air bottle. There was no need to say anything – it was empty. Furiously now, the three sailors tried to turn the heavy engine by hand, but the terrific compression was too much for them. We stood aghast. And with each moment the engine grew colder and made the job still more impossible.

The fickle sea joined in the conspiracy. Once again a wind whipped the flat calm into a seething water. The boat tossed about like a cork. With the engine running, it would have ploughed through the waves and mastered them, but now we were helpless. We ran a sail up on the mast. Alexis slipped and nearly fell into the sea, but we got the sail up. For a moment I thought we would even yet beat the hoodoo: but disillusionment came fast. It was blowing a full Easterly gale. The boat spun round and began racing back to Greece . . .

Dawn found us close to Kythnos, an island we had passed hours before. Here, we played straight into the Jinx's hand. Like all the other islands Kythnos was a huge mass of rock jutting out of the sea. One of the few natural harbours lay directly ahead, and without so much as crossing our fingers, we sailed in, beached the boat, and began the Enquiry.

George was the most eloquent. 'What the hell did you do?' he demanded. 'Why wasn't that tank full? Where's your spare air bottle?' He went on without giving Cold Bean a chance to reply: but there was no reply. One look at the skipper's guilty face showed that.

The story came out gradually, and not without odd promptings. It illustrated how easily even the best-laid plans can come unstuck. Cold Bean hadn't bought any spares. He had every confidence in his boat. So much so that he didn't even bother to check it. For three days he and his crew enjoyed a monumental spree on the safety money. They drank nearly a vineyard apiece, and not a spanner nor a nut nor a bolt found its way into the toolbox. They left Piraeus sober enough, but with the fuel tanks half full, and one air bottle empty. The engine was all right. The only trouble was they couldn't re-start it. If the gale had blown the other way even that wouldn't have mattered. We were within thirty miles of Smyrna when the tank ran dry. But this was Kythnos, not Smyrna. We realized that abusing Cold Bean from now till midnight wouldn't get us an inch nearer.

Frank took charge. All these islands had Italian garrisons. They were small, but effective, and so we had to work fast. He sent Cold Bean to find a village, and then a blow-lamp, and gave him a special instruction to keep his mouth shut as much as possible. If we could heat the top of the engine sufficiently the strong men might start it by hand. If no blowlamp came, there was still a way. We could knock the bottom out of a bucket, heap hot embers inside, and try that. In the meantime we got busy making another sail. If bucket and blowlamp both failed we would have to reach Turkey the hard way.

Just before dark the gallant skipper returned. He was waving the blowlamp above his head and displaying much the same modesty as a Crusader who had found the Holy Grail. An aroma of cressi preceded him. He had done the deal in a tavern and had stayed to celebrate. No doubt the customers all knew our Christian names by now, but it couldn't be helped. He had the lamp; and for Cold Bean that was Duty Nobly Done.

Frank and George decided to leave next morning. It would take that long for the patrol boats to get positioned again. It also meant another night in the Cyclades, and most of us spent it in a stone hut near the beach. It was warmer than the island rendezvous, but the fleas nearly ate us. There were thousands of fleas in that hut. They queued up to feed, and then gorged themselves: but we endured them. Spirits were rising. Turkey was once again only a day away, and the future was hidden: which was as well.

In the morning we refloated the boat, and the crew set to work. One blowlamp was enough, but it promised to be a long job. Gradually the Greeks abandoned sailmaking, and climbed aboard to spur on the efforts. Eventually Frank, Roy and I were the only ones left on the beach.

It was a pleasant morning. The gale had died down, and the sun's warmth and the peacefulness and serenity of the little bay lulled our caution. Nobody felt the imminence of fast-approaching disaster. Frank put the finishing touches to the sail, and we were just straightening up when a faint chug-chug sounded. Instantly everyone stiffened. The sound grew louder and a boat appeared from behind the cliff. Momentarily it continued on its course. Then it turned in a wide arc and headed into the bay.

SEVEN

What happened next happened at speed. Frank breathed the one word 'Run!' and we were away like the wind. A warning shot rang out, but the three of us only fled faster over the hard sand. Fifty yards up the beach a small hill threw out a protecting shoulder. Behind this was safety. A volley now sounded. I heard the angry Zip! Zip! of flying bullets all around me.

Another fusillade followed. The Italians were blazing away with everything they had. Roy disappeared behind the bend, with Frank close on his heels. They were safe anyway. Sheer panic lent wings to my feet. Still another volley echoed into the hills, but the shots missed. The range was a hundred yards. Later, we counted fifteen Italians, which all told made rank bad shooting.

But we weren't safe yet. Around the bend I was expecting level ground. It never occurred to me it could be anything else. Behind that crag I found a hill that looked a mile high. Frank and Roy were already clawing a way up. The Italians only needed to walk to the foot to pick us off, and as bottom man I was most aware of that.

I wasn't surprised at being last. In his spare time Roy had been an All Black three-quarter. Frank got his Running Blue at Oxford. I never got anything anywhere, but the thought of what might be below made up for it. We reached the top together. There wasn't much I could do after that except wheeze like a stranded whale. My eyes were popping out with strain. My heart was beating like a trip-hammer. Roy and Frank looked on sympathetically, but a couple of minutes' grace was enough. Then we crept back to the hill-top.

It was galling to find we could have walked up in complete safety. The Italians hadn't bothered to pursue us, but they had the rest of the Greeks in the bag. George and his friends were clustered under an armed guard in our own white speedboat. The patrol vessel now had a tow-rope attached. As we watched, it started up and chugged slowly out of the cove. A few ripples spread over the silent water and broke noiselessly on the shore. The high cliffs looked down dispassionately.

Three Greeks escaped the round-up. George had sent them to fetch water an hour ago, and the hullabaloo warned them something serious had happened. They made up their minds quickly. Two of them turned back. They went to the far side of the island, took a rowing-boat and set off home. The weather was kind to them and they made the trip safely. It was a sensible thing to do. The third Greek, a young Athenian named Costas, thought the boat idea too risky. He joined us instead; so four men were left stranded on the island. It was ten miles long and two wide.

Frank summed up for all of us. 'There were fifteen Wops down there,' he commented. 'At a guess I'd say there's about fifty in the garrison. They'll hunt us, I expect, but we've got the advantage. The islanders'll be on our side. If it comes to a push we should get a boat from them.' I began feeling more cheerful. We were in a fix, but the way Frank put it, it didn't sound too bad. I was about to speak when he continued. 'That's if we need it, of course. But we'll have to see about the others first. Maybe we can help them.' Roy nodded. It seemed fair enough to him, but I felt icy hands on my spine. The real chill was coming. 'Perhaps we'll get our own boat back,' mused Frank. 'It's worth a try, anyway. Tell the Greek, Bill, will you?'

I retailed this to Costas. It did me good to see the pallor creeping into his face. So he wasn't a hero either. That was comforting: but whilst out of pure shame I kept my feelings hidden, Costas had no inhibitions. The magnitude of the scheme dawned on him. He exploded.

'But it's suicide,' he protested. 'We can't do anything for them. Those Italians are armed. They've got rifles.' His voice took a sudden falsetto. 'They'll shoot,' he squeaked.

That was exactly what I'd thought. The Italians would shoot, without a doubt. If we got a hundred yards start, it wouldn't be too bad, if to-day's marksmanship was anything to go by; but we mightn't get a start. And how Frank reckoned to spirit nine captives out of the garrison clink beat me altogether. Still, if he and Roy were for the idea, it left no option. I'd have to be, too.

We did try. We did all we could, even to dodging sentries and spying out the garrison H.Q. at night-time; but it was soon clear we couldn't help. The Greeks were locked in cells in the main building. Before they could be released, we'd have to lay out the entire garrison. It was a job for a task force. To give him credit, Costas came with us, but he aged in the process. I was relieved myself when Frank called off the rescue. He was disappointed, but he was no fool.

His next plan was a perfect one. We were to sail back to the mainland, walk to Athens, re-equip, and then try again for Turkey. The idea called for a motorboat, but if necessary we were prepared to row the thirty-mile stretch of sea. That would be no sinecure. In one of the sudden January storms an open boat stood very little chance; and however hard we rowed it would still take about ten hours. The risk of being intercepted was there, but it had to be faced. We couldn't stay on Kythnos indefinitely.

Merika was an automatic choice. It was a small fishing village on the West coast, where the Italians kept one of their two patrol boats. According to the villagers, only eight men guarded it. The villagers were very free with advice. They helped us too, with food, lodgings, and warnings of any searching posse of Italians. The whole island seemed to be watching the manœuvres with the zest of a cup-tie crowd.

The next day we were at Merika, hiding in a barn waiting for darkness to fall. I was in high spirits. The thought of storming that garrison didn't haunt me any longer, and as for the sea trip – well it was a fifty-fifty chance. I couldn't ask more than that. Roy lay beside me, sleeping peacefully. Frank sat disconsolate, mostly because he felt he had abandoned his friends, and partly because his cigarettes had run out again. Costas, the fourth member, looked very worried indeed. For the life of me I couldn't understand why. This wasn't a raid-the-garrison venture. With any luck we'd be away before the alarm sounded; and once away none could pursue us. There was no other motorboat on this side of the island. Before H.Q. woke up – the luck continuing of course – we'd be halfway to Greece. Even a general alert along the coast wouldn't help the Italians then. We could land in darkness, sink the boat, and no one would be any the wiser. If there was a hitch, even before we got the boat, the odds were still with us. It would be dark, and we had the wind in our feet.

I put all these arguments to the Greek, to cheer him up a bit, but none did any good. Costas refused to be comforted. His wind wasn't confined to his feet. Violent stomach pains were troubling him, he said; and as it was obvious what was really wrong, we left him.

Just before midnight, three men came out of the barn, and crept silently down to the shore. A half-moon shed a weak light on the line of small boats drawn up on the beach. We inspected them. Some had oars in, which was heartening. It meant that if there was any snag over the patrol boat, the second string was there, ready. We sat down by the side of a fishing smack and took off our shoes. A few whispers followed, and Roy vanished. He was going to reconnoitre and come for us if he found the stage all set.

It was a good idea. Roy could move almost like a ghost, and just now he needed to. Already one or two of the village dogs had given querulous barks. We cursed those infernal dogs. The slightest sound would set one barking: and if it didn't stop immediately, every dog in the village would join in.

Frank and I settled down to wait. Somewhere a dog barked once, and then held its peace. Uneasy minutes passed. Then Roy returned as quietly as he had left, and blasted all our hopes. The boat was there, just by the darkened guardroom. The engine was still warm, and would probably fire at once – but the stick he had thrust into the tank showed that it was almost empty.

The reserve plan became the only plan. We decided to row to Kea, sink the boat when we got there, and use Kea as a stepping-stone to the mainland. Perhaps the Organization would trace the bereaved owner and compensate him: but whether it did or not made no difference. We had to have a boat. That was all that mattered. But at that moment we stopped thinking about boats in any shape or form.

I had learnt my first Italian phrase at the Levadia roadblock. 'Viene qua!' means 'Come here!' Even Ricco's gruff tones couldn't conceal the musical qualities of his language. The second lesson was easier. A squat figure appeared before us, waving a long rifle menacingly. 'Alt!' he challenged, 'mani in alto!'

Obligingly we put our hands up. It was the guard. The cursed dogs had roused him and he had followed Roy back to us. The rifle swung in little arcs, covering us. 'Who are you?' demanded the sentry. 'What are you doing here?' He spoke in Greek, and I felt sudden hope. So he didn't suspect we were English. It occurred to me then there was no reason why he should. I replied in Greek.

'We've come for the oars. This is my boat. I left the oars in it and I'm frightened they'll be stolen. These are my brothers.'

But there wasn't a chance. The guard had got his Greek from a phrase book. He didn't understand a word of what I said. Even if he had there still wouldn't have been much hope. It doesn't need three men in stockinged feet to carry one pair of oars. Not at midnight, especially.

The Italian seemed to think along these lines. He stood about six feet away, motioned towards the guardroom, and added strong warnings, this time in Italian. We set off, still with our hands in the air, and with the guard on the *qui vive* behind. The newborn optimism died. The still silent guardroom was only fifty yards away and I knew that once there we were sunk. Roy and I walked ahead resignedly. It looked like the end of another chapter – but we were reckoning without Frank. With about ten yards to go, he dropped one of his shoes, and groped on the ground to find it. Unconsciously, the guard closed up. Like a flash, Frank dived under the levelled rifle and took him by the legs. We turned to see both men struggling furiously for the weapon. The next moment it went off with a report that shattered the night.

It was too much for the Italian. He was shot. In his own mind he was certain the bullet had got him. He reacted strongly. A shriek of pure unbridled terror bubbled from his throat, sand churned up from his flying feet, and suddenly the guard vanished. His yells died away and I saw Frank smile: but the terrific din had bounced every Italian above us clean out of his bed. All the dogs in Merika began a fierce sustained uproar, and lights clicked on.

We were already in full flight. It was every man for himself now, with a vengeance. I lost the other two as soon as we started running. A shot rang out, and then another. Then a ragged volley. I was heading towards the barn at top speed, but not in any panic. Those Italians were only half awake. They were firing blindly and there was a lot of empty space to fire into.

One of my shoes came off, and for a minute or so I ignored the increasing fire to search for it. One of the islanders had given me a new pair to replace the battered city shoes. The replacements were good. They were made from pieces of motor tyre, with thongs of goats' sinews to hold them on. Even with gun-happy Italians around they were too good to lose. A stray bullet clattered into the pebbles nearby. There were regular volleys now, aimed at different parts of the compass. The guards didn't know where we were, but their idea was sound. Half a dozen bullets whistled overhead, and I gave up the search: and going again at top speed up the valley I charged into an unseen wall and turned somersaults on the other side. Getting up, I jagged my unprotected toes full against a rock.

Behind, the firing grew less, and in the next field Roy hailed me. Five minutes later we saw Frank; and despite the agony of mangled toes I had to smile. This was the real Frank, replete with the good old English *sangfroid* that so many people mourn as being extinct. He was unruffled. What was more, he had the rifle; and if the last half-hour's frolic had disturbed him, he didn't show it. 'You all right?' he asked. We nodded, doing our best to feign indifference. Frank approved. 'Well, we'd better see how Costas is getting on,' he said.

That was a waste of time, as all three of us anticipated Costas had forgotten his ailments as soon as he heard the first shot. I would have laid odds he was still running. We found the barn door swinging on its hinges and knew it would be foolish looking any farther. Frank dallied longer than was necessary, but at last we set off up the valley. It was a narrow path, strewn with thorns and pebbles. My foot smarted painfully. I wrapped my cap around it, tied it on with a handkerchief, and found the improvised bandage a great help.

The moon had set now, and we plodded on in pitch darkness. All went well for a space, and then Frank missed a turning and walked over a precipice. Fortunately it was only a ten foot drop. He turned a complete somersault, and landed on his feet unharmed. By a miracle, the loaded rifle neither went off nor impaled him: but this time, as we hauled him up, he relaxed sufficiently to say a few things about the night, the rifle and the Italians that cheered the three of us. So far there had been too much unsaid in this venture.

We were halfway up the valley before the garrison went into action. A good way below, two sets of headlamps suddenly flashed out. They twisted and turned as the cars sped at breakneck pace along the solitary island road. We sat down to watch. There was silence for some minutes, and then the counter-attack opened up. Rifles flashed somewhere near the barn. Staccato reports echoed up to us. Half a dozen marksmen were loosing away at their sunseen quarry, and I remembered the sheep grazing below. The grenadiers went into action. At the savage cra-ack! of grenades I began feeling sorry for those poor sheep. They would be dashing about in the darkness in blind panic. Probably the Italians thought they were tackling a troop of Commandos.

But our own business was urgent, and we left while the battle was still on. It was pretty certain the whole garrison would be out at dawn, and before then we had to find a good hide-out. Motorboats were now out of the question. Equally so was any further stay on Kythnos. To-morrow night we had to get a rowing boat and move to another island. Saros was the nearest, fifteen miles away. It was in the wrong direction, but that couldn't be helped. Very soon this place would be too hot to hold us.

For some reason none of us could understand, the next day was quiet. We ventured out of the stone hut, scouted far and wide, and never saw one Italian. A thought struck Roy. 'Maybe they're all confined to barracks,' he grinned. 'After last night's do they deserve it.' What was more serious was the complete absence of boats. We didn't see a single one. I quizzed innumerable Greeks without any success. Most of them had heard all about the Merika battle, and the cup-tie fever was at its height. They pressed more food and wine on us than we could have consumed in a month; but none admitted to owning a boat.

In the end I struck oil. An elderly islander agreed he had a 'barca'. 'Yes, you can have it,' he said. 'It's a spare one. Perhaps someone in Athens will pay me for it sometime.'

I stopped just long enough to reassure him, before calling Frank and Roy. 'It's O.K.' I said, modestly. 'It's fixed. This chap's got one.' But the due measure of praise didn't come. My friends seemed suspicious. The long search had been a trying business, and if there was a boat, they wanted to see it first. 'Where is it?' asked Roy. I pointed out to sea. 'His son's out fishing in it now. He'll be back about six. That's his usual time. All we've got to do is wait.'

That last remark was ill-chosen. I saw the instant hostility in Roy's eyes. 'I don't believe it,' he said, flatly. 'I'm not waiting.' Frank was as firm. 'Nor am I,' he said. 'You can, if you like, but I think you'll find the old boy's romancing.'

We settled the affair quite easily. I understood Greek better than they did, and felt convinced that this boat was genuine. Frank and Roy remembered too many promises that had been made in the past. We agreed to part. In one way it was a good idea. The Italians were looking for three men. If Frank could hide the bulge of the rifle he was still carrying under his long coat, two might pass unchallenged. They walked away, and I followed the islander into his cottage.

Needless to say the boat didn't arrive. The Jinx was at the top of his form. An hour after it was due, the old Greek suddenly remembered something, and his face fell. His son had spoken that morning of going to Saros if the weather kept fine. I looked at him disgustedly. The sea was like glass. The sun had set in a blaze of crimson glory that would have done credit to midsummer. A red sky was promising a wonderful day to-morrow: and the sailing trip was off. I thanked the old man for his pressing offers of hospitality, and said 'No'.

Next evening I was back in Costas' barn at Merika. It had seemed a stupid idea at first, but not after second thoughts. The Italians would be looking for us, despite their apparent inactivity. The guard would have told a rare tale about three armed desperadoes, and clearly the island couldn't settle down until such dangerous men were safe behind bars. But where were they now? It seemed a safe bet the Italians would decide they were as far from Merika as possible. Two nights before the little fishing port had proved a hornets' nest. They'd hardly try there again. And thinking along these lines, I went back. They say lightning never strikes the same place twice.

I didn't advertise the move. Nobody saw me going to Merika, and I didn't venture on the beach until well after dark. I sat motionless, fifty yards from the guardroom, and watched and listened for nearly two hours. After that I walked confidently towards the line of boats. There was no guard to-night. In all those two hours there hadn't been a move or a murmur. No doors had opened or closed; and most convincing of all, I hadn't seen a match flare up, nor a cigarette glow in the dark.

The boats were all drawn well up on to the beach, excepting one small one which lay at the water's edge. It had a pair of oars in; and I felt that much luck was about due. I unlashed the oars, and made sure the rowlocks were in firmly: but getting the boat launched put years on me. Sand crunched noisily with each heave, and a series of echoes reverberated over the bay. I was working as quietly as I could, but the noise seemed terrific. Every second I expected to hear a fatal bark, and was poised for instant flight. But no bark came. The boat slapped flatly into the water. I waded knee-deep alongside and climbed in. There was still no summons. And wondering whether the luck had really turned, or if there was some monstrous catch behind all this silence, I rowed gently out to sea. The boat passed like a wraith under the silent guardroom, with the oars dipping feather-light, and a revealing trail of phosphorescence behind: but except for a faint snoring that drifted down, the night remained as silent as the grave.

About half a mile out I abandoned caution and gave the first real pull on the oars. With that, luck went back to normal. The boat turned a brisk half circle to port. I found that a strong pull on one side and a light one on the other maintained an even course. I pulled light and heavy, and two minutes later the rowlock on the heavy side jumped overboard. We *were* back to normal. It was how the Jinx liked to work. I found a spare rowlock under the seat, jammed it in hard, crossed my fingers and carried on.

About two miles slipped past without incident. Then the Jinx had another go. Suddenly, water began slopping around in the boat. It slowed down quickly as I left the oars. 'Good God,' I thought, 'we've sprung a leak!' It was worse than that. The bung had come out. The water was six inches deep before I could find the hole and plug it. It took a long time to bale out the water. I used my cap and an army vocabulary, and continued the ill-omened journey. By now I was growing blasé to disaster. I was feeling a bit dogged about it, too. It only remained for hidden rocks to rip the bottom out of the boat. If that happened, well, I'd swim to Kea. I was going to get there somehow.

But the Jinx was satisfied with the night's work. Nothing else went wrong, and I got safely to the tip of the island. The sea was like glass. There was no hint of approaching bad weather, and the moon had risen, as expected. In the distance I could see the rugged outline of Kea. It seemed about five miles distant, and I did some quick calculating. Those five miles were fifteen on the map, and it was 3 a.m. by the moon. The point was – could I row that far before seven o'clock? Regretfully I decided no. With a decent boat it would have been worth a try. With this drunken old tub, with its bad oars and faulty bunghole it was asking for trouble. I'd need at least seven hours. It might be an idea to fix the bung and the oars before I started, too. Best leave it, I thought, and start early to-morrow night.

The luck now changed again, this time for the good. Behind a ridge of rock jutting out opposite the boat, was a tiny natural harbour. It had a narrow entrance, but once inside, the boat was completely hidden. It floated snugly in a little lagoon, and I could laugh at the Italians. Both patrol boats would be out searching as soon as it was light. The guard corporal at Merika would probably be on the carpet soon after, but that was his affair. What concerned me at the moment was food, and if possible, some sleep. Item Number 1 meant contacting the islanders again. In turn that meant scaling the cliff in front of me, and more logic advised climbing up before dawn.

It wasn't easy. A little to the right the vertical cliff lessened into a steep slope covered with moss and vegetation. It was climbable, but only just. I couldn't see too well, and I was dead tired. Halfway up it began to rain. They were gentle drops at first, but soon they developed into a semi-tropical downpour. The rocks grew treacherous. Below was a black void, and above, a cliff of unknown height. I grew careless with fatigue and slipped on the edge of a drop. Only a wild and desperate contortion saved me.

It was the last straw. Every muscle in my aching body was pleading for rest. I lay down on a flat rock, pillowed my head on a small bush, and was asleep in an instant. The rain fell steadily. My clothes became saturated, but I didn't wake. It was a warm night and there was no wind.

I had climbed about 500 feet, and the morning revealed only another hundred or so above. A house not far from the top would have been welcome, but perhaps that was too much to expect. I climbed up, and viewed the deep rockstrewn valley below without resentment. It took three hours to descend it and get up the other side. This time I did better. A quarter of a mile away was a cluster of houses with smoke curling up from the chimneys.

I had long since learnt to love chimney-smoke. It meant warmth, and hot food, and Greeks who were mostly willing to give the shirts from their backs. The young Greek who answered my knock was no exception. I sat by his fire, pulled off some of the wet clothes, and listened to him.

His name was Nicos, and he knew all about the missing boat. The Italians had checked up a couple of hours ago and the patrol boats were already circling Kythnos. Nicos had got this via the islanders' bush telegraph. The Greeks themselves weren't sure what to make of it. They did know only one man was concerned, but whether he was now in Kea or at the bottom of the Aegean was anyone's guess. Most of them favoured the sea-bed. Apparently the old boat had a fierce reputation.

Nicos shook his head. 'You shouldn't have taken it,' he admonished. 'Why, I wouldn't trust it ten yards. Didn't you have any trouble?'

But I was ready for this. I lied, hard. 'No, it went all right. It was a calm night, of course, but the boat's not as bad as you're making out. You must be biased against it.' I had reason for lying. It was one of the worst boats in the Aegean, I was well aware, but then it was the only one available. I needed the old tub to get to Kea: and I didn't want Nicos to start dissuading me. In any case, detailing its iniquities didn't mend them: and the longer I talked the farther away was breakfast.

But Nicos' wife was already attending to that. The Greeks aren't saints. They are excitable, prone to pessimism, have a weakness for telling tall stories, and possess assorted minor faults: but one great virtue counteracts all the weaknesses. They appreciate a man who owns up to having a belly. They admire him for it, and staunch characters like Mrs Nicos will do their best to help him fill it. She started me off with a bowl of lentil soup, and followed up with corn bread, *tiropeta*, figs, nuts, wine, and a big slice of baclava. Being about eighteen hours behind on my meals, I ate the lot, thanked her and her husband, and accepted the offer of a blanket. This was real hospitality. Without the Greeks none of us would have lasted long.

The weather had changed by the time I woke up. It was about two in the afternoon and should have been the best time of the day, but the door and windows were all rattling in the wind. One of those unpredictable Aegean storms was setting in. There was no chance of sailing to Kea now. Only the flattest of flat calms would do with my boat, but uneasiness drove me out of the warm house. That boat was the link with Freedom, and I was worried about it.

It wasn't idle worry. I got back to the cliff and began climbing down, but a spur of rock hid the lagoon from me until the last moment. By now I was really alarmed. The sea was running high, and white horses rode gaily on the crest of each wave. The storm had a majesty that would have gladdened any Nature lover. What entranced me was the muffled roar reverberating from the foot of the cliff.

I rounded the bend with both fingers crossed, but it didn't work. One agonized glance was enough. Where last night had been a motionless sheet of water was now chaos. Big waves battered in vain against the rugged cliff, but they were surging triumphantly through the opening and hurling themselves savagely into my lagoon. It was a fury of seething tempestuous water. The boat had gone. Not even a splinter of wreckage could be seen in the maelstrom.

EIGHT

Nicos was sympathetic. He realized that a whole night's effort had been wasted, but he had news of his own to soften the blow. It was big news. He had found Frank and Roy in a barn about half an hour away: but that was only the hors d'œuvre. What really electrified him was the sudden remembrance that his brother was due to-night from Samos. 'Your troubles are over,' he exulted. 'Giorgos comes once a month in the caique. He'll take all of you back to Piraeus. The Italians will still be looking for you when you're back in Egypt.' He took a breath and raced on. 'They're getting worried now. A ban went on yesterday and we've got to get permission before we leave Kythnos. That means that nobody can give you a boat, even if they want to: but there's no check on boats coming in. Not yet. The caique only stops ten minutes but it's timc enough for you to slip aboard. The patrol boats won't know a thing about it.' He slapped me on the back in great humour. 'Your luck's changed all right, Vassiliou!'

The new plan did seem A.1. The sea was going down again, and even my eager pessimism couldn't find a flaw in this idea. I grew jocular, which was a new mood for me. 'We'll send you a battleship before long, Nicos,' I promised.

The trip to the landing beach began after dark. We collected Frank and Roy en route, and this time they grew almost as enthusiastic. I told them about my boat and its sad end, and listened to their account of the last two days.

Their star wasn't in its zenith either. After I left them they went on into the main village, where the Italians had their Headquarters. They intended to take the patrol boat, but the Commandante, who had guessed as much, was a move ahead. He mounted a triple guard and a searchlight and sat back confidently. Frank and Roy turned to the local craft, to find they had been checkmated there as well. The farseeing Commandante had ordered all boatmen to remove oars and rowlocks: and feeling rather low, the two searchers gave up. They broke into the island's single hotel, which was closed for the duration, and slept on spring beds. A hospitable Greek met them next day. He filled them with good food and offered a boat which didn't materialize. They waited all night in vain, and spent the rest of the time in the barn, ignoring fleas, and catching up on back sleep. Now we were all together again, another boat was in the offing, and we were raring to go.

It was a pity it didn't turn up either. Nicos was mystified. He couldn't understand what was keeping his brother. 'But he must come,' he said flatly. 'He always comes. He's never missed in three years. Let's wait a bit longer.' We sojourned another two hours, until even Nicos realized it was hopeless. He was almost in tears with disappointment. So was I, for that matter, but I spent some minutes comforting the Greek.

'Don't worry, Nicos,' I soothed. 'It'll be all right. You've done your best and we can't ask more than that. You've been very generous too. We'll get a boat all right. There's been one or two upsets so far and maybe there'll be more, but we'll get a boat sometime. It's only a question of waiting. We're not impatient.'

It was a neat speech, and Nicos felt relieved, if no one else did. We shook hands all round, and after a renewed spate of good wishes and much *Bon Voyage*, he left us.

In the clear January night we reviewed the situation. There wasn't much on the credit side. We were still free, of course, but it was a freedom within limits. The trouble was we seemed unable to expand these limits. For a week now, individually and collectively, we had grasped every opportunity and taken every conceivable risk – and had got nowhere. Such continued ill-luck was getting wearisome. It was baffling, too. None of us had done anything silly, and by rights we should all have got away several times. Only the most outrageous ill-fortune had landed us in this pickle in any case. But holding a wake didn't help, any more than it had done over Cold Bean. We were up against a hoodoo: what was needed was another dose of the same old prescription – action.

An hour later we spotted a likely craft. It was a small white yacht, moored in an unfrequented bay. It looked ideal for the purpose, and light-footed Roy went off to reconnoitre. Frank and I, waiting for him, had a repetition of the Merika affair, all barring the guards and the fireworks. A solitary dog barked once and then held its peace. Roy met it on the beach, but he promptly walked breast high into the sea and left the dog to work that one out. He swam to the yacht and lay concealed under the overhanging side. Unfortunately, the crew was aboard. One man came on deck, and Roy pressed closer against the side; but he wasn't suspect. The sailor relieved himself and went back to bed. We weighed up the pros and cons of this latest venture, and decided No. The Greeks couldn't give us the yacht, and the search was too keen to risk a commotion.

We sheltered in one of the little stone churches that abound in these islands. Roy slept on the stone floor in his wet clothes, and shivered a little: but he was none the worse when morning came. We were all far too busy to catch colds.

The quest continued. Towards six o'clock next evening we were at the extreme Southern tip of Kythnos, near the village where the two Greeks found their boat a week ago. Frank was working on the principle that where there's one there may be another. It reminded me of my favourite axioms about lightning and shells, but I said nothing to him. I hadn't the heart.

The village must have been the smallest in the Cyclades. It lay at the bottom of a 500 foot cliff, and consisted of two houses. There seemed a poor chance of doing business here. We looked down on to the bay, but saw no sign of a boat. It seemed as elusive as ever. We began to descend the cliff. Even if it was another frustration, there'd be a night's rest here, and maybe something hot to eat. But somebody must have been praying for us. Halfway down, Frank gestured. I turned and saw a solitary boat shooting into the bay, with two pairs of oars dipping strongly. I nearly lost my hold in relief. That was *our* boat. There wasn't a doubt about it. *Meum* and *tuum* are fine principles to have, but not when your liberty hangs on them. We couldn't afford sentiment. If the Greeks would part with the boat willingly – good. It would save some bother. If they wouldn't, it made no difference. This was probably the last chance we'd get, and that boat was going out again tonight.

With us in it.

The rowers reached the shore before we did. They pulled their craft out of the water and took the oars with them into one of the two houses. We had expected that, and being the most fluent in Greek, it was my cue. Roy came with me to the house. Frank, still holding the rifle, stayed on guard outside. He had hung on to that weapon through thick and thin. There was now a chance it might pay a dividend.

The Greeks seemed pleased to see us and quickly put two more stools in front of the fire. I wasted no time. It was nearly dark now, and we were going to need every minute of it. I told them how we were fixed, and how urgently we needed the boat. 'We must have it,' I said, 'but we don't intend to steal it. That's why we've come here first. Outside that door there's a British officer. He's armed. He says I'm to give you a written promise of 50,000 drachmae. Our government will cash it after the war.'

The oars were leaning against the wall. I could see Roy sizing things up.

'But the Italians . . .' began one of the Greeks.

'You won't have any bother with Italians,' I assured him. 'You can tell them we took your boat by force of arms. We'll fire a shot outside to prove it. Someone will hear, so you'll be all right. All you have to do is sit tight and say nothing about the 50,000 drachmae.'

But the Greek was getting worried. 'They'll punish us,' he protested. 'And we lost one boat last week. You can't take this one.'

'But we must. There's no other. One of your friends will lend you a boat in the meantime. That money will buy half a dozen soon.'

'But you mightn't pay . . .'

It had gone on long enough. Hurriedly I wrote out the I.O.U., went out to Frank, got it signed, and gave it to the Greek. We each took a pair of oars, but another Greek was now barring the way. He was a little man, who had lost an arm somewhere. He waved his stump in our faces.

'The Italians cut my arm off,' he shouted. 'We'll all be shot to-morrow.'

Roy and I were on the way out. The one-armed man began bawling, and the other Greeks, as yet uncertain, caught his panic and joined in. Frank fired the rifle, and the din ceased abruptly: but as we ran to the beach I heard a shout 'Get the pistols!'

It was pitch dark outside. We ran like hares, intent on getting into the boat and away: and in the excitement none of us remembered an elementary precaution. Kythnos is a poor place for farming. The islanders cultivate what soil there is in terrace fashion. We forgot all about this until the tumble over the first drop. Just ahead of me I heard a thud, followed instantly by a curse. Then the ground vanished under my own feet. I flew through the air and landed in a heap about six feet lower down. But the ground was soft, and somehow I clung on to the oars.

It was too dark to see ahead and we were in too much of a hurry to slow down. The thuds and curses increased. Then the rifle went off again. Frank had automatically reloaded and was still clinging to his talisman. The bullet smacked into the ground near Roy's feet. Roy accelerated. He was an easy first, and the heavy boat was already moving when we reached it. We pushed it into the water, threw in the oars, and scrambled after them. There were confused noises behind, but no pistol shots. It was probably a bluff. We moved away from the shore and the cries became more distant. Eventually they faded away altogether.

We were elated. Here at last was the promised boat, with not one, but two pairs of oars. The luck had turned. We couldn't fail this time. Two happy oarsmen pulled strongly and the boat grated on a rock. We shuddered to a halt.

I lost my head slightly. 'We're aground!' I shouted, jumping overboard to push off. The calm waters of the bay closed peacefully over my head and cut off further observations. I came up gasping. We weren't aground. My friends hauled me aboard and began examining the boat anxiously. It was still sound. We had run on to a narrow shelf of rock that luckily was flat. A little judicious bouncing soon got us back into deep water. I was still coughing when the boat cleared the bay and entered the calm waters of the Aegean.

Frank decided to get well out before starting the trip to Kea. We had the ten miles length of Kythnos to cover, plus the open stretch that had beaten me two nights before. That made twenty-five miles all told, but we weren't perturbed. We had a sound boat, and ten hours of darkness lay ahead. We could hardly ask for more.

The sea was once again near perfect; but it was full of phosphorescence that illuminated the boat and made the oars dazzle at each dip. It was a dangerous phenomenon. We were lit up like a Brock's Benefit.

Roy had his ears cocked. Suddenly he listened acutely and drew in his oars. 'Something's coming,' he said tersely. Frank stopped rowing and the boat slowed down. The gleaming wake behind flickered and died away. Then we all heard it. It was the ominous 'chug-chug' of the patrol vessel. Frank whispered 'Get down!' and we crouched silently in the bottom. Those shots had carried farther than we thought.

The motor boat drew nearer. A powerful searchlight was stabbing into every nook and cranny along the shore; an equally brilliant wake streamed from the stern. For a moment it seemed to head straight for us. Then, veering, it passed between us and the shore. We could see dark forms standing on the deck. Our boat rocked slightly, but remained unseen. A few crags were jutting out of the sea nearby and we merged thankfully into their anonymity. The patrol moved away.

The Italians had nothing to go on, of course. They had heard firing, and no doubt suspected their three mystery men were at the back of it, but finding them was another matter. Probably none of them dreamt we were already in the middle of the Aegean. The motor boat disappeared around the bend of the island, and we took up the oars again. It was safe now. The Italians would go back and report a blank. With any luck our boat mightn't be missed for a few days. Certainly the one-armed Greek wouldn't rush to tell them.

We reached the northern tip of Kythnos at 1 a.m. which was two hours earlier than I'd done on my own. We were all fresh and the sea still glassy, but Roy was looking worried. At home he had a yacht, and he knew a thing or two about weather. 'I don't like it,' he muttered, sniffing the slight breeze. 'There's a blow coming.' We stared at him and then laughed.

'There'll be more than a blow coming if we don't get off this blasted island,' I said. 'It'll be red-hot to-morrow.'

Frank nodded, 'Yes, I think we'd better try,' he advised. 'We should do it in about four hours.'

But Roy was unconvinced. 'Maybe,' he grunted, 'and maybe not. I think there's a cross-current farther out too. But dirty weather's coming. You mark my words.'

Frank and I swayed the balance. Kea looked closer and more enticing than ever, and it seemed to us the breeze was dropping. We weren't experts on weather, but we did know it was going to be unhealthy staying in Kythnos any longer: and that was putting it mildly. In the end we convinced Roy. 'Perhaps you're being too pessimistic,' Frank said. 'Anyway, we'll do it before the weather breaks.'

Partly because of Roy's prophecy, we moved really fast. The grim cliffs of Kythnos faded into the mists behind us, and Kea loomed encouragingly larger: but we had a long way to go Those fifteen miles were genuine ones, and fifteen miles is a long way. We were still strong. Each man was rowing half an hour and resting fifteen minutes. With a clear run we would have landed on Kea about 4 a.m.: but Roy's nose hadn't misled him.

The weather broke when we were still about six miles out. The Aegean is always a fickle sea, but in winter its temperament is mercurial. Now it took just over ten minutes to wheel through a full circle. In that time the calm changed to a gale.

It was a full-blooded gale. It roared straight at us, marshalling endless ranks of heaving billows before it, and lashing every wave top into frenzies of flying spume. The wind became a howling fury. It snatched one pair of oars, and flung them far into the night. It battered us, flayed us, and tossed the boat about like a cork. We had no chance to row. With all the water coming aboard Frank and I had to bale for our very lives. We kept on baling. Roy sat grimly at the tiller, fighting the gale with set teeth, using his yachting skill as he had never done before, dodging giant waves, riding crests, always keeping our head into the wind. We owe him our lives. For two hours he fought tooth and nail, and then the Goliath gave in. Miraculously, the sea's fury abated. The waters stilled. And despite the tiredness that hung on us like heavy weights, we began to row.

The gale had blown us nearer to Kea, but not much nearer. Mostly it had carried the boat before it along the channel, and at a guess, we were still six miles out. We would have done it easily, but for the current Roy had also foretold. Two miles off shore we felt it grip the boat and force us back. I gave my oar to Frank and he and Roy strained savagely at their work. We made progress, but it was desperately slow. After ten minutes I relieved Roy. We crept in farther, but only at a quarter of the former speed. We rang the changes constantly, until all three of us were soaked with sweat, but the current won. When dawn broke we were still half a mile from safety. Directly above us was a white coastguard station.

There was still a chance. The war had by-passed this island-studded sea, and it was Sunday morning: and of all mornings surely this was the ideal one for happy coastguards to roll over and forget what had brought them to Kea. After all, it was still only the crack of dawn.

The sun peeped over the eastern horizon to urge us: and spurting in a final all-out effort we beat the current, grounded the boat and jumped out. Above us rose the cliff, with the white building perched on top. Awaiting us, quite calmly, in an almost friendly manner, were two Italian marines, each holding a short carbine. The Jinx had struck again.

NINE

I didn't like the officer. He was a suave efficient man, and one look at him was ample. He was one of that unlikeable breed who Get Things Done and keep both ears open for the applause. There are too many of them. But for this one, the Marines would still have been snoring.

In this quiet place we were a Godsend. The officer had already phoned his Headquarters and got the Commandante out of bed. He spoke a little Greek, and I tried to convince him we were fishermen, but it didn't work. We weren't fishermen. We were a Roman holiday. He did have good reason to doubt my story, admittedly. No one had yet rowed through a winter's gale to pay him a social visit, so the mere fact that we were on Kea was suspicious. The Italian rifle in the bottom of the boat also needed some lengthy explaining. All told, the officer felt quite happy. He stood facing us with a levelled revolver in his hand. 'You will wait,' he said firmly.

The two Marines came back wearing battle harness, and listened to a series of crisp orders. Then we all moved off. One Marine led the way, three doubtful fishermen followed him and the other Italian covered the rear. Frank still carried his rifle, but now he was short of bolt and bullets.

It was a rough track. Nicos had given me another pair of shoes, and I was all right, but Frank's footwear was in a bad way. Before long it disintegrated. He continued for a while in bare feet, until the sharp stones drew blood. Then he stopped. We stopped with him. It was no use going on like this. The guard at the rear howled to the guard in front, who had gone on, and both of them began shouting at us. That didn't cut any ice either. Frank lifted his bleeding feet, explained 'Kaput. No go. Finito,' and sat down again with an air of finality. We joined him. This was the guards' pigeon.

They reacted strongly. They patted their rifles, roared louder, and signalled us to get moving. Both Italians then raised their weapons, took careful aim from five feet, and began counting. It amused Frank. It was the one and only time I ever heard him guffaw. Roy and I were wearing ear-to-ear grins. Even an Italian could hardly miss from five feet, but it was a watery bluff. They didn't dare shoot. Old Man Caligula of the White Tower was on our side now, and we knew it. The sailors knew it too.

They gave in. One of them moved back, knelt down and kept us covered. His mate disappeared. After a while he came back with a mule, and Frank thanked him courteously. The journey continued. For the rest of the way Frank rode in comfort and with considerable dignity.

It was a good ten miles to Kea H.Q. I was tired enough to drop when we got there, but we weren't to rest just yet. The Kea Commandante was in wireless touch with Kythnos, and apparently Kythnos hadn't finished detailing the case against us. We waited a solid hour. 'Tell them nothing,' Frank advised us before we went in. 'Only your Army number and rank, and that you escaped in Greece. That's all they're entitled to know.'

I was first. It was a large room, and I found the Commandante striding about with a dog whip in his hands. He was a youngish man, dressed in the rather flamboyant style peculiar to Italian officers. Two orderlies were looking on, together with a very nervous civilian interpreter, who spoke Greek and Italian. The officer continued his tour of the room, lashing at tables and chairs as he passed. Each thwack of the whip made the Greek shudder. He had a huge cyst, about the size of a billiard ball, in the centre of his forehead. The distended skin went white at each shiver, and unconsciously I stood clear.

The Commandante opened up with his big guns. He roared at the Greek, who asked me who I was and so on. 'Don't understand,' I replied. Surprisingly the interpreter switched over to English, and the Commandante's eyebrows lifted. He stopped walking about. 'Are you English?' he demanded. It seemed he understood the language too. I answered 'Yes' and gave the details we had agreed on. The officer waved his interpreter aside and sat down. We were bigger game than he had thought.

He flew into a rage when I refused further information. I got a blow in the stomach to encourage me, but the heavy clothes deadened the whip. 'I can't tell you,' I repeated. I was too tired to care much what he did. The Italian calmed down abruptly. He switched over from bullying to guile, and began asking questions about the Army. It was a bad lead. Most of his queries were in the Brigadier's province, not mine, and at my best I couldn't have answered them. It was a stupid business. Being pressed for a reply, I told him so. That brought the dog whip in again.

Frank was next. He answered the preliminary questions, and through the half open door we saw the Commandante looking relieved. If this prisoner was a Captain, perhaps he wouldn't be as dense as the other fool. But there was no change coming out of Frank. The Italian picked up a Greek passport from his desk and pounced. 'You say you're a British officer,' he accused. 'But you're in civilian clothing and you have this passport. That makes you a spy. Well, you know the usual treatment. Spies are shot.' Then, tentatively, 'Tell me, are you an agent?'

Frank was unruffled. Technically he was, but after this tactless reminder about shooting he wasn't going to boast about it. 'No,' he said. 'I'm not a spy. None of us are.'

'But you must be. This passport —'

'The passport's nothing,' Frank said patiently. 'Every escaped prisoner has a passport. Use your head a little.'

That stumped the Commandante for a moment. The colloquialism was beyond him. 'How do you mean?' he asked, wrinkling his brow. 'Use my head —'

'We're not spies,' Frank repeated. 'Think for a moment. We've crossed from Kythnos in a rowing boat, in the middle of a gale. We were nearly drowned. If we were spies wouldn't we be organized better than that?'

The poser got Frank outside again. Roy went in for his turn, but by now the Commandante was getting tired himself. He got nothing out of Roy.

Soon the three of us were led into another room. Here we stripped naked before six fresh Italians. Three of them examined us – soles of feet, mouths, armpits and all the crannies they could think of. The other three set to work on our clothes. The spy suggestion wasn't dead yet. They cut my sandals to shreds, got their cypher expert on Roy's belt, because of its studded pattern, and took the lining from Frank's waistcoat. It was a great search, and it was dark before they finished. In the end they gave up, said 'Niente' to each other in despair, and handed back what was left of our clothes. Some bright soul then remembered we had stomachs too, and probably nothing in them. He brought soup and bread. We ate gratefully. We had walked ten miles and rowed twenty-five since the last meal.

The posse lodged us in a cell and marched off. Only one soldier remained on guard, but he was a bad choice. It so happened that the guard at Merika beach was this man's bosom pal. News of the unhappy exploit had now reached Kea, and the garrison was chuckling, but our man outside saw nothing funny in it. He took his friend's part. The full length of a bayonet stabbed through the bars, and Frank shook his head sadly. He had been wondering what the chances were of getting a smoke.

I was more concerned about the cell. I was in my bare feet, and had already felt the dampness of the stone floor. We saw beads of moisture on the walls, and that didn't augur well: but worse was coming. A breath of foetid air wafted towards us from the far wall. At the foot of it we found a shallow puddle which gave off an unmistakable smell. The wall above was like a damp sponge. Next door, overflowing into our cell, was a lavatory.

We went back to the door. 'The Commandante!' we ordered. 'Go and get the Commandante!'

But the guard ignored us. He was still musing over his friend's misfortune. This was obviously another of the Inglese's little games, but they weren't getting away with it this time. He'd see us in Hell first. To emphasize it, he kicked the door and spat into the cell.

That warmed us. We weren't sleeping in a urinal for him or any other Itie. We began battering the door from our side. Roy kicked it. Frank and I had no shoes, so we put in some good work with our fists, and the Italian, now furious, thudded with the butt of his rifle. The door creaked under the strain. It was left to Roy to put in the finishing touch. He found a large stone in a corner and hurled it as hard as he could. A panel cracked wide open. Almost immediately there was a shot, and a little hole appeared in the woodwork below. The bullet passed under Frank's arm, grazed Roy, and smacked into the wall behind. We jumped out of range as the Italian reloaded.

Silence replaced the din. We waited expectantly. The whole garrison would be here any minute now, and there'd likely be a rough-house, or at the very least some concentrated bawling:

but if either got us out of this place it would be worth it. Minutes passed. But nothing happened. No one stirred. The night was quiet. It dawned on us then, slowly, but very clearly, that this sentry was the Boss. We had made enough noise to wake the dead, even before the shot: and if shots were going unquestioned there was no doubt who held the whip hand.

We slept on that stinking floor after all. In the small hours the fatigue grew until we were out on our feet. In unspoken assent all three of us lay down, and sleep came instantly.

The Italians were in good humour next morning. They brought us out, counted us very solemnly, and tied our hands behind our backs. That done, we were fed, which wasn't easy, marched to the shore, and lifted into a caique. At midday it started, but we saw nothing en route to Kythnos. Down in the hold, now with our feet tied as well, we weren't meant to. The dozen soldiers in the escort placed us as far apart as possible and forbade conversation. Periodically, one of them came down to examine the ropes. After each scrutiny he went round and tweaked each nose in turn. It was the highlight of the trip.

At Kythnos they untied our legs and we walked ashore. Half the garrison was waiting, every man armed, and none of them looking too pleased to see us. These were the men who had fought ghosts on Merika Beach a week ago, to the amusement of the Aegean Command. With some of them it rankled. Roy got a cuff on the ear as the transport lorry drew up; but he gave prompt value. Roy has failings, like the rest of us, but tame submission isn't one of them. He wheeled, kicked his man solidly on the shin, and sent him down in a heap. The Italian began bawling his head off.

The assault galvanized his friends into action. Six of them jumped on Roy, shouting, and beating at him with their fists. Frank and I, gripped firmly on either side, watched helplessly. Under the savage assault Roy was beaten into unconsciousness. His arms were still bound behind him and he rolled awkwardly on to his face. Several more men gripped a suddenly berserk Frank.

The guards hustled us into the lorry, lifted Roy, and dumped him in. He had a gash in his forehead and blood trickled from one corner of his mouth, but Roy was tough. He fought back to consciousness. His eyes flickered open, and a fighting spirit began reasserting itself. At that moment the Italian who had caused all the trouble limped up, leaned over the tailboard and struck a crushing blow on the side of Roy's head. He passed out again.

Six men piled into the lorry, all with drawn revolvers. They were nervous men, those Italians. I had two guns aimed at my stomach all the way, and when the lorry began bucking over unmade stretches of road, I wondered if we would arrive in one piece. Roy came to before we stopped, and got down without assistance. The blood had run and congealed, but a bleak look in his eye signified a spirit as yet unbroken. Roy had had a hammering, but he was ready for more. So far as his bonds allowed, he was going to give as good as he got; and if he went down, he'd go down fighting. I was glad he wasn't put to the test.

The Kythnos Commandante was very different from the swashbuckler at Kea. He took us into his office, made us sit down, and sent for a medical orderly to attend to Roy. Frank even got his long awaited cigarette. It was awkward smoking with arms bound, but the Italian did what he could to help. At intervals he took the cigarette away and gave Frank a chance to unscrew his eyes. The sleeping problem was more difficult. The Commandante wanted to be humane, but officially Kea had sent him three desperate men. He was guarding us for only one night. In the morning we were off to Siros, the Aegean Command H.Q., for further questioning: and as we were an unknown quantity, it behoved the Kythnos officer to play safe.

In the end he found an answer that suited everyone. He didn't ask for a parole, or loosen the ropes. Instead, he had fetched down two spring mattresses, mounted two guards, and said a polite 'Goodnight.'

Inside five minutes we had untied each other and gone to sleep. The guards were nervous for a while, but neither interfered. In the morning we submitted meekly to a tying-up process before the Commandante appeared.

At Siros, H.Q. had everything nicely organized. A squad of black-shirted carabinieri met the boat and escorted us to jail in a Black Maria. They even untied the ropes, which was a sporting gesture. None of us bothered memorizing roads. After being trussed like chickens for a day and a half, we had too much limbering up and circulation-restoring to do to bother about roads. It wouldn't have done us much good, in any case. This wasn't an ordinary island. Next to Rhodes, Siros was the biggest naval base in the Aegean. Four thousand soldiers and marines were stationed here.

The authorities weren't sure what to make of us. Only garbled accounts had come from Kea and Kythnos, and they had nothing to go on. It was understandable. We hadn't told Kea anything, and Kythnos certainly wouldn't boast about what happened there. To be on the safe side the Siros Italians took the worst view. Once again we were spies. I was beginning to believe I really was a spy. For good measure we were also classed as criminals of war. This was a new one, and didn't sound too good. A super searching squad did its best, and then the Intelligence took over. Both failed, as their colleagues before them had failed. After a couple of hours we were flung into jail.

It was a big cell, with a light, and a dry floor, but it was very full. Thirty-odd Greeks crowded around us, and I learnt that some had been here as long as six weeks. They were all civilians, mostly thieves or black-market offenders, and the more they told me about this new place the less I liked it. The food was bad. 'You'll get soup twice a day,' said one Greek, 'and three fingers of bread. It's all right, except when the bread's mouldy.'

The overcrowding was much worse. At night twenty Greeks huddled on a long wooden bench that had room for ten. The overflow slept on the concrete floor. We were amongst them. A different kind of overflow came from the rusty bucket in the corner, but fortunately the slope favoured us. Each day we got ten minutes' grace to go to the lavatory. For the rest, we stayed behind locked and barred doors, killing time and fleas.

On the third day official recognition came to our criminal-of-war status. On the sixth, the Greeks moved out, and conditions improved. We were off the floor at last, we got more to eat, and we got some exercise; but it was still far from being enjoyable. On the ninth day we improved again. An officer came in to announce that the C.O.W. business had been dropped and that we were now P.O.W. Five cigarettes each confirmed the promotion. The same afternoon, a lorry whisked us away to a new home, and we didn't know whether to feel glad or sorry about it. During the last two days we had been talking escape. Something might have come of it.

The new cell was infinitely more comfortable, but it was escape-proof. The walls were solid and over a foot thick. The door bolted and double locked on the outside, and sentries guarded it day and night. The two windows let in all the light we wanted; but each was criss-crossed with iron bars. The place would have baffled Houdini: but it was pleasant, and for that much we were thankful. We now slept in army beds with three blankets. We got two hours' exercise every day, instead of five minutes; and best of all, perhaps, full army rations. Frank's came from the officer's mess. We pooled everything and did nicely.

The new Italians were a friendly lot. The company barber came in, chopped off three respectable beards, and gave us each a first class haircut. We had a long overdue bath, and got our clothes doctored in a steam boiler. They were full of fleas from Kythnos and lice from the civilian jail, and needed it. It was wonderful not having to scratch every two minutes. We seemed to have landed in Easy Street, excepting for one big snag. The cell was too tough. It would have held three gorillas in safety. We spent three months in it without the remotest chance of getting away.

I put the time to good use. The Commandante sent in an Italian-English grammar, and for want of something to do I began attacking the new language. It was easier than expected. Fluency came quickly. I worked hard and at the end of two months could manage fairly well. I kept plodding away at it. Some day this knowledge might prove very useful.

During the third month the prison population increased. Four new men came into our cell, and a bigger party of twenty went into another strongroom next door. All bar two of the newcomers had been captured on an island called Antiparos, and we began listening to men whose bad luck had eclipsed even ours.

One of the Athenian organizations had collected the party together. Three British officers were put in charge, Cairo H.Q. obliged with a submarine, and a rendezvous was agreed at Antiparos. They got there safely, and the sub actually came in. Everyone in the party relaxed. They were as good as home now, or almost; but the sub commander soon pricked that bubble. Since leaving Alexandria fresh orders had come through. 'I've got a job to do,' he told the waiting refugees. 'You chaps had better stay here. I'll be back in ten days, and you'll be in a Cairo night club three days after that. It's a promise.'

He left, and the party settled down to wait. A week went by safely. On the eighth day the balloon went up. Six hundred Italians from Siros raided the island and captured the entire party. The officers put up a fight, but it was no use. One of them lost a leg, and was still in hospital. One Italian was killed. Thirty-six hours later the submarine came back and waited in vain for an answer to its signals.

Jock and Harry, the other two men in our cell, literally walked into trouble. They took a yacht from Argos, on the coast, and headed for Turkey. All went well until they hit the same storm that nearly sank us. The two men, both experienced yachtsmen, ran for shelter and found it in a bay in an island called Kythnos. There are hundreds of islands in the Aegean, and they got into Kythnos in time to miss us by one day. It was a beautiful yacht too. If they had stayed on it, perhaps the Jinx would have spared them even then, but Jock and Harry insisted on helping the hangman. They decided to go ashore and stretch their legs. Nobody was there to tell them Kythnos was lethal. They were a hundred yards up the beach, blissfully ignorant of the goings-on of the past few days, when a squad of Italians, bristling with machine guns, grenades and every other light weapon short of a Breda, walked into them.

The submarine party, including the two officers, left for Rhodes after a few days. That left five of us in the big cell, but not for long. Soon afterwards, a major catastrophe occurred. The Italians had been investigating Frank's movements for some time. Now it appeared they had got hold of someone in Athens who knew of him, and who was prepared to talk. The informer didn't know enough to get Frank condemned out of hand, but he said plenty. The Contra Spionaggio, suspicious from the start, but now grimly confident, went on searching. The evidence they had was strong. Only a few links were missing. In the meantime they sent word back to have Frank put in solitary confinement.

We moved into the other cell, with orders not to speak to him, or to attempt any communication. We had exercise periods at different times, and never did see him, except at his window, but he kept in constant touch. Frank had had a presentiment that something like this might happen. The communication line was simple. We wrote messages and hid them on the lintel above the lavatory door. Frank collected the missives on his visit, and in turn left replies and requests. I took my four ration cigarettes out each day. No doubt they cheered him up considerably. The service was never suspected.

This period lasted for the whole of March '42. It was a dreary month, and a bad one. Singapore fell, and the Italians grew jubilant. Their soothsayers gave the war six months, and everyone, from the Colonello right down to the sanitary squad's latest whipping boy, mellowed in happy expectation. Half the garrison wore Iron Crosses awarded for defeating the French, and even the medals clinked louder in anticipation of victory. The Axis star was fast reaching its zenith. To the four prisoners in Cell B, the fortunes of the Allies looked grim indeed.

We were much worse off for the change of cells. Frank's room was a big airy one, with two large windows that gave a good view of everything going on outside. Our new quarters were cramped, and we had no window. There was a hole high up in the wall, but it was little better than a skylight. There was another hole in the floor, a smaller one this time, where a mouse lived, but it was no wee sleekit cowrin' tim'rous beastie. It was a truly dogged he-mouse with the tenacity of a bulldog.

At first it annoyed us. We stuffed the hole with paper and left it to starve, but the little animal gnawed a way through contemptuously. It defied fire and flood, and overnight left a trademark in Jock's dixie to indicate its scorn. Jock got heated about that. He promptly hammered a stone into the opening and sealed it. 'That'll cook your goose for you,' he muttered, 'you impudent little bastard.' But Jock underestimated the opposition. The giant-hearted rodent ate through successive layers of stone, sand and plaster, and emerged farther along the wall. We gave in. Courage of this order couldn't pass unnoticed. We forgave the mouse and put it on the ration strength. The once-murderous Jock spent a whole evening making a bowl for it.

Perhaps it was the mouse that got us thinking of Bruce and his spider. They hadn't admitted defeat either, and thinking of it, there seemed no reason why we should. We got up and went over the room again, this time inch by inch. In the far corner, under some rubble, Jock found a grating. It electrified us. Strong arms levered it up, and we looked down at the black chasm below. Was this the way out, after all? If it was a sewer, and there were no bars farther on, it could easily be. We could crawl through, take a boat somewhere, and enjoy a whole night's start over the Italians. Only the thought of having to abandon Frank tempered the enthusiasm.

It was a good scheme. Roy, who had done so much of the dirty work already, lost the toss, and went down headfirst to reconnoitre. He held a burning newspaper in his hand whilst Jock and Harry held on to his feet: but no hoots of joy floated up to rejoice us. We hauled him back and saw the look of disgust on his face. It was no go. What we were hoping would be a nice wide sewer, preferably not too dirty, and with an opening not too far off, was nothing more than an underground water tank.

In one way it was as well we were disappointed. If we had gone, Frank would have been left on his own at a time when he most needed moral support. Besides that, we would have missed the Easter celebrations.

Pasqua is a big event in Italy. It means as much to Italians as Christmas does to us, and the exiled soldati made a bigger fuss than usual. We went to Sunday Mass, although none of us belonged to the Catholic faith. Frank came too, and during the service I learnt that he was up for trial as a spy. And knowing what that meant – most probably a firing squad at the double – I felt very upset. Incongruously, Frank did the comforting. 'Don't worry,' he whispered, 'there's life in the old dog yet.' That was true. There's still life in the old dog to-day, which reflects well on his guts and resourcefulness. But it cast a blight on the festivities.

After Mass, the garrison cooks really went to work, and about mid-day a procession drew up outside our door. It swung open, and two beaming guards ushered in an exalted and very superior personage. It was the Head Cook. He was supported by a bevy of lackeys, who all bore covered dishes. There was an awed silence for a moment; and then the Cook, inspired by the occasion, delivered a speech. 'Oggi è Pasqua,' he announced. He reviewed the waiting dishbearers, and continued. 'Non c'è rizi.' That ended the oration. He had said all that mattered.

The maestro now waved to his subordinates, and into borrowed dixies went a full measure of first, minestrone, and then pasta asciutta, made as only Italians can make it. A third flunkey offered us rosy apples, the fourth poured out Chianti, and a fifth weighed in with nuts and figs: but the showpiece was left to the Boss. He took this dish from his acolyte, whipped off the cover, and unveiled his masterpiece. I don't think there was anyone, English or Italian, who wasn't overwhelmed. Before us were genuine, piping-hot Hot Cross Buns. Even the guards joined in the applause. The Cook bowed, not once, but many times, gesticulated modestly – 'Niente' – wished us 'Buon Appetito' and finally shepherded his flock through the door.

That was a day. We sat down on the beds, grinning at each other, and started on the most delectable feast in two years. We needed a sleep after that, but the spirit of Pasqua was strong. We didn't forget the mouse. He came out afterwards, enjoyed his macaroni, finished the sip of Chianti and dragged a piece of Hot Cross Bun back into his hole.

We left Siros a week later. All the original Piraeus party, plus Jock and Harry, met again in the hold of a tramp steamer. George, Alexis, and the others had been kept in a civilian prison not far away, where they had heard we were bound for Rhodes. The elder George was in bad trouble. He was now charged with assisting an enemy agent, which meant Frank, and if Frank was found guilty, George automatically came up for the high jump. The two men conversed in low tones. It seemed the Italians had dug up more evidence against them. George also knew that the Organization had found the informer, and had settled him, but that was cold comfort. It didn't make their prospects any brighter. Both men knew the coming trial would be largely a farce. They also knew that escaping and living were now synonymous.

The escape plan was conceived in Roy's fertile brain. On the third day out he squatted on his heels before us, and gave the details in a calm almost nonchalant voice. I was amongst the several who felt their bowels turning rapidly into water.

Roy had thought it out well. The only exit from the hold was up a vertical thirty foot ladder which was guarded at the foot by six Italians. Three hundred soldiers were billeted aft the bridge, so no sentries had been detailed to guard the top of our ladder. We were allowed up once a day to visit the unhygienic lavatory, so we'd know when to strike. Briefly the plan was this. Jock, who was an amateur boxer, was to approach the one watchful sentry at about 3 a.m., ask for a cigarette, and lay him out. The rest of us were to jump on the other guards and tie them up. Armed with the captured rifles, Roy, Jock and anyone else who was willing would then climb the ladder and rush the bridge from two sides. The Breda guns on the bridge could be reversed, which would check any sorties from aft. That would be easy, as only two doors opened on to the deck. By this time the ship would be steaming straight for the Turkish coast. Once it beached, we were to stop acting in concert. Then, it would be every man for himself.

We passed the plan. I voted for it, not being willing to admit foreseeing a dozen or more snags; but Cold Bean and one of his mechanics trembled too much to vote either way. They weren't heroes either.

We decided to strike as soon as the ship entered the narrows between Rhodes and Turkey. The strait was fifteen miles wide, so if the ship steamed down the centre, we wouldn't be more than seven or eight miles from Turkey. Nobody knew what currents might be running; but neither Frank nor George worried about that. In the water there was a chance: in Italian hands there was none. If we could get the ship beached, well and good. If we couldn't, they were still going overboard.

The days went past slowly. Much too slowly for the two imperilled men, and also for Roy and Jock. They were all thirsting for action, which was more than Cold Bean and his pal were doing. When we tied up at the last island stop before Rhodes both of them were cracking under the strain.

TEN

In a tale of fiction, all this could have been built into a grand yarn. A few minor snags to increase the tension, a last-minute crisis to bring it to fever pitch, a frenzy of rollicking action, and then a finale of success – and safe home. It would be easy to write it.

But at this last little island a company of infantry boarded the boat. The accommodation was already taxed to the limit, and so the newcomers had to sleep on deck. About fifty of them stretched their blankets on the hatch above us. We heard them cursing at the cold, and even Roy admitted it was hopeless.

At Rhodes we lost Frank and all the Greeks. They waved goodbye as the prison lorry swept out of the gates, and four years went by before I heard of them again. The majority of the Greeks got off lightly. Some received sentences as short as two months, but George and Cold Bean weren't amongst them. They were indicted, with Frank, on capital charges, and kept for trial by the Supreme Military Court. All three knew what that meant: and realizing that he too would probably end up as a target, Cold Bean changed into a different man. Some hidden source began pumping courage into him. In the two years that followed neither of the other two once faulted his nerve.

Frank had foreseen this Supreme Court business. He knew it was only a piece of legal jargon, and that eventually the Court would shoot him just as efficiently as any less long-winded body. He knew only one way of escaping the bullets. After three weeks of confinement he took it. He and his friends climbed the prison wall and escaped.

Rhodes is a large island compared with Kythnos and Kea, and given an hour's grace to leave the prison, the three men could have remained at large indefinitely; but the evil fortune which had pursued them through the Aegean was still potent. An informer told the Italians ten minutes after the escape. All three men were recaptured, and thrown into the punishment cells. Frank went before General Rosse, the Italian Commandante. He expected severe treatment, knowing that Italians don't take kindly to escapees, but this time his luck was in. The General had been a prisoner himself, during the 1914/18 war. He had escaped, too. In addition, he held the British Military Cross, and in short, Frank found an ally instead of a judge. The General saw to it that living conditions were bettered, and his benevolent interest made life much more bearable than before: but all were guarded well, and found no opportunity to get away again.

The Military Court was eventually set up in Samos, and a strong escort took the prisoners there. The General's patronage ceased, and they resumed their unpalatable diet of boiled maize. Frank and George were aware of the imminent danger. They knew the trial would be little more than a formality, and that death was close at hand. Promptly, they accepted the challenge and escaped again. It was more difficult this time, but they managed to force the cell window, and with Cold Bean, climbed on to the roof. It should have been easy to drop into the street, reach the end of the island, and if necessary, swim the four miles to Turkey, but the usual Jinx was awaiting them. Several Italians were sleeping on the ground below.

The trio on the roof held a whispered council. George wanted to wait until the guards patrolling farther down had left, and then drop there, but Frank was against that. At length each decided to go his own way. The Italians slumbered on as Frank landed lightly near them, and he got clean away. The others waited too long, and were caught. A large posse went after Frank and found him at the pre-arranged rendezvous.

Back in prison it was soon clear that the Axis was taking no more chances with such slippery customers. Guards now stayed in the cells with them day and night. Their living conditions deteriorated to a sub-human standard, and sewer rats and vermin tormented them. Nearby, the Italians were busy building a special escape-proof dungeon. When they were transferred to it, all hope disappeared.

They stayed in Samos for eight months, as their trial was repeatedly postponed. Eventually, in March '43, they were taken to Athens, and soon afterwards heard the inevitable verdict. The Supreme Military Court sentenced them to death by shooting. As a soldier, Frank was granted a concession. He would face his executioners, and be given an honourable death, but the civilians, George and Cold Bean, were to be shot in the back. As would be expected, Frank showed no emotion. George took it like a man too, and Cold Bean, all honour to him, was rock steady.

They were lodged in the condemned cells at the infamous Averoff prison, and all seemed lost. They had fought as men should fight. They could do no more. But although Frank got no glimmer of hope from the outside, great interest had been taken in his case, and strong efforts were being made on his behalf. British Headquarters in Cairo offered five Italian officers as an exchange. Damaskinos, Archbishop of Athens and all Greece, personally intervened with the Italian Commander-in-Chief, and three Foreign Ministers followed suit. Even the Vatican authorities showed interest.

The net result was a continued postponement of the execution. Daily the condemned men expected the firing squad, and each night was one of grim suspense. The execution was first fixed for the 13th July '43, and repeated postponements followed. On the 9th September, they learnt of the imminent Italian collapse. This made things worse rather than better. The Italians might easily vacillate until peace was declared, but the Germans were of a different fibre. They could be relied upon to clean up the condemned cells in their usual brusque fashion. It became imperative to Frank and his companions to get out at once.

The Italians were now hesitant, uncertain as to which side they owed allegiance. Frank took advantage of their dilemma. He offered to take with him all those who wanted to collaborate, and quickly got himself released. George and Cold Bean walked with him out of the grey prison into sweet liberty. Their freedom was Frank's first concern. The Bishop of Samos had given him a pair of boots with twenty gold sovereigns hidden in the heels, and the two jailers concerned were sensible men.

It was too dangerous to keep together, and each of the trio went his separate way. Frank stayed at the Swiss Consul's house until an unknown person 'phoned, and said briefly, 'Get out.' The Gestapo had arrived. Frank left just in time. He stayed with the Archbishop for a while, survived a Gestapo search of the house, and finally arranged to leave for Turkey by caique.

It was 1941 all over again. He reached his rendezvous in Athens on the back of a tandem bicycle, and travelled from there to the departure point on the coast in a police car. The Gestapo knew all about him. He had been their prisoner originally in Crete, and his photograph, fingerprints and details were in the German files – but first catch your hare. The Germans knew he would try to leave Greece. They set up roadblocks, but Frank, seated comfortably in the back of the police car, went straight through. It hadn't occurred to the Nazi soldiers that forces of law and order could be enlisted to aid a fugitive.

So Frank boarded his caique after all, despite the intensive search, and the large reward being offered for him: and this time the Jinx relented. He reached Turkey safely, and soon afterwards was home in England. Nearly two years had passed since that fateful day when he, Roy Natrousch and I walked ashore at Kea into Italian captivity. Two long and weary years which Frank had spent in prison cells and dungeons, often in unspeakable conditions: but he was still full of fight. On New

Year's Day 1944, he parachuted back into Greece. He had false papers, and wore a beard, but even so, his mission was dangerous in the extreme. He contacted various friends in Athens, and reorganized and reopened the escape routes. He was not recaptured. In the months which elapsed before the Germans left Greece, this very gallant officer, risking his life daily, sent a constant and undetected stream of escapees safely out of the country.

ELEVEN

We had an easier passage. The Italians gave us a haircut (short back and sides, and shorter on top), and the clerical staff put in half an hour's tabulating. After that a lorry took us to a transit camp ten miles away.

I knew Rhodes was the last chance. We were being sent to Italy, and if any escaping was going to be done, now was the time. Too many escorts travelled with the lorry to offer any hope there; but I missed a big chance that same day. Which goes to show that in this kind of life you shouldn't relax: at least not unless you want to stay put.

Three soldiers took us outside the camp to fill palliasses. They were watchful for a while, but the fern gathering was a long job. At length, the guards sat down for a smoke. I wandered on, plucking ferns here and there, and for perhaps a minute I was out of their sight. A wood lay about ten yards away. The Greek population would have given all the assistance they could, and quite likely I would have made Turkey inside a week. I went on plucking ferns. It never occurred to me, during that one vital minute, to run. For three nights afterwards I didn't sleep a wink.

But if we learn from others' mistakes, this aberration of

mine may yet prove useful. Very few of our overseas troops can now laugh at the idea of being captured: and to those who don't – a few words in season. If you should be captured and intend to escape, get away as soon as you can. The best time is just before the bag closes. The next best, just afterwards. There will certainly be a dozen opportunities then for every one that crops up later. Also, your own forces won't be so far away, and your captors will be fighting men, not prison guards. There's a world of difference.

To give an example. At Kalamata the Germans took about 10,000 British prisoners. For two whole days after that mass capture any one of those men could have walked away without let or hindrance, but only a few did. They were the wise ones. I was slow, but it was still easy even when I left.

In Germany escaping was a different proposition. Men dug tunnels that took months to complete. Even when the tunnelling was successful it still left them in enemy territory, with every hand raised against them. Escape Committees tried to cope with that. They provided false passports, civilian clothes, food, money, maps and suchlike to give the men a fifty-fifty chance. It took a dozen experts to equip one man, and that only in the minority of camps which had Escape Committees. Most didn't. The galling part is that all that paraphernalia should have been largely unnecessary. In most cases, the real opportunities had come in France, Norway, Africa, Greece and Crete, and had passed by unnoticed. Hence all the tunnels and disguises and so on.

The moral is obvious, but bears repeating. If you are going to make a break, grab Time by the forelock – and hang on. Don't wait until you're in a permanent camp that's been built specially to hold you. There'll be a chance en route somewhere. Take it!

The journey to Italy wasn't pleasant. None of us was expecting much, but we all thought there would be a limit. The sea trip reached that low level of expectation and then went three or four stages lower. It was a British boat, Clyde built, sturdy, and very old. The sanitation would have shocked an aborigine. The guards walked about with laces undone and lifebelts on their shoulders, all ready to dive overboard. We were kept in a stinking hold. After Roy was caught it was battened down and covered with a tarpaulin. If the ship was sunk, presumably we were to take a deep breath and wait for the salvage people.

Roy really deserved to get away this time. We anchored in Piraeus bay, so near the shore that most of us could identify at least one of the houses in sight. Each evening we were allowed on deck, one at a time, and given about two minutes to get a breath of fresh air. When Roy's turn came, he took in a big breath, took it overboard with him, and struck out for the beach. He knew that once ashore he was as safe as the house he was heading for. The two guards looked on stupidly for a moment, and then woke up. The prisoner was gone, granted, but Porco Dio! they still had their lungs. The hullabaloo shook every man in the ship. Both guards rushed to the side, and loosed off their entire magazines; but Roy wasn't worrying. He was swimming underwater, and he knew the Italians could only fire blindly. No one can aim a rifle in the dark.

The firing died away, and the din above us lessened slightly. Sharp orders rang out. I breathed a prayer for the intrepid Kiwi, but he was not yet to escape. The Jinx was still in charge. One of the ship's tenders was just leaving for Piraeus and the occupants found Roy about fifty yards from the beach. He was unconscious when he came back. It was partly from exhaustion, and partly as a result of the vicious manhandling he got; but when his eyes opened, the same bleak look was there that I had seen at Kythnos. Nothing could daunt this man's spirit.

The Italians left a few planks unbattened, but to be on the safe side, they draped a canvas cover over the entire hatch. The next night their surprise count went wrong. They were a man short. The poor guards nearly had a fit. They lined us up, counted in ranks, in threes, and individually, but always ended up a man short. It panicked them. They scrambled up the ladder, bawling for the officer, and as alarm bells began ringing Roy dropped down from the top of the hatch. He had been sitting there for two hours hoping to slip overboard again, but there was no chance now.

The officer came, lined us up, and got his total right first time. He fumed at the sweating N.C.O.s for a trio of fools; but he guessed something was afoot. As soon as he left, the canvas swung away, and down came the hatches. We were battened down like rats in a trap. We stayed like that until the boat was well out to sea again.

Being cooped up had one advantage. We now got five minutes' warning of counts, which was a fairly safe margin. The hatch covers came off the hold below easily enough, and we tried our luck there. It was no go. There were no portholes so far down, and therefore no escape, but Signor Baldi's parcel made the sortie worthwhile. It contained ten pounds of raisins, a tin of olive oil, and some figs, and was legitimately in transit. Vittorio Emanuele's Royal Mail was guarding the parcel, but George VI's subjects ate it. The thought amused Harry. 'Maybe they'll sue each other,' he grinned.

At Bari we climbed out of the stinking hold to find an armed escort lined up to greet us. There was more escort than prisoners, so everyone got safely to *Campo di Concentramento di Prigionieri di Guerra, Numero* 75. That name was a mouthful. The camp looked formidable too, with all its multiple barbed wire fences, but it wasn't as tough as it seemed. We had room to move about, the air was unrationed, and the food passable. It made a pleasant change from the ship.

I was even more pleased than the others. I roamed about, enjoying the comparative liberty, and bumped into Joe Pollak. And here comes another story. I had already bumped into Joe twice before, once in Greece and once in Kythnos. I reckoned I knew him well by now. We seemed to have much in common, too: and if circumstance had made the other meetings brief, well, it looked as if time was now on our side.

Joe was Austrian and a Jew. I was English and a Gentile, but neither race nor religion made any difference to us. It was the man who counted, and from my point of view the man in Joe couldn't help but appeal. He gave the impression of being a good lad in a tight corner.

Joe's war had been going on since 1938. He was in Prague then, studying quite happily for his degree, when a whisper came of an intended Gestapo *putsch*. Joe left the University

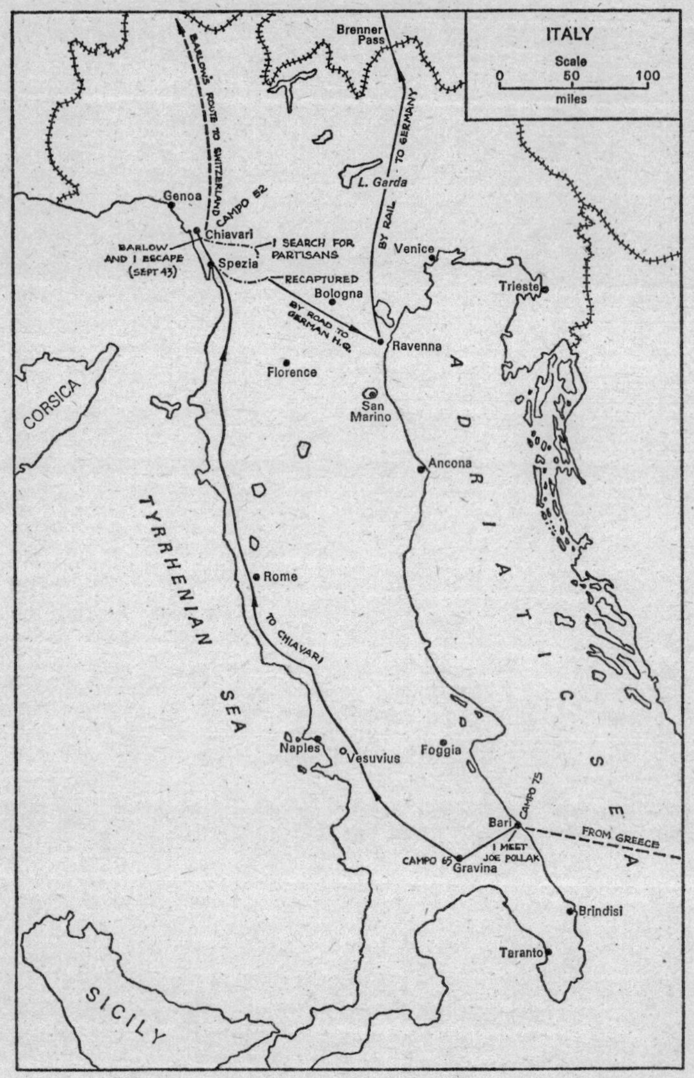
ITALY
Scale
0
50
100
miles
Brenner Pass
BARLOW'S ROUTE TO SWITZERLAND
BY RAIL TO GERMANY
L. Garda
Genoa
CAMPO 52
Chiavari
I SEARCH FOR PARTISANS
BARLOW AND I ESCAPE (SEPT 43)
Spezia
Venice
RECAPTURED
Bologna
Trieste
BY ROAD TO GERMAN H.Q.
Ravenna
Florence
CORSICA
San Marino
Ancona
ADRIATIC SEA
TYRRHENIAN SEA
Rome
TO CHIAVARI
Naples
Vesuvius
Foggia
CAMPO 75
Bari
FROM GREECE
I MEET JOE POLLAK
CAMPO 65
Gravina
Brindisi
Taranto
SICILY

for Palestine next day, beating the *putsch* by twelve hours. His departure was unauthorized, but he knew the ropes and spoke seven languages. His wife and two children were already in the Promised Land. He stayed a year with them before he was away again, this time to join the British Army. Greece followed, and capture, but Joe wasn't a prisoner more than a day or two. He lived in Athens for a year, trying all the time to get out of the country, and like so many more of us, finding it wasn't easy. He added Greek and English to an already impressive list of languages. One day, in Omonoia Square, he met a Palestinian friend who greeted him warmly. The friend had a car, and offered a lift. Inside, Joe found two more friends, both wearing Gestapo uniform. It was the usual routine of informers.

Three weeks in jail followed, and then Mr. Pollak got an idea himself. He pleaded sickness and went with one Italian guard to the German hospital in Kephissia. The Italian wasn't a brainy man. He waited outside the lavatory door far too long. By the time he broke it down, Joe, who had left via the window, was halfway across Athens. Once bitten, he was very shy. He walked warily, and made no more mistakes until he joined the Antiparos submarine party. That disaster was beyond his control.

We were mates from the beginning, with a policy of 'all for one and one for all'. From the first we decided on action, which meant getting out. There were already a hundred British officers in Bari, and Stage 1 was accomplished when we were appointed batmen-interpreters. Joe spoke fluent Italian. I could get along passably enough, and as liaison between the officers and the Italians, we got to know both sides quite well. Stage 2 was entry into an escapers' circle. About half the officers were perpetually planning escape, but most of them were going round in circles. One clique, headed by a Lt.-Colonel, approached the problem more soberly and were glad when they enlisted us as interpreters.

The Colonel was a skilful organizer and a good man to team up with; but he faced a big problem. For a start, there was no one who had any experience of escaping in Italy. Nobody had any equipment either, and our one solitary map was scaled at 200 miles to the inch. That wasn't much use. We knew

Switzerland was 600 miles away, which made walking rather pointless: but walking was the only way. We couldn't go by train. Train journeys demanded passports, money, civilian clothes, fluency in Italian, a knowledge of railway schedules, and a good start. The Medaglia D'Oro could have been added to the list for all the difference it made to us.

In the end the planners agreed that the first attempt would have to be a hit-and-miss affair. Getting away wouldn't be too difficult. The inevitable weak spot in the wire had been found weeks ago, and as the Colonel remarked, disguises and documents weren't any longer a hindrance. 'It's a pity the Swiss border's so far away,' he said, summing up. 'We couldn't be much worse placed than we are here. As we've agreed, conditions outside this camp remain an unknown factor. That means we must cut our walking to a minimum. The only course open, therefore, is to abandon the Swiss venture, and follow the coast southwards. By night, naturally. We'll take the first boat that offers, and cross the narrows into Albania. If we get there, we won't be free, but we'll be freer. Pollak and Jones will be useful as regards language difficulties. I'm afraid we're leaving a good deal to chance, gentlemen, but then this is only a first attempt. We leave in ten days' time.'

The Colonel knew his astronomy. The moon had ten nights left in it, and a dark night was essential for the breakout. Joe and I were almost as essential, and both of us were looking forward eagerly to Stage 3. So far, this project had gone like clockwork.

The Colonel must have been annoyed when the Italians transferred us to Campo 65 at Gravina, two days before the breakout. The move came without warning. It was so sudden that neither of us had a chance to contact the Boss, or even to leave a message. Possibly he didn't find out until next day, when his shaving water didn't arrive. By that time we were in Gravina, and not liking it a bit.

Bari was a good camp, as these places go. Gravina was a hell of a place, on the edge of the Pontine Marshes, in one of the most barren and inhospitable parts of the whole country. There couldn't have been a worse spot.

We found 9,000 men already installed in the four barbed

wire compounds. Prisoners and guards alike lived in white sandstone barracks with no heating arrangements, and poor lighting. There was water, but it was pumped from a station some distance away, and more often than not the pumps were on strike. During the 'on' periods water was flagrantly wasted. The builders' ideas hadn't run to taps. Instead, they put in long pipes, drilled holes in them, and left the rest to chance. Every day the engineers pumped so many gallons through and then stopped: and if prisoners weren't there with cans and water bottles at the right time, well, that was just too bad. There were agile men who managed a bath before the supply went off. Usually there was a bigger number all soaped up to the eyes who stayed like that until the water came on again.

Lieutenant Ivo Verzola, the Adjutant, didn't love Gravina any more than we did. He counted us, opened the gate, and pulled a face when Joe mentioned that the place didn't look so good. 'È bruto,' he agreed. 'È brutale regione.'

An early brush with authority didn't leave us any happier. It transpired that two men had to return to Bari, and hearing this, Joe and I decided to give Chance a helping hand. We could see the Colonel's planning behind the move. He was giving us an opportunity to get back, and trusting we'd have the sense to grasp it. We did. We addressed a letter to the Commandante, and not caring for half-measures, threw in the offer of a parole during the journey.

That same day a sergeant came looking for us. He escorted us to what was called the 'Bread Palace', where the warrant officers lived in splendid isolation, somehow managing a better standard of living than the rest of the camp. We found the R.S.M. waiting. He had intercepted our letter and was now holding it at arm's length, as if it were a live cholera swab. A bevy of lesser lights were standing by, all tuned in to the Great Man. He brought us to attention, and picked up a translation of the letter.

We had thought our effort a good one. It was well-phrased, well-written, and had a lot of thought and psychology behind it: but the R.S.M. didn't agree. He was patriotic. He read the epistle, finished it, and paused a moment. Nobody stirred in the awful silence that followed. 'Did you write – this?' he asked, in a half-strangled voice. His neck was fitting his collar tightly. 'Yessir,' we agreed, smartly. The response brought a look of contempt, of utter abhorrence. I began feeling I had crawled from under a flat stone. 'And you're dressed like soldiers,' commented the R.S.M. bitterly. Then the floodgates opened. 'And who the hell d'you think you are?' he roared. 'D'you realize this is a prison camp, you bloody Quislings? So you'd crawl to the Ities with your paroles, eh? I'll give you parole! By God, I will! Do you know your first duty as a prisoner is to escape?' Four loaves sitting on the table jumped as the R.S.M.'s fist crashed down. 'You're for a court martial when you get back,' he promised savagely. 'I'll see to that. Both of you. Now – get!'

We got. It hadn't been a fair interview, nor particularly enjoyable; but there wasn't much we could do at this stage. We should have told the R.S.M. everything at the beginning. Now it was too late. He wouldn't believe a word we said. Worse, he'd have it round the Bread Palace in a minute, and that could easily wreck the Colonel's plans. It was too risky.

The two men left next day. Neither of them spoke Italian, and we knew the Colonel would soon be cursing; but that couldn't be helped. We had to stay at Gravina.

Campo 65 lived up to every bad impression it had made. The food was a rude shock, but after a month or two the low rations grew worse. The daily 'stew' became more watery, and almost everyone grew thinner. There were exceptions. The warrant officers, for instance, didn't seem to lose much weight. The happy gang of fiddlers also waxed fat, and a stranger could have picked out the cookhouse staff to a man. We weren't getting anything like our proper rations. They were depleted before they got to the camp. The cookhouse boys dealt them a few telling blows when they did arrive, and fiddlers, stationed all along the delivery line, showed little more mercy. As a result, what we got mocked what went into the dixies.

What it added up to was the first Black Period. For some men it was the only one. The standard of health deteriorated and disease came to the camp. It found easy prey. Dysentery ravaged underfed bodies: malaria-carrying mosquitoes came in hordes from the marshes, bringing sickness and death with them. We grew accustomed to the slow funeral processions.

I escaped the malaria, but began having blackouts every time I stood up. Joe was in the same boat, and it drove home more firmly what we already knew – somehow we had to get extra food. The trouble was – where? The 'Bread Palace' was out of the question. We were *persona non grata* there, in quite a big way. The cookhouse was almost as hopeless. Every cook had his mate as heir apparent to any vacancy, and there was a queue waiting to get on the waiting list. Only one other élite corps – the racketeers – remained. Their activities were a monument to free enterprise. They weren't a closed shop, didn't rely on influence or graft, and anyone who had the brains or the 'know-how' could join them. Once a member he became automatically one of the Gravina royalty.

I managed it, as much through good luck as good management: but for a long time, it left a nasty taste, because I was on my own when it happened. Joe wasn't there to share the spoils. In August '42 he was transferred to a camp up North. With him went Roy Natrousch, Jock, Harry, and most of the Old Brigade from Siros and Rhodes. I stood at the barbed wire fence and watched them walk out of my life. I mourned especially for Joe. The rest of that day was misery. Next morning, the first delivery of Red Cross parcels delighted the rest of the camp; and the day after I got my foot on the bottom rung of the ladder.

The old R.S.M. had left with Joe's party. The new one brought some old-fashioned military discipline with him, and on his first day things began to hum. For the first time in twelve months blankets were folded instead of being tossed to the end of the bed. Everybody who could stand had to come out for 'pep' parades, and the slovenly and the unwashed changed their habits in a hurry. Even the Italians began to smarten up.

That R.S.M. was a one-man revolution. He was a terror, and he didn't mind who knew. In many ways he did us all a deal of good. His best effort, without any doubt, was appointing me interpreter, so he could lash out more effectively at the Italians. Verzola and 'Farmer Joe', the Colonel, were on the hop for a whole week. Before it was over they sent an agonized appeal to H.Q. It succeeded. The dynamic R.S.M., with an Italian corporal meekly carrying his kit, left us for a new camp. He raised instant hell there, too. Before the war finished, the mention of his name was enough to give any Commandante in Italy the shudders.

A third R.S.M. arrived, and the camp waited expectantly: but this one had been hand chosen. He went to his suite in the Bread Palace and troubled nobody. Conditions quickly reverted to normal. The habitually unwashed parcelled up their soap and the sleepers crawled back to their beds. I sought out the new man as soon as I could.

'D'you want me to-day, sir?' I enquired briskly.

The R.S.M. looked up. 'No. Who are you?' he asked.

'Interpreter, sir. At the office. On duty every morning.' The job wasn't going into disuse if I could help it: but the new boss was looking interested.

'Yes,' he said. 'It's a good idea. Right. Be there this afternoon. I may need you.'

I stayed on as interpreter. It was a good job, that kept me alert and off my bed. There was a cup of boiled rice attached to it as pay, but that didn't count for much. Bigger things than boiled rice were in the offing. Verzola, the Adjutant, mentioned that good watches were getting scarce in Italy. Next day I brought him one, and after dark collected fifty loaves in a sack. The man who owned the watch had asked me to try for twenty. I gave him twice that many, and became his blood brother.

From then on, more commissions came in than I could handle. Personal parcels were coming through, and it soon got around that the interpreter was way up on the other dealers. The transactions weren't ethical, but nobody worried about that. Ethics are things you think about on a full stomach. At Gravina, if a man preferred to eat his new pullover rather than wear it, that was his business. If he brought it to me, he got three quarters of what Verzola gave, and went away happy.

Sometimes it occured to me that 'flogging' these goods was a furtive and rather shoddy business; but the regrets were always short-lived. No dealer could afford a conscience. In any case, some of the gifts that came from home couldn't have been worse chosen. Loving hands made beautiful patchwork quilts that never reached the loved one's bed. They would have been louse-ridden in a night. Instead the recipient went hot-foot to a middleman, changed his quilt into loaves, and probably wrote back for another. Mistakes happened, too. Occasionally, violent rainstorms sent flood water surging past the barrack doors. 'There's a river flowing outside,' commented one man in his letter. A fishing rod came for him post haste. It ended up with Farmer Joe. He had entered the lists with Verzola, which suited me nicely. It put the prices up.

Being in daily contact with the top men gave me a big advantage over most of the business community. To begin with, my loaves weren't thrown over the wire. I could combine three or four deals and bring back a sack load of civilian bread at a time.

We racketeers were shady characters. We didn't pretend otherwise, and weren't very interested in codes of morals; but one unwritten rule was always observed. No dealer ever undercut another. It kept prices at a constant high level.

The more scrupulous prisoners were also doing some brisk business. If a man could turn a piece of wood or metal into something useful, he was entitled to sell it. A good many could and did. We had some real talent at Gravina. There were watch-repairers, curio-makers, wood-carvers, weavers, and the like, all turning out beautiful work, and all selling it at a tithe of its value. One man made himself a set of false teeth. Another built a clock from old tins and odd bits. It took him six months to complete, and had a tick like a trip hammer, but kept time to within ten minutes a day.

The 'blower' originated in this camp. 'Blowers' were portable stoves which could boil a quart of water in two minutes. By 1943 no prisoner was complete without one. Early models worked on the bicycle pump principle, but hand-driven fans soon made them obsolete. But graft beat honest industry every time. In an officially sponsored 'brewing-up' contest an engineer started off a ten-to-one favourite. One of the cook-house boys left him standing: and only a few of us knew the winner had boiled his wood fuel in sugar the night before. In Campo 65 the weak and not-so-wide-awake went to the wall.

Soon after Joe left I found a new friend. Cecil was a modest lad, ex-public school, popular with everyone, and with more refined speech and manners than most of us. I liked him for his character. No dealer was ever short of fair-weather friends, but what every dealer yearned for was a comrade who wouldn't leave him as soon as trouble cropped up. Cecil was the perfect answer. I had a feeling that he wouldn't have cared if we had been on the one ration loaf.

He tried to help with the business, although obviously it wasn't in his line. At one time I had a contract with an Italian who brought three dozen fresh eggs in every day. They cost me twelve two-ounce packets of tea. As soon as the Italian left, I would go into the barracks, stand in the middle of the floor, and bawl at the top of my voice 'Eggs! Fresh Eggs! Eggs for tea!' In no time I was surrounded by purchasers. The next day's tea-packets poured in at two eggs a time, which left me a profit of a dozen eggs. It was good quick business, and everyone was satisfied. They were good big eggs too, and replaced if bad, so everyone had a right to feel pleased.

Cecil made hard work of the job. His method was to walk up to a bed, wait until he wouldn't interrupt, and then murmur, 'I say, old boy. About an egg. Er – are you interested?' It didn't work. Our customers were a conservative lot, a tough bunch used to loud-mouthed vendors and aggressive salesmanship. They distrusted Cecil's approach. It made them distrust his eggs as well, and after one trial he gave up. We were equally relieved.

The food parcels were coming in regularly now. There were twenty-seven different nationalities represented at Campo 65, and about twelve different languages spoken, but the only thing we were ever unanimous upon was our debt to the Red Cross people. Without their help three-quarters of us would have died. With it, almost every man got a pass to health and a weekly morale-boost that did him a world of good. As always, there were exceptions, but they were few. A stretcher party took one man to hospital where the doctor diagnosed malnutrition. The orderlies who went to investigate found five unopened parcels under the sick man's bed. He had been keeping them for a rainy day.

Other men managed to keep their sanity, but still let the prison beat them. Their trouble was laziness. They grew slack, didn't shave, and spent most of the day on their beds. One or two were forcibly washed and needed it. They probably did themselves permanent harm and certainly made the biggest call on psychiatrists after the war; but the vast majority of prisoners took up the challenge. They realized that their biggest enemy was boredom and that boredom had to be defeated. The 'Bourse' was one way of doing it. As soon as food parcels were given out, tins began changing hands. Everyone was trying to make two tins out of one, and some spent all day at it. The man next to me set off regularly with his ration loaf. It weighed seven ounces. Usually he came back late at night with a 'grandi' – a military loaf weighing over a pound – looking as pleased as Punch. Probably forty or fifty exchanges covered the transition.

The Red Cross deserve credit for more than their basic success in providing food. They sent sports equipment, books, and so on, and tried to accommodate every taste. Periodically we got new boots, which almost as frequently caused trouble. The weekly parcel would keep a man in health, but even with the Italian ration, there wasn't enough to satisfy him. As a result anything that could be sold was sold, and boots commanded a high price. The R.S.M. knew this. He didn't approve of people eating these gifts, and he held regular parades to make sure they stayed on the right feet. Offenders went straight to 'clink'.

The cooks were known universally as the 'Forty Thieves'. Every now and again there was a change of staff, but it never did the rations any good. We didn't expect it. At Gravina honest men went hungry, and each new cook took this to heart. He knew that he mightn't hold the job for any length of time. Consequently he made all the hay he could whilst the sun shone. It would have been better to put one lot of rogues in and have done with it.

The Red Cross made only one mistake. They sent tea, milk and sugar, and forgot we had to boil water. Very soon there was nothing left in the camp to boil it with. Beds were wooden affairs, and every bed quickly sacrificed most of its boards to the tea ritual. The blowers were efficient, and would make tea in double quick time, but they ate fuel. A wood market promptly sprang up, but only the rich ever patronized it. The prices were terrific. Wood was worth its weight in bread. Sometimes it wasn't far short of its weight in tobacco. It got to be a desperate business, tea-making, but nobody ever thought of going without his brew. Tea was more than a habit. It was a tradition.

Most of the camp were forced to use the outdoor cookhouse stove. It wasn't a good one. That was why it was outside; but in its all-too-brief free periods every square inch of space had a can resting on it. Frequently the tea boiled over before the agonized owner could get it clear. More frequently still, cans dissolved into a scalding hiss of steam, but the tea-makers were a stubborn lot. When the stove smoked their faces turned black: when it roared at white heat they had their eyebrows singed off: but seldom a man withdrew before someone shouted the magic formula – 'You're boiling!'

Now and again there was a break. Odd crates were spirited into the camp to lead short but well-guarded lives. Once, and once only, a sentry's hut came over the wire.

That epic rates with the best achievements of World War II. Just after dark one of the guards found himself being offered a gold watch for ten loaves. The Italian had only eight concealed in his tunic and down his pants, but he knew the watch was worth at least a hundred. No fish ever rose better to the bait. When the Italian came pelting back, out of breath but triumphant, his contact had disappeared. His little wooden hut had gone too. During his five minutes' absence ten men had bridged the wire with bedframes and manhandled it into the compound.

It was some time before the hysterical guard could get the duty officer to believe him. It took longer to get a search squad ready, and by then the sentry box was in a thousand pieces. Nobody was caught despite the search. When it finished, the gang collected all the bits and made a celebration brew. After that they had no fuel worries for a week. The sentry, who went to jail, had none for two months.

TWELVE

Gravina was almost as bad, as far as escaping was concerned, as Bari. We were still remote from Switzerland, still without civilian contacts, and no one had the faintest idea what papers or documents were essential. During the first six months the majority of would-be escapers were also too weak to try. Now they were fitter, it was a different story. After all, men get away from Devil's Island, and Gravina wasn't as bad as that.

Two warrant officers from the Bread Palace were the first to break the ice. They persuaded the Cypriot traders to hold a bargain sale at one end of the wire. When the guards were nicely bunched together, the W.O.s cleared the fence and set off. Dummies in their beds fooled the Italians for two days, and by that time the two men were sixty miles away. It was good going. They might have reached Switzerland safely if the language barrier hadn't tripped them. On the third day, an old peasant gave them a cheerful 'Buon giorno,' and got suspicious when no answer came. He mentioned it to a carabiniere farther down the road. Next day an army lorry brought the W.O.s back to Gravina. Their return took a load off Farmer Joe's mind and instead of the harsh punishment they had been expecting, the escapees got only a week 'inside'.

It surprised us all; but the matter didn't rest there. Farmer Joe had been doing some thinking lately. The double escape spurred him to action. If prisoners could get away as easily as those *sergenti-maggiori* it didn't say much for the defences. He knew his superiors would probably echo the sentiment. And as for that sentry box affair! *Dio mio!* Right from under the guard's nose! The mere possibility of H.Q. getting to hear of that made Joe shudder. He pictured the amused grins of his fellow colonels, winced at the thought, and rang for Verzola. Something would have to be done about this pretty smartly.

A couple of days later, three lorries loaded with barbed wire rolled into the camp. It was proof that the lethargic Joe could move when he wanted to. Another fifty names went on the white rice list, and work began straight away: but the fence was a slow business. Both Joe and Verzola supervised personally, and both complained that 'go-slow' tactics were being adopted. That was strictly true. The newly employed wiremen were doing a good job, but in their own time. None was keen on working himself out of a job: or a ladle of white rice. The new fence could have been erected in a week. It took a month, solely because the gang couldn't make it drag out any longer: but when it was done, prospective escapers took one look and turned away. That avenue was closed from now on.

Farmer Joe's fence left only two ways out – the gate and tunnels. We weren't organized sufficiently for tunnels, and there was always a danger from informers; which left the gate. For a while it looked promising. So promising, in fact, that I gave up the lucrative interpreter's job and had a shot myself.

Another barracks was being built just outside the camp. It wasn't hard to bribe one of the official working party, and for two days I took his place. The first day was for reconnaissance. On the second I came out of hiding at about seven o'clock, detoured the camp, and set off on the 600 miles trek. I had maps and the usual escaping kit, and about 597 miles to go when an old man stopped me. He was suspicious before either of us spoke. He asked for my passport and I knew that was the end of that. Unless I murdered this old nosey-parker, the carabinieri would be out within the hour. If I did cosh him, it would only delay the search.

Still, the old boy wasn't bad at heart. We walked back to the camp and approached the sentry. 'Who's this man?' he demanded. 'A prisoner,' said my escort, and then lying nobly, 'He's been out with me on a special job. Colonel's orders.'

We shook hands, and the gates clanged shut. Effort No. 1 hadn't got very far: which left the water cart as the last hope of leaving Gravina. It came in every day with five hundred gallons of water for the cookhouse. During the fortnight I spent checking it in and out of the gates, it was never once searched. I made the usual preparations. On the fifteenth day I did a practice jump into the back of the lorry. No one saw me, but it wouldn't have mattered if they had. The big tank occupied most of the covered space. The dark corner where I might have crouched down quietly was there too; but the driver had a mattress spread in the back. On the mattress were his eating irons and part of his kit. Another good idea was strangled at birth.

But the gate wasn't invulnerable. A week later twenty men walked through it in broad daylight, and left prison life for good. There was a catch, of course. The Italians had been putting out intensive appeals for war workers, and this group had volunteered. They collected brand-new kit, had their names taken for future reference, and left with jeers and catcalls ringing in their ears. Campo 65 had no use for traitors. The one sailor who went got the worst abuse of all. There were only fifty naval men at Gravina and they had always managed to maintain a high standard of discipline. The affair hurt them more than they admitted; but they got the last laugh. They got it twice. The mutineer half-turned at the gate and a bad apple caught him fairly between the eyes. A week after he left, the whole naval contingent got sudden orders to pack. They had been included in an exchange of prisoners.

The war workers had their own reasons for going. Few men in the camp ever got enough to eat, and the promise of extra rations tempted some. Others were too fed up after ten months at Gravina to care what they did: and quite a few were thinking of women. None of us had seen a girl for nearly a year. Perhaps the guards received orders. Possibly they talked the way they did spontaneously. Whatever way it was, very few men failed to get the idea that there were women workers at Napoli, and not all of them chaste.

The Italians themselves weren't over pleased at this move. They had been expecting hundreds of volunteers, and the organization they laid on was largely wasted on twenty. There were nine thousand men in Campo 65. A score was hardly a flash in the pan and so far they hadn't unearthed a single technician. To give them due credit, it should be emphasized that there was never any question of compulsion. There was no forced labour in Italy.

The next move was more subtle. We all got long forms asking for details of our occupations and hobbies. Farmer

Joe, who wanted to know which men would recognize a turret lathe when they saw one, sent a box of pencils into each compound to help. A blurb at the top of the form pointed out that if more was known about us, maybe more could be done towards making life easier; but we suspected Joe's good intentions.

The completed forms showed it. They went back fast enough, but they didn't help him. It was too bad there weren't any lathe operators or capstan turners at Gravina, but in case any were found it seemed we had an Archbishop ready to bless them. A Zulu chief and an explorer were also standing by to do what they could. The 'occupations' revealed some unexpected versatility. In our compound was a burglar, two guess-your-weight men and a Fairy Queen. Next door to us was a marathon runner and a sprinkling of long-distance cyclists. Lower down lived other unusual characters, including a gigolo, and one optimistic chap who claimed experience as a frothblower. In short, the appeal was a flop.

The months slid past. 1942 ended. Inside the Gravina *reticolato* we said 'Thank God' for that, and began hoping '43 would see us home.

The new year began well. In Africa the Allies started advancing from both Libya and Tunisia in what we hoped would be a giant pincer move. As early as January there was a real burst of optimism. Tripoli fell to the 8th Army, and in Stalingrad the Russians trapped the whole of the German 6th Army. Perhaps '43 would be The Year after all. We heard about the terrific bombing raids the R.A.F. and the Yanks were making, and hopes began soaring. We almost felt sympathy for the Italians when their own 8th Army was sent back from the Russian front.

Spring came and more victories were won. It was pretty obvious now who was going to win the war, but not so easy to say when. The Germans were once again proving tough foes. From the scattered reports we got it seemed they were the same old Huns they always had been. There were hints of brutality and atrocities, but it was clear the Germans were fighting back hard. But the Gravina Italians knew they were supporting a lost cause. Not even Musso could stir up much enthusiasm with our guards.

In June came an event that momentarily put the war news in the shade. About three hundred men got the usual hour's notice to leave, and Cecil and I found our names listed. In the speculation that followed as to where we would end up, everything else was small talk.

It was a long journey. For some unknown reason we travelled in first class passenger coaches with every imaginable luxury. It was just possible that somewhere down the line a band of V.I.P.s were staring goggle eyed at their cattle trucks, but that didn't concern us. We spread out over the plush seats and registered a vote of thanks to the Transport Officer.

At dusk the guards came round and pleaded with us not to escape. It seemed they would lose some leave if we did; but so far as I could see they were safe enough. There were only two doors to each carriage, and they were guarded. Jumping out of the window was too risky. The train put on speed as soon as darkness came, and dropping eight feet into a black void appealed to nobody. Railways have a lot of obstacles along the permanent way, and no one relished the idea of being wrapped around a concrete post. Not at 40 m.p.h.

I sat up the whole night, but the engine never faltered. The rhythm of click-clicking wheels was as constant as a clock. 'You'll break your neck. You'll break your neck. You'll break your neck,' it said.

Early on we saw the glow of distant Vesuvius. Several times flashes of gunfire illumined the train, as nearby ack-ack batteries opened up. The flashes grew more frequent as we sped North. Now and again, especially during the small hours, I thought I felt a slackening of speed, and got ready to wake Cecil: but it was all in vain. The driver never once slackened pace.

We pulled in to Chiavari about nine o'clock next morning. It was a fair-sized town fifty miles East of Genoa, and about 200 miles from the Swiss border. We had been going in the right direction anyway. It struck me that we were now only a third of the previous distance from Switzerland. The French-Italian border was less than that.

A train puffing slowly past interrupted these thoughts. I

glanced out of the window. Four wagons slid by, with four anti-aircraft guns pointing menacing noses at the sky. Then came a number of long flat trucks. On each was an enormous field gun, with a crew of lithe young Germans in attendance. More ack-ack guns followed, some of them multiple-barrelled jobs. I caught a glimpse of shoulder flashes. It was the crack Hermann Goering division moving South to Sicily.

THIRTEEN

One look at the new camp was enough. It lay at the foot of a wooded valley, with terraced hills and green slopes rising gently on either side. A sprinkling of white houses dotted the hillsides, some buried almost roof-deep in masses of green foliage, others standing sharp and clear against their background. The air was incense. Flowers and herbs were pouring out generous perfume, and bees filled our ears with incessant droning. Men looked at each other wonderingly. At Gravina there had been no bees, nor flowers, nor anything except dreary desolation. Someone raised a cheer.

Campo 52 stood on the far side of a stream that ran parallel with the road. We crossed a shaky wooden bridge, passed through some trees and bushes, and surveyed the place. It was up to expectation. We saw trim wooden huts, raised well off the ground, and evenly spaced inside a vast barbed-wire triangle. There was any amount of room. The latrines seemed less primitive than at Gravina, and washing facilities more extensive, although still the same hole-in-a-pipe system. There was even a *Refetorio*. It was a large building that could be used as a common room, or a theatre, and the few camps that had such places appreciated them. We were all smiles. If the food was passable here, we were on a good thing.

But there was another side to all this. The Italians had done their best to make the place comfortable, but they hadn't overlooked the defences. A double fence ten feet high ran around the entire perimeter of the camp. The wire sloped inwards at the top, and every sentry box had a press-button floodlight above it. At each of the tree corners stood a 'tiger-box' with searchlight and Breda machine gun at the ready. Chiavari camp was intended to be a tough proposition. So far it hadn't failed its makers. In all the eighteen months of its existence no man had yet escaped.

There had been attempts, naturally, but not via the wire. A gang of tunnellers started work in an end hut soon after the camp was opened. They reached the outer wire before one of the carabinieri tripped over a forgotten bag of earth. After that, tunnels were 'out'. The guards concreted the entrance, began inspecting huts regularly, and sent in 'ferrets' to prod the ground with iron rods.

With tunnels taboo there was no way left to escape. Dodging away from a working party would have been plain foolishness. Each guard signed for five prisoners, was held responsible for them, and fussed over them like an old hen. The average working party was counted once every two minutes. When a man escapes, he needs hours as currency, not minutes.

We went through the heavy gate and sat down for the counting ritual to start. I got a book out and began reading. The guards would need three or four tallies on the run before they were happy, and a book seemed indicated. A cigarette would have gone well with it, but I had run out. I was sitting down resignedly when a packet of ten landed at my feet. At the same moment a well-known voice shouted jubilantly, 'Hi-ya, Joney!' – and there was Barlow waving at the fringe of the crowd.

We had only half an hour to wait. By a happy fluke the counting squad got three correct results consecutively, and decided not to risk a fourth. They dismissed us. I hoisted my kit and ran immediately to where Barlow was standing.

A stranger would never have guessed the feelings behind that reunion. We shook hands, pummelled each other, did a spot of violent horseplay, and said none of the things long-lost friends are supposed to say. Our friendship went deeper than that. We had joined up together. We went abroad, feasted and fought together, and wherever Barlow was, it was a safe bet Jones wasn't far away. And vice versa. In captivity we fasted together, and missed several chances of easy escape. The association continued until Randle jumped from the train in that Peloponnesian tunnel. The break then lasted two years. During that time neither of us knew whether the other was alive or dead. Certainly we never dreamt we would meet again in Italy.

'What happened?' I asked. Barlow looked puzzled, and I realized I had been thinking to myself. 'In the tunnel,' I explained. 'After you hopped off the train.' My pal looked up, enlightened.

'That was easy,' he grinned. 'I rolled a bit but there was some kind of a drain by the track. It soaked me, but that was all.'

'And how d'you go on then?' It had never been easy getting Barlow to talk.

'Middling,' he said, doing his best, gallantly. 'I was loose five months and then got caught. Woke up one morning and found half a dozen Ities looking at me. I ended up here six months ago. What happened to you?'

I told Randle of my ups and down, and after that recital, approached a more important matter. 'What's the camp like?' I asked. 'You know, grub?' I didn't like the look that question brought.

'It's bad,' Randle said. He grimaced. 'The grub's bad. You wait till you see it. There's no fags either. Those are my last.'

'Any parcels?'

'No, none for three months now.'

'Any rackets?'

'Yes, but you won't smell them. There's a gang here called the "Ring". They've got everything taped. The guards don't deal with anyone else.'

This sounded bad, but I persevered. It was as well to know everything. 'Can you get out?' I enquired. 'I mean on working parties. You know, do a bit of trade outside?'

Randle squashed that one too. 'No,' he said. 'Not a chance.

There *are* working parties, but the Ring are the only ones with contacts. If you've got a belt, pal, get ready to pull it in.'

This account of Campo 52 wasn't so good, and I soon found that Randle hadn't exaggerated. The food *was* bad. In the first couple of days I forgot all those pretty thoughts about birds and bees and rolling hillsides. The ration was much the same as at Gravina, but I was accustomed to getting more than that. And much better. Here there was no chance. The Ring had a cast-iron grip on all trading and the usual crowd of fiddlers and cookhouse pals were making the usual inroads on scanty rations. Even so I was better off than I should have been. Randle had a job in the *Refetorio* moving furniture about, and got an extra loaf every other day. The seven ounce bun only teased his stomach, but he inisted on sharing it. I went on eating half his pay for three weeks. It took that long before I learnt the ropes and struck out on my own account.

A spot of luck helped. I was in the *Refetorio* helping Randle when the Colonel came in. He was the camp Commandante, didn't speak English, and was looking for the R.S.M. Nobody understood him. I took the plunge. 'Scusatemi, signor Colonello,' I volunteered, 'ma non è qui addresso. Partì un mezz'ora fa.' The Colonel looked up, surprised. Randle had already told me that nobody in 52 spoke much Italian. Both interpreters were carabinieri and so nobody got any practice: and without practice, and plenty of it, you can't learn any language.

I had quite a chat with the Colonel. It turned out that he had visited London just before the war, and had stayed there several months. We discussed London. He told me about Rome and Milan and Venice, but what he said after that was more interesting. In the morning I was to go to his office and start teaching him English. The Colonel had been looking for a teacher for some time. 'I think a lesson a day,' he mused. 'Yes, each day. An excellent idea.'

Randle got that one and gave me a barely perceptible wink. The ship was coming home at last. Back in the hut we did a Victory dance, embraced each other, and kissed goodbye to the famine.

But we were a little premature. The Colonel had his mind

on lessons, not food. He knew his prisoners were entitled to the same ration as a backline soldier, and he knew that sufficient food went into the camp. He saw it going in, and that satisfied him. We were well fed. He knew nothing about middlemen or fiddles, and it wasn't up to me to enlighten him. Nor to mention that a backline Italian's ration wasn't much use to an Englishman.

The lessons went on a whole week without either side raising the question of a fee. Randle was disgusted. 'The old cuss must be blind,' he complained bitterly. 'Why, you *look* hungry. You're a walking famine.' That was going some, but I let it pass. My friend gave me a harrowing look. 'And he's seen *me*,' he added. 'Well, if that doesn't work, nothing will. If there was a grain of compassion in him, he'd send a bread van.' It was more exaggeration. Randle's well-muscled figure didn't suggest starvation, but there was no doubt he was hungry.

We did play one ace. I told the Colonel his pronouns were weak and set him an essay entitled 'Myself'. From it we learnt he was a lawyer in civilian life, in his 43rd year, and had a wife and four daughters. The thought of all those female fingers intrigued Randle. He meditated for a whole afternoon before the inspiration came. At the next lesson I gave the Colonel an army 'housewife'.

The ladies were delighted. They sent their compliments and thanks, and a big parcel full of fruit and white rolls. A note inside apologized for the bread being a day old. It amused us. Our own black buns took a week coming from the bakehouse and over thirty people counted them and handled them before they were issued.

The bounty lasted three days. It was most enjoyable having civilized food again, even for this short time, and we were sorry it was so emphatically a once-only levy: especially as we had half-a-dozen spare housewives. But the resumption of parcel deliveries saved us further scheming. They never came at a more opportune time.

The Commandante's lessons continued. They were easy, mainly because he was an intelligent man and wanted to learn. He grasped most rules at the first explaining, made a point of learning five new words each day, and progressed so well that only an odd lesson was uphill work. But I was still doing it all for nothing. Randle and I were considering the idea of setting another essay, this time about a labourer and his hire, when he saved us the bother.

'By the way,' he remarked. 'I must pay for these lessons. You should have reminded me.'

I pooh-poohed the idea. 'It's a pleasure,' I said. 'I enjoy them as much as you do.' But the Colonel insisted. I was hoping he would.

'No,' he said emphatically. 'I must make some return. It's only fair.' He waved a proprietary hand. 'I want you to ask me a favour. Now think. What would you like?'

Well, here it was at last. At long last. The top man at Campo 52 was asking me what I'd like. It was an auspicious moment. Randle's bread van flashed into mind and flashed out again, as more entrancing ideas replaced it. A bicycle and an hour's start. A key to the gate. A helicopter. – Come on, Jones, I thought. Make your mind up. He's waiting. But I was only making pretence of being difficult. Randle and I had been play-acting this scene for the last fortnight. I had my part off by heart.

The Colonel listened as I put in the request and then sat back. 'Is that all?' he asked. He seemed surprised.

'Yes,' I said. 'We'd like the exercise.' Which was partly true.

The Colonel reached for his pen and scribbled a brief note. An orderly came, took it and went to the Italian cook-sergeant as instructed.

The lesson resumed. 'Now let us speak in English,' said the great man. 'I fast. You fast. He fasts . . .' he recited. It does no harm to plug a subject.

The plan carried without a hitch. At two o'clock that afternoon Randle and I were escorted to the woodpile behind the Italian cookhouse, and installed as official Woodchoppers. Lord High Executioners would sound better, perhaps, but even that job couldn't have offered more scope. We had arrived. From now on we were safe. The parcels might keep coming in, and again they might not. There could be anothei famine not so far distant; but whatever the future held for others we were all right. There was only one man other than Barlow whom I was concerned about. That was Cecil, who had also found a mate at Chiavari. It was a 'Blow you, George' attitude, but a damned comforting one.

The woodchopping brought in a full Italian ration, and more besides. Everyone knew that Mario, the cook, would stand on his head for five Players. We sweetened him on the first day, and came back with two dixies crammed tight with pasta asciutta. It was more a hobby than work. Anything which took a man out of camp confines was welcome; but this was really enjoyable. We worked hard and got lathered in sweat, but a couple of hours at this pace did a day's work. The afternoon session was bliss. We gave the guard a cigarette to keep him quiet, filled our woodsack with assorted contents, and then sat back to enjoy the comparative freedom, the sunshine, and more often than not, a bottle of chianti from Mario.

We started trading after the first few days. Personal parcels were rolling in once again, with all the usual crop of quilts, knitted vests and like impedimenta. Getting the stuff out was easy. Mostly we wore the clothing through the gates and came back dressed in shorts. And because we were taking the delivery risk, we charged the Italians double the normal prices. Some customers complained, but not for long. 'All right,' I told them. 'Don't buy anything from us. Go and throw your bread over the wire. It's cheaper that way. But don't blame us if you get caught. There's one of your chaps doing fourteen days now, but maybe the carabinieri won't catch you.'

For every Italian who stuck out against the new price list, three or four accepted it. After all, trading over the wire was risky, and with us there was no danger. Not for them, anyway. They went on grumbling, but it was half-hearted protest that wasn't expected to be noticed.

The price of goods varied according to conditions inside the camp. It was never static. In good times there was a marked tendency towards keeping salable goods in reserve, or at least demanding a fairly high price. When men were feeling the pinch they would often sell for next to nothing. On the average the Ring paid four loaves for a vest. They sold it for six or seven and the Italian who bought it did the transport both ways. Barlow and I introduced a new system. We offered a stock price of eight loaves for every new vest, and charged the soldati twelve. Soon we had a queue of customers at both ends.

We had the bread delivery fairly well organized. A sack of chippings, one of the 'perks' attached to the job, was allowed us twice a day. The idea behind that was to ease the acute fuel problem. Wood was like gold in Campo 52. It was worse than at Gravina, but the brews went on regardless. Tea was more than a ceremony here: it was a holy ritual. All the bed-boards had vanished long ago, and had been replaced by wire. Odd rafters had also been sacrificed, and the hut next to us had lost some of its main joists. It still stood, but it was shaky.

The wood shavings we brought in managed to keep most of our room mates supplied, but we emptied the sack ourselves. It was a specialist's job. On top was a covering layer of bark and rubbish: underneath, half a sack of wood cubes that fitted nicely into the blowers: farther down might be ten or twenty loaves, and at the very bottom, either potatoes, or a bottle of wine, or even a few eggs carefully wrapped in moss. It was more a lucky dip than a woodsack. It was heavy too. Normally I carried it as far as the gate before handing over to Barlow. His job was to get it inside without the Ring interfering. Their men did watch closely, but none made any move. They had seen Randle win the light-heavy championship, and maybe the set of his chin did something to deter them.

But the Ring bosses didn't intend to submit easily. For over a year trading had been their monopoly, and until now the camp had danced to whatever tune they had thought fit to play. No pair of sprung-up cheapjacks was going to put them out of business.

Their first move failed. They put the Vigilantes on to us, but they did it too late. By that time some of the anti-trading police were getting special terms and we had sweetened the rest. It made the Ring disturbed. Eight loaves for a vest wouldn't see them doing much business, if it went on. No one had ever heard of such prices. A delegate came to see us and pointed out we were breaking a monopoly that wasn't ours to break. We told him we knew. It was a virtual declaration of war, and the Ring weren't slow to accept it. The next time we came in, four bruiser types came from behind a hut and made straight at us. They had the advantage of surprise, and we barely got time to put the sack down: but the attackers overlooked a couple of points. We were fit from swinging axes and sledgehammers, and they were taking on Barlow.

Randle looked hefty, but even his build belied his phenomenal strength. He was as strong as a bull. He was easy-going and as a rule avoided quarrels, but not far below the placid exterior was a rare fighting spirit. He relished a real scrap like a connoisseur does a vintage wine. When he opened up something drastic happened. His blood seemed to get supercharged with adrenalin. It turned him into a raging fury that only a pickaxe handle could subdue. I took on one of the attackers and managed to keep my end up. Barlow, overjoyed, fairly sizzled into action. I'd done my bit in getting the job. Now it was his turn. He was about as gentle as a flamethrower and almost as efficient. In two minutes it was over.

We had no more trouble after that. The Ring left us alone, and because we weren't bothering to trade on a big scale they eventually dropped their hostility. It was sensible of them. With 3,000 men in the camp, all flogging odd vests and shirts from time to time, there was no need for dog to eat dog.

Life would have run too smoothly during this period if there hadn't been a fly in the ointment somewhere. We collected a large fly with a larger appetite. He answered to the name 'Lodger', because he lived in the bed above us and rarely left it. The record listed him as James Henry Gleason. If it had bothered to ask his hobbies it would have put stomach and bed, in that order.

Neither of us quite knew why we liked the Lodger. It was our undoing. In a weak moment, and not realizing what we were letting ourselves in for, we asked him would he like to do batman. He was off his bed like a shot. 'What's it worth?' he demanded; and then more cautiously 'What d'you want doing?' We felt we knew the Lodger better after the bargaining finished. He wasn't as dense as he looked, for a start. The parent Gleasons had bequeathed the infant James a quick brain, for all his doltish looks, and captivity had sharpened it. Under the rigours of prison life he was growing expert at living on other people's efforts. We were to learn that soon enough.

Under the terms of the Contract, the Lodger was our Batman from now on. He was to make the beds, draw camp rations, do all the washing, and collect any mail or parcels. As an afterthought I decided to trust him with the camp end of the business. He would fiddle it, of course, but he was too intelligent to do anything noticeable. It was worth that much to have it off our hands. In return for these services, we offered our evening 'stew', a small loaf every day, and a big loaf on Sundays. I thought that was generous pay, but the Lodger didn't. He began consolidating. He mentioned 'perks' and stuck out for a bottle of wine once a fortnight, any double issues of stew, and all the gnawed loaves. The arrangement assured him of three times as much food as the average prisoner.

Gnawed loaves 'happened' fairly frequently. We kept a hollow log near the base of the woodstack for those timid customers who didn't like coming in daytime. They stuffed it full of bread overnight and we collected next morning. Sometimes field mice would nibble at the end loaves. If they did, it was the buyers' lookout, and usually there was no fuss about replacements. The night birds weren't the type to argue overmuch.

The new job made a changed man of the Lodger. Whenever we got back to the hut we found the beds made, a brew standing ready, clean washing hanging on the makeshift line, and a ration loaf sitting in the geometrical centre of each bed. Generally our noble servant was there too, tucking into three dixies of stew, but he always looked fresh. It puzzled us. All these jobs made a lot of work for two hours. What was more, we couldn't see any sign of skimping, which was the Lodger's trademark. I felt that some acknowledgment was due. 'You're doing a damn fine job,' I complimented him. 'I didn't think you'd be as good as this. Don't strain yourself.'

The reason for the slow smile that spread across his face dawned later. Three sub-contractors came to us on the quiet, and protested at the way they were being slave-driven. It seemed the Lodger was a hard master. 'It's hardly worth doing,' the spokesman complained. 'We get one loaf a day amongst the three of us. That fat bastard sits on his bed there doing sweet Fanny. He's robbing you and he's half-killing us. You sack him and we'll do the job properly.'

We didn't take that advice. The Lodger was doing the camp end of the business himself and making a success of it. As I had guessed, he was far too bright to fiddle overmuch. We felt that a man with his initiative was worth keeping.

We were now in the middle of the Sicilian campaign. The Allies continued their advance and the Colonel's interest in his lessons increased. He seemed to think a knowledge of English might yet be useful. When Catania fell the enthusiasm redoubled. He could speak English fairly well now, but was finding it hard to understand. The 'Geordie' and West Country accents baffled him absolutely. 'I understand no word,' he said miserably. 'It is – what you call it? – a noise. It means nothing. We have two lessons each day. Yes?'

We began having the two lessons. I didn't mind. The Colonel was an affable chap, quick to call for another bottle when necessary, and the lessons weren't boring. I was rubbing the rough edges off my Italian, too: but an unexpected voice protested.

It belonged to the Lodger's flying dhobi. Normally the dhobi washed two pairs of shorts a day, and considered that plenty. The rub was he had to use his own soap. Now there were four pairs: and he reckoned that a loaf, shared with the chef and the bed-maker cum odd-job man wasn't enough. The Lodger took up his protest. He still thought we were in the dark about his sub-contractors. 'What the hell d'you want four pairs washed for?' he glowered. 'Don't you think I do enough work as it is? Now you expect me to be a bloody laundry as well.'

We took no notice. After all it was the Lodger's staff who were complaining and therefore his job to keep them happy. In any case, it was the Colonel's fault. Our afternoon lesson followed a bout of sawing, and I didn't relish the idea of sitting down with sweat dripping off me. I asked Randle to sluice me with Mario's high pressure hose. He liked doing it. The Italians liked it, too. They came from far and wide to watch this eccentric going-on, and nothing pleased them more than to hold the pipe. Often we stood together under its full force whilst delighted soldati took turns to hold it and bellowed for still more pressure. When they finished we put on clean shorts. From there the Lodger's worries began.

The Colonel improved rapidly with the extra lesson. We were on the friendliest terms, but there was always a certain amount of play-acting before we got down to work. It was in the interests of comfort. He knew I was fond of Chianti, and I knew he preferred English cigarettes to any of the Italian brands. We got the ritual to a fine art. He would open with 'Buon giorno, Guglielmo,' and offer me a Principe di Piedmonte, which is a passable cigarette compared with the horrible Army 'Milits'. That was my cue. I offered him a Players and dropped the packet conveniently near his elbow. The Colonel then poured out two glasses of wine and we got down to work.

The polite hypocrisy finished there. After that, if I felt like another drink I poured one out; and when he got bothered with conjugations or syntax he would reach absent-mindedly for a Virginia. I always forgot to collect the half-empty packet, and he never failed to top up the flask for the next session. It was real teamwork.

The Colonel was pardonably conceited over his quick progress. On the day he got through a whole lesson without error his vanity welled over. 'I'm doing fine,' he announced. He also had a weakness for colloquialism. 'Now I think we will have a short rest. Would you and your friend enjoy a walk to Monte Allegro?' I saw the anxious look in his eye. He wasn't sure about that bit. 'Do I say it correctly?' he asked. I assured him he did. My friend and I would very much like a walk to Monte Allegro, or anywhere else for that matter. The Colonel thought for a moment, then closed his eyes and attempted some harder going. 'I would have asked you before had I thought of it,' he said. He repeated the sentence once or twice and opened his eyes to note my reaction. I gave the all-clear. He clapped his hands delightedly. 'È difficile, Guglielmo,' he exclaimed. 'È molto difficile ma l'ho fatto. Va bene. Partiremo alle nove domattina.' He stopped short. 'No,' he said pensively. 'It must be in English. Always we must speak in English. The time is short. Nine o'clock to-morrow morning. Yes?'

That trip was the highlight of three luxurious months at

Chiavari. Even when the Black Periods came back in all their gnawing intensity, the memory of it fortified me for the better times that I knew lay ahead. It was a wonderful day.

We climbed a track to the top of the mountain. The Colonel had brought his Adjutant with him, and also the three British officers resident in the camp. A solitary carabiniere followed discreetly behind, but he wasn't really necessary. None of us intended to escape on this trip.

It was almost midday before we reached the Sanctuary. By this time the sun's rays were beating down fiercely and we were glad to rest awhile. We gazed down the far side of the mountain. Below us lay what the Americans are fond of calling a panorama, but none of their superlatives would have been out of place here. It was a scene of exquisite beauty. The towns of the Italian Riviera – Nervi, Voltri, Savoni and Noli – all lay shimmering in the heat haze far below. In the distance, and only just visible, was San Remo, the most important of them all.

The stout wires of a cable railway descended in dizzy fashion before merging into the anonymity of the mountain below. In happier times it was the easy way to visit this lofty Sanctuary. We sat drinking it all in. Even the pleasant surroundings of Campo 52 were drab and lifeless in comparison. Here, surely, was the antithesis of all that prison life stood for.

The Colonel broke the spell. He opened a basket which the sweating carabiniere had been carrying all morning, and made the little speech we had practised together. It did him credit. 'Well, gentlemen,' he announced, 'here you have Italy at her best. When you are ready we will serve luncheon.'

There was still much to see after the meal was finished. We left the carabiniere to clear up and went into the Sanctuary. It is famous throughout Italy for the miracles which have been wrought there: and if the stacks of crutches, leg-irons and surgical aids piled against the walls meant anything, the reputation was well-justified. Their owners, most of them incurably crippled, had journeyed to the Sanctuary with faith in its Healing Spirit and trust in their own hearts.

A gravelled path led from the Sanctuary to the summit of the Happy Mountain. It was spaced at regular intervals with marble and granite columns, all beautifully inlaid and each representing one of the Fourteen Stations of the Cross. At the highest point of all was the final attraction. A wooden hut, locked, bolted, and weathered by winter storms, stood on the peak. A notice informed us that from here Marconi had sent the first wireless signals to San Remo over forty years ago. And with that, except for the journey back, the momentous day ended.

FOURTEEN

The summer months slipped past. August came, and the tempo of the war increased. Most of us had a feeling that the long travail was now nearly over. The rumours that spread like wildfire through the camp did nothing to suppress the idea. It was astonishing to see how readily they were believed. We should have been immune to rumours by now, but there was something electric in the air.

A variety of repatriation schemes were suddenly announced. We were in on every one of them, of course. Nothing much materialized, but the rumour mongers had more aces up their sleeves. The Fifth American Army sailed from Gibraltar with the entire British fleet acting as escort: the Germans were abandoning Italy (and us) rather than risk being cut off: Turkey had come into the war – which was the twelfth time by my reckoning: and gem of gems, R.A.F. troop carriers were already landing at Pisa, eighty miles to the South, and taking prisoners home.

Even if the rumours were all poppycock it was clear that the war couldn't last much longer. Our morale soared.

But the Italian newspaper *Il Popolo* didn't print any of our news. Nor did any of its contemporaries. Instead they talked about the Germans regrouping south of Cittanova, and promising stiff opposition. All through the first days of September they kept harping on this subject.

It worried me. I read the accounts to Barlow, and we had a serious chat. The Huns weren't retreating as fast as the camp news made out. They still had plenty of time to collect us, if the mood took them.

'If we were in Capua or Gravina it wouldn't be so bad,' Randle said thoughtfully. 'But we're not. And that Cittanova place you mentioned's a couple of hundred miles South. There's nothing to stop them whipping us off to Germany, so far as I see. I don't like it.'

I agreed. 'Nor do I. Our army's coming North, but. . . .'

'But they'll get here too late,' interrupted Barlow. 'How about going to meet them?'

'When?'

'To-morrow. We could dodge away from the cookhouse. If the guard goes to sleep again, we'll get an hour's start. If he doesn't we'll make do with five minutes.'

It seemed quite feasible. Usually we had to wake the guard when it was time to go. He kept late hours and got in his back sleep when he was with us. 'O.K.,' I said. 'To-morrow it is. And here's to it.'

That to-morrow was like those in the songbooks. Next morning Mazzotti, the sentry, made no move to open the gate. 'Come on, *pigro*,' I shouted. 'Stop dreaming. Open up!' But the Italian stood firm. 'No,' he said, 'nobody's allowed out to-day. Colonel's orders.'

That shook us. I was more concerned when no summons came for the daily lessons. It was the same on both following days. I never saw the Colonel, and none of the messages I sent through had any effect. By the third day I was getting alarmed: but on this day the news everyone was tensely awaiting came through.

At first it was whispered, but an official denial left us wondering, sky high with uncertainty. Then the R.S.M. confirmed it and the camp went wild. Italy had collapsed. Men danced with joy. They sang patriotic songs, went around in jubilation backslapping and shaking hands, and all the saved-up food came out in glorious free-for-all parties. The war was over. The three and four years' old separation from wives and families was nearly finished. We were free men at last. 'Hi de ho!' sang the delirious crowd. 'Roll on the boat!'

At six o'clock everyone assembled in the big *Refetorio* to give the R.S.M. a hearing. He was briefer than I expected. 'Good news has come through,' he began. 'Italy has collapsed. The armistice was signed at two o'clock this morning. You are now . . .' But a mighty wave of cheering drowned his words. It was a full minute before he could be heard again. 'You are now under army discipline,' continued the R.S.M. 'Nobody leaves this camp until our forces arrive. Anyone attempting to go will be court-martialled. Good-night.' We stood up, and for the first time in two years Chiavari camp heard the British National Anthem.

As the last notes died away Barlow and I got together and compared notes. 'I don't like this either,' my pal began. 'Why doesn't the fathead open the gates? If there's any hitch in this business you know what'll happen, don't you? We'll be stuck. Nobody's got out of this joint since it was built.'

He spoke my own thoughts. Campo 52 was about the toughest escaping proposition in the whole of Italy. It needed only one man in each of those tiger-boxes, and its reputation would be safe. It struck me it would be as well to get moving. 'The boss said something about court-martials,' I mentioned. 'That scare you?'

Barlow grinned. 'Yes,' he said, 'but you won't notice it. Reckon we'd better go now?'

I reached for my coat. 'I think so. I'm on one court-martial already, so another won't make much difference. You'll be all right, Randle. They'll let you off as a first offender.'

We found a quadrupled guard at the gate. It was locked, but Mazzotti was still there. His face was now one big smile.

'What's the idea?' I asked. 'I thought the war was over?'

The Italian pushed his hand through the wire to congratulate me. 'Si, si,' he replied. 'The war is over. Now we are at peace. È buono, Guglielmo. È molto buono. Viva Italia! Viva Inghilterra!'

He would have gone on like this if I hadn't butted in. 'Then what are your pals doing here?' I demanded. 'And why is the gate locked? Suppose the Germans come? What then?'

Mazzotti slapped the butt of his rifle and made a brave gesture. 'Never fear,' he said, stoutly. 'You are safe. We, the Italians, are protecting you. If the Germans come we resist.' He looked at his three partners and added valiantly, 'By force of arms.' His speech stirred the others. They braced themselves, struck heroic poses, and brought their weapons to the 'present'. It was superb histrionics. At that moment it only needed someone to shout 'Charge!' and they would have tackled the Wehrmacht.

But this tomfoolery wasn't getting us anywhere. I lowered my voice and spoke to the principal protector. 'Look here, son,' I said urgently. 'You go to the sergeant and get the key. Bring it back right away. Tell him Guglielmo sent you.' A fifty lire note changed hands and Mazzotti came down to earth. He went, running, and at that moment four burly sergeants came up. The R.S.M. was making sure his orders were obeyed.

A variety of proverbs could have told us how to cope with that impasse. They all say more or less the same thing – 'Do it now!' – and it was our fault we didn't. One of us was to pay for that mistake. We could have gone. The sergeants might have turned a blind eye, but even if they hadn't we would probably have gone just the same. I had Barlow with me. And knowing our liberty might well be at stake, I think my pal and I could have persuaded those four men. When he got steamed up properly, Barlow was a versatile fighter.

As it was, we hesitated and were lost. Randle looked at me uncertainly. I shrugged. 'What odds,' I said. 'Let's leave it till to-morrow. If there was any real danger the gates would be open. What do you say?'

We shall never earn much at soothsaying. Next morning a *Feldwebel* and six German soldiers appeared without warning. They manned the empty tiger-boxes, fired a couple of bursts to let us know who was boss, and three thousand 'liberated' men went back into the bag. A brown-skinned young Nazi strode up to the gate, took the key from Mazzotti's nerveless fingers, and dismissed him with a contemptuous jerk of his thumb.

Our gallant protector looked pretty small beer at that moment. The R.S.M. was looking a trifle sick too, but he was quicker to make amends. He had more reason to. But for his stupid court-martial order last night, the gates would have been open hours ago. We would have had that formidable wire barrier pierced in a dozen places. And now because of his idiocy, seven men had captured all three thousand of us. I felt sick.

The R.S.M.'s new instruction '*Sauve qui peut*,' didn't help. Some men were already obeying it, but they were being careful. Reinforcements of lithe young Germans had joined the *Feldwebel's* squad, and it was as well not to take risks. Our new guards were fresh from the battle line. They held life cheaply: prisoners' lives least of all. The diggers were wise to post sentries of their own.

During the night two tunnels pushed out towards the wire. The first was the old one the Italians had found and concreted over. The other was a brand new one which the South Africans started under the stage in the *Refetorio*. During the long night both bands of sweating tunnellers heard the vicious rat-tat-tat of machine guns.

The Germans kept a good watch. Searchlights flashed on and off regularly and a patrol kept circling the camp. Every sentry box was manned; but eight men still managed to get away. They had listened to the R.S.M., and like us, hadn't been impressed: but their tactics were better. To be on the safe side they had made their own private hole in the wire. No one else got away. The Germans repaired the fence, and to discourage any similar efforts, spent a whole afternoon planting spring bombs and booby traps.

The tunnels were still unsuspected. The older one went well for a time until a stony patch slowed it down. The South Africans, who had the bigger labour force, worked round the clock. They needed to. Their tunnel was planned to cross a small field and open at the river bank, a hundred yards away. It was an ambitious idea. When it was finished there was no reason why half the camp shouldn't escape.

Barlow and I joined up, and did half-suffocating shifts at the end of that long hole. It was dangerous work. We hadn't time to shore up the sides and everyone knew that one fall would be enough. Whoever was digging when that happened could forget there was a war on. We got past the wire in two days, and found it easier going in the field beyond. Some bright individual rigged up a ventilation system, worked by blowers, which helped enormously. Another expert lit the tunnel from the camp mains and cheered us more. Up to now everyone had stood an even chance of being suffocated in the dark.

The other tunnellers weren't doing well at all. They had hit solid rock, and no deviation seemed able to by-pass the barrier. They made a quick decision to abandon it, and then joined us.

On the sixth day our engineer calculated we were half way. It put new heart into us. The reinforcements had brought the labour squad to over the hundred mark, and fresh men were continually at the face. The ventilation expert got his blowers and pipes working so well that the air was fresh all the way along. Spare men braced the tunnel for over half its length and the disposal gangs were often queuing up. It looked for all the world a 'cinch'. It was a grand tunnel On the eighth day, when the Germans suddenly evacuated the camp, we had less than thirty yards to go. . . .

Barlow and I left in the second party. We lined up in the middle of a batch of 150 men and towards noon began the 15 Km. march to Chiavari station. Rumour had it we were bound for Germany. It seemed probable that rumour had got it right for once.

We were strongly guarded. Two Germans marched in front, half a dozen spaced themselves along each side, and two more followed at the rear. All of them carried sub-machine guns, and all managed to convey the impression that very little provocation would be plenty. An N.C.O. marched up and down the column once or twice, patting his weapon and looking at us questioningly. Those who were keen on getting away decided to let him cool down first. I didn't propose to end up at the station if I could help it. Nor did Barlow, but neither of us was putting a foot wrong whilst this super vigilance lasted.

It was very hot. Five of the 15 Km. passed, and most of us

threw away the heavier bundles we were carrying. At 10 Km. we passed Mazzotti, the Great Protector, now wearing a nice line in civvy suits. The guards seemed as alert as ever. We plodded on in the increasing heat, and Chiavari drew nearer. I was beginning to feel desperate. Somehow we had to get away. It might be our last chance: but in this flat country there wasn't an earthly. I put it to Barlow. 'You still going, Randle?' He nodded. 'It's a bit risky,' I suggested. 'Think we'd better separate?'

Barlow looked at the guards in front, sneaked a glimpse behind, and weighed up the chances. 'I think so,' he said. 'We'll never do it together. You try first, if you like. And good luck to you.'

The column approached Chiavari. It wound through the outskirts of the town, and I felt abrupt hope. We had veered in to the side of the road – to my side. Farther ahead, between the houses, were occasional narrow passages.

I looked around. On the left, the danger side, a guard was walking one pace ahead of me. Big round bullets in the magazine of his Schmeisser automatic grinned wickedly. I felt my knees going weak: but it passed. That guard had his back turned. The real danger was in the man three or four yards behind. If he saw me go. . . . But there was no time to ponder what might happen. We drew level with one of the houses which had a passage alongside. I gave Randle a brief 'Cheerio!' and without looking round, stepped out of the ranks and walked away.

As on a previous occasion I didn't dare run. That would have been fatal. As also happened in Greece, a slight heat haze helped, and the guards didn't see me. But each of those ten yards was a mile long. Every second I could almost hear the raucous shout that would herald the bullets.

I turned the corner of the house and came into a small garden. It was hedged in with a thick fence of prickly roses and was deserted. For a moment or two I stood still, not quite knowing what to do next. A bellow came from the road. I moved like greased lightning. In a split second I was head-first through the fence and fleeing for dear life. I don't think I ever ran so fast before. Merika Beach was dawdling compared with it. These were Germans, not Italians.

The sheer impetus of that rush took me to the bank of a river about 300 yards away. I stopped for urgent breath. There was now a wood between me and the road, and danger wasn't so imminent. But I knew danger would never recede far from a man in khaki. A peasant came walking along the path and an idea formed. Five minutes later the Italian continued his stroll, resplendent in new battledress, and rustling two 50 lire notes in his pocket. I adjusted his old clothes as best I could, and gave thanks that he was no smaller.

On the far side of the river I sat down. I was already missing Barlow's company, and for the first time it dawned on me why my pal had said 'You go first.' The second man to leave would have a far harder job than the first. One man might not be missed. His neighbour could move into the outside file and leave the gap in the centre: but two empty spaces was a different matter. That shout I'd heard could only mean one thing. I'd been missed. The Germans had slipped up and no doubt would be mad about it, but they wouldn't do it twice. I felt rotten. There seemed precious little hope for Barlow now.

I could have spared the regrets. If only I had known, Randle was a couple of hundred yards from me at that moment. He was almost within earshot.

I had guessed his 'You-go-first' motive correctly. As soon as I left the column he stepped into my place. Twenty yards farther on, he stepped out of the ranks himself, and walked up another passage. It turned out to be a cul-de-sac but Randle kept his head. He went in through an open door, said briefly to an astonished old lady sitting by the window, 'Here's a present for you, Ma,' dumped the bucket of Red Cross food he was carrying on the table, and continued through the back door. By the time she got up Barlow was hidden in a ditch twenty yards away. He heard the guard bellow, and knew he'd been missed. He crawled deeper into the ditch.

After half an hour the old lady came up. 'It's all right now,' she said. 'They've gone.' She spoke in English, and back in the house Randle found a set of clothes laid out ready for him. When Signora Bien returned from America on her husband's death, she brought his clothes with her. That was a stroke of luck for Barlow. He told her about me, and two local boys crossed the river about an hour later. By that time I was five miles away. I was still feeling acutely for the captive Randle, and still meeting nobody who could do more than wish me the best of luck.

Barlow stayed with his benefactress for two months. She was a brave woman, that little Signora, and no thought of refusing sanctuary ever entered her head. She was also a good organizer. One evening, an ambulance drew up at the door. Two uniformed attendants went into the house, and carried out a man whose head and face were swathed in bandages. He groaned as they struggled to lift the heavy stretcher, and two German soldiers who were passing stopped to give a hand. The ambulance drove on for over four hours before it reached the foot of an Alpine pass. Barlow took off his wrappings and got out. The driver, who was Signora Bien's nephew, told him the route to take, and gave him a small parcel of food. He thanked them, and set off. Next day he was in Switzerland.

A year passed before the repatriation papers came through, and Randle put it to good use. Amongst other activities he found time to become an ace skier. The night before he left for home he met the Swiss champion at foils and wasn't disgraced.

FIFTEEN

I pushed on. Various ideas were simmering, but only three of them seemed to have any chance. I did know this was going to be THE escape. That much was definite. I wasn't in Greece now, but the Italian peasants seemed friendly enough. Perhaps I'd get help from them. Whether or not, the main object was unaltered. This was an escape, not an attempt. It meant eyes open and steering clear of Germans at all costs.

None of the three ideas was simple. The easiest was Switzerland, 200 miles away. Most of the route lay through the densely populated Lombardy plains, but that didn't worry me particularly. Where there's a crowd, generally there's safety. The snag with Switzerland was that it didn't aim high enough. I could get there, granted; but supposing I did, what had it to offer except a milder form of captivity?

Reaching our own forces was a better idea, but correspondingly harder. They were fighting 400 miles to the South. It meant going progressively deeper into the back areas, dodging sentries, penetrating the German front line, skipping across no-man's-land, and chancing snipers from our own side. Or rather, from both sides. No, that programme didn't appeal either. If the Jinx was still around, and the luck anything like the usual brand, it was as good a form of suicide as any.

The middle course was the only one left. I would be a partisan. Not on my own, of course. The villagers had confirmed that there were partisans, so all I had to do was locate the local bandit chief and offer one able man's services. Having joined up I could more or less mark time until the Eighth Army came North. Once a partisan, I wouldn't be so impatient: and if an odd spot of action enlivened the wait, well, so much the better. It sounded fine – when I said it fast.

The trouble was that no one knew the precise whereabouts of the partisans. Nobody could provide a guide to take me to them, but there was no shortage of other ideas. I stayed the first night in a priest's house and listened to plenty. He knew as much about bandits as I did, but he stood me a rare supper. After the meal we listened to the B.B.C. news on his wireless. It appeared that over four hundred ships of the Italian fleet, including most of the heavy stuff, had gone over to our side. That rather tickled the cleric. It seemed that he had never been wedded to Fascism, despite the slogan '*Credere! Obbedire! Combattere!*' that covered the wall of his house.

Most walls in Italy bore some phrase from Mussolini's speeches. 'Believe! Obey! Fight!' was the most frequent. Time was when the Italians were only too willing. That was around '40 and '41 when they were treading the victor's path, but the easy conquest the Duce promised hadn't come off.

Mussolini had been a first-rate ruler until the Napoleon bug bit him; but since those rosy days two years back his stock had gradually sunk lower and lower. Now the final blow had fallen. Italy was split in two. What might have hurt the Duce even more was the number of his slogans disfigured with freshly-thrown mud.

I spent the second night as the guest of one Antonio Petardi, a hardworking peasant. Antonio needed to work hard. He had always yearned for a son, and had never quite given up hope. His wife had done her best too, but the Petardis had had bad luck. So far the score was eight girls, with a ninth on the way.

Perhaps Antonio was glad of a spot of male company. He brought out several large flasks of vino and we set to. It took less than ten minutes to convince us both that Signora Petardi's latest was a boy. It was bound to be a boy. Two or three flasks later, Antonio, forgetting he had an heir on the way, asked me to stay and be his son. I declined. In a vague, kind of fuddled manner, I remembered having heard that one before. I slept in his barn that night and again the following night. The next day I moved on. The partisan brother-in-law hadn't turned up, and there was no point in staying any longer.

Antonio and half a dozen of the daughters disagreed. 'Stay with us,' they chorused. 'You'll be safe in the barn. Stay till the war ends.' I said '*A rivederci*', again more firmly. I had no intention of staying. If there were any partisans around here it wasn't likely they'd make a pilgrimage to the Petardi barn. It was up to me to go and find them. It was no time for dallying, even with a flock of handmaidens all anxious to help speed the hours. In any case I wasn't partial to barns, with or without attendance.

For ten days after that hectic farewell I walked along stony tracks in the Tusco-Emiliano Appennines without finding a single bandit. I was now an Italian soldier trying to dodge the new German mobilization order and hurrying home to distant Udine. It passed unquestioned. A good many ex-soldiers were doing precisely that, and the villagers sympathized with all of them. My accent also passed. Italy is a land of a thousand dialects, and Udine was a long way off.

I sat on one hillside for two whole days. At Campo 52 the

final bush-telegram had given Spezia as the port to which the Fifth American Army was sailing. It was a very hot tip, allegedly from the head carabiniere, but the Armada was a day late when I got to the vantage point. It didn't seem to be hurrying. Towards the end of the second day I went down into Spezia itself to see if there was any news, but the Germans were there in force, which made it bad policy to linger.

Big notices were already posted up all over the town. Most of them concerned the mobilization order but there were two others that made the trip worth while. I read that there was to be an eight o'clock curfew from now on. Anyone out of doors after that hour would be fired at. The second placard announced that British ex-prisoners, all of them enemies of the people, were at large, and were to be given short shrift. As encouragement it offered 5,000 lire to any Italian who handed over a British soldier. I read that part again and decided to stick closely to the Udine story. Five thousand lire was big temptation to a poor peasant.

In one way the reward offer was cheering. I had gone around for eleven months in Greece with 2,000 Drachmae on my head. I remembered feeling at the time that the Germans could have valued their ex-prisoners a bit higher. I wasn't the only one who felt that way. Two thousand Drachmae was worth £4, and Jim Thompson had valued Jericho, his old donkey, at more than that. Now justice had been done. Four pounds wasn't head-money to write home about, admittedly, but £70 was different. Values were going up.

The Germans knew what they were doing in offering that reward. A good many men had escaped. At Chiavari we heard of Italy's collapse only twelve hours before the *Feldwebel* and his six men came: and thanks to our fatheaded R.S.M. the gates had stayed shut. Very few prisoners got away from 52, but other camps acted sensibly. They broke the gates down, slashed the wire, and kept watch in case the Wehrmacht should approach.

Most of their men got clear without any trouble. In many cases, particularly farther South, there was good luck in abundance. Partisans, even British agents, contacted the escapees and led whole parties safely to our lines. The numbers who got through fostered the idea that it wasn't too hard after all: but probably the successes weren't ten per cent of the total number of men involved. The Germans weren't dense. They sent out search patrols, bribed the Italians, and had their own agents posing as British soldiers. These activities put paid to hundreds of attempts to win through.

I kept to the mountains for the best part of another week. The people were as helpful as ever with food and news of partisans, and I averaged three good meals and one red herring each day. Finally, in a little village called Santo Giuseppe, the chase ended. Two of the most ardent Hun-haters in the whole of Italy gave me dinner, toasted Italia and Inghilterra, cursed the Tedeschi, and offered to take me to the local Partisan chief.

The house was in a larger village three miles away. The chief was smaller than I had expected, but his welcome made up for the lack of inches. We chatted for a while, and I told him about Chiavari and how I had escaped. That part seemed to amuse him. 'Those German swine,' he chuckled, 'all brawn, no brains.'

In the middle of supper a knock came at the door, and two soldiers walked in. They were both Germans. The partisan chief whipped out his revolver, and I got ready to duck; but there were no shots. He was pointing it, not at the Germans, but at me. His lieutenants, who had brought me here, gave the intruders the Fascist salute, smiled at them, and indicated where I was sitting.

I gathered it was my army boots that had first made them suspicious. All the anti-German talk that followed was merely bait to test the suspicion. I had fallen for it, hook, line and sinker: and now the three smart 'partisans' would soon be splitting 5,000 lire. It shows it pays to be observant.

We went to the German H.Q. As it happened there was no cell there. It was a requisitioned hotel, and I spent the night in a locked room on the first floor. The officer, who spoke good French, made one or two comments before he went. 'I wouldn't think too much about that window if I were you,' he advised. 'There's a sentry outside. If he sees you he shoots. He's a good shot, too.' He picked up my boots, and the ghost of a smile flickered over his face. 'We wouldn't like to lose you,' he confided. 'You may be a spy for all we know. If you are it's just too bad.'

I had a look through the curtains later on, and found the German wasn't bluffing. A sentry was standing by the hedge ten yards away. After two hours his relief came up and had the window pointed out to him. I gave up. There'd be no leaving this hotel without paying the bill.

In the morning I got my boots back and was given a good breakfast. None of the Nazis seemed resentful about the extra guards they had done, which bore out a point I often heard made. Fighting troops mostly do the right thing by their prisoners. The tyrants and petty dictators of the prison camps seldom get as far as the danger area.

After breakfast I was taken away in a staff car, presumably for investigation. It was an hour's ride, with two escorts in the back, and once again, no earthly chance of getting away. When the car stopped, I quit thinking about escape altogether.

The jail was a well-chosen place. A carabiniere slid back two massive bolts in the iron door and motioned me to enter. The door swung to, bolts slammed home in their sockets, and the escort marched away. They had no worries. So far as anything in this world could be certain I was booked to stay here until called for.

It was a big cell, but not well-lit. That was because the single window was set high in the wall, and had three iron bars obscuring the light. If I had been strong enough to rip the bars out, it wouldn't have got me anywhere. A good architect had designed the cell. The window narrowed outwards through the thick wall, and ended up as a hole about a foot square. On the outside, throttling most of the light which tried to enter was another set of bars, bigger, tougher, and more firmly set than the first.

Three days went by without much discomfort. It wasn't pleasant, of course, but then it wasn't intended to be. Once that idea gets home a cell is much like any other place. You know you won't be there for good. Each hour is one nearer the time you come out; and so long as you don't count those hours time passes tolerably enough.

But the third night was different. Somewhere about nine o'clock, the bolts pulled back and an elderly man in the uniform of police captain came in. I lay on the wooden planks, hands clasped behind my head and wondered what next. The visitor stood watching me for a while. 'I expect you're finding it dull here,' he began. 'It's a bit bare. No?' I agreed with him. He had something there. It was a cell, and could hardly be mistaken for anything else, but he hadn't come at this hour to discuss cells. I waited. The captain wrinkled his nose at the place and came to the point. It got me off the bed like a flash. 'You can have dinner with us if you wish,' he offered. He made a deprecating motion with his hand. 'It's Emilia's idea really. The guards have gone and there's only us here. Nobody need know about it.' He shot an appraising glance. 'I'll need your parole, of course.'

He got it. If the Gravina R.S.M. had been present with a dictograph I wouldn't have hesitated. Not with a chance like this: and still wondering, I followed him into a brightly lit room where the table was set for a meal. A pretty girl of about twenty was sitting by the fire. The captain introduced her as Emilia, his daughter, and remembering my etiquette in time, I gave a bow and thanked her for the invitation.

We sat down. It was a wonderful meal, exquisitely cooked and served in a way I had almost forgotten existed. Emilia smiled at the bewilderment on my face. 'I suppose you're wondering why we asked you here?' she said.

I turned to the dark, big-bosomed girl and nodded. 'Yes, I am wondering. But it's very kind of you. I must thank you again.'

She waved the thanks aside. 'You don't need to,' she said, smiling. 'My fiancé's in Egypt. He's a prisoner, too. I had a letter from him to-day and he says he's very well treated. He buys cigarettes at a Naafi. He says your soldiers go there too. Tell me, what does Naafi mean?'

So that was it. Emilia's man must have landed himself a depôt job. Mustapha Barracks in Cairo was full of such prisoners. They had the run of the place – no guards, no overseers, and so far as we could see, only as much work as they felt like doing. Most of the time they seemed to be queuing up at Naafi canteens. I didn't wonder at the captive Italian writing reassuring letters. He was better off in Egypt than he'd ever been in the Regio Esercito.

I told her about Naafis whilst she served ravioli. The old man filled my glass and started off on a long yarn of his own about his Great War service. He had fought with the British. 'Perhaps with your father,' he suggested. 'You know, we were good allies then. We should be to-day.' He paused a moment before going on. 'Why is it you must fight against us now?' But I wasn't to be drawn on that one. To-night, politics were taboo. The food, the wine, and the nearness of the dark-haired beauty opposite me were far too enjoyable to permit argument.

The self-assurance of the couple surprised me. Neither the old man nor his daughter seemed at all apprehensive, and we chatted away like old friends. I could have got away easily. Barring the parole and the fact that they had asked me here, I would have done. The captain had his pistol, admittedly, but the holster flap was buckled. If the table had overturned he wouldn't have kept it long. But I knew I would never do it. I think they knew too.

To me, it seemed typical of them that in this land of rapidly changing allegiances, Emilia and her father were still loyal Fascists. The girl especially was a fervent admirer of Mussolini, and I had to listen to a good deal about the great man he was. I agreed with her about his domestic policy. Until he meddled in foreign affairs Mussolini was perhaps the best thing that could have happened to the Italians. I kept my opinions quiet after that.

Suddenly Emilia glanced at her watch and hurriedly switched on the radio. We were just in time. 'In two minutes from now,' said a voice, 'Il Duce will address the nation.' The captain offered me a cigarette, and we waited in a silence broken only by the crackling of the wireless. Then the announcer spoke again. 'Il Duce,' he said, simply. Emilia, eyes shining with fervour, turned to her father. 'È lui,' she breathed, as a familiar rasping voice filled the room.

'Italiani,' it began, 'Io sono stato incarcerato dagli traditori. – I have been imprisoned by traitors. I have been released, thanks to the Fuehrer, by our German friends.' The rumbling tones went on for a while, and then gained sudden volume and aggressiveness. The Duce had finished with preliminaries. Now came the pith of his message. 'The war will continue!' he shouted. 'We will win – because we must win! Italians! Patriots! Take up arms and fight! Fight to the death if need be, against the Allies! Fight for Italy! *Viva L'Italia!*'

It was a good rousing speech. There wasn't any artistry of words in it, but Mussolini's fanaticism and oratory carried all before him. Suddenly the Fascist anthem broke the renewed silence. We stood up. As the last notes died away, I thanked my companions for their hospitality and made to go back to my cell. Nothing else remained. The old man paused on the threshold and then offered his hand. Humanity had battled with patriotic feelings and won. 'I hope you get home safely,' he said.

On the hard bench I put in some considerable reflection. It seemed all wrong we should be fighting people like Emilia and her father. They had shown kindness and courtesy where neither was expected. Nor safe. Their generosity could easily have told against them, yet they had trusted me, a complete stranger. And for all the cameraderie and hand-shaking and good wishes one fact stood stark. They were still enemies. Conceivably I might yet have to kill them, or they me. I gave up. It was too confusing.

I wasn't destined to sleep that night. A couple of hours later, the bolts went back again, but it wasn't the Captain this time. Two German soldiers were standing at the doorway, beckoning. I followed them into the dining room, now cleared of all traces of the meal, and saw a lieutenant sitting in the old man's chair. He was flanked by a couple of soldiers holding automatic rifles. It was the investigation; and a God-forsaken time they'd chosen for it.

The officer spoke good English. He was a young man, barely above twenty, and obviously very keen. He fired questions for the best part of half an hour. The Greek passport, that veteran of so many searches, lay before him, and at first he tried to make something of it. I was a spy and might as well admit it. The passport was all the proof necessary. In the next war I get involved in, I will be a spy. It will save time all round.

But I knew the German was only fishing for information. The 'partisans' would have already told him I was an escaped prisoner, and the Italian records in his possession would have confirmed it. The spy business was a preliminary, part of the softening-up process. What this German was really concerned about was whether or not I'd contacted any of our agents in the hills. He knew I spoke Italian, too. 'That's suspicious,' he remarked. 'Very suspicious. You say you have no rank and yet you speak Italian. And French also, I believe. No, you're lying. You're a spy. It's quite clear. . . .'

But I interrupted the flow. 'Nonsense!' I burst out. Nobody takes kindly to being called a liar; least of all at this time of the morning. 'I was interpreter at Campo 52. You know that. You've had the best part of a week to check it. And an interpreter must know the language to get the job. That's sense, isn't it?'

It was, but it didn't suit the lieutenant. He stood up angrily. 'I will ask all the questions necessary,' he reminded me, gratingly. 'You will answer, not ask. Remember that.' The atmosphere was noticeably chilly after those remarks. I wasn't told why the interrogation was taking place at 2 a.m. and no one volunteered any information. It didn't seem good policy to ask just then, either.

The talking continued. It was mostly one-way, and after another ten minutes or so, it finished. The officer got up, pulled on his gloves, and led the way to a truck outside.

The roads were deserted. The shoot-at-sight curfew had seen to that, and we drove swiftly for over two hours. I had no idea where we were going. The direction was roughly North, but at this rate it looked like being Germany first stop. It puzzled me too, why so much trouble was being taken over one prisoner. Still, the farther North we went, the better. So long as we didn't cross the Brenner, it brought Switzerland all the nearer; and when the 'heat' was off I might get another chance. 'If I do,' I decided, 'it's going to be Switzerland: and to hell with the Eighth Army.'

Two of the three guards in the back dozed over their rifles, but the third remained alert. Suddenly both the sleeping men woke up. The driver had turned off the main road, and the truck was beginning to bounce over rough stretches. Through the partition I saw the lieutenant look at his map and speak to the driver. The truck slowed to a crawl. It negotiated one or two sharp bends, went another hundred yards or so, and then stopped altogether.

The two men in front got out. A moment later the officer called to my guards. They got out too. I could see we were in a quarry, and for some reason gooseflesh began creeping over me. All around us were high stone walls glistening with damp. Pools of water at the foot of the quarry gleamed sinisterly in the moonlight. I tried to stop thinking why we had come here. A few yards away were five armed men, and it didn't do to get over-imaginative.

The officer lifted the flap and beckoned to me. 'Get out,' he said. 'We want you.' I obeyed slowly. I wasn't scared now. There wouldn't be a dog's chance and when all hope has gone a man isn't frightened of death. There was only dull resentment that it had to come like this, and in such a place.

I stood still, waiting. The four soldiers eyed me curiously, but none of them moved. They seemed to be waiting too. I noticed with a kind of detached curiosity that the driver was unarmed. His rifle was still in the truck. Then the lieutenant spoke again, this time with some asperity. 'Come on,' he instructed. 'Don't stand there like a dummy. Give a hand to turn the car. We've come the wrong way.'

We were about twenty miles farther on, and speeding to make up for lost time, before I recovered properly. Outwardly I looked calm enough. At least I hope I did. Inwardly I was stiff and taut with the tension of a man snatched from the firing squad. One experience like that is enough in a lifetime.

An hour later the truck stopped outside a squat building in the middle of a village. It didn't need a second glance to identify it, and in another ten minutes I was behind bars again. The Germans left, and I groped around to find the wooden bed. The quarry scare was wearing off now, but one thing was still puzzling me acutely. Why all this fuss and midnight excursion for one recaptured prisoner?

It wasn't a good cell. I can't comment more accurately

because I never saw what it was like. There was a tiny grille in the steel door, so small that I could only look through with one eye at a time. Opposite was a brick wall reaching almost to the ceiling. Apart from a faint glow that filtered through the grille, the cell was pitch dark.

I stayed there six days. The carabinieri allowed two five-minute breaks each day, but they were scared of the Germans, and timed the breaks to a second. No sooner did I leave the Black Hole than I was back in again. I even had to eat in total darkness. 'It's a hell of a place,' consoled the Italians sympathetically, 'but we can't help it. We'd let you stay out longer, if it wasn't for the Germans, but they come here by the minute. We daren't risk it.' That was too bad.

After the first day I realized 'too bad' was an understatement. Being penned up in darkness is bad punishment. No prison in England will permit it because it can send a man crazy. Towards the end of that stretch I began having cold sweats. Sometimes it was a big effort not to hammer and claw at the walls. It took more self-control to stop thinking that they were closing in all the time.

But on the last two nights the carabinieri relented. They gave me a couple of hours' blessed freedom, and although I had to be ready to dodge back if the Germans came, the respite worked wonders. The escorts who came on the seventh morning seemed surprised to find their prisoner had weathered the place so well.

An incident en route to H.Q. pushed my morale up to normal. We passed the English-speaking lieutenant, and the two guards gave smart salutes. He halted them and spoke for a moment. After that we carried on, but not as before. The two soldiers now walked some distance from each other, and both covered me with levelled rifles. I was being mistaken for someone. I knew that, but I didn't care. I felt grand.

At H.Q. I saw my Greek passport torn up. This was a hard blow. The little red folder had been with me so long, and had come successfully through so many searches that it was almost part of me. It had been in salt water a few times and the wear and tear of two years had left it rather battered, but it was the only memento of Greece I had left. It would have made a grand souvenir. That wild-looking hairy man in the photograph would never have aged. The years would have given him an air of romance that the mysterious Greek cipher and official stamps could only have heightened. When I am old and doddering, if I get that far, Vassiliou Zoneras, the bearded man in the *taftotita* would have enthralled grandchildren, and remained for ever what he was – a strong and virile reminder of more dangerous times. I never mourned anything so much before.

The H.Q. interrogation went on. I was quizzed, cajoled and threatened, and then dismissed. The civilian clothes vanished and I got a makeshift Italian uniform instead: but none of these goings-on left any impression. I was still mourning the precious *taftotita* as I climbed into the German half-tracked vehicle.

In the army a man never knows where he is going until he gets there. As a prisoner it is much the same, and for four hours the vehicle drove on without my being any the wiser. I wasn't alone now. By my side sat a South African captain, pips up and very spruce: opposite us were a couple of hard-bitten Afrika Korps veterans, with revolvers in their laps and willingness in their eyes. In front was the driver; and by his side, completing the party, rode my old friend, the English-speaking officer.

All the signposts were down, as a precaution against invasion, but the driver knew the route. The big lorry roared on, through mountain passes, up steep hills and along interminable straights. Before the journey was half done I got one thing settled. The High Command would have less petrol by the time they'd finished these investigations.

We recognized Ravenna from the wording above some of the shops; and here the long journey finished. The captain and I ended up in a barbed wire compound holding about a hundred other Britishers: and if a demarcation line could be drawn, I suppose it was here we stopped being mystery men and were relegated to ordinary prisoners. That didn't mean the guards were slack. The place was more a fortress than a camp, and if there had been very little chance of getting away en route, here there was none at all. Armed sentries patrolled the perimeter with Alsatian dogs accompanying them. Search-lights stabbed out questing beams throughout the night. In the background, quiet, but with the ace of trumps at their trigger fingers, were watchers vigilant in high towers.

Next day we went to the railway station under strong escort. We were bound for Germany, all of new recruits into Fritz Todt's international labour force, and with a future that didn't look too bright. Those who had ideas were planning to cash in on them somewhere South of the Brenner. We memorized footholds and handholds on the outside of the cattle wagons, and nodded approvingly at the unwired windows. So long as the train wasn't doing above forty it would be worth risking the drop and possibly a few shots. It was our last chance. No one had illusions about that.

I decided to wait until we were somewhere near the frontier It would mean less walking to do and less time spent in Italy, and I wanted the minimum of each. It also meant trusting the Italians again, but perhaps the people farther North wouldn't be as pro-German as the Santo Giuseppe 'partisans'. In any case it couldn't be helped. I needed food and a route through the mountains, and they had both. I glanced idly at the crowd watching us, and found myself hoping that the Northern Italians would look more intelligent. Only one person in the group near us seemed to have any idea what was going on. The rest stood there, with faces like shop window dummies, devoid entirely of sentiment or wit or recognition.

In a way, I suppose, it was little wonder. Events of the past few weeks had shocked most of the Italians into a kind of mental apathy. They were between the devil and the deep blue sea. Little Vittorio Emmanuele, their well-beloved King, had gone over to the Allies and was now proclaiming their cause; but the newly-rescued Duce was singing a different tune. He was still on the German side, and not wasting any of his time. He had dug out all the old slogans and introduced a few new ones. They were having some success, too. Fascists were painting '*Morte agli Angli-Americani*' on the walls of Ravenna, and furbishing up the old '*Credere Obbedire Combattere*' injunctions.

Italian loyalties were suddenly in the melting pot. Twenty years of habitual obedience made the people tend to follow Mussolini, but for once their natural instincts were in revolt.

Behind the imposing Fascist façade Italy was and always had been a monarchist country. The newspapers hadn't exaggerated when they spoke of '*il nostro ben-amato re.*' But now, little Victor was on one side and Benito on the other. The Italians were in a flat-spin. They weren't sure whose side they were on, or what they ought to do. Our misfortunes troubled them least of all.

The one exception in the station crowd was a rather stout lady. She didn't seem upset about the split in her government, or very concerned at the Savoia-Duce clash; but she was interested in us. She pushed a way to the front. 'There's no need to worry,' she assured us. 'They'll never get you out of Italy. Your Air Force has blocked the Brenner, and all the lines are up. Trains have to stop fifty miles South.' She beamed at us and dropped her voice to a stage whisper. 'That's from London only an hour ago,' she confided. 'You know – the B.B.C.' Two guards sauntered up and the newsflow ceased abruptly. The stout signora gave us an encouraging smile and disappeared into the crowd.

We were already feeling better. If the lines were bombed, and the Brenner blocked, as she had said, we stood a chance. A good one, too. Anything could happen now. Alexander could overtake us: the Germans might get the wind up and abandon us: the Italians might rise in revolt: even at the worst, this breakdown should delay the transfer to Germany – once again, *if* it was true.

The train started after another hour's delay; and with its first feeble snorts we felt happier still. We weren't on an express. We weren't even on a normal slow train. The antiquated engine pulling us wheezed up every incline, clattered along the downgrades, snorted and grunted on the straights, but never once touched 20 m.p.h. It was devastatingly slow. It must have been painful to the other passengers, but we exulted. 'Bloody old slowcoach!' we thought happily. 'It'll be money for jam.'

Towards dusk we stopped altogether, which was better still. The Brenner was only thirty miles distant now, and as soon as Methuselah started up again, most of us intended to jump. But Methuselah showed no inclination to get moving. Half

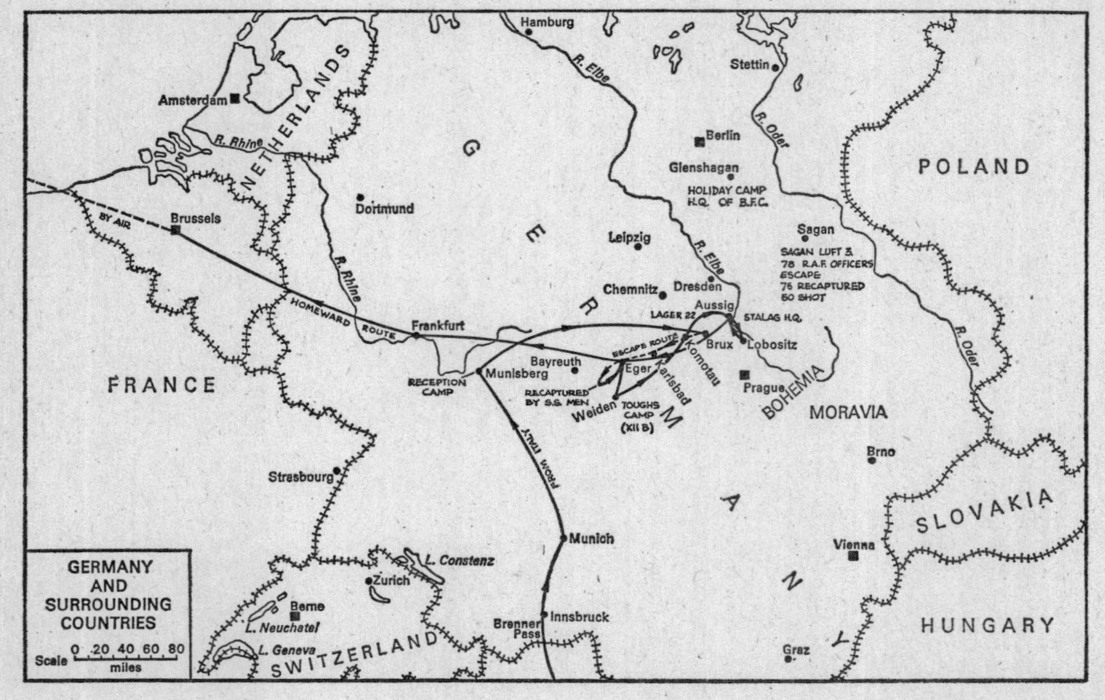
GERMANY AND SURROUNDING COUNTRIES
Scale 0 20 40 60 80 miles
NETHERLANDS
Amsterdam
R. Rhine
Hamburg
R. Elbe
Stettin
R. Oder
Berlin
Glenshagan
HOLIDAY CAMP H.Q. OF B.F.C.
POLAND
GERMANY
BY AIR
Brussels
Dortmund
Leipzig
Sagan
SAGAN LUFT 3.
78 R.A.F. OFFICERS ESCAPE
76 RECAPTURED
50 SHOT
Chemnitz
Dresden
Aussig
LAGER 22
STALAG H.Q.
HOMEWARD ROUTE
Frankfurt
ESCAPE ROUTE
Brux
Lobositz
Komotau
Bayreuth
Eger
Karlsbad
Prague
BOHEMIA
MORAVIA
RECEPTION CAMP
Munisberg
RECAPTURED BY S.S. MEN
Weiden
TOUGHS CAMP (XII B)
FRANCE
FROM ITALY
Brno
Strasbourg
SLOVAKIA
Munich
Vienna
L. Constenz
Zurich
Berne
L. Neuchatel
Innsbruck
Brenner Pass
L. Geneva
SWITZERLAND
Graz
HUNGARY

an hour passed. The wagons banged against each other once or twice, but we put that down to termperament. Nothing else happened. An hour went by, and guards were still walking up and down the permanent way. At last the observer at the window waved his arm excitedly. 'They're getting on,' he said. I edged nearer the window. I wanted to be amongst the first to go.

A sudden jerk ended the long halt, but a second or two later every mouth gaped open in dismay. The wagon was thrusting forward in powerful rhythmic jerks. We all surged towards the window. I got my head through and saw unfamiliar wires glinting overhead. Below us, the wheels were click-clicking rapidly over the rails. As the train turned a bend I saw a trail of sparks flying from the huge electric engine which had replaced Methuselah.

SIXTEEN

We got to Germany intact. The train never slowed below 50 m.p.h. all the way to the Pass, and once there, sentries, with dogs and torches, wrote off the last hopes of escape. When morning came, nobody mentioned the word. We were heading farther and farther into the heart of the Reich, and all hope had gone. To rub in the disappointment, the new engine pulling us was a twin brother of the Italian relic. It rumbled in all its joints, wheezed asthmatically, and plodded along at a brisk cycling pace.

Innsbruck had passed by early on. The train chugged over a high viaduct spanning the River Inn, and we got a brief view of the cathedral. The Southern Bavarian countryside was at its best. Under different conditions we could have waxed ecstatic about the picturesque wooden houses that harmonized so well with the landscape; about peasants dressed in Tyrolean costume, with leather trousers, embroidered braces and feathered hats; about rolling fields, and distant snowcapped mountains, and other scenic gems: but nobody seemed appreciative. We were seeing it all for nothing, but that had no appeal. Conversation languished and then died away altogether. There was no more talk of escaping. The Alps were already over a hundred miles to the South, and receding with every click of the wheels. In any case, getting out of the truck was a night job; and by nightfall we might easily be once again on the wrong side of a barbed wire fence. We felt gloomy. We were gloomier still when the five-day trip finished.

Muhlsberg came almost as a welcome relief. It was a reception camp, situated in the geographical centre of Germany, that catered for such waifs and strays as were periodically delivered into German hands. It was also a permanent camp for shot-down aircrews.

We found it full. Partisans from Yugoslavia (where there really were partisans) mingled with Super-Fortress men shot down the week before. Pretty well every Allied country was represented. There were soldiers in the shabby dress of the Soviet army, smartly uniformed Americans, English, Dutch, French, Greek, Norwegian, Belgian – a score of nationalities that embraced such extremes as a bearded Pathan and a French-speaking negro from Mauritius. I heard a dozen languages in five minutes and saw as many different uniforms in half the time: and all around, keeping this polyglot community intact, were the inevitable barbed fences and high watch towers that most of us knew so well.

Muhlsberg had a really efficient staff. Four years of specialist duty had made every man a past master in his job, and few arrivals stepped off the conveyor belt system without feeling a gudging admiration for it. We began with a horse-clipper haircut which took the barber about six sweeps and fifteen seconds. After that we undressed, had a hot shower, and walked naked into a long room where pipes ran the full length of walls and ceilings. The doors closed and the pipes began hissing; but nobody panicked. The gas-chamber parades weren't public knowledge until the war finished. Perhaps it was as well. A man feels less brave without his clothes.

These pipes were innocuous. They gushed out a stream of hot air, dried us all in about two minutes, and saved the staff a laundry bill. The end door now opened, and revealed a Russian prisoner waiting for us, with a bucket of blue fluid and a mop. As each man passed, the Russian dabbed him with disinfectant, and still naked, we passed on to Stage Three.

It was here that the Reception Committee proved itself an international affair. Four Italian medical orderlies, working in pairs, vaccinated every man and gave an injection as well for good measure. My vaccination 'took', which was more than the British Army had ever managed, but the injection was probably wasted. I never felt any effects and never discovered what immunity it was supposed to give.

At this point we got our clothes back. They had been cooking in a big steam boiler, and the insect population was dead. It took nearly twenty minutes to get dressed, mainly because no one could locate his own clothes in the huge steaming heap. I managed to get my own boots back, but the rest of my kit was 'foreign'. Still, everyone got something, and if some more than others, perhaps they put it down to good luck. The German in charge seemed satisfied. He kept shouting 'Schnell! Schnell!' to hurry the slower men, and eventually got us all into the Records Office. We had reached the final stage.

The Records Office hummed with acitivity. Squads of clerks filled in huge forms, doctors passed us, photographers distributed chalked name boards and took us in groups of six, and the last official gave everyone an identity disc. We were now certified as being disease and vermin free, we were cleansed, card-indexed, numbered and tabulated, and over the last hurdle: and from that moment I was no longer Jones. Jones had gone. In his place stood a bald-headed cypher Number 248897 in the great army of Germany's forced workers.

A few days afterwards, a column of newcomers marched into the prison compound at Brux, in Sudeten Germany. We were a mixed lot. For most of us this was our first German camp, but for some it was the first prison camp of any kind. The original Italian contingent was no longer intact. We were now spread all over Germany, and in this column veteran escapees from Greece marched with R.A.F. crews who had been in England the week before.

The Air Force men were still to face the hardening-up process that every prisoner goes through. We old hands knew the ropes, and were better off in that respect, but the new boys had an initial advantage. They were warmly dressed and well shod. We weren't. I wasn't, in particular. I was still wearing mixed Italian uniform, and a bald head didn't give it any dignity. The top half of me was *Regia Marina* and the bottom *Regio Esercito*. The naval coat was on the big side and all the warmer for that, but the army trousers made a bad match. They were three-quarter length. To make things worse, my boots were worn out. Miles of heavy going in the Appennines and constant wading through mountain torrents had finished them. One had only the upper left. The Germans had no boots either, at least not for us, and the best they could offer was a pair of wooden clogs three sizes too big. 'Stuff the toes with straw,' advised their storeman. 'You'll get your right size that way.'

He was a liar. The things fell off about every third step, and in the end I had to tie them on with strips of blanket. That left me less a Beau Brummel than before. The huge coat enveloped me like a tent. The trousers were tight and exposed a three inch gap of bare shin that suffered in the cold winds. Huge clogs at one end, and a knobbly skull at the other finished the picture, and even well-meaning chaps had to laugh. My legs, which were always half-frozen, stopped me from joining them. It was six weeks before I got proper battle-dress. The Red Cross, who should be canonized, sent it.

But forced work didn't amuse anyone. Brux was an industrial town, built around a group of enormous installations all making ersatz petrol. Collectively, these were known as the 'Factory'. They were already employing 60,000 'slaves' and about 40,000 civilians; and after the first day no one had any doubts about the slavery part.

We got up at 4 a.m., had a cup of ersatz coffee, and marched out of the gates at a quarter to five. Long columns trekked two miles to the Factory in total darkness. The work lasted twelve hours without any break for food, because we had no food, and at five o'clock we marched back, once again in darkness. At the lager, a bread ration and a meal of 'stew', that any self-respecting mongrel would have scorned, awaited us. The bread was supposed to be for the next day, but it never lasted that long. Most men promptly crawled into their bunks and went to sleep. Until the life-saving parcels caught up with us, very few had the energy to do otherwise.

Those weeks seemed about the blackest anyone had ever encountered. Not even the Dunkirk 'long-service' squad could remember worse, and the poor R.A.F. tyros had a rough time. Things were bad. A blanket of apathy spread gradually over the whole camp. Hope seemed to fade, and even the inherent humour of the British soldier wilted under the strain. Days and weeks of savage toil on a starvation diet took their toll. All the usual accompaniments followed. Black-outs and collapses grew as numerous as the fleas, and each day saw some poor chap carried out to his grave. If war has any glory, there was none here. We were the Legion of the Lost, the Walking Dead.

The Germans didn't worry. We weren't men to them. We were units of labour. The Reich came first, and so long as we could work they would see that we did. If we died, well, it didn't matter all that much. There were more prisoners.

The spark that kept us going was the knowledge that it couldn't go on for ever. Some day there'd be a homecoming and happiness and full stomachs; and every day was one nearer. Without that spark we might have given in.

The tragedy of it was that not everyone was destined to get home. There were captives whose names were written on bombs stacked in the fields of England: there were broken men who were to die miserably in makeshift hospitals with no loving hands to solace them: men who were to be shot in attempting escape: two of my friends who were killed in a motor accident on the way home: and one unfortunate who was to celebrate the Armistice with a lethal dose of wood alcohol.

What was worse than even this privation was knowing that the war had cheated us. That was a galling thought. We knew that some day we'd be liberated and become the dependants of a real fighting army. They'd give us kind words and sympathy and then go on to finish the war without us. We wanted to be in at the kill. Above all else we wanted to flaunt the beaten German and know the surging triumph of victory. But it wasn't to be. All we'd have would be old memories – timeworn recollections of struggles against hopeless odds, of retreats and still more retreats, of rearguard actions that were brushed aside, of final stands that collapsed, and of capture. Even those memories were growing dim. Long subjection to the enemy and years of degradation had all but effaced them.

These thoughts troubled me at times. They troubled Sergeant Wally Walpole and Varney, the Commando, more often. Their war had been short, but they had seen more action than most. The other members of the team, Taffy Owen, the Welshman, and 'Arryock', the Liverpudlian, weren't immune either.

All five of us had been in Italy. The other four had cheered, too, when Vittorio Emmanuele and the Duce fell out, but none of their fond hopes came to anything. And now, with Brux as it was, and every prospect as vile as it could be, not even the good luck that kept us out of the Factory seemed of much account.

We had all wondered what the 'special' occupation would be. We indulged in a little gentle phantasy about counter-espionage on the German Staff, and even of being sent on missions to England, but it didn't do us any harm. The thoughts coloured our daydreams and so had value. That was as far as they got. We were in Germany, not Wonderland, and were quite prepared for cloak-and-dagger visionaries to emerge as odd-job men. The first bit of odd-jobbery – stuffing palliasses with straw – would have tumbled any dreamer.

It was still a remarkably good job compared with anything the Factory had to offer. For a start, Herr Schmidt's barn was only a mile from the lager, which cut the walking to half. Working conditions weren't bad, either. Most of the Factory gangs stood all day in the open, doing pick and shovel work, with arbeit-fuehrers on top of them. Our barn was walled in on three sides and fairly warm. The work was easy – fifteen mattresses a day – but best of all, our work-fuehrer was

Schmidt.

This doesn't mean that Schmidt was pro-English, or sympathetic, or even a friendly man. He wasn't. He was the cartoonist's Hun to a T – a full-blown Party member, an arrogant bullet-headed Prussian, and not a nice chap to know. But like all the other little Hitlers, he had his weaknesses. One was for good tobacco: another for the little comforts of life to which his Spartan Nazi training had said a vigorous 'No!' After a day or two he sounded our guard, and the pair of them found they were twin souls. From then on we worked in the barn, unsupervised. Schmidt and his new friend stayed in the hut nearby, and kept the fire going: and two men could always burrow into the straw for a quiet sleep without any fuss being made.

When the parcels came, Schmidt showed the bigger chink in his armour. Locally, he was a big noise. He could get a lot of things that were denied other people, and was up to his neck in various rackets; but the one thing he couldn't buy was good tobacco.

It was his downfall. We lit up, puffed out blue smoke and opened full packets under his eyes. Schmidt stuck it for two days. On the third, he waylaid the last man out and tried to frighten him into giving up a cigarette. The attempt failed. Schmidt promptly turned over a new leaf. He began saying 'Good morning' to us, gave us grimaces that were meant to be smiles, and even volunteered to make the brew. That didn't work either. There was only one way left. The arbeit-fuehrer took it. He swallowed his pride and began cadging openly.

It was the start of a new regime. We allotted Schmidt two fags a day, and the sentry one, and took over the reins. The midday break doubled itself and became an hour. We began taking morning and afternoon breaks as well, and decided to complain about the amount of work that was set. It had never bothered us, but then we had the whip hand and might as well use it. The fifteen mattresses promptly dropped to twelve.

That made life easier still. It gave us time for all kinds of pursuits. We played cards, slept, chatted with Czech civilians and learnt some of their outrageous language, and made eyes at a couple of fräuleins living close by. In odd half-hours, Taffy, who had a natural bent for sabotage, looked around for things to break: Varney, who had been in the task group that tried to capture Rommel, told us about Commando exploits: Sergeant Wally, who had left the dreariness of the Stalag for a working camp, congratulated himself: and Arryock, who was Harold Ockleshaw on the books, caught up further on his back sleep.

Schmidt soon lost whatever status the cigarette business had left him. We were trading with him now, and had the thumb-screws on. Food had stopped being a worry. Bread was plentiful, and in comparison with Italy, dirt cheap. Under the Duce it once soared to 140 cigarettes a kilo. With the Fuehrer in charge, we paid ten; and because Schmidt had no other buyers, occasionally beat him down to five.

Wally's idea put a millstone round the German's neck. He paid forty cigarettes in advance, and took an I.O.U. as security. Schmidt delivered the bread next day, but by then the I.O.U. was lost. It dawned on the Boss that he had made a fool of himself.

From then on we dropped all pretence of obeying orders. Schmidt knew what his Haupt-fuehrer would say, and do, if that I.O.U. ever turned up, and he had an uncomfortable feeling that given cause, it might. He wasn't far wrong: and so long as we kept an eye open for the all-powerful Haupt-fuehrer we did as we liked. Schmidt no longer counted.

The B.B.C. news was the best item in this New Order. Basil, one of the Czechs, had a set that could get London, and every day one of us slipped up the back stairs to his flat. It was a dangerous business. Listening on this wavelength was a capital offence, and the Gestapo weren't short of informers. Only recently, nineteen Czechs had been shot in Prague in one day.

Basil took no chances. He kept his hand on the tuning dial and we had to strain hard to hear. Still, enough came through to furnish a news bulletin that cheered the whole camp. The Allies were on top, and their supporters were feeling happy. Basil, getting good news from the B.B.C. and good pay from us, was feeling doubly happy, which was more than some were. There were Germans who found the London news too much to bear. Sebastopol, the last Nazi stronghold in the Crimea, fell, and the secret listeners mourned. Some time afterwards Schmidt brought in a blood soaked mattress and asked Wally to clean it. One of the fainthearts had waited a week for the *Zeitung* to confirm the loss. That night he took a razor to bed with him. Wally was sympathetic. 'Poor man,' he mused, 'he'll never get over this.'

In the Spring of '44 we left Schmidt's barn and went on a number of roving commissions. Schmidt was still the Boss, although there was precious little bounce about our arbeit-fuehrer these days. That business of the lost I.O.U. was getting between him and his sleep.

But new afflictions weren't long in coming. At the first job, a Wehrmacht store-fuehrer spent about fifteen minutes warning us what would happen if we stolc anything. That night knives, forks, tins of polish and other valuable bric-à-brac went back to the lager. Arryock had to strip to the waist to find his new towel. Varney had a replica of his beloved Commando knife, and amongst other things Taffy produced half a dozen cleaning dusters.

Nobody quite knew what he wanted dusters for. He wasn't sure himself, but then Taffy had been feeling queer for some weeks past. Stuffing mattresses for other prisoners wasn't war work, and his conscience was clear enough on that point. What was worrying him was the way his destructive instincts were being thwarted. He had 'murdered' dozens of mattresses already, but no one cared. They were shoddy things at best. If he ripped a hundred, it didn't matter. If he had set fire to the barn even that wouldn't have made H.Q. bat so much as an eyelid. If prisoners had to sleep on bare boards why should they worry?

But Taffy's chance was coming. One day he walked into a storeroom and saw a great pyramid of cups stacked on the stone floor. It was an enormous heap. All told there must have been about a thousand cups in that pile and the Welshman's long-suffering inhibitions did a war dance. A sigh of relief escaped him as he gave the bottom rank a long raking kick.

Huge waves of crockery shattered down to disintegration on the hard floor. Three of the top civilian bosses rushed white-faced into the room, and Schmidt, who was behind them, went suddenly grey.

That 'accident' cost Taffy 6,000 marks. It was his Kriegsgefangener pay for the next twenty years, but he didn't care. He felt the memory alone would be worth that much. The ones who really got the mallet were Schmidt and the three civilians. They had to explain things to the Oberst, and the Oberst was not an even-tempered man. When he finished shouting, he docked each of the unhappy quartette a month's pay and put their promotion prospects in permanent cold storage.

We were sacked on the spot. The Store-fuehrer came back from his interview looking as if he could throw a case of knives at each of us. He worked fast. A lorry was at the gate in ten minutes, and in another two we were on it and away.

The new warehouse was twenty miles distant, and once inside, we began to see the German's point. The place was stacked to the roof with bales of straw, each weighing about a hundredweight. With any luck one of the high ones could topple over: and if it did, there was no harm in hoping that Gottverdammt Engländer would be underneath. In any case, argued the Store-fuehrer, this was the one place where we couldn't do any damage.

He was wrong there. The crockery episode had only whetted Taffy's appetite, and for days he sat high up in the roof thinking and searching for inspiration. It was warm up there, despite the hard frosts of the last week, but Taffy's brainracking produced nothing. He went to sleep and dreamed about lighted candles in the roof, but he knew that was no good. It would have to be something more subtle than candles. They could be traced back. What was needed was a foolproof scheme that would do the damage when we were miles away and in such a manner that we wouldn't be suspect. It was a big undertaking.

Taffy had almost given up when the idea came. It wasn't any flash of genius on his part. He was on his back snoring when a drop of water hit him in the face, and awakened him. Taffy blinked. Suddenly, he got up on his feet. Running along the wall was a water pipe leading to the next building. From a pinhole directly above him an odd drop was falling. A feeling of sudden exhilaration radiated through the Welshman.

That was Friday afternoon. We still spent Saturdays in Schmidt's barn, so there was no call to go back to the warehouse for three full days. The week-end saw Herr Schmidt's crew doing a lot of meditation. Taffy looked benignly happy. Natural instincts that had been repressed for years, barring the golden moment with the cups, were feeling satiated. Now and again he took out his jack-knife and smiled at it: and ten miles away a semicircular cascade of water fell unheedingly on stacked bales. The dry straw absorbed it like blotting paper. Such a volume of straw lay in that shed that even on Monday there was no sign of the leak. The caretaker opened up at 6 a.m. and heard unfamiliar swishing noises. He climbed up to investigate. After one horrified glance, he rushed down again and phoned frantically to his arbeit-fuehrer, his Haupt-fuehrer, and every other fuehrer he could think of. In a moment of wisdom, he also phoned for a plumber.

We had a wonderful time. About a hundred of the top bales were masses of sodden pulp. Another two hundred below were waterlogged and more still, damaged. Schmidt and the strawshed fuehrer went pale with fright, but they didn't try to blame us. They couldn't. By pure chance the night before had been exceptionally bitter, and burst pipes were legion everywhere. An icicle was suspended from the very door of the warehouse. We had a ten minute inspection by a gentleman who wore patent leather jackboots and a forbidding look, and then the affair was closed. Nobody asked why the pipe had burst inside, where it was warm; but perhaps that was just as well.

It was the best job of work Taffy ever did. It took three lorries a week to dump the ruined straw, another week to transfer damaged bales, and after that we were left in peace. That was a happy time. The only wrong note was Schmidt sitting brooding in his corner. He had plenty to worry about, but in the end his glumness proved too much for Wally. 'Beat it, Schmidt,' he ordered. 'Go and buy us a bottle of schnapps. And for God's sake, try and look a bit more cheerful, you old crow.' Schmidt took the money and went. Wally never mentioned I.O.U.s these days, but Schmidt knew where he stood.

The schnapps came. We toasted Taffy and all his ideas.

Two Russians sneaked in from a working party and we toasted Churchill, Stalin and the Anglo-Soviet Union. Joe was a prime favourite in those days. We gave the Russkies a loaf of bread to cement the alliance, and weren't surprised at the way it disappeared.

The two unkempt prisoners wolfed that loaf. Even in the hardest times we were never quite so ravenous, but then we were never quite so far from some kind of help. The Russians were forgotten men. They wore rags, of course, but that was usual. No Soviet prisoner ever seemed to wear anything else. For food, they were desperate. The official allowance was just enough to keep body and soul together, but a good many of them had to survive as best they could on less. In Germany, only the dreaded E gang lived worse than the Russians.

There were several reasons for all this. Mainly it was innate German hatred that worked so much against them and produced such callous treatment; but the Soviet wasn't altogether blameless. The Russians have a different system from ours. When one of their soldiers is captured – he is finished. His name gets struck from the active list and to all intents and purposes he is forgotten. Russia is not one of the Geneva Convention nations, so no parcels or new clothing or other kit ever reach the captive. Worse still, no inspectors ever look over his camp. It gave the Germans a free hand.

The Kremlin had a ready excuse. They had lost five million men in the German push of '41, and no country at war can hope to carry that many passengers. It was more than twice the number of men Britain had under arms at the time. Moscow took the easy way out and didn't try to help them. We had our rough times, and some were grim enough, but in contrast with the Russians we lived like lords. The parcels made the difference. They were 'in' more frequently than not, and even as memories they helped us weather the gaps. The Russians had nothing. Their mass hunger must have rivalled any Biblical famine. And for every British prisoner, there were twenty Russians.

The Red Cross didn't stop at nourishing us. Two million French and Belgians also benefited, and during the second half of the war, got much the same as we did.

The Germans made no organized interference with parcels. As might be expected, odd crates went astray here and there and mostly ended up on the black market, but the bulk of the Red Cross stuff got through intact. The Huns are entitled to that much credit, but it comes harder to believe they were being altruistic. As prisoners we knew them well. After 1945 everybody knew them too well.

But they were good organizers and also good psychologists. There was a terrific alien population in Germany – imported workers, slaves, prisoners and so on, and Goebbel's ministry made strong efforts to win as many as possible to the Nazi cause. Not much propaganda came our way. We were reckoned poor prospects, too insular in character to respond properly, and too stubborn to make the effort worthwhile. Not much was directed at the Russians either. Most of them were illiterate, and almost all of them too hungry to bother their heads about anything except food. Men who have to grub around on refuse heaps for odd potatoes become very single-minded.

But with the French and Belgians it was different. There was fertile ground here, and the Germans knew it. Belgium was split in two over the Leopold question. France was at odds over Petain, with one half of the French favouring the old marshal and the others swearing by de Gaulle and the Free French. Into this welter of divergent opinion the wily Germans threw Philippe Henriot.

Philippe was a journalist. He was probably one of the best journalists ever. It was a pity, for his own sake, that he wasn't patriotic with it. Soon after Dunkirk he introduced himself to his fellow-countrymen as editor of *The Patriot*. He told his readers that in future this newspaper would be their link with la belle France, and would be sent to every lager in the Reich. What was more, it would be free.

Philippe didn't mention who his sponsors were, but it didn't need a second edition to guess. That was a point to be lived down, of course, but he made a good job of it. The first issues were deceptively mild. They printed just the news that every homesick Frenchman was longing to hear, and lagers soon began clamouring for more copies.

It wasn't until everything was set that Philippe took the

gloves off. The cycling news and other reader-attractions continued, but new items began to appear alongside. They got more and more space until it became clear what the paper was trying to do. Its first aim was to split Anglo-French concord: its second, to win pro-English, anti-Vichy Frenchmen back to the fold.

Philippe played on this dual theme for over three years. Because he was in the top flight of journalists he had fair success. Everything the British had ever done was wrong and directed against French interests. Everything de Gaulle did and was doing was the same, only more so. Phillipe dug out a lot of dirty washing and hung it up for public gaze. It won fresh converts. His masters congratulated themselves on having found such a first class man, but Philippe didn't tell that to his readers. He was never pro-German. At least not openly. His heart and soul lay with France – Vichy France – and his only purpose was to open his countrymen's eyes. 'If I can do this,' he once wrote, 'I will die happy.'

Once again it was a pity – this time that he had to meddle in prophecy. One Saturday he published an article about le grand Charles that did de Gaulle's reputation no good at all. Philippe had pulled out all the stops and dipped his pen in vitriol. Two newly-conscripted French workers disagreed with his views. They were passing through Berlin at the time, which was bad luck for *The Patriot*'s editor. He knew nothing had gone wrong until the door of his office burst open and the self-appointed critics charged in. They were carrying automatic pistols.

The next edition carried Philippe's swan song. It was another vicious attack on de Gaulle, and was framed in mourning black. A note at the foot mentioned the assassination and offered a big reward. Men of Henriot's calibre were few and far between, and the Germans felt rightly annoyed. Later they increased the reward, but they never caught the gunmen. The paper deteriorated quickly. It had always been more or less a one man show, and none of the new mainsprings could ever touch the original in quality.

I was reading Philippe's article when the straw warehouse 'holiday' finished. Authority had caught up with us again;

but the local fuehrers seemed slow at learning. At the last two places, 'accidents' had happened that should have made the woolliest minded of them think twice; but the warnings went unheeded.

The new job was to be a delicate one. A civilian Boss came, told us we were being sent to a railway siding and stressed that it was a job needing care. 'The wagons are full of furniture,' he explained. 'It has been evacuated from Berlin owing to the bombing, and some of it is fragile.' We looked up at this. So the Forts were giving them hell in Berlin? Well that was all right with us. The civilian droned on. 'Some of it is quite valuable. You must be careful. Most careful.' Taffy's eyes suddenly lit up with a familiar gleam.

We broke nothing the first day. Too many civilians were fussing about for comfort, and none of us wanted to lose the job just yet. According to the new 'gaffer', more wagons were coming in, and we wanted to see what was in them. Also, we had an idea the supervising wouldn't last long.

It didn't. On the third day only Schmidt turned up, and like a fool, backed the lorry against the wrong side of the truck. The doors opened on a medley of furniture that would have baffled an expert. Schmidt tried to solve the jam himself, and failed. He looked worried. Then, like a bigger fool, he called Taffy and the little Welshman jumped to it. Schmidt frowned at the crashing noises that followed, and we hid our grins. A big table that was causing the blockage came out minus its legs. 'O.K.' grunted Taffy, 'now I'll get weaving.' He vanished inside and soon cleared a space. More table legs came out in the process, along with arms of chairs and odd drawers. All Schmidt had said was 'Get them out.' Taffy, obeying the order literally, was making the most of his opportunity.

But it seemed we couldn't go wrong. The warehouse fuehrer accepted the battered furniture without question. Things did get knocked about these days, and after all, they weren't his: but we soon stopped kicking chairs to bits. Some of the Berliners had left parcels in their cupboards and had locked the doors for safety. We began watching for locked doors. Each of us had acquired a hefty screwdriver, and those parcels were worth having.

Within a week we all wore civilian underclothing and had a spare set in the lager. Soon after, Basil the Czech was giving away new clothes to his friends. I had a complete head-to-toe civilian kit, donated by a Berlin citizen named Funk. I opened Funk's cupboard, liberated his parcel, and relocked the door. It was a neat job and for once the screwdriver left no mark. It took three journeys to get everything back to camp and stowed under the floorboards. The suit exceeded all my hopes and fitted like a glove. That was grand. I burnt the cardboard case, cut off all the name tabs and dropped the bereaved German's thick spectacles down a grid. Arryock laughed at this precaution. 'If old Funk needs specs like those,' he said, 'he'll have a hell of a time finding his parcel.'

That was true enough. Perhaps I was being too meticulous, but I had good reason. In the past all my efforts to get away had flopped because of some unforeseen fault, usually a trifling one. This time there weren't going to be any mistakes – not if I could help it.

Escape talk was never absent in Lager 22. At almost any minute of the day there was sure to be somebody airing views on how to go about it, what to do, what not to do, and so on: but usually the vocal experts were safe. Very few of them went further than talking about it. Escaping is a serious business and if you mean to 'have a bash', you don't broadcast the details. That was partly the reason I didn't confide in Arryock. He was a good fellow but he might talk in his sleep. I did tell Ronny Martin, who was a special pal, but then he slept next to me where I could hear him. What was more, I needed his help.

The informers were the main reason for keeping dumb. We had two in the camp, and more than once the Germans had made unexpected swoops. One of the informers was clever. He kept the guards *au fait* with a lot that went on, and we could never catch him. We didn't even know who he was: but the second Judas was easy meat. He had a job as bath-house attendant, and for some time had been on better terms with the *Feldwebel* than there was need. After one particularly suspicious incident, the Australians decided on action. They 'tested' their suspect first. Two of them stood under his window and discussed a proposed escape in immoderate tones. A third Aussie, watching, saw the informer creep up and listen.

There were two secret meetings after that. The Germans raided the hut in question, but they found nothing. The inmates, for once equally up to date with authority, had been through it with a toothcomb. Now it was their turn. Being just men, they waited until the angry *Feldwebel* rebuked his lackey, and then a body of them set off for the bath-house.

The crowd had attracted me, and I pushed through to the front to see what was going on. From the bathman's viewpoint it was more than enough. A tall Australian was standing over him. 'You yellow German ba-astard!' he snarled. The lovely Australian long 'a' was twice its length. 'You'd squeal, would you? Well, start now!' A succession of open-handed smacks landed on the informer's already puffed face. He moaned, gibbered, and began to collapse, but it didn't work. The Australian was at fever pitch. 'Get up, you swine!' he hissed, 'there's more yet!' The informer staggered up again, with a hobnailed boot helping him. Then it happened. The Aussie gripped him in one hand and inflicted such murderous punishment with the other that before he was finished I had to turn away: and my stomach wasn't a queasy one.

In the end, eyes blackened, teeth missing, and face unrecognizable, he was flung to the ground. It would be some time before that chap did any more eavesdropping.

I thought he might die, but he didn't. About an hour later, he staggered up and lurched towards the First Aid centre; but there was nothing doing there. Nobody would lift a finger to help him. He reeled away, managed to reach his own hut, and was promptly cuffed and kicked out again. The R.S.M. came and conducted the unhappy man to a storehouse, where he locked him up for the night.

That was the first bit of luck the informer had. He never knew just how lucky he was. By now the news had travelled around the camp, and one small group of extremists was hunting high and low. Four of them met outside the storehouse, and swore because it was too strong to break open. The fifth stood on guard at the wash-house. Behind him, a rope, dangling from one of the beams, was swaying gently in the night breeze.

The informer left first thing next morning. Nobody saw him go, and until two Brux men landed in his new camp, he managed to keep his secret. He even got an identical job, and for all we knew, set up as a stool-pigeon again; but the Brux newcomers spoilt things. They had got as far as Strasbourg before being caught, and they were sore about it.

The informer got another dose. Late that night he was in the camp hospital, where once again, nobody would speak to him. The two would-be escapists nursed bruised knuckles and felt a good deal more cheerful than before.

SEVENTEEN

Funk's suit stayed in its hiding place under the floorboards. It was only February '44 as yet, and I didn't reckon to move off until May. I didn't pick May out of the hat, either. It was a carefully chosen time when the danger of snowstorms should be past, but when it would still be early enough to lead the Homeward Bound summer rush.

Brux was a restless place during the Spring of '44. The war was moving faster, and we all felt that big events were in the offing. Basil's B.B.C. news kept us up to date. We learnt that in Italy, British troops were at the Anzio beach-head, thirty miles from Rome, whilst the Fifth Army, flat out in an attempt to reach them and to link up, hammered furiously at the Gustav Line. On the Eastern front, the Russians were making up for their bad showing in '41 and '42. They had chased the Nazis back over the Estonian border. Better still, they got the whole of the German Eighth Army encircled in the Korsun pocket, and to quote the radio, 'the process of liquidation is going on.'

It seemed that Berliners were also far from happy. They were busy having their first thousand-bomber raids in daytime. In France, Fritz Todt was putting the final touches to his Westwall; whilst across the Channel, the invasion armies began to mass.

We had enough news to talk ourselves silly. The rumourmongering brigade, never slow on occasions like this, did the job for us. They captured Rome a few hours after Anzio began; they got the Germans out of Greece and Crete, and had Hitler die all over again. There never was such a galaxy of victories. Perhaps that was why the whisper about the Secret Service agent didn't attract many customers. With whole armies on the move it was small beer: but I listened to it. Probably it was moonshine like all the rest, but I heard it several times from varying sources and for some days was intrigued with the possibilities.

The report said that a British agent had parachuted down near Brux, and was using the camp as a base. If he was, it was a clever move, but I never knew. After a while I stopped thinking about it. If there was an agent amongst us he would hardly declare himself. There wasn't much hope, then, of getting home on his ticket, which left me much as I had expected, to my own devices.

But a much more important issue than the agent was baffling even the Rumour Kings. Neither they, nor we, nor anybody else could understand why the Factory was missing every raid. The Germans were doing their best to keep the installations secret, but they were well aware that Bomber Harris knew all about them. Such an enormous area of buildings couldn't be missed. The vital contribution they were making to Germany's war effort couldn't be ignored either, but the expected raids didn't come. The Germans didn't know what to make of it. They began persuading themselves, incredulously at first, but then firmly, that maybe it was a secret after all. Action followed. Anti-spy posters appeared on the hoardings almost overnight. '*Der Feind hört mit*' shrieked at us a dozen times a day, and civilians took suddenly to looking over their shoulders.

It was a stupid move, born of panic. Some men had got

away from Brux, and had got home – and they had worked in the Factory. Perhaps the Sudeten Germans forgot that, but there was one thing they couldn't overlook. Sixty thousand 'slaves' were still doing twelve hours' 'arbeit' every day, and none were doing it willingly. No spy worth his salt would need to listen in cafés or trams. He'd have all the contacts he wanted.

But the bombers flew over Brux and dropped nothing. The factory's roar went on day and night. Sunday became a working day, and more wagons than ever filled up with ersatz petrol and rolled away to distant battle zones. And during this lull before the storm that was coming, I made another effort to shake off the shackles.

In some ways, I suppose, it was a daft thing to do. Life in Lager 22 was dull, admittedly, but there were compensations. We had the storehouse crammed full with three months' reserve of parcels. That was phenomenal security in itself, but added to it, every man had a 'famine' reserve of cigarettes too.

Our own little gang was doing splendidly. We had B.B.C. news every day, the black market 'taped', and a very obsequious Schmidt running round in circles. Conditions couldn't have been better than they were: Brux couldn't have been worse placed for escape attempts. It was nearly 500 miles from Switzerland, farther still from France, and every inch of both routes lay in hostile country.

Sensible men, some of them seasoned Dunkirk veterans, laughed at the idea of trying. There was no Escape Committee, they pointed out, and no one to offer any help; and from their viewpoint that put the top hat on what was always a perilous undertaking. What they forgot, of course, was that it *had* been done. By the end of '43, no less than 114 prisoners had run the German gauntlet successfully, and in devious ways had got home.

What troubled us was that they took their methods with them. That meant that every fresh attempt had to start from scratch. A far greater number of escapees had been recaptured, but their accounts didn't help. They failed for all manner of reasons, and in recalling them, the pessimists looked happy. As they said, there was only one way to guard against such a variety of catastrophes. It was the simple way –

stay in camp.

But 114 voices could have protested against such a dictum. It wasn't impossible, as they had shown, and one last point was equally above dispute. If you don't try, you certainly won't get anywhere.

A small matter of personal prestige was also goading me. The years since '41 had all given varying spells of liberty – some long, some short. I was growing in experience, if not in wisdom: and I did know the bounty of '44 wasn't going to slip by through funk or apathy. A grain more luck, a spot more grey matter, perhaps just one more 'do,' and maybe I'd make it. It was worth a try.

I was shaved and dressed before the rest of the hut awoke. The early birds stared at Funk's blue serge suit and neat collar and tie, but a khaki overcoat soon hid those details. The other informer was still going strong, and it didn't do to court trouble.

I marched in the outside file, in front of my friend, Ronnie. He had been a big help. The small scale map in my pocket, now with the route to St. Gallen neatly traced, had once belonged to his boss. Half the 'hard tack' in my haversack had come from Ronnie, too. He had very much wanted to bring the rest and come himself, but we hadn't argued long over that. The odds were too heavy, and he knew it. Besides, I still needed his help.

The tramp-tramp of hundreds of feet was now echoing down the highway. I was just behind one of the guards, but guards with their backs turned are seldom dangerous. Not if you step quietly. In any case, it was 5 a.m., pitch-black, and the German was three parts asleep.

A mile down the road I put on Funk's trilby hat, and freed my arms from the greatcoat. We were approaching a bend, and a lot depended on what happened in the next minute or two. At this point we were accustomed to meeting a group of unescorted Frenchmen who pushed their way cavalier fashion through our ranks. They had been doing it for months, and I was banking on them doing it to-day. If they failed – well, it would be awkward explaining the collar and tie.

But the Frenchmen didn't let me down. As we rounded the

bend they came up dead on time, and began filtering through. I glanced back at Ronnie. He nodded and muttered a brief 'Cheerio'. A couple of Frenchmen sidled into our rank, passed in front of us, and Ronnie gripped the collar of the greatcoat. It came off in his hand. I stepped out of the file and followed the French civilians to the far side of the road.

It was the third time I had left marching columns. It was by far the easiest. Out of sheer curiosity I tailed the procession for a hundred yards or so, but nothing happened. The guards plodded on like automatons, and none of the men looked back. Possibly no one but Ronnie realized what had happened, nor that the tally would be one short to-night. That didn't matter overmuch. The night tally wasn't expected to be accurate. To-morrow was Saturday, but I felt confident a dummy would pass one day undetected. On Sunday our gang didn't work and there was no count: so all told I had three days' start. It was ample to clear the Brux area. With any luck I hoped that the next three days would show noticeable progress towards St. Gallen.

I was in Komotau, twenty miles away, by midday. I walked all the way, which was no less than I'd expected. This trip was going to include a great deal of walking.

I realized long ago that a Brux escape could never be one of those slick organized affairs with everything laid on. Expert forgers alone would have been a great help. For instance, I would have liked a passport to certify I was a French civilian worker. I would have felt happier with a number of documents allowing me to travel from one region to another, and above all, would have valued a permit to use the railways. With it I could have boarded the 9 a.m. train from Brux and gone all the way to Munich.

But I had none of this kit, so it was no use heartburning over it. An Escape Committee could have done wonders at Brux. It could have supplied me with sufficient forged documents and enough advice to give this journey a fifty-fifty chance at least. Real efficiency would have made it safer still: but we had no Escape Committee. That let the railways out, for a start. Taking a private car wasn't on the agenda either.

It would be stopped inside fifty miles; likewise a motorcycle.

I was pinning my hopes on being able to 'liberate' a bicycle somewhere, but as yet, this idea wasn't going too well. Like the Dutch, the Germans and the Czechs are nations of cyclists. They ride to work and they ride for pleasure. I knew this and had been building on it: what I didn't know was the depth of affection between man and machine. In the factory areas there were thousands of bikes – all chained up in special frames. In rural parts there was also any number, but none was left unattended. It was a setback, but I had come prepared for disappointment. About 480 miles lay ahead. If in all that long distance a bicycle didn't show up somewhere, well. . . .

For the moment I decided to keep my eyes skinned and not worry. I slept in a wood during the afternoon, and after a hot drink, started walking again. It was around 5 p.m. now, a time that coincided with the home-from-work rush and made the main roads fairly safe. Towards nine o'clock I was fifteen miles to the other side of Komotau. It wasn't bad going for the first day. I still felt fresh, but the bicycle problem was as acute as ever. There'd been no lorry lifts either. That was the second line of defence. In some ways it seemed safer than cycling, but as yet it was equally unproductive. I didn't care. A sign post opposite me said 'Brux 50 Km' and it was good enough. There was always to-morrow.

It was a bad night. All the barns I tried had dogs sleeping in them, and the ditch wasn't warm. On the second day I covered over forty miles and got well beyond Karlsbad. There was still no bicycle, but two lifts provided nearly twenty miles of free transport. A farm tractor came first. I jumped on the trailer, and went right through Karlsbad – along all the main streets, past policemen, past marching prisoners, and past one column of soldiers wearing the double thunderbolt flash of the *Prinz Eugen*. They were singing '*Wir fahren gegen England*' in rousing style. It made me grin. I had much the same idea but I was riding, not marching. It was more comfortable. Also, I wasn't making so much noise about it.

The second lift was disappointing. The French prisoner driving the lorry only took me five miles. He stuttered badly, and I misunderstood him. It was after the lorry had gone that I realized I could have travelled another twenty miles with him.

After dark I tackled the bicycle problem seriously. I had to beat this hoodoo. It was uncanny, the way every machine I'd seen seemed to be under vigilance: but even cyclists who are glued to the saddle by day have to sleep by night. It appeared the only way to get a machine. After all, they would hardly take the things to bed with them.

The first two farm outhouses yielded nothing. The third had a bicycle – chained up, and the fourth, one with flat tyres. There was no sign of a pump. Probably it was under the owner's pillow, but I found four fresh eggs to make up for it. I was getting tired now. At the next place a brace of chained dogs raised such a commotion that I fled through the farm gate and raced back to the road. I slept in another ditch and didn't notice how much colder it was till morning.

That third morning wasn't good, either. Last night the sky had been full of dark clouds, and a chill breeze now pierced through three sets of underwear. I stopped in a wood, boiled the eggs, washed and shaved, and felt much better. The shave especially was a tonic.

A lorry was passing as I got back to the road. I dropped off outside Eger, and toured the town on the lookout for a machine: and at long last I got one. It wasn't before time. It was a sports model, propped up outside some kind of a municipal office. I took a good look around, went in, stayed a moment or two in the office, and then came out and sailed away on the bicycle. No one gave a second look.

The next hour was all sighs of relief. I was set now, and all laid on for Switzerland in five days: but the hoodoo had a card up its sleeve. Ten miles past Eger a huge nail gashed the front tyre. There were spanners in the saddlebag, but no puncture outfit; and the bike suddenly became a liability. A good cyclist doesn't ride on the rim. More important, in Germany, hardly any of the polizei would allow him to. Perhaps that machine is still hidden in the copse where I left it.

A few miles farther on the countryside began to change. It grew more rugged and exposed until finally sentinel pine trees from the great Bohmer Wald began lining the road. I had reached the edge of the forest. The weather was growing worse, too. The morning's cold wind had come back and was now nipping my ears and nose and sending icy fingers through the thick woollen vests. Above, a leaden sky offered no prospect of change or hope.

I couldn't understand this weather. We were in the month of May, and by all the rules it should have been warm and sunny. But where were the birds and bees and flowers? What had happened to the roads that should have been shimmering in heat? It was May, but it seemed more like December. A Siberian blast whistled down the road and ran full tilt into me. I shivered. Towards one o'clock the one catastrophe I had so confidently ruled out, happened. It began to snow.

At first they were only feathery wind-blown flakes, but that phase passed. The Christmas card variety came, and soon I was trudging through a white carpet an inch deep. It was dangerous, but I couldn't stop. In this desolate country there was nowhere to stop. I was beginning to look like a snowman, too, which was worse. Very soon people would be asking the obvious question. What business had I being out in a storm like this?

I should have stopped, of course. The eager gang of pessimists in Lager 22 would have raised satisfied eyebrows at my mistake in going on. I could almost hear those smug philosophers. 'It's impossible. We could have told you all along. It can't be done.' But I anticipate.

A civilian in one of the small villages glanced at me and then vanished into his house. Outside the village I dodged into a clump of trees and stayed there half an hour: but no one followed. I went back to the road. The only living creatures in sight were a couple of birds perched on the telephone wires. One of them began to sing, and as if it were a signal, a weak sun battled through the clouds. It had stopped snowing. Patches of blue were rapidly coming into the sky and I felt better for seeing them. Perhaps it was only a spot of freak weather after all.

After another two miles I approached quite a big village. It stood at a cross-roads and the chances of a lift seemed brighter. With any luck I thought, there might even be another bicycle. There was now no trace of snow on me. There was nothing unusual about my appearance at all, and I had no premonition of danger. If the old Grecian Jinx was sitting on my shoulder, I hadn't noticed him as yet.

Half way along the main street three men stepped from behind some trees. Their leader wore S.S. uniform. He stopped squarely in front of me and blocked the way. 'Wohin gehen Sie?' he demanded. Something told me this was the end, but I tried a bluff. 'Weiden,' I answered, trying hard to look perplexed but in no way dismayed. Then, in bad German, 'I'm taking some food to my brother in the French lager. He's sick.' 'Who are you?' snapped the S.S. man. 'Where've you come from?' 'Eger,' I said, 'I'm French. French Kriegs-gefangener.'

It sounded plausible enough. I had been rehearsing little anecdotes like this ever since I left Brux, but it had me worried. How did these men know I was coming? And why a posse for one lone traveller? And why pick on me, anyway? A breath of wind in the wires overhead answered all three questions. It was obvious. My expression didn't change, although inwardly I raged at being so damn stupid. A raw novice would have thought of those telephone wires. So that was why they hadn't bothered to chase me at the last village! But something else was making the Jinx smile. It shows just how chancy this escaping business can be. Germany was 'escape-happy'. A month ago 78 officers had made the mass break from Sagan Luft III, and the biggest hue-and-cry the Reich had ever known was now at its height. Nobody in Lager 22 had ever heard of Luft III.

But all hope wasn't gone yet. The three men were looking puzzled, as if uncertain what to make of all this. My story was a reasonable one. Everybody knew how these Gottverdammte Franzose wandered from town to town without so much as by-your-leave. They seemed to think the roads belonged to them. The Germans looked still more uncertain: but I feared what might come. If only we had had an Escape Committee. . . .

'Your name,' snapped the S.S. man. 'Guillaume Vermont,' I said. 'Number 618432.' Perhaps if I gave enough detail he might forget to ask that all-important question. 'Where's your brother?' 'In the French lager at Weiden. He's been ill a month with jaundice. This is the first chance I've had to go and see him. I've got two days' leave.' 'Why didn't you go by train?' 'Couldn't afford to. I've spent all the money I had on food.' That was nearer the truth. Then came the part that had been keeping me on tenterhooks. 'Well, it seems all right. Let's see your papers and you can go.'

There were two more S.S. men at the police station. One of them was an officer. He looked up as the little procession marched in, and a half-anticipatory smile flitted across his face. He seemed pleased. It was a sleepy outpost, this, a dead-and-alive hole if ever there was one. I guessed any diversion would be welcome.

The S.S. guard barked 'Halt!' clicked his heels, Heil-Hitlered, and explained about my having no papers. The officer took over. 'Where is your Ausweis?' he asked sternly. 'At Eger,' I said, 'In the lager. I thought I had it with me, but of course I'm going back to-morrow.' It was a low hand, but I wasn't throwing it in yet. The officer fired questions rapidly. 'What's the matter with your brother?' 'Jaundice. He's had it a month.' We'd been over this part before. 'When were you captured?' 'June '40.' 'Where?' 'Breteuil. Between Aumal and Noyon.' This bit was well rehearsed. 'And your brother?' 'Same place. He was with me. We joined up together.'

The officer began looking disappointed, and my spirits rose. The pair of deuces seemed to be doing uncommonly well: but it's a queer poker game where deuces sweep the board. The German grunted and reached for the telephone. 'Gottverdammte Kriegsgefangenen,' he muttered, half to himself. Into the receiver 'Give me Eger.'

I got to Eger after all, but not to the French lager. It was some distance from the jail. A monocled Wehrmacht officer unlocked the handcuffs, searched me, filled in a huge form, and brought out an inking pad. Two thumb prints and all the eight finger prints went on record. For good measure the officer added both my palm-prints. He'd know me again. After that I lost braces and shoelaces and went in ungainly fashion to the cells. And so ended that escape. All that remained was the pay-off.

There were four cells. Each had a massive door set flush in the wall, and secured on the outside by bolts that would have held an elephant. Two steps forward, I found the bed. It was a firm one, brick-built, with loose straw on top in lieu of a mattress. In the straw were colonies of fleas, all starving. There was no light. We were home again.

I stayed here a week. It could have been worse. Some daylight filtered through an unexpected grille, and the food was unusually good. I got out for five minutes each day; and having some experience of this mode of life, I ignored the vermin and settled down to wait. A great thing to remember in Kriegsgefangenenschaft is that there will be loads of waiting, but it will always end sometime.

The week passed. Two escorts called, and were obliging enough to wait whilst I washed and shaved. That took time. I had a week's beard and a lot of dirt on me. There were two surprises waiting. The monocled officer gave me my kit back intact, and we travelled to Weiden in a third-class railway carriage. With one last surprise. I wasn't handcuffed.

Weiden was a distinct change for the better. It was a toughs' camp, reserved for the ill-behaved and ill-mannered, but its surroundings were surprisingly gentle. Stalag XIIB was set in a lovely place. Only half a mile from the triple fences lay a fringe of the great Bavarian Wald. The nearer trees were nodding gently in the evening breeze, but behind them rose a solid wall of green, a massed motionless profusion of leaves and branches that sent forth errant breaths of pine-laden air to hint subtly of freedom in the wide forest beyond. Neither triple fences nor tiger-boxes could subdue that challenge.

I liked the Belgians best. They were a jolly crowd, quite unperturbed about the long sentences the judges had awarded. Every man jack of them was in for rape; but that didn't reflect upon them or upon Belgians in general. In Germany, rape was an elastic word. A prisoner could have a dozen mistresses if he wanted, and rape the lot for all the Germans cared, so long as the ladies were non-Deutschers. If a prisoner did rape a German woman he was shot: but none of the Belgians had fought for their pleasure. Rows of photographs on the barrack walls confirmed that. The Belgians' crime wasn't so much making illicit love, as being found out.

The French were not so cheerful. That was because they were split into two factions over the everlasting Petain – de Gaulle business. The Germans knew this, and as usual, were doing all they could to foster discord. Very largely it was a waste of time. On the surface, the tension was fierce, but underneath, the French were solid. After all, politics and personages are transient. Their loyalty – their true loyalty – was for 'La France' and all the mother country meant to them.

The one real friend I made at Weiden was Sergeant Major Degraux. He was undisputed leader of the French, partly because of his rank, and partly because politically he was neutral. If he had wanted to, he could have explained the neutrality, but he had good reasons for keeping his mouth shut. I got a pretty thorough testing before he told me: and when he finished I understood why.

Sergeant Major Degraux didn't exist. His papers were flawless, naturally. Official German stamps had been impressed several times alongside the first forged marks, and everything was in order, but then that kind of thing happened in those days. There was still no S.M. Degraux.

Captain Merry O'Brien, late of the Canadian Air Force, had made three attempts to get out of Germany. The first came within a hairs'-breadth of success. Fifty men breached the Oflag fence in '42, leaving a couple of dead guards behind them. They separated, but all got to the coast rendezvous punctually. That would have been miraculous in itself, except that Secret Service agents, *au fait* with the situation, had a lot to do with it.

Two of the three M.T.B.s came in punctually, too. They went away loaded, but the third was an hour late. It was one of those unpredictable misfortunes that escaping always incurs. When it did come, it was too late. The Germans had reached the coast, and the M.T.B. crew walked straight into captivity. In the mêlée O'Brien got away. He remained free another two days, which was long enough. When he was picked up, all traces of the Air Force officer had gone. The reserve plan was in operation, and as S.M. Degraux, he went behind the barbed wire again.

The second escape got him nowhere, except that he learnt one or two useful tips. The third also failed, but once again only by the smallest possible margin. O'Brien locked himself into a goods wagon and reached Paris without incident. That was mainly due to the way he entered the wagon without breaking the seals, but the method is too long to explain here. Also it might come in useful again sometime. At the Paris marshalling yards only the easy stage remained. He dodged the sentries, and being in civilian clothes, should have got clear altogether; but like so many of us, O'Brien had a gremlin. A mile away a friend was waiting with newly-forged papers, food, money and a passage to Marseilles. The Canadian knew this, but the knowledge wasn't much use. He could hardly tell the two German policemen his passport was almost within hailing distance. He had landed in Paris at the height of a sudden identity check.

A few days later he was back at Weiden. So far, none of his other schemes had come to anything, but he wasn't discouraged. You can't hold a good man indefinitely, not even in as tough a spot as Weiden.

There was one other friendship at XIIB, but it only lasted an hour.

Guido Rinaldi had just been booked as a dangerous prisoner. He was the only man who had yet got away from the camp, which, in German eyes, put him automatically on a par with Churchill, Stalin, and der Teufel. His break had lasted half an hour. From the first it hadn't an earthly chance, but that made no difference. Rinaldi had blotted the camp record and would have to pay the price. Irate guards locked him in my strongroom, left a man outside and went away to decide what to do.

But the camp knew Guido far better than the Germans did. He was the one sole innocent amongst this cut-throat crew of thieves, rapers, and escapers. There wasn't an ounce of harm in his whole make-up. On the day I landed at Weiden, Guido reached breaking point. He was homesick and utterly miserable. His wife's letter had just arrived and recollections of the carissima moglie and the bambini and sunny Calabria were coming back too vividly. Something snapped. Guido got up and walked towards the wire. He was going home.

He climbed the double fence at a point midway between two tiger-boxes. He continued across the German compound and scaled their wire, too, but nobody saw him. Providence had taken a hand in the game and the sentries were all looking the other way. The outer patrol had just passed, but that was Providence again, not Guido. He had no room for any thought of danger. The moglie, the bambini and Calabria were calling, and Guido heard them. There was a mountain of determination in him, but no subtlety. He didn't bother asking which way to go. It didn't even occur to him that blue uniform might be conspicuous. He was on his way home and that was enough. The police picked him up in the first half-mile.

Tears were still wet on Guido's cheeks when I saw him. He was himself now. The fearless wire jumper had gone, and in his place was a very humble and pathetic little man.

The guards came back and I barely got time to give Guido fifty cigarettes and a tin of meat before we parted.

My own marching orders came soon after. I was the only Englishman in XIIB and the cheerful Belgians insisted on making yet another present of food and cigarettes. A noisy throng accompanied me to the gate. Merry O'Brien gripped my hand firmly and gave me a brief wink. 'Keep trying,' he said. 'We'll make it yet.' The merry band of rapers behind almost drowned him with their vociferous farewells. 'Vive l'Angleterre!' they bawled. 'Vive la Belge! En bas les Boches!' From one little chap somewhere at the back came a strident 'Et vive les jolies femmes!' And with this storm ringing in my ears the gates of Weiden closed behind me.

It was a film star's send-off.

EIGHTEEN

I had an idea the new trip would end at Stalag H.Q. Kriegsgefangenenschaft has an axiom that no man is punished for escaping. Only those who fail get jumped on, which is as it should be. It makes them more careful next time. The German penalty for being caught usually ensured that they were: and outside the Kommandant's office at Aussig H.Q., I guessed that whatever might be brewing up inside, it would hardly do me any good.

We didn't start off well. The Hauptmann was one of those Germans the cartoonists dream about. He had a bullet head, short stiff hair and a liberal amount of neck over the back of his collar.

He was an irascible man. 'Who helped you escape?' he demanded. The interpreter translated. It was always far better not to speak German with a Hauptmann about.

'Nobody,' I answered.

'But some Czech has helped you. He must have done. Where else did those clothes come from?'

I said nothing. It certainly wouldn't help bringing Funk into this. The interpreter repeated the question but there was still no answer. At a third asking, the Hauptmann grew red in the face. I had a nasty feeling that at any moment he might send for a squad of 'gorillas', but that had to be risked. Until then, and possibly afterwards, he could find his own information.

The haranguing went on, and the Hauptmann began letting off steam. Fortunately, the interpreter was slow in translating one passage and the officer promptly turned the attack on him. I think he welcomed the diversion. It was much more satisfactory cursing a subordinate than a blankfaced alien.

But despite his aggressiveness the Hauptmann made a comparatively mild inquisitor. I was lucky. A good many officers would have called in the strong-arm brigade and let them beat the daylight out of me to begin with. Gestapo officers would have gone further.

The bullnecked Hauptmann didn't believe in these measures, and for that much I was grateful: but I wasn't getting off scot-free. The German went up to white heat, roared and bellowed at me, and made various threats, but eventually cooled down again. The cross-examination ended abruptly. Soon after, I was lodged in a cell.

This doesn't sound too bad. Thinking back on it, it doesn't seem so bad now the years have blunted the sharp edges of the picture: but I remember at the time being convinced that it was the worst, the vilest, the most stinking and abominable hole in all Germany.

It was a little cupboard of a place about six feet square and eight feet high. It had one of those solid smells you can carve with a knife. It had no windows and no ventilation. It was down in the bowels of the building, near the boiler room, and insufferably hot. And it had a million bugs.

During the first three days I never slept. The wooden bed which took up most of the cell space was 'walking', but for every hundred bugs I killed, a thousand streamed out of the walls to replace them. A new odour, the nauseous smell of crushed bug, began battling for lebensraum with the all-pervading stench of sweat and stale urine.

On the fourth day the luck changed. One of our own men, stationed at the Stalag, managed to visit me. He had already sweetened the guard, and so no notice was taken of the parcel that remained behind. It contained fifty cigarettes, a box of matches, a tin of bully and a huge tin of anti-louse powder. Years have passed, but even now, I would still recommend that unknown hero for every medal on the list.

The whole picture changed abruptly. I didn't know how long I was going to stay in this hole. Probably that was the Hauptmann's idea – to encourage stray misgivings that it might be for good. Apart from one bowl of soup a day, and that short-filled, I wasn't getting fed either: but hunger and confinement had lost their original sting. Bugs and tobacco-fever hadn't. Both had been getting a little overpowering, too, but now, thank God and the Good Samaritan Kriegie, I was able to cope with them.

The louse powder was good stuff, even outside its chosen métier. I sprinkled the whole tin over the bed, decimated the hosts within, and discouraged fresh invaders. The bully went in one meal. After that I felt A1 for a week to come. The cigarettes lasted until the door opened, four days later.

The Hauptmann had a parting word to say. It wasn't a kindly one, with any now-let's-be-friends motif, nor did he look any better disposed. 'I am sending you to a schwerarbeit camp,' he growled. The interpreter, looking nervous, made a good job of it. 'There you will work,' continued the Hauptmann, severely. 'You will work hard. You will sweat. It will do you good. And if you try to escape again you will be shot. Mark that. Nobody can escape from Germany.'

I had my own views about the last remark, but didn't air them. I didn't ask any questions until we were well clear of Aussig; but even then nothing much came from the guard. All he knew was that we were going to a heavy workers' camp, that there was extra food, and that the Kommandant was a good man. The food part was the only comfort.

The train stopped at Lobositz, a village in Sudeten Germany. Pleasant surprises followed immediately. The 'camp' turned out to be a converted Gasthaus, built almost on the bank of the Elbe, and like XIIB, amidst exquisite surroundings. It was only five minutes from the station instead of the usual hour, and was a far more homely place than I had been expecting. Another happy augury was that the young Kommandant seemed a reasonable man. He took a few brief particulars warned me to do well to warrant being equally done by, which was fair enough, and with that dismissed me. I went inside.

The shirt-sleeved spectacled man who came up wasted no time introducing himself. 'I'm Robinson,' he said. 'Sydney to you. Where're you from?'

I liked this direct approach. 'The mush,' I answered. 'The clink, Sydney. At Aussig. It stinks.'

Sydney nodded agreement. 'Yes, I've heard of it. What were you in for?'

I accepted the cigarette he offered and lit up. 'Escaping,' I said. Then quickly, 'No, not escaping.' Here was I forgetting the old axiom. 'Being caught. And right now I need a bath.

What's the chances?'

Sydney looked at me thoughtfully. 'You could do with a cup of tea, first,' he said intelligently.

Such was the start of another friendship, this time one lasting nine months. I got my bath and heaved every stitch of clothing I had through the window. Sydney dug out some spare clothes from a well-stocked case. He had been here nearly four years and none of his personal parcels had gone astray. Other men, just back from work, made up a complete kit.

It was a friendly camp, and in some ways different from any other I had been in. All the forty-odd men were old hands. Most of them had come straight from Dunkirk and Greece, and this was the only permanent lager they had ever known. It seemed I was the first punishment case to arrive in four years. There were twelve Cypriots here too, but only one spoke English. That promoted me interpreter on the spot.

Food was the best ever. The cellar was stacked full of parcels, German rations were good (by German standards), and the usual market was providing all kinds of luxuries. The place was clean, fairly spacious and compared with some, vermin-free. A few odd fleas roamed about, but they were timid creatures and had no teeth.

At first the slack discipline of the guards surprised me. They held a check in the morning and another about bedtime, but both were cursory affairs. There were no night patrols, and only steel-shuttered windows blocked the way out. They weren't insuperable. It wouldn't have been difficult to fake the morning count either, at least once, and unconsciously I began sizing up the chances of a getaway. By Oflag standards this place seemed a gift from the gods: but a couple more days brought second thoughts. I noticed that the Kommandant, who knew every man by sight, held a watching brief over the parades. He was no fool, despite his easy ways, and I realized that a truant would be lucky to get a day's grace. It wasn't enough. With Lobositz even more centrally placed than Brux, something like two or three days' start was essential.

I decided to lay off escaping for a while. After all it was cosy here, and I'd had my share of jails. It might be as well to give the bull-necked Hauptmann time to forget, too.

It was easier understanding the heavy rations at Lobositz. About two miles away was a stone quarry, where most of us more than earned the extra bread. I started work the day after I arrived. At 6.30 a.m. we marched out and trekked two miles, mostly uphill, to the quarry. It was a huge place. A wall of rock rose sheer above us, in places to a height of 300 feet. At the foot was an amphitheatre, criss-crossed with small gauge railway tracks, all converging on a concrete bunker which fed the crushing machines below.

Our job was simple. We had to break stones blasted down from the cliff face, lift the pieces into a truck, and take the laden truck to the bunker. Twelve such journeys were reckoned a day's work.

What surprised me initially was the way almost every man buckled into the job. I went over to the chap on the next truck and had a word with him. 'Yes,' he agreed. 'I am working hard. And I'll tell you why. As soon as these bloody wagons are done I'm off. Finished. You watch me, mate. I'll be gone before dinner.'

He kept his word. About half past eleven he brought the empty truck back for the last time, picked up his coat and wandered off, unescorted. I had finished two wagons. By two o'clock I had another to my credit, but all except two of the regulars had gone.

It was an example of first-rate German psychology. The arbeit-fuehrers knew that no prisoner would sweat on the Reich's behalf unless he had powerful inducement. This finish-and-you-can-go business provided the spur. The absent stone-loaders had only worked half a day, but every man had broken twelve tons of stone. An unwilling worker could easily spin that out to last a week. Going back unescorted was more bribery. It didn't give enough time for potential escapers to get moving, but it did allow those with black market contacts or female friends a chance to make their assignments.

I walked over to where Panagioti and Ramadan, the Cypriots, were working. Unlike the others, they were going at a snail's pace. Their knocking-off time was five o'clock, the same as mine, so there was no point in getting excited over the work.

Panagioti and Ramadan were the only men in the lager who had consistently refused the German bait. In all their eighteen months on the black list, neither of them had ever done a full day's work. They didn't believe in it. Eight wagons between them was the highest yet, and even that was an accident. On that day a fall of rock toppled into their empty wagon and filled it for them.

Herr Wertzig, the boss, didn't like either Panagioti or his pal. Baldy, the grizzled little under-boss, hated the sight of them, but the Cyps didn't mind. They came from a free country, and allowed generously that a man could think what he liked.

Wertzig had already tried everything. In summer he kept them at the quarry until nine o'clock. In winter he turned them out on Sundays; but neither of these ruses got him anywhere. Panagioti and Ramadan were past masters in the art of going slow. Between them and Wertzig was a state of undeclared war.

The three of us were standing idle when the Boss came up. Perhaps he was afraid the black sheep would be tainting the new man, and perhaps he wanted to display his authority. Whatever it was, his action was ill-chosen. Ramadan watched him walk up, and then carefully turned his back. 'D'you notice a smell round here?' he asked. He spoke bad German, but it was good enough. Panagioti took his cue. He looked everywhere, looked right through the fuming Wertzig and held his nose. 'Yes, something does stink,' he said, looking puzzled. Suddenly the swarthy Cypriot beamed. 'Ah!' he cried. 'It's Herr Wertzig! Ramadan! Wertzig's here!'

I enjoyed the little comedy. I was more than interested, though, to see what Wertzig would do about it. After all, he was the arbeit-fuehrer and supposed to have authority; but if prisoners could call him a smell and get away with it, well, I had a few scruples that would soon be going overboard.

Wertzig didn't like it. He purpled with rage and gripped his stick until the knuckles showed white: but he did nothing. There was no guard near us and he was too scared to do anything himself, even in white fury. Somebody had once told him that every Cypriot carried a knife, and both Panagioti and Ramadan, beaming at the furious German, had their right hands ominously inside their trouser bands. It was a bluff, of course, but Wertzig didn't chance it. He stood at a safe distance, and cursed instead. It was a silly move.

The Cypriots were always pleased when things went this way. People had been cursing them for three years now, and they knew all the answers. 'Gottverdammt Schwein!' roared a foolish Wertzig. 'Saboteur. . . .' Ramadan raised a protesting hand and stopped the flow. 'Halten Sie die Schnauze, Herr Abort,' he chided gently. Ramadan still hadn't finished when the furious Nazi turned and stumped away. He looked back once, with black hatred written all over him. Panagioti, waiting for it, clapped a hand to his nose and pulled an invisible chain. It was the final insult.

I was frankly bewildered. Anywhere else in Germany such flagrant abuse would have been impossible. It would have meant the 'mush' at the very least, and probably a beating-up to go with it. I turned blankly to the two smiling Cypriots for an explanation.

It seemed that it wasn't so far-fetched after all. Circumstances were peculiar here. Wertzig was a civilian. He was a red-hot Nazi, a Party member, and a big noise generally, but still a civilian. A missing eye was keeping him out of uniform even at this late stage. As a civilian he carried no weapons. His authority depended on the Kommandant's backing, and with it, he could have had the Cyps in jail in an hour. He would have been invincible: but the two bosses had a feud. It was a long-standing one, and because they were enemies, the Kommandant cheerfully ignored all One-Eye's complaints. 'Where's your proof?' he would ask. 'These men say they haven't spoken to you to-day. Did anyone else hear them?' Wertzig could never get over that hurdle. Panagioti and his pal were careful to abuse him only when the guards were elsewhere. At all other times they were as meek as lambs.

Wertzig had enough sense not to go over the Kommandant's head. He knew better than that. The Aussig authorities were too busy with the war to waste time in squashing a couple of rebel prisoners. That was the arbeit-fuehrer's pigeon.

I didn't join the Cypriots' strike for some months. From a patriotic viewpoint they were undoubtedly going a good job, but there are two sides to every question. This was only one. On a good 'pitch' and especially after a fresh blast, it was hard to do less than seven or eight wagons in a full day. Even that meant going dead-slow, and was more tiring than the morning flat-out session. And besides his patriotic duty, a prisoner must needs look after himself. The people who prate most about Duty usually do it from the safe side of the wire.

Our Kommandant was one of those rare Germans who could keep their nose out of other people's business. He believed in live and let live. So long as Aussig didn't send him complaints he didn't interfere with us. Parcels came regularly, mail wasn't delayed or 'lost', and we had no unnecessary parades. It was more the reverse. Wc enjoyed a good many privileges we shouldn't have had. There were walks, football matches, bathing parties, even boat trips on the Elbe. There was no doubt about it, the Kommandant was doing his bit.

I weighed things up, and joined the majority. It was hard work filling those twelve trucks, but it was worth it. After midday I was free until next morning, and the virtual *carte blanche* we were all given to enjoy the freedom made it very tempting. If I keep this good pitch, I decided, I'll finish. If Wertzig tries any dirty tricks – well, that'll be another story.

The Kommandant was a rare man for turning a blind eye. At Lobositz we worked like horses and ate proportionately. There was no shortage of food. Every stone-loader was strong and fit and virile, but of course, still captive. The result was inevitable. To a greater or less degree we all became woman-hungry.

It wasn't a sudden change, nor an alarming one. For most of us, nothing much came of it, either. There wasn't enough talent in the neighbourhood for fair shares all round, and unfortunate newcomers, who had to start from scratch, got nowhere. All the available belles had been booked up long ago. Their swains went out to see them regularly. Camp mechanics had 'fixed' one of the windows, and about twice a week, the steel shutter was lifted quietly from its moorings as two or three Casanovas slipped out. Others even went farther afield. Russian women were billeted on the local farms, and most of them seemed keen to make assignments. Inside the Gasthaus we had a big notice pinned to the wall. It warned all prisoners that anyone having intercourse with a German woman was liable to ten years' imprisonment; in serious cases to the death penalty. The Commander-in-Chief of the Wehrmacht had signed the order, and he wasn't joking. Weiden was proof enough of that: but there was a handy loophole in the order There always is, if you look for it. The C.I.C. had only mentioned German women. He said nothing about Polish or French or Russian girls, for the good reason that he wasn't interested what happened to them: so as far as Authority was concerned we had no need to court trouble. I didn't keep any appointments, despite this. About three-quarters of the Lobositz men were also celibate, although it wasn't the ten years, or superior morals, or satisfaction with the status quo that stopped any of us. What deterred us was the fear of contracting disease. With the terrific influx of people into the Reich, V.D. was widespread. There were some obvious cases, but you could never take anything for granted. Two minutes away from the lager there was a woman who was always willing. You knocked twice on the door and produced five cigarettes. Because of her three of our boys were already making weekly visits to Aussig hospital. One of the Cypriots was an inpatient there. He had contracted syphilis from a Russian wench, but none of us knew who she was. There are some things in life that are not worth the risk.

My pal Sydney never got back to the lager before five o'clock. He worked at a railway siding two minutes away, and despite the longer hours I was soon envying him his job. The other stone-loaders had been doing that for years. We had to slog two miles uphill every morning and work like niggers to finish our twelve wagons. About an hour after we left, Sydney and five other men meandered leisurely along to the Bahnhof where they did much as they liked.

The secret was the light workers' tickets they all had. This priceless document classed each of the six brainy Bahnhof 'invalids' as partly disabled, and forbade heavy work. It was the one order they religiously obeyed. In all their years at the Gasthaus none of them had ever sweated blood at the quarry face.

They even liked their job. All the local and war news reached them first hand, they had access to every black marketeer for miles around, and were on nodding terms and sometimes more than nodding terms with every safe woman in Lobositz. They had no complaints.

Officially they were the last link in Wertzig's production chain. At the quarry, crushed rock was loaded into trucks and sent down to the Bahnhof by cable railway. Six descending trucks, their speed regulated by a Czech brakeman, hauled up six empties, which were then ready for another load. Sydney and his gang were the transport men. They uncoupled full wagons, tipped the stone into huge silos, recoupled the mile-long cable, and gave the waiting Czech the O.K. by telephone. Six of them were on the job, although at a push one man could have coped with everything. There was a slight if ever-present risk attached, admittedly, but none of them worried about it. Wertzig liked to drive men and machines as far as he could. Amongst other things, he was inclined to over-estimate the life of wire cables and to run them after flaws had shown up. It was foolish of him. Twice in the memory of old hands, the stout wire had snapped.

The double track merged into a single line about three-quarters of the way down from the quarry. On the first occasion, the runaway wagons fouled the points. They shot off the track, and wheels, axles, and twelve tons of stone spread themselves over the best part of two fields.

The second time, the wagons took the points successfully and hurtled down the steep slope to the Bahnhof at over 80 m.p.h. Fortunately our boys heard the high-pitched scream of racing wheels and jumped clear. The wagons flashed past. By this time they were probably touching the hundred mark. They roared straight at the wooden hut where the brains trust took their meals, demolishing it, and catapulted on to the road thirty feet below. Strong steel trucks disintegrated. Various bits and pieces bounced off the hard highway like so many rubber balls, almost as far as the Elbe. The twelve tons of stone vanished completely.

That was a great day at Lobositz. Up at the quarry, heavy-arbeiters clapped each other on the back and cheered like schoolboys. To them, the smash meant a fortnight's holiday. To Wertzig and Baldy, whose faces couldn't conceal their despair, it meant sixteen hours a day putting the transport system in order again. To the Kommandant, back in the Gasthaus, it was the best joke in years. He laughed until the tears ran down his face.

NINETEEN

I was at Lobositz a month before the Hauptmann's shadow fell. It was in the first week of June '44. I tipped my last wagon somewhere about noon, rode down to the Bahnhof on the Wertzig express, and promised Sydney a cup of tea on the dot of five.

But Sydney never got that brew. I found the Kommandant waiting for me at the door of the Gasthaus. There was a letter in his hand. 'Yo-ness,' he said, not unkindly, 'Yo-ness, you've got to go to the bunker for seven days.' I looked at him, and promptly called for the sergeant-interpreter. There was a mistake here somewhere.

Our sergeant read the letter, and a puzzled frown came over his face. 'Yes, you've got seven days all right,' he said slowly. 'It says so here. This letter's from Aussig H.Q.'

'But what for?' I exploded. 'Are you sure it's me?' The sergeant read the letter again.

'It's still you,' he affirmed, 'and it's for escaping.'

'But that's nonsense!' I protested. 'Why, I've been in about four clinks since then. I was in Aussig for a week.'

But the sergeant shook his head. 'I know,' he agreed, 'but it seems that didn't count. You were awaiting trial then. Now you've been tried and you've got seven days. It's the way they do things here. There's nothing you can do about it. You've got to go now, too, but there's one consolation. It isn't the Stalag mush this time. It's somewhere farther down the line.'

That wasn't as consoling as the sergeant made out. I didn't relish going into any kind of jail; but I knew it was a waste of time complaining. What the Stalag said, went: and rightly or otherwise seven days' clink lay ahead. There was no getting out of it.

Not much time was left for preparation, but I made good use of what there was. I bandaged two packets of Players on the inside of each thigh, split open the shoulder tabs of my tunic, put matches in there, and had a good feed. There were still ten minutes or so left before Schmidt got back from the quarry, but no one was surprised at that. Schmidt was only acting true to form.

Our guards were first-class malingerers, all four of them. Joe, the youngest, was lame. Sometimes he would forget, and limp with the wrong foot, but he made no mistakes when officers were around. Joe had been at Lobositz since the war started. So far as it lay within his power, he intended to be there when it finished, too. His friends, Hans and Rudolf, had been wounded in Africa, and they didn't intend to recover just yet, but old Schmidt put the three of them in the novices' class.

Schmidt had heart trouble. Four doctors had certified the heart as being in bad shape. In reality it was as sound as a bell, but Schmidt knew the ropes better than most soldiers. He was a clever man who didn't want to go to the Russian Front: and now the Wehrmacht had accepted his diseased valves, he took good care that no one forgot about them. He never hurried.

We made slow progress to the station. Both of us knew the path was visible from the Gasthaus, and Schmidt didn't take chances. At the halfway mark he sat down for a rest. On the station steps he had another rest. He was rightly proud of his attention to detail. I watched admiringly. Any number of weak hearts, flat feet and varicose veins were doing yeoman service on both sides of the conflict. The cure for most of them was not so much death as Armistice.

Schmidt bore the journey well. His bad health didn't stop him smoking my cigarettes, and he made an affable companion. I enjoyed the train trip. We got to the jail in fine fettle.

But the two guards who were waiting weren't Schmidts. They were a cold, business-like pair, curt, full of Teuton efficiency and fuller still of their own importance. For all that they were a pair of fools. They searched my pockets, looked inside my hat, patted me around the waist, ran their hands down the outside of my legs, and finally agreed I had no contraband. The four packets of cigarettes escaped unscathed. Nine Wehrmacht men in ten would have found them.

It was a peculiar prison. The Germans had built it inside the grounds of a wire-making factory, but why there, no one could tell me. It was a low white building with only two cells, and one of those was empty. I seemed to be keeping two guards occupied simply through being in the place; but neither guard had the least fear that I might escape. The prison was too strong. Both the outside door and the cell door were locked and barred, and it took a full minute opening them. That suited me. I needed that long to waft away all traces of tobacco smoke.

As prisons go, it was comfortable. There was the usual board bed, and there were no resident guests. A ten minute inspection didn't find a single flea or bug. The latrine bucket was brand new. The walls were newly plastered and in one corner stood a radiator. It didn't work, of course, but that didn't matter. It made the place look homely. The cell had only one bad point. The window was covered by a fine-mesh screen fixed to the outside; but even that was less hindrance than it looked. If I stood near enough I could see out without trouble.

The week passed easily. What with the unaccustomed cleanliness and the Frenchman, Louis, it slid past, although there were the usual ups and downs. The factory was far too noisy. It clanged and banged all day long, and I got no peace until six at night. The noise started again at 6 a.m. but I was always wide-awake at that hour. The less civilized of the two guards got up at the crack of dawn so he could come and whip the blankets away. There were lots of little Hitlers in Germany.

The food was poor. I got bread and water for the first three days, and a subsistence meal on the fourth. That was a rank swindle. I forfeited the day's bread, and in return got a can of lukewarm gummy bilge which the guard said was soup. I couldn't have eaten it for my freedom, but fortunately Louis brought something special on that day.

Louis was about the best of all the good points. On the first day I kept an eye at the grille and whistled the Marseillaise whenever anyone passed. I was on the fifteenth rendering before Louis came up. He heard me, stopped, and we chatted awhile. From then on it was plain sailing. I was allowed to visit the toilet opposite every morning. From the second day onwards, I reached to the top of the cistern, took down Louis' parcel, and hid it in my clothes. The Frenchman collected the five cigarettes I left, later on, by which time I had usually eaten all his bread and margarine, and read most of the *Aussiger Zeitung* it was wrapped in. On Subsistence Day, my Gallic pal left a neat parcel of cake as well.

I had already got the Invasion news from Louis. He came hotfoot with it on the second day, and each night since, a bevy of his friends had brought up-to-the-minute details. A lot of speculation went on by that cell window.

The *Zeitung* editor wasn't as happy as we were. At first he tried to play down the Invasion as something in the nature of a Commando raid, but events dictated his policy. On D day + 2 his headlines were boasting 'We will repel the enemy!' Next day's edition used bigger print. 'The West Wall is impregnable!' it bellowed. Underneath was the assurrance 'Our Fuehrer leads us,' but I guessed that didn't ring a bell with the Editor. He knew his Fuehrer was leading him, but he wasn't sure if it was up the garden path.

Schmidt came for me when the week finished. He was looking pleased about something, but we were on the train back before I discovered what it was. He accepted one of my last cigarettes, lit up, and then disclosed that the Fuehrer had just passed the total mobilization order that made every man in Germany a Volkssturmer.

'Does it include you?' I asked. I was most interested. Perhaps our leadswinging expert had met his Waterloo at last.

Schmidt inhaled deeply and a wide grin spread over his face. 'Nein,' he said. 'You forget, I'm a sick man, Yo-ness. The doctors have passed me again. This is the fifth time. I'm a permanent noncombatant now. Ja, Yo-ness, I'm sick. I'm a *very* sick man.'

TWENTY

I found Sydney waiting for me at the lager. He had wangled the afternoon off, and his battered old teapot was steaming a merry welcome. He was just as brimful with news as Schmidt. 'Hello, Bill,' he greeted, 'd'you know we're on the Cherbourg peninsula? It's due to fall any minute. We're going through Normandy like a dose of salts. Boy, oh boy! What a war! What I'd give to be there!' He shook his head and smiled ecstatically. Then another thought occurred. 'Oh, by the way, there's two fag parcels for you. They're both thousands.'

I didn't get a chance to tell Sydney about the 'mush'. We talked war until dinner time, and when that was over, my pal and two of his Bahnhof cronies brought out a huge map and a box of little red flags. For the next hour or two, the three of them, Sammy, Joe and Sydney, were busy men. They deciphered the *Zeitung*'s version of the Invasion and planted flags in a tight ring around the beach-head. Sammy then produced a written copy of the B.B.C. news, which had come from Franz, and started reeling off names. Another wider circle of flags went down.

At this stage the budding generals began to argue. As far as I could gather Joe and Sydney were textbook militarists. They were nervous of the enemy's strength, and wanted an orthodox war, consolidating as they advanced. Sammy, the blitzkrieg expert, said No. He favoured a lightning push to the Rhine. 'I'll have the damn thing finished before you're out of Caen,' he said contemptuously. They were still going strong an hour later. I gave up all hope of recounting my adventures, and went to bed.

Technically, Franz was boss over the Bahnhof staff; but the relationship wasn't what it used to be. Since the end of '43, Franz had been doing his best to forget the 'boss' part. More recently, since June 6th to be precise, he had obeyed the red lights that were flashing, and had become a staunch colleague.

He was always a man of divided sympathies. Like so many of the Sudeten-Deutsch, he was half Czech and half German, which from the start gave him a choice of loyalties. Our new ally had never made any bones about it. He supported the winning side every time, and it had been interesting to watch his weathercock allegiance.

Until '43, Franz was very much his father's son. He was ardent in his Nazi convictions and Heil-Hitlered with the loudest. The rout of Rommel's Afrika Korps stopped this carry-on. When the Allies landed in Sicily, Franz climbed uneasily on to the fence. The capture of the island finished his conversion, and the former Superman changed completely. He realized he had been backing the wrong horse, but it wasn't too late to change sides. With Teuton thoroughness, he did. Overnight he became more staunchly pro-Allied than any of us. He dropped Rommel and took up Ike and Monty instead. He praised Winston. He even tuned in to the banned B.B.C. news and passed the details on to us. There was one good point about Franz. He didn't do things by halves.

So I never told Sydney about the wire-works after all. We didn't see each other during the day, and at night, as soon as dinner was over, he had his generals' conference to attend. Sammy was becoming adept at flag-sticking, and the circle of flags marched deeper and deeper into the heart of France.

The end of the war really did seem to be getting near. In the lager the three generals concentrated on their maps and strategy with true professional detachment, but the rest of us, the rabble, weren't so cold-blooded. We thought of our own D day, and wondered how long it would be before we were back in England. On one thing all ranks agreed. We wouldn't spend another Christmas in Germany.

The months went slowly past. In October '44, some of us

began having faint doubts about getting home for Christmas, but we said nothing. In November, dark suspicion spread like measles. In December, Rundstedt started his Ardennes push, and the doubts vanished. They were now certainties and it was no use evading facts. Very glumly we realized that the Christmas trip was off.

Early in December I ran into trouble myself. Wertzig also found his path becoming far from smooth, but the two events weren't directly connected. Baldy, the under-manager, put a light to one fuse. He had been doing some bitter complaining of late. My wagons weren't full, I was loading snow as well as stone, I was unco-operative, and was apt to fiddle the wagon tally. I wasn't entirely innocent of these charges, but Baldy wouldn't let it rest there.

Somehow a sledgehammer gravitated into the bunker and stripped the teeth off the cracking machine. Baldy promptly came up and accused me. He was dancing with rage. 'You did it, you Englischer Schwein,' he bawled. We both knew that this accident meant a three days' holiday all over the quarry. I produced my hammer for inspection. Baldy should have known there had been a spare one lying around for weeks. 'I didn't do it, you Deutsch Hund,' I told him. 'Very likely you did, though. You're getting old now, you know. You don't know what you're doing half the time.' Baldy went apoplectic. He lashed out with his stick, but I dodged and taunted him again. Wertzig came up, heard the story, and all three of us went down to see the Kommandant.

The two civilians were red-hot. They rampaged into the office and demanded a charge of sabotage on the books right away. The Kommandant's flat refusal didn't help them to cool off. That old enmity had always paid a big dividend. 'But Yo-ness says he knows nothing about it,' argued the Kommandant. 'It's up to you to prove he does. You say he had his hammer intact? Well, now, what can I do on that evidence? And another thing. You might knock before you come into my office.'

The two stone-fuehrers took that defeat badly. It rankled, as the Kommandant no doubt hoped it would, but the luck was changing. A week afterwards I was caught red-handed.

For three days running I was on a beautiful patch of stone. It came in long straight slabs that cracked almost at the sight of a hammer. It was too rare an opportunity to miss. I built bridges in the wagon, piled rubble on top, and ran the faked loads to the bunker at the rate of six an hour. For two days it worked like a charm. Then I grew careless. I forgot Baldy would be watching like a hawk, and didn't tip the wagon as fast as I should have done. The little overseer pounced at the bunker's edge, and began prodding about with his stick. Very soon the bridge collapsed. The rubble dropped, revealed the wagon only half-full, and Baldy shouted with joy. Yo-ness was for it this time. Being a fatalist, I grinned at the thought of the rumpus there'd be when the balloon went up.

Wertzig came along. It was the first time anyone had ever seen him run, but at the moment One-Eye didn't give a damn for his dignity. Yo-ness had been caught red-handed. His prayers were answered, and this time he had proof. The load was in the bunker now, but Granpa, the doddering old German who kept the tally bag, had also seen it.

I lost my good pitch and was banished to the dirtiest spot in the whole quarry; but I didn't fret. It had been a good job while it lasted, and I'd had a fair run. Perhaps more than I was entitled to. Now it was time to join the Cypriots and go on strike. Wertzig felt much happier after the showdown, but his other worries, which had nothing to do with me, soon tempered the joy.

A week ago, six new men had come to Lobositz. They all descended on the same day, each from a different camp, and each one ignorant as to why he had made the sudden move. For a time it had us guessing too.

It was pretty obvious that strings had been pulled to arrange the transfer, and even clearer that the new men were expected. Normally a Kommandant vetted his recruits very carefully. No lager Fuehrer wanted 'wild' men in his camp, and as a rule, if a conduct card wasn't satisfactory, its owner got sent back in a hurry. Our Kommandant waived this procedure. He went to the gate to meet the new men. We saw him greet them like long-lost brothers, escort them into his office and hand out cigarettes all round. It stunned us. No one else had been honoured like that before. The newcomers were no beauties, but even now the Kommandant's 'Guten Morgens' seemed to be reserved for them. There was an almighty smell of fish about the whole business.

A chance item of news about a week later made things clearer. We learnt, with undisguised regret, that our Komandant was leaving. For some unknown reason Aussig H.Q. was pulling him out of his easy job and sending him to the Russian front. For a time the news dazed the lager Fuehrer, but as soon as he got over the shock he began thinking. He couldn't help going now. He'd been posted, and there was no getting clear of that, but before he went, he intended to settle scores with someone. For all his easy-going ways the man was a fighter.

He didn't have to look far for an opponent. Herr Wilhelm Wertzig, who had smarted a good deal after that sledge-hammer fiasco, was now wearing a wide grin every time he came near the office. The Kommandant thought back on the threats that had been uttered, and remembered that Wilhelm was a Party member, in touch with all the big shots at H.Q. Well, he'd certainly pulled a fast one. The Kommandant smiled rather grimly. It was one up to Wilhelm, he reflected, pushing aside his official correspondence, but maybe two could play at that game.

Next day, six lager Fuehrers in different parts of the Sudetenland pondered over the rather curious communications they had received. None of them had any idea what their Lobositz colleague was playing at. They weren't at all sure if the war hadn't unbalanced him slightly, but none of them hesitated on that account. You don't examine gift horses too closely. The deceptive body of prisoners who marched into the Lobositz stone lager was proof of that.

The new boys soon showed their mettle. Each of them was a hardened malingerer, a veteran of countless clashes with authority, and owned a conduct card that stank. No other word would be strong enough. All had been drummed out of more camps than they could remember, and as a group, had probably caused more headaches than any other six men in Germany. We began to see the light.

On their first day three of the new recruits reported sick. Being expert at this kind of thing, they stayed sick and Wertzig never saw them. Perhaps it was his good fortune. Jock, a tall Glaswegian, rubbed ersatz butter into a cut on his arm, and developed a minor skin infection. Curly, from Bow Bells, had a swollen wrist. He tapped it with the back of a spoon for half an hour before it swelled sufficiently, but he knew that five minutes a day after that would be ample. Harry, the third invalid, was out of action with a bad foot. It didn't bother him until Germans were around, but he wouldn't disclose details. 'It's a professional secret,' he said.

The other half of the contingent soon put years on Wertzig. Two of them worked together, and took over an hour to load one truck. They tipped the stone into the bunker and then sent the truck in for good measure. It was midday before that lot was put straight. The third man piled an enormous load on his wagon and derailed at the busiest points. If Churchill had been there he would have decorated them.

By this time Wertzig was looking pale. He gathered the trio together, went back to the lager, and found the Kommandant on the point of departure. There were tears of protest in Wilhelm's eyes. He was really sorry for himself. Who had sent him these terrible men? he asked. Where in God's name had they come from? A bland Kommandant was full of sympathy. They did seem bad cases, he agreed. It would be hard to find worse. Maybe, he suggested, that hammer-in-the-bunker episode had been a bad omen after all. And picking up his kit, he patted Wertzig's shoulder, and pressed the conduct cards into his shaking hands.

Christmas came. It was the Christmas we had all intended to spend at home, with stone-bashing and lagers and Wertzig things of the past. But that bubble had burst. We were still here, still captive, but thank God warm and with plenty to eat. We had the day off. We made the best of it, and after dinner most of us perched comfortably on the Gasthaus wall and watched the people passing below. It was easy to identify them. The Czechs, Poles and Russians were all smiles, but then Victory wasn't far away, and they had something to smile about. The Germans were nearly all glum and morose. It was

Christmas Day, but the news they had didn't bring them happy thoughts.

Their crack divisions had all been severely mauled, and were now being annihilated. The whole of Von Paulus' Sixth Army was lost at Stalingrad, and countless homes were paying the price of defeat. The General Staff were desperate for more men to fill those appalling gaps in the Wehrmacht ranks. Germany had been drained almost dry of manpower.

In the end the General Staff decided to enlist prisoners; and once the decision was made they put in some fast work. On Boxing Day, each man in our lager got a pamphlet from H.Q. It was well phrased, but too longwinded. 'Following express and repeated requests from the many British personnel who recognize the menace of Bolshevism,' said the preamble, 'the Fuehrer has consented to the formation of a British Free Corps.' At this point, some of the Fuehrer's stone corps stopped reading. They liked their literature light, and this kind of verbal dropsy pained them.

But they missed the best part. Lower down, and stripped of its fancy rhetoric, the pamphlet indicated that Adolf was willing to do a deal. All we had to do was join his B.F.C. and go fight Stalin's hordes. That wasn't asking a lot. In return, the Fuehrer offered a new German uniform with a distinguishing Union Jack on one sleeve, full Wehrmacht status, a promise that no one would fight on the Western Front, and a priority passage home after the war was won.

We liked that bit especially. It solved all our travelling problems. We asked the new Kommandant for more pamphlets. A prisoner has a thousand uses for paper printed on one side only.

The B.F.C. did get some recruits after this offer, but nothing like the number that was expected. Maybe the organizers forgot we didn't like Nazis. The Russians didn't mean all that much to us, but at least we weren't on fighting terms with them. Not many men in British P.O.W. camps felt strongly about the Russians, one way or the other. There were fewer still who yearned to freeze in the Polish snow for either Joe or Adolf. By and large the appeal failed. We used some of the pamphlets for writing purposes, put the rest in the Abort, and forgot about them.

A week or two later the High Command tried again. This time they trod more warily. The lager got a huge wall map of Europe, with London and Berlin linked by a thick red line. There was a heartcry below. 'Stop this fratricidal struggle,' it exhorted. 'Let us combine to fight the Reds!' It didn't mention the B.F.C. It didn't tell us how we could stop the war, either, and none of us stayed awake wondering. We hung the map next to the 'German-Girls-Verboten' placard, and sat back again. Something told us another text would soon be on the way. After ignoring us for four years, it looked as if H.Q. now intended to pester us with these *billets-doux*.

Some other officer tried his hand in Effort No. 3. He adopted an unfamiliar hail-fellow-well-met style, and told us not to escape. That was a silly theme. None of us intended to escape at this stage. There was a lot of detail in the message about new 'death zones,' where guards shot first and asked questions afterwards. The author stressed that nobody knew where these zones began or ended, which sounded odd. He signed off with a hint that the B.F.C. had room for more men, and added a gem from his phrase book. 'Well, chaps,' he asked heartily, 'what about it?' The chaps could have told him.

But it's an ill wind that dries nobody's washing. A few days later a new Geneva rule came out and the whole lager trooped off to Aussig for tuberculosis X-ray tests. To give them due credit, the Germans were prompt in obeying these instructions.

A huge throng of prisoners was already assembled when we got to Aussig. We waited behind a crowd of Italians; and the contrast between the Lobositz men, all spick in new suits, and this poor motley, made me reflect once again how well Italians seem to fill the P.O.W. rôle. I had seen them in Egypt and Palestine and Greece; and here, as there, they were much of a type – shabby little men, docile, friendly and lousy.

A stout Alpini Major seemed to be in charge of the group, and I learnt from him it was the remnants of his company. 'We were in the Peloponnesus,' he told me. Then reflectively, 'It wasn't bad there. At least we fed regularly.'

I offered a cigarette. There were a lot of things I wanted to know. 'How did you get here?' I asked. 'And what about the

Armistice? I thought it meant you chaps were finished with the war.'

The major grimaced. 'We thought so too,' he agreed, 'but things didn't work out that way. We got in the train all right —' he puffed out blue smoke appreciatively '— Now we're here. I suppose we'll have to make the best of it.'

The thought struck me that English P.O.W.s weren't the only ones with Jinxes; but I had another point. 'How do you stand with the Germans?' I asked. 'Are you a prisoner too?'

The Italian shrugged. 'No, not exactly. We're supposed to be workers for the Reich. The Duce did get that concession, but it hasn't done us much good so far. Look at those men. They're half-starved. We don't get food parcels, you know. If we had half as much as you we'd be well off.'

That was true enough. Now we were stripped, the comparison between the stone-loaders and the Italians was more pronounced than ever. We were well-fed, muscled men. They had no beef on their bones, and here and there a pot belly hinted suspiciously of oedema.

But the food problem was only half the story. What was bearing the Italians down just as much as hunger was lack of morale. We had victories to cheer us. Even in defeat we earned respect from the Huns, but they had neither victories nor respect. They had never known either.

I noticed the Alpini major looking on curiously and realized I had been day-dreaming. The officer took a last puff on his cigarette and tossed away the butt. A dozen men scrambled for it, and I came back to earth with a bump. Here was something I could do. I produced two full packets and handed them to the major. Tobacco hunger is the worst of all privations. 'Have these,' I offered. The major thanked me, doled out the Players, and in a minute a score of Italians were puffing happily.

That reminded me. 'Do you read *La Patria*?' I enquired. It was the Italians' German-sponsored newspaper.

The major smiled. 'Yes, it's interesting to learn how well we're being looked after!'

'Then you remember that article about our cigarettes? The one that said they're being adulterated with horse-dung?'

'Yes.'

'Well that's a sample you've got now. What do you think of it?'

The Italian breathed out a curl of blue smoke very slowly. He looked at his cigarette, and his lips creased in a smile. 'Well, he said, pensively. 'Maybe it is horse-dung. I wouldn't know. But I do know this. They're damn good horses.'

TWENTY-ONE

Back at the quarry, relations between the overseers and the bad men were rapidly growing worse. Every day some fresh trouble arose, but the culprits were always the same. Wertzig's life became a real penance. He did his best. He put the three new men who weren't invalids at one end of the quarry, stationed Panagioti, Ramadan and me at the other end, and hoped for the best. As he feared it would be, hope was still-born.

Early in February things came to a head. Ramadan and I took a load of dirt to the refuse tip and accidentally tossed the wagon. It hurtled down a fifty feet slope, demolished several trees, and ended up a wreck. Wilhelm charged up, breathing fire. 'Schwein. . . .' he began. I left it to Ramadan. He was good at these exchanges: but after calling Wertzig a latrine and casting doubts upon his female ancestry, Ramadan produced a surprise packet. 'It's Baldy's fault,' he accused. 'These lines aren't straight. You can see that yourself.' He was right. The lines were faulty, and Baldy was responsible for all the tracks. I grinned at Ramadan admiringly. Wertzig glared at both of us and stumped away to find his henchman.

Poor Baldy had no idea what a load of trouble was hanging over him. He had been preparing a blast all morning. As soon as Wertzig had delivered his 'rocket', the little overseer touched off his charges, and blew down a large section of cliff. The frown on his face melted as soon as the dust cleared away. It was a lovely blow, expertly prepared and expertly accomplished. Five minutes later Baldy was shouting and gesticulating at Wertzig and at the same time doing a queer kind of dance. Three more experts at the other end of the quarry had just told him they couldn't work any more. Their picks, shovels and hammers were all immobilized under about three thousand tons of rock.

That day finished us. Herr W. had been goaded beyond all endurance. He went the same night to Aussig, and poured all his troubles into the official ear. He was past caring about his own status. But on one thing he was determined. Those Englische Schurken had to go.

I was sorry to leave Sydney. He was a good pal, but I had warned him from the start that something like this might happen, and probably would happen. In Kriegsgefangenenschaft friendship was always a precarious business.

Wertzig didn't spare the horses. On Monday morning nine of us assembled in the Kommandant's office and were told we were going to Lager 22. I brightened up. Lager 22 was at Brux. It was the one I had come from originally: and at Brux were Ronnie Martin and Wally and Arryock and a host of others. That wasn't so bad. The Kommandant spoke again. He seemed rather puzzled. 'I don't understand this,' he said, giving each of us a shiny new conduct card. 'These came this morning from H.Q. Herr Wertzig brought them specially. He says your old cards have been lost. It seems very strange.'

Perhaps it did to him, but the stratagem didn't mystify us. We all knew what choice and endearing remarks were on those 'lost' cards. We were well aware that no Kommandant in Germany would accept such prisoners save over his dead body: and we knew that Wertzig was just as well informed as we. Wilhelm wasn't taking any chances. When we left Lobositz he didn't intend that we should come back.

The ever-faithful Schmidt was roused from his beauty sleep to act as Zug-escort. Before long we were in the train heading for Brux, and I watched Lobositz fade into the distance without emotion. Barring a twinge of regret at losing Sydney, I was neither glad nor sorry. It was a move, and moves were too frequent to allow for sentiment. I wrote off Lobositz as another chapter in this by no means unentertaining captivity, and turned my thoughts to Brux.

It was a slack morning. There was hardly anyone on the train and we got a compartment to ourselves without difficulty. Everything seemed set for an interesting journey. The scenery was pleasant, the seats comfortable, and the atmosphere free and easy. We lit up and offered Schmidt a cigarette. In return, knowing we wouldn't give his little game away, he told us a thing or two about passing doctors that made even Harry open his eyes in admiration. Schmidt was certainly a man of parts.

The Brux I got back to was very different from the one of May '44. It seemed the R.A.F. hadn't forgotten the benzine works after all. The Yanks had also left visiting cards, and what now remained of the giant installations didn't seem worth two pfennigs.

It was almost unbelievable chaos. Great gaping bomb-holes lay everywhere. Tall buildings were reduced to twisted frameworks, huge oil tanks were buckled and concertinaed, and heaps of rubble stood as high as a house. It was difficult to recognize the place. Schmidt's barn, the landmark I was looking for, had gone. It had got a 500 lb. bomb all to itself and two months' supply of palliasses were buried under the débris. I heard that old Schmidt had been bereaved that night. He was sleeping there and got to the funkhole just in time. His leather pants, the envy and admiration of all our eyes, stayed behind to perish.

I found Ronnie as soon as I got through the gate. We entertained Arryock and the rest of the team to a reunion brew-and-bite and I was brought up to date with the local news. Like the tea, it was a mixture of good and bad. I gathered that the whole camp had settled down to await Victory Day. It was February '45 and common sense told everyone the end couldn't be far off. Even the tyrannical arbeit-meisters in the Factory had seen the red light and were being polite for the first time in years. Some of them were finding civility a bit of a strain. We were nearing the end of a long long trail. . . .

But not everything was as bright as the war news. Food was running low in Lager 22, and successive weeks had each brought a new cut in the ration. Red Cross parcels had finished a month ago, but work didn't. It increased: and now, to add to the double strain of short commons and rubble clearing, there was the constant fear of another air raid. I learnt that stray bombs had already killed nine men in this camp.

The authorities announced a vicious ration cut on the very day I got back. When I learnt just how little would be on the menu in future, Lobositz and Wertzig took on a sudden rosy hue.

Ronnie and I were all right for a few days. Then my own food stock ran out and the few possessions I had began travelling a familiar road. My best trousers went to Basil for a week's bread. My overcoat kept us going for ten days, and odds and ends fought the wolf a little longer. But capital never stands being lived on. The day came when we had nothing except the bare ration. It was a bad day, and worse were to follow. The rest of the camp, all barring the cooks, had been hungry for weeks now, but they were used to it. I wasn't. I had come straight from the stone camp where I had been eating big meals.

Another month passed by. Victory marched ever nearer, but by now privation was making most of us feel apathetic about it. We did know that one day soon we'd be released and that God willing we'd get back to civvy life and three meals a day. Mainly we left it at that. We were living from day to day and had neither time nor inclination for castles-in-the-air.

I found my own strength slipping away fast. I had reached the black-out stage and was beginning to walk round humps in the ground instead of over them. Nobody who was in Lager 22 in March/April '45 will forget those days in a hurry.

We marched to work as usual, although men dropped from exhaustion before they ever reached the Factory. Very few did any real work. We either dodged into some hideout and went to sleep, or if that was impossible, held shovels and spades and went through the motions. The arbeit-meisters knew what was good for them, and kept quiet, but even the pretence was a drain we could ill-afford. And until April, when a convoy came through from Geneva, Lager 22 men had a rough time. Each day we got ten ounces of black bread, four small potatoes and a scoop of hot soup. There was a sugar, meat and ersatz jam ration too, but it went on a rota. It was too small for any other method of distribution. On this diet we had to march up to four miles a day and were supposed to work twelve hours: and when the sirens blew, which they did often, run like hell for shelter.

Nobody did run. It wouldn't have done any good. Every building in the Factory had a Luftschutzraum, built of reinforced concrete and strong enough to withstand even the punch of Ten Ton Tessies; but these shelters weren't for us. The top men – executives, key workers and arbeit-meisters – used them. Lesser lights, Czech civilians and the general hoi polloi had to shift for themselves. The nearest safe place was a mine known as Julius V, but Julius V was four miles away. We stayed where we were and chanced the bombs. The gamble came off. Although the Factory somehow achieved the miracle of getting back to quarter-production, neither R.A.F. nor Yanks revisited it.

Ronnie and I escaped the pick and shovel work. He was in my old place in Schmidt's gang, and with Wally's connivance I got back too. None of us even pretended to work. We spent most of the day foraging for food, but it was scarce everywhere. Basil's wife brought a bowl of soup out occasionally, which was good of her, but it didn't help much. One bowl amongst six men doesn't go far.

The shortage of cigarettes made life even worse. It was weeks since any of us had seen an honest Virginian fag, and ersatz German tea made a poor substitute. But we rolled tea fags, and what was more, smoked them. They had a deceptively sweet aroma, and at the back of it, a kick like a mule. With my first, I took a good long pull and inhaled deeply. The next morning a thunderbolt hit me. Forked lightning ran up and down my outraged throat and a giant hand reached down and cleaned out my lungs with a barbed wire brush. For five minutes I lay coughing and gasping for breath. It was like smoking old carpet mixed with gun cotton. It was lethal – but I smoked it just the same. There was nothing else, and like the rest, I got accustomed to it; but I never inhaled again.

Towards the end of March, Ronnie and I stopped going out

to work. He got a job as camp maintenance man, and congratulated himself. I got an abscess of the middle ear and didn't. Probably it was present bad conditions, allied with a spot of untreated Libyan bomb blast, that brought on that abscess; but while it lasted I didn't bother analyzing the cause. For nearly a fortnight I sat in a sleepless Hell.

It was an operation job, and should have been tackled immediately. That was too bad. All the Medical Room could offer was Aspro, warm poultices and the best of luck. On the tenth day I was in a bad way. On the eleventh, I learnt what agony was, and in rare moments of relief, wished I'd led a better life. On the twelfth, the thing burst and gave me instant relief. I stopped worrying about the past. Life had been fairly entertaining so far, and I wouldn't have changed it.

The abscess discharged itself through the broken drum and I mended quickly. A week later I left the hospital, a bit groggy on my feet and stone deaf in one ear, but with the flag still flying.

The one consolation I had was being put on the sick list. I joined Ronnie, and being in camp all day soon opened our eyes to what was going on. We spotted one or two cookhouse rackets that made us wish more than ever before we were cooks. We noticed chaps who came in regularly with supplies from mysterious sources; three or four men who seemed too friendly with the guards, but looked fit on it; and most of all, the Dodgers.

Dodging the column was a great game. Up to a month ago it had been easy, and we had stayed in the lager more often than we went out: but when the absentee list soared to 25 per cent the Germans sat up and took notice. They clamped down a veto, and it wasn't a half-hearted one. Within two days the majority were back at work. It was less exhausting there: but a small minority ignored the ban.

They pitted their wits against Authority and a ding-dong battle resulted. At first the guards went to each hut and bawled at still-sleeping men to get up. Soon they began using their bayonets, but none of the cognoscenti got prodded. Their beds were made up correctly, but they were sleeping underneath. That ruse was soon discovered. The guards now began poking about with bayonets but it didn't worry the wide boys. They had pushed up the ceiling boards and were roosting in the rafters. The Germans got angry over this. They fired occasional shots through the boards, and the men they were seeking, now prone underneath the floor, kept very quiet.

The danger period only lasted half an hour. As soon as the marching columns passed through the gates, not enough guards remained, and the 'hot' part of the search was over. Recluses emerged from all manner of hiding places. A hard core of about thirty men was always missing. They refused to work; and because they had nimble brains most of them got away with it.

Sick men had a special stamp impressed on their arbeit cards, but there were too many sick for prowling absentee catchers to examine every one. They wouldn't have inspected the right cards, in any case. They were conspicuous in field grey uniform and the leadswingers didn't tempt Fate. This disadvantage irked the Germans. 'We catch some of them,' they complained, 'but as soon as they've done their week in the Bunker, they start again. That means we have to catch them again. It's harder the second time.' They fretted over it until in the end some bright Hun had a brainwave. 'Let's mark the Schwein,' he suggested. 'Then we'll know them.'

Like all really good ideas, it was simple. Soon afterwards a batch of prisoners with shaven heads paraded for work. Every Dodger who was caught got the compulsory haircut and the number of bald pates in Lager 22 went up rapidly. Those men couldn't risk dodging again, but they were mainly amateurs. The elite kept their hair on. By now they had formed a Union and were working in co-operation. They thought up bright ideas, brooded over them, polished them and kept them strictly as Union secrets.

At one stage, every accredited Dodger had his card stamped 'Sick'. The Germans were baffled with a run of blank days; but when they discovered that deception it was too late. The forgers had moved on to a new racket. It was their best ever, and fittingly, their last. Unsuspecting medical orderlies impressed the new and complicated 'Sick' stamp on Union cards right up to the last day.

The British Medical Officer was an overworked man. He had a meagre stock of medicine, precious few instruments and far too many customers. Every night he had to deal with a long queue of malingerers who lined up with the genuinely sick. They were all trying to scrounge a day off, and because he knew this, the M.O. was ruthless. He had to be. The Germans would exempt only a limited number of men. His job was to see that genuine cases got relief.

He cured a mild epidemic of stomach trouble by prescribing hot water before and after work. It was never any use having spots before the eyes, or a touch of 'flu, or vague internal maladies. To be sick, a man had to have visible symptoms or a temperature. The M.O. developed a sixth sense. It got that he could tell which men were trying to pull a fast one even before they spoke. Amateur leadswingers dropped out by the score.

It speaks highly of the Union's efficiency that they chose this time for their biggest coup. One after another, the members marched in, registered the necessary 100 degrees, and were packed off to bed. An hour later they were all normal again. One of them, a chemist in civilian life, had brewed up a concoction that raised the most stubborn temperature for half an hour or so. So long as they took their elixir at the right moment the wide boys were on a winner every time.

Dodging the column and hoodwinking the M.O. weren't 'illegal' so far as we were concerned. They were reasonably sporting activities, one needing luck and the other brains, and these days it was very much every man for himself. But we did draw a line. The food situation was now desperate. We were nearly on our knees, but the Factory men still had to footslog twelve hours every day and in some cases work really hard. When bread rations began mysteriously to disappear, all Hell was let loose. Bread was vital. Bread was Life, and there was no replacing a lost ration. It meant another twenty-four hours on soup and spuds. Because we were living on the edge of starvation it frequently meant collapse as well.

But the thefts continued. They even increased, and warning notices went up without effect. Hunger was goading some men too powerfully for scruples to deter them. When the first thief was caught over a score of bread-bereaved prisoners were waiting for him.

Judge Jeffreys would have approved the treatment. It was sheer savagery. Blazing inquisitors kicked and battered the thief into unconsciousness. As soon as a bucket of water revived him, he was picked up and smashed down again. He ended up looking worse than the wash-house informer, and he got about as much sympathy. Scattered around him were his bedding and all his possessions. From that moment, the man was a pariah. No hut in the camp would allow him through the door and he had to fix up a home in the wash-house. As a final degradation he was named as a thief in the Daily Orders.

But despite this vicious punishment, the thefts went on. I didn't profess to understand why. More thieves were caught and each one got the same terrible thrashing. The wash-house filled up and a special hut had to be allocated to the offenders. It was known as the Thieves' Den. Every man in it was ostracized like a leper.

But we had all had more than our share of misery. We were overdue for a brighter patch, and as usual, the Red Cross people provided it. On the third of April their Geneva convoy got through.

Saying it like that is easy. Describing what it meant to the three thousand near-starving men of Lager 22 would be a job for all the masters of literature. I know we went wild with joy. So much so that even the outcasts of the Thieves' Den shared in the great outburst of comradeship that flooded the camp.

Ronnie and I got our parcels and sat on the bed, nursing them and holding them tight. The man next to us wasn't so demonstrative. He was a Scot, a hard craggy man, but even his dourness broke down. He put the precious package on his bed, walked around it, sat down, and patted it affectionately. 'Well, you old bastard,' he beamed, 'so you've come at last, eh?'

They were American parcels. Each one held 100 cigarettes instead of the usual fifty, and after the first glorious spree we stopped smoking, and went easy on the food. God alone knew when the next delivery would come; or if there'd be another one at all. Fags were too precious to smoke. Five cigarettes would buy a kilo of bread, and we had got into the way of thinking with our stomachs. Bread wasn't so much the Staff of Life as Life itself.

I had another use for the cigarettes. The M.O. had arranged for me to visit a specialist in Brux to get treatment for the damaged ear. I went there, put five Camels on the great man's desk and got my card marked for another visit. When he saw the cigarettes he took the card back and banned work until further orders. That specialist was a distinguished man. He was one of the best in his line in Germany, but the magic token was infallible. Next week I slipped two fags into the drawer and put a bar of chocolate on his desk. The chocolate was to say 'Thank You' for meticulous treatment. He acknowledged it, but he ignored the cigarettes. That was business, and business ethics forbade any show of interest; but he marked the card again. We played fair. I paid the 'fee' regularly, and although I was soon fit again, I never did another stroke of work until the war ended.

It was only a question of weeks now. Every day a whole armada of bombers passed overhead en route to Chemnitz and Dresden, and Allied fighters began cavorting above the camp itself. Air raid alarms were a dozen a day. They were even more frequent at night, and life moved nearer the edge of the precipice. The Factory was picking up again and no one could say just when the bombs would fall. We felt sure they must. Petrol is the lifeblood of war, and the Factory's ersatz stuff was going out again in quantity.

But although the danger was great, we didn't run to Julius V any more. A better 'ole had been found less than half a mile away. It was a disused mine shaft with a steel staircase that was supposed to descend 400 feet. Nobody went down that far for the good reason that he'd have to climb up again, but the huddle at the top felt happy. There, they were safe from everything bar a direct hit.

Night alarms became continuous. The banshee wailing started soon after dusk, with first the normal alarm, and then six short blasts to intimate that raiders were coming our way. It was a signal to get moving. Usually about three minutes passed before the dreaded warbling note sounded. It meant 'Raiders Overhead' or 'Evening Prayers' according to how you felt. When the planes passed, the sirens went into reverse – six blasts for 'Moving Away' and a melancholy two-minutes blare for 'All Clear'.

At first it was a good alarm system, but it deteriorated. The operators lost their nerve and before long a flock of birds was enough to set the whole circus going. The Germans opened the gates on the express condition that nobody escaped. They were safe enough. Nobody intended to, not at this stage of the war, but after a day or two less than half of us bothered to seek shelter outside. We stayed in bed, kept the fleas safe from pneumonia, and ignored the raid. There was some sense in that. If we had to die we might as well do it in comfort.

TWENTY-TWO

The war moved faster. Lager 21, a mile away, began painting BRITISH P.O.W. CAMP in huge white letters on the roof, until the Germans stopped them. The Ack-Ack got some new shells and brought down six bombers in one day. On May 4th I went to Brux for the last time. There I found far bigger news. The shop windows were all cleared, and a bust of Hitler stood in each one. Nazi flags, draped in mourning black hung, lifelessly in the streets, silently proclaiming news the world was waiting for. The Fuehrer was dead. Adolf Hitler, Man of Destiny, Leader of the Herrenvolk, Idol of the Reich, had gone at last.

In Brux, everything was suddenly A.1. I knew that in a day or two we'd be free men, and homeward bound. It was time to rejoice. Schmidt could get better, Joe could forget his lameness, and flat feet in a dozen countries could regain their lost arches. The Brux placards announced Admiral Doenitz as the new Leader. The gallant ex-Fuehrer, they said, had met a hero's death at the head of his troops and was now in Valhalla. All Germans were to transfer their loyalty to the Admiral. Everyone would stay at his post, and fight to the bitter end. There would be no surrender. And so on, in detail.

Little remains of my own story. The Allies received the surrender of whole armies and made final advances into the resistance pockets. We found it a mixed blessing. We were right in the centre of one of these pockets, with the Erzgebirge mountains surrounding us on three sides.

On V.E. day, Henlein, the Sudeten-Deutsch leader, ignored the 'Cease-Fire' order and threw the remnants of his Blackshirts into a death struggle with the Russians. During the morning, the boom of gunfire came nearer. At 11 a.m. the first Russian shell fell in the camp. It roused us faster than the Geneva convoy had done. At 11.01 a.m. the gates burst open and a great mob surged out. More shells crashed down. One or two huts collapsed as the last stragglers flew out of the gate and hit the trail to Karlsbad.

Most of us lost everything. Ronnie and I left our washing on a homemade line and a pan of water bubbling away beneath. They didn't matter, but I did regret leaving my propaganda library. Now it had gone I was finishing the war without a single memento.

We were well in the van of the fleeing horde. We passed through a Czech village two miles from the camp, and smiled at the hammer and sickle flags already waving in the breeze. A soldier in the forbidden blue uniform of the Czech Army was standing at ease, complete with rifle and fixed bayonet. We gave him a cheerful 'Dobridra,' pushed two of our last cigarettes into his hand and pressed on.

We walked nearly fifteen miles before the faint thunder of battle died away. All along the route the Czechs were cheering and waving flags. They gave us what food they could spare and we felt our strength flowing back. But fifteen miles was heavy going. Near Komotau a panzer-wagon roared up with a large trailer behind. We jumped on. It was taking a chance, but life had long been a chancy affair. Luckily the German crew didn't object. They weren't in battle any longer. Their war was over, and they were going hell-for-leather for the American lines.

From their gestures we gathered they couldn't get there too soon.

The steel tracks of the big vehicle ate up miles steadily. We had one bad moment when a box of grenades came out, but it was a false alarm. The boys on this battle wagon were genuine pacifists. They flung the grenades into roadside pools, heaved the box overboard, and smiled at us.

We got a long lift on that trailer. Just as it was growing dark, the driver pulled up in a small village where a whole convoy of tanks and trucks had halted for the night. The panzer crew were feeling easier now. They were safe from Russian pursuit, and Eger was only ten miles away. To-morrow would see them all prisoners, but what of it? The Russian bogey was laid, and nobody had to worry any more about Siberian snow. A burst of singing floated towards us.

We leaned on the newly-established amity to the extent of borrowing a couple of dixies. We weren't concerned about the Russians either, but it was a long time since we had eaten anything. We got a first course of macaroni and beef without any questions being asked. It was the best meal we'd had in months. Next time round the cook looked doubtfully at the Wehrmacht's latest recruits, but he handed out ladles of cornflour automatically. They were good too. I had an idea cigarettes were being handed out somewhere, but our luck didn't stretch that far.

Then Dame Fortune relented, and decided to do the thing in a big way. We walked along the line of vehicles in time to see a staff car starting up. A minute's conversation did the trick. The Oberst asked Ronnie to get in the back, and as there was no more room I wedged myself between wing and bonnet. I was quite happy. It was the last lap of a momentous journey. Ever since the day Greece fell and Tobruk surrendered we had been visualizing something like this. Now it was happening.

We travelled fast. Lines of pine trees flashed by in the car's headlights as Eger grew rapidly nearer. Periodically the Oberst opened the door to hand me a lighted English cigarette. It was thoughtful of him; and between puffs came odd memories of those four years of intermittent freedom and captivity.

Mostly they concerned the quicksilver patches of comfort

and happiness; but now and again I reflected, in a nostalgic way, on escapes that might have been but never were. I remembered errors that had been made and wouldn't be made again; and felt I'd like another try. I wanted those chances over again to make better use of them; and all through this dreaming came glimpses of men I had known, from the superb Macaskie at one extreme to bread ghouls at the other. The ten miles passed like a flash.

I was still meditating when we reached the end of the dark horror that is imprisonment. A tin-hatted American stopped the car and tapped me brusquely on the shoulder.

'Say,' he demanded, 'where've you Krauts come from?'

I turned and faced him. 'Brux,' I said, grinning. 'The other side of Karlsbad. And you've made a mistake. Only half of us are Krauts. That fellow by the driver's an Oberst. Colonel to you, pal. The other chap's English. I'm English. And I'm damn glad to see you.'

The sergeant's eyes widened. 'English?' he repeated. A puzzled frown came over his face. 'Well, wadda y'know about that? How the hell. . . .'

It seemed that between them the panzer-wagon and the Oberst's car had won the Brux-Eger marathon. We were the first ex-prisoners into the place, but only just. More were close behind. All through that night the vanguard of Lager 22's 3,000 men trickled into the town.

Ronnie and I didn't waste time; but before going off to find bed and board we did one job that had been overdue since the first day in Reich territory. The Yank had marched off with his Oberst. A few yards from us a group of Germans were descending stiffly from a lorry. We walked towards them. I barked the order 'Achtung! Offizier!' and from sheer force of habit the Germans stiffened to attention. Ronnie took over. He broke into fluent German. 'You are now prisoners of war,' he began. He paused, savouring both the exquisite moment and the words on the tip of his tongue that had so often been addressed to us. 'For you the war is over,' continued Ronnie. 'You will be well treated. Now place your weapons on the ground, and report to the sentries farther up the road.'

The Germans marched off, with the leading man fluttering

a white handkerchief. We experienced peculiar emotions. It had taken four years to get this far.

We selected a brace of pistols apiece. For good measure I added a Schmeisser automatic. I had been at the wrong end of these things too often to resist the temptation. A bed was the next item; and with a Mauser 38 bumping theatrically on each hip and the fat bullets of the Schmeisser winking in the moonlight, I felt grand. If only Wertzig and Baldy had been there, the cup would have flowed over.

In the morning we put a sack of pistols into the Oberst's car and set off for Belgium. We didn't hurry. After five years abroad a few days either way didn't weigh heavily. All down the line, souvenir-hungry Americans supplied petrol, PX rations and other necessities. I traded the Schmeisser for a couple of uniforms and got top-sergeant's stripes sewn on for a Lueger pistol. After that nothing could go wrong. We fed like fighting cocks. We commandeered the best rooms in every Gasthaus we stayed in, and had mine host dancing attention. The mere mention of 'requisition' was enough to put any innkeeper into a flat spin. There was snow-white linen, minor miracles from the kitchen, and the pick of the wine cellar.

At one Gasthaus a pair of buxom waitresses took pains to see that everything was just so. They were sisters, Hilde and Berta. Later on they came back and offered to show us our rooms. We realized there was more in the offer than that, and unconsciously our shoulders braced as we went upstairs. It seemed we were men again. . . . I kissed Hilde's blonde hair as she smoothed back the coverlet. . . .

All the way to the Belgian border we enjoyed the victors' march that had once seemed so remote. White flags hung out everywhere in token of surrender. We passed endless columns of prisoners trudging towards their barbed wire isolation. Smiling Americans saluted the Union Jack and Old Glory, now fluttering jointly from the car's bonnet, and waved us on.

The devastation we saw astounded us. Bomb-scarred Brux seemed newly-built in comparison. Whole towns were flat. In others only shell-pocked tottering walls remained to brood over vast heaps of rubble. Near the Rhine we crossed one of the few bridges that were still intact. It had almost escaped the war, but not quite. A roving Yankee gun crew had passed on V.E. day and the Yanks had made whoopee. The row of headless statues spaced every few yards along the bridge bore silent witness.

At Brussels we reached the end of the road. A Lancaster bomber carried us over the last lap, and for once the old phrase 'For you the war is over' came to have a real meaning.

We were glad, deeply and profoundly glad. We were feeling a relief we couldn't put into words, but it was none the less powerful for that. We had sojourned too long in those little Englands whose borders were marked by tripwires and guarded from tiger-boxes for us to have facile tongues. But we knew the Germans: and perhaps more than most, we realized what we and Britain as a whole had escaped.

Well, we won the war, that's certain. The fruits of victory are ours for what they're worth, but maybe greater perils lie ahead. Perhaps we have yet to face them. I'd like one wish that everyone will echo – may we never jeopardize the precious liberty that six years of blood and sorrow bought for us, nor ever come to realize just how bitter is the taste of defeat.

THE END